SHOCK FRONT

A TRIGGER MAN THRILLER

AIDEN BAILEY

INKUBATOR
BOOKS

Published by Inkubator Books
www.inkubatorbooks.com

ISBN (eBook): 978-1-83756-499-6
ISBN (Paperback): 978-1-83756-500-9
ISBN (Hardback): 978-1-83756-501-6

For my good friend Sarah Townsend

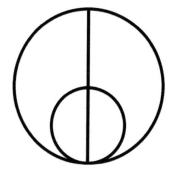

1

Patna, Bihar, India

Blood smeared the door handle and spilled onto the softly lit porch, then transformed into a crimson trail that disappeared into the makeshift safe house, showing where persons unknown had dragged a freshly killed body. In the driveway, a four-by-four's engine block leaked steam from where the vehicle had crashed into a ditch. Further blood on its bonnet mixed with the heavy monsoonal rain crashing down on it.

A man approached this scene of carnage with caution on his mind. He was with America's Central Intelligence Agency, a CIA Ground Branch operator named Mark Pierce, and he wasted no time reaching behind his rain-soaked shirt to withdraw his suppressed 9mm Glock 19 semi-automatic pistol from his belt. Then he waited in the shadows and watched, because he sensed trouble.

That trouble proved to be only seconds away, as a Toyota Glanza screeched into the driveway, churning heavy sprays of mud as it shuddered to a halt. Two assailants hurriedly stepped out with CZ P-10 semi-automatic pistols in shooter grips. Each wore civilian clothes overlaid with plate carriers and chest rigs and moved with the professional ease of seasoned killers. But neither assailant had bothered to check their blind spots, and therefore had missed Pierce, who had ducked behind a row of banana trees, and had walked straight past him.

With their backs to Pierce, the first man spoke into his earpiece as he approached the blood-smeared porch. "Vali, you copy?"

There came a moment of silence as the man called Vali presumably responded, but Pierce couldn't hear what he said as the men listened to their instructions via their earpieces.

"Say again?" said the first man with a questioning frown. "Kill everyone inside? You sure...?" The man tensed as he was interrupted, then expressed subservience when he answered with, "Yes, sir! Confirmed. We *will* kill everyone, including the wife."

Then the conversation ended, and the men advanced again.

Silently, Pierce aimed his pistol and shot the two assailants in the backs of their heads, killing them both instantly with a suppressed coughing noise barely heard in the heavy rain. Stepping out of the shadows cast by the banana trees, he shot them both in their faces just to be sure they were dead, then kicked their pistols into the darkness. More blood flowed from their corpses, mixing with the deluge of muddy water gathering everywhere.

With the pistol out in front and aimed, Pierce listened for further assailants but heard nothing over the downpour. He glanced left and right, seeing only the night's dark expanse but sensing nothing. Any danger that lingered, Pierce concluded, now waited inside, or was yet to arrive.

Stepping onto the porch and glad to be under the shelter of its veranda, he pressed against the door.

Already unlatched, it swung open with a hushed creak. Inside, a lamp flickered in the hallway. Half in shadow, a soaked man lay crumpled against a faded yellow wall. The right hand gripped a Beretta APX, ready to shoot anyone who entered, except that he never would, for this man was dead. The bloody trail from outside led to his corpse. Two bullet holes decorated his chest.

There might have been further entry and exit wounds, but the folds of clothes and dim light made it difficult to see. With a honed muscular physique like Pierce, the dead man would have also been a CIA Special Operations Group paramilitary officer like himself. He had just made the ultimate sacrifice, protecting the interests of his country at the cost of his own life.

Pierce pocketed the Beretta and the man's spare magazines, then snuck further into the safe house. Now the rain sounded more like tiny pebbles than water droplets as the incessant impacts bounced off the roof.

Ahead, he heard fast, shallow pants from a wounded woman in a room just off the main corridor, while nearby light footsteps suggested another person attended to her. Drops of blood on the tiled floor showed the way.

Weapon raised and eyes forward, Pierce entered the room lit by soft coffee table lamps. The woman was half in shadow and half cast in the dull yellow light. She lay slumped and listless on a sofa, where she pressed a blood-soaked pillowcase against a stomach wound. Her water-drenched business attire was that of a smart middle-class professional, with flat shoes for running. If the dead man was the muscle, she was the brains. Pierce guessed the woman was the team's field intelligence officer who, two hours earlier, had flash-called for Pierce's presence.

The second woman, standing nearby, was not CIA. Pierce could tell by the constant clenching and unclenching of her fists, a jiggling leg, and eyes focused only on the dying officer. Her shiny black hair was long and flowing, her figure was curvy, her age was early thirties, and her only jewellery was a large diamond ring. Although much blood covered her too, it didn't seem as if any of it was hers. Water dripped off her nose, earlobes, and from her drenched clothes.

When she noticed Pierce standing at the door, she screamed and stepped back.

"It's... okay..." panted the prone woman as blood dribbled from her mouth. "He's Mark... The operator... I called for..."

Pierce nodded to them both. "The house secured?"

The dying CIA officer nodded.

He lowered his weapon. "I take it you're Daniella Estrada?"

The intelligence officer nodded, then asked, "It was... Abdul Ibrahim... who sent you?"

Pierce nodded again. Chief of the CIA's Special Operations Group Abdul Ibrahim managed all Ground Branch officers and had personally requested that Pierce take up this operation after learning of the decimation of Estrada's team and their precarious situation in the heart of India. "I was on transit from Jakarta to Doha. I was in the area."

She nodded again, then tensed from the pain growing in her abdomen.

"I dispatched two men outside. How long before the rest of their team finds us?"

Before she could answer, Pierce imagined the sequence of events leading up to this moment. Assailants had ambushed Estrada and her team somewhere nearby. Only three of them had made it from the kill site to the safe house. Only one would now live long enough to walk out alive. Estrada lay in a puddle of too much of her own blood to be that lucky individual.

"We shot out... all their vehicles... except one. Half... an hour... Maybe."

Pierce looked to the civilian woman wet with rain and Estrada's blood. "You have a name?"

"Roshini."

Pierce wondered if she was the "wife" the men outside had mentioned. "Get changed, Roshini. Spare clothes will be in the bedrooms. Wash if you need to, but you have five minutes only. Then we're leaving."

Roshini looked at Estrada.

The dying CIA officer nodded. "It's okay... You can trust Mark. He'll... get you to safety."

Roshini turned to Pierce. She had the look of a terrified woman about to put her life in the hands of a stranger, which was exactly what was about to happen. He gave a smile to show he cared. In response, she forced an upturned mouth, then disappeared.

Pierce crouched next to Estrada. Fresh sheets and pillow-cases lay on the tiles nearby. Pierce grabbed one, folded it several times and pressed it against her wound while discarding the soaked cloth.

"Thanks... for coming." She grinned through gritted

teeth. "I know... I will not make it, and... I presume Samson didn't either?"

Pierce guessed she meant the dead man in the hallway. He shook his head. "What do I need to know?"

"Roshini Jahandar... is her name. She's holding... important intel... You must get her to... CIA headquarters... in Langley..."

"You've checked her for bugs?"

"Yes."

"Including her diamond ring?"

"Double-checked that... Nothing."

"What's the exfil route?"

"We had one... It was... compromised... Hence..." She shook her head. "You'll need to find... another... way." She coughed up blood, and for a moment Pierce thought she had reached the end. Then in a quieter voice, she said, "You must go dark... until she's out... of the country..."

"Why? Who's chasing her?"

"She's... critical, Pierce... The information she has... We gave our lives for... You should... too... Don't worry about... the paper files... or the... videos... They... weren't... important. Something new... came up... We had... to move quickly... Only that intel... is critical."

Pierce nodded. "What format is the critical intelligence?"

"Roshini has it... on her..."

"And?"

Estrada's breath became faster and shallower. Blood gurgled from her mouth. With great effort, she lifted her left hand and gestured to her throat as if she wore a necklace, but no jewellery adorned her. "A... data stick..."

Then Estrada's hand fell, and her breathing dropped away.

He waited a few seconds for her to say more, but nothing came from her lips.

He felt for a pulse. Nothing.

In respect, he closed her unfocused eyes and let her body fall back on the sofa.

Pierce stood and considered his operational situation. Down the hall a shower ran, barely heard over the storm-front crashing down outside. He checked his wristwatch. Roshini had three minutes remaining, according to his count. Three minutes to prepare the safe house and ex-filtrate.

Pierce remembered how two hours earlier he had received a flash call from Ibrahim, requesting his help in aiding two surviving compromised operatives and their asset. Their names were Samson, Estrada and Roshini, so that had checked out. The private CIA Gulfstream, flying him from a recently completed mission in Indonesia, happened to be in the ideal location to assist, resulting in a diversion to a private airfield outside of Patna in eastern India. From there, he had secured a vehicle and driven to the safe house. He had no information yet on who the CIA team were running from, and Ibrahim had been reluctant to share too much over a potentially compromised line. He had told Pierce, however, that his regular handler, Mitch Hawley, would brief him on the mission details later. The most important aspect of his mission right now was to secure Roshini and the intel she had in her possession, and then steal her away from any and all danger.

From down the hall, he heard Roshini Jahandar turn off the shower. Her name was familiar to him, but Pierce couldn't place the context.

Returning his focus to the moment, Pierce searched the

safe house. He discovered a sports bag stuffed with rupees equivalent to thirty thousand US dollars, another Beretta APX pistol with spare magazines, and several fragmentation grenades with trip wires.

Pierce went to work.

A minute later, he found Roshini standing over Daniella Estrada's corpse, one arm across her own waist and the other at her mouth. Tears gushed from her eyes. She'd dressed in a suit with flat shoes similar to the dead intelligence officer's attire. Perhaps the outfit was from Estrada's travel luggage. The clothes were dry but wouldn't be as soon as they stepped outside. It impressed Pierce that she had readied herself well within her allotted five minutes, and the blood was gone, so she wouldn't stand out when they needed to move in crowds.

She said in a croaky voice, "Is Daniella... dead?"

Pierce nodded. "We leave, now."

Roshini returned the nod and followed him. He noticed her tremble.

He stopped her before they exited and pointed to a thin, almost invisible wire at ankle height. "I've positioned trip wires at all the entrance points, set to detonate deadly grenades. Step over this one carefully."

Roshini did as instructed.

Outside with his Glock 19 raised and ready for threats, he led Roshini past the three corpses to his Maruti Gypsy four-by-four parked down the road. Houses with high walls and weathered apartment complexes crowded the street, but no people were about to notice them.

He looked to Roshini. The monsoonal downpour hadn't let up since Pierce's arrival in India, and the wet weather had now soaked her as much as it had soaked him.

"Get in."

She climbed in, and within thirty seconds of exiting the safe house, they were on the road and headed southeast on a crowded night-time road headed away from central Patna.

A minute later they heard a distant explosion.

Roshini let out a squeal and covered her head even though she was not physically harmed.

Pierce looked back through his rear-view mirror. Despite the obscuring rain, the light from an inferno lit up the sky behind them.

The enemy was closer than he had hoped.

2

"What's our destination?" Roshini asked of Pierce as they sped into the monsoonal night.

Pierce glanced from the slow-moving traffic of people, bicycles and pedestrians all competing for road space in the heavy rain, and tried to gauge her state of mind. Controlled fear was his only impression as passing headlights dappled her in waves of bright yellows and oranges.

When a truck raced past, splashing their windscreen with a deluge of muddy water, Pierce returned his attention to the traffic. He spotted a sign for the highway and followed it. The dual-lane transit corridor was congested with cars, trucks and motorcycles like all of India's city roads, but at least it was faster moving. He merged with the traffic, knowing they could cover greater distances in a shorter time period on the highways, but it was also an obvious route for their pursuers to look for them. So far, however, no tails had appeared in the rear-view mirror. The trap he had set at the safe house might have worked in their favour.

"Mark, where are we headed?"

"Sorry!" He realised he hadn't answered her questions, or even properly acknowledged them, distracted as he was by their predicament. "We're headed east, for now. When I have a moment, I'll arrange your exact extraction point from India, and then we'll head for that location. A CIA team will meet us there to fly us to America. In the meantime, want to fill me in on what's going on?"

She twisted her diamond ring around her finger so that the headlights from other cars caught in its highly refractive crystalline structure and sparkled back. "You mean you haven't been briefed already?"

An interesting choice of words, thought Pierce. "Briefing" was a word intelligence and military personnel used to describe the pre-mission planning and instruction process undertaken before an operator like himself was sent into the field to complete an assignment. A civilian would have asked if Pierce had been "informed", "filled in", or "told" what the situation was. Not use the word "briefed".

"No, Roshini. I know as much as you. Less, in fact."

"But you're CIA?"

Pierce nodded. He supposed he was with the United States' Central Intelligence Agency, a sanctioned para-military operator and an off-the-books asset sent into the field to "fix" problems after the CIA had exhausted all other conventional and legal means to get the job done. He was also deniable, should a mission go wrong, and he found himself captured or killed. But he liked operating independently and alone in the field, where he could make his own decisions and follow his own rules to get the job done, so deniability suited him. This was the nature of his current mission, and he felt a comfort that this situation was entirely in his own hands to control.

"Yes, Roshini, I am CIA."

"You've secured defectors from hostile countries before?"

"Secured." "Defectors." "Hostile." Roshini's words, spoken in an Indian accent but with a hint of English education in her inflections, were those of an individual active in the spying profession, but her actions back at the safe house and in this moment suggested she was a civilian. An example of this was her lacking situational awareness skills, for she stared only at the taillights of the car in front of them rather than constantly scanning all directions for threats, as he did.

He cleared his throat and answered her. "Yes, many times."

"That's a relief." She breathed deep, then held the air in her lungs for a count of five before expelling it again.

"Roshini, who are we running from, and why?"

Again, she held her breath, then said, "I have many encrypted video files uploaded on the Dark Web. Of the director-general of the FIA and my husband making deals with the terrorist group al-Qaeda where they hide out in the Federated Tribal Lands and Hindu Kush regions of Pakistan."

"FIA? The Federal Investigation Agency?"

She nodded.

Normally when the CIA dealt with Pakistani intelligence, it was with Inter-Services Intelligence or ISI, the foreign arm of the country's many intelligence apparatuses and the most powerful and influential agency in the country. But FIA was internal and responsible for counterterrorism, counter-espionage, and sanctioned to halt smuggling and other federal crimes within the country's borders. If ISI was equivalent to the CIA, then the FIA was equivalent to the American Federal Bureau of Investigations, or FBI.

"What is the FIA doing in India, when foreign intelligence is not their mandate?" Then a realisation struck Pierce. "Wait a second! Is your husband Fawad Jahandar, assistant director of FIA's Technical Wing?"

"Yes."

Pierce couldn't quite believe what he was hearing. "You mean the same man responsible for Pakistani counterintelligence and counter-proliferation?"

She nodded. "You know him?"

"Only by reputation."

Pierce processed this information. He should have guessed this earlier when he had first heard Roshini's surname. He asked himself why the CIA were taking a risk in orchestrating the defection of the wife of a senior head from a powerful and allied intelligence agency. If this mission failed or if the FIA could prove CIA involvement, it could cause serious diplomatic strains between Pakistan and the United States, which wouldn't fare well for the never-ending global War on Terror that both sides expended considerable resources and money on trying to halt. No wonder the CIA required Pierce to go dark when he had secured Roshini, and why Abdul Ibrahim had barely briefed him on the mission details. If the FIA captured or killed them, or the defection failed in any other way, he at least was deniable and knew very little to give up under interrogation or torture.

"Why are you defecting?"

Tears filled her eyes. She touched her stomach. "Pull over!"

"What? Why?"

She started gagging.

Pierce slowed onto the shoulder, ignoring the horns of cars behind him. Once stopped, she flung open the door and vomited, not caring that the rain pounded the back of her head. In the three minutes it took to empty her stomach, Pierce kept an eye out for pursuers. They were an easy target, parked on the side of the busy highway with cars racing past, and tires splashing muddy water over them. He had to presume the worst, that their pursuers were professional intelligence officers and paramilitary soldiers and well equipped for the hunt. A drive-by shooting would be an effective strategy to now end her defection. He kept his Glock 19 close to his chest, ready for action.

Her face ashen, Roshini climbed back inside with his help. She was soaked again, and so was he, but at least the subtropical weather kept them warm. They wouldn't shiver from being wet.

Pierce returned to the driver's seat and eased into the traffic. Then he passed her a bottle of water, which she drank in small sips.

"Thank you." She cleared her throat. "To give you context, while the FIA probably knows by now that I'm defecting, they're unlikely to know the CIA orchestrated it."

He was surprised she was ready to talk again so soon after violently expelling the contents of her stomach. "Let's hope so."

"But after the earlier shoot-out, I'm sure they'll eventually figure it out."

"Why are you defecting?" Pierce asked again. Her actions made no sense.

"Okay, let me explain."

"Please do."

While she prepared herself to tell him her tale, the thought crossed his mind that she might be pregnant, but he would keep that speculation to himself for the moment.

3

Pierce had never seen this much falling water in his life, had never believed this much rain was possible. India's monsoon was as much an enemy to them as their pursuers were, with the volumes of water washing over them and the road network they traversed.

Another truck rattled close past their Maruti Gypsy, splashing further muddy water over their windshield. For a second Pierce thought it was about to run them off the road; then it sped away. Pierce was already pushing the odometer at one hundred and twenty kilometres per hour. Faster speeds would be perilous in the rain-soaked, late-night traffic, but speed took them further from the enemy.

Roshini Jahandar, rigid in the passenger seat, said, "Let me start at the beginning."

"Okay."

"I'm originally from Patna, the city you are driving us from. I'm a lawyer. When I first met my husband, Fawad, many years ago during a period of my life when I was working in London, I thought he was a lawyer too." She showed Pierce her diamond ring. "He too was working in the United Kingdom, and within three months of dating, we were deeply in love, so we married and moved to Pakistan to be with his family in Islamabad. Pakistanis and Indians don't often see eye-to-eye on many subjects, so it was a big choice for me to make, but that's what wives do."

"But you soon felt lonely, leaving your family?"

"Yes, Mark." She gave him a surprised look when he had guessed correctly. "Fawad had all these friends whom, he told me, were lawyers, people who were my peers and intellectual equals. So I'd thought I'd easily make friends in Islamabad, but it wasn't the case. Everything had been easy in London, but when I was in his hometown with his friends and co-workers, I always felt they shared a long-standing joke I was never a part of. I constantly felt I was on the outside, and this made me lonely instead. But more importantly, I eventually realised too late what that joke was, that my husband and his associates weren't in the legal profession, as they all claimed to be, but intelligence officers."

Pierce said nothing. So far, her story sounded plausible. It could be a ruse, but if it was, she was a superb actress.

"I realised I'd met Fawad during an operation in London, when his cover was that of a Pakistani lawyer, and he'd just stuck with that cover since because it suited him that I believed he was a kind and just defender of legal rights. I believed him for years."

Pierce frowned. "But he's FIA? What was he doing in London then, operating outside of his jurisdiction? Shouldn't the operation have been with the ISI?"

She shook her head. "I don't know about that. I'm not in the intelligence services, just unwillingly messed up with it.

It's old history, so does it really matter why or which service he was with at the time?"

Pierce shrugged. "Probably not."

"Mark, what I'm trying to say is I realised too late I had given up everything for a lie. At first, I accepted the deceit, pretended I didn't know Fawad's real profession. But it became increasingly difficult when Fawad came home with bruised knuckles, or he'd be angry for no reason. Sometimes he was as white as a ghost, like he'd almost died, and that was probably the truth of the matter. Like he had just walked away from a shoot-out unharmed when everyone else had died. He'd be angry more times than not and refused to talk. I kept telling myself he was a good man... That he protected his country and his people from terrorists and criminals..."

Her voice wavered, and she ceased speaking.

Pierce sensed her desperate need for him to believe her, but he held his tongue so she could continue her story uninterrupted, knowing he was testing her. She could still be a plant, sent to the CIA as a double agent or a saboteur of some kind. Not that Pierce thought it likely, but he did have to consider and assess all potential options. He turned to look at her for a moment but found himself staring at her longer than he intended. She was attractive, and the raw vulnerability appealed to him in a way he could not clearly articulate.

"One day I discovered two human bodies in the back of our family car." She gagged again while recalling this traumatic memory, but nothing came up. "Someone had beaten them all over. I also saw raw wounds around their wrists and mouths where someone had tied and gagged them."

"Fawad caught you, with the bodies?"

Roshini nodded. "Because I screamed. At first, I didn't

believe Fawad was responsible for their deaths. I'd thought the bodies were sent to our home as a warning, or that someone had targeted my husband for assassination and this was a message he'd be next — or something like that. I expected consolation. Instead Fawad became angry with me, ordered me to forget what I'd seen. He locked me in our bedroom and disappeared for many hours, presumably to dispose of the bodies or do whatever it is intelligence officers do with deceased, tortured victims. When Fawad returned, he acted like nothing had happened. I tried to ask him about it, but he raised a hand as if to strike me. For the first time I witnessed the fury in his eyes. He was different, not the man I had fallen in love with and married. I recognised he would beat me if I asked again. I didn't."

Pierce kept his eyes on the road. Finally, the rain's intensity was dropping, and visibility was improving despite it still being late in the night. The scents of diesel and other fuels soon overpowered the air-conditioning ducts. He kept glancing in his mirrors and out the side windows, uncertain if someone was following them and unable to detect any signs that they were. While he listened to Roshini talk, it became clear to him that he'd need to call Mitch Hawley soon and finalise their extraction pretty damn quick. He was sitting on a powder keg here with this woman and her perilous situation.

"I got a little crazy. I started spying on Fawad, which was insane, risky behaviour when I look back on it. But I wanted to get back at him for fooling me for so long, and for threatening me like that. So I started tailing him, putting GPS trackers in his car." She shuddered as another horrific memory returned.

"Something else happened. Something worse?"

She sobbed. "I had a friend, Yasra. Another lawyer in the Islamabad firm where I worked. She helped me spy on Fawad. We were stupid together, but she was my only friend, and we couldn't help ourselves. The man who supposedly loved and cherished me was a fake, and I wanted to know who he really was, and so did Yasra. Then one day, Yasra disappeared. No one knew what happened to her. Her family became distraught, and so did Sahir, her husband. But I got the message, leave my husband's work alone or face the same consequences."

"And yet here you are, ignoring the threat and defecting. Exposing your husband's deceit in exchange for a ticket to America."

"You make me sound heartless when you put it like that."

Pierce nodded. "In my profession, most words I hear out of other people's mouths are lies."

"You think I'm lying?"

Pierce remembered what Estrada had told him about Roshini just before she had died. "No, I don't think so. Every question you've answered is consistent with your overall narrative. Elaborate lies fall apart under scrutiny."

"You're testing me?"

He nodded and grinned. "You're a lawyer. You know as well as I do, people lie all the time to protect themselves."

"I'm not lying, Mark. The videos are insurance. Information that, if released, will be worse for Fawad than for me. I want my husband to have good reasons not to come after me or my family."

Except that he was, thought Pierce, and judging by what he had overheard the two killers say back at the safe house, Fawad was willing to kill Roshini for her indiscretion. Instead of voicing his concern, he said, "See, that explanation makes sense. That's why I believe you." He felt she wasn't lying to him, but also sensed she didn't understand the full picture here.

She smiled with relief.

"But that's not everything, is it?"

"What do you mean?"

"Daniella Estrada told me, and so did my boss, Ibrahim, that the critical intelligence you have in your possession, that your husband really wants back, are not the video files of Fawad making deals with al-Qaeda, but something else."

Roshini seemed to shrink into the passenger seat. "You know about that?"

4

Pierce looked back at the traffic through his rearview mirror. All he could see were headlights, but none seemed to be moving erratically or accelerating to catch them. For the moment, he felt their pursuers had still not found them.

"It sounds to me like you had a carefully planned defection worked out, but something changed in the last week. Suddenly, you had to speed up your timetable, and it had something to do with the data stick now in your possession, right?"

The lawyer nodded as she visibly paled. "Estrada told me that the CIA needed to get me out straight away, not wait a few weeks longer as we had originally planned. Suddenly, she wanted me to snatch everything I could from Fawad's house safe — he had no idea I'd worked out the combination long ago — and that included multiple physical files, cash, which is in the bag you saw earlier, but most importantly the data stick you speak of. The paper files we lost during the assault at the first failed extraction point, when we were first attacked. As I said, the cash is in the bag on the back seat where you put it. The data stick, however..."

When she had paused for several seconds and not spoken further, Pierce said, "It is or is not on your person?"

"On me. I'll show you, later, if you don't mind? I'm trusting you with my life here, Mark. Please don't let me down and snatch it away because that is all you need from me, and then leave me high and dry in India to fend for myself on my own."

He turned to her again, noticing her staring back at him with wide eyes. She was fighting herself not to appear vulnerable before him. "I won't do that."

"Please don't."

He reflected on what Roshini had said so far. Despite her tears and trembling, she gave the impression she was methodical and had likely spent months if not years working through the details of her defection. She might not be a spy, but she had taught herself the basics of the profession and what she needed to do to protect herself. That impressed him and left him feeling respect and admiration towards her. If she was pregnant, then her actions were also to protect her unborn child. It could all still be a lie, some kind of FIA mission to feed false information to the CIA, but he sensed she spoke the truth. He decided to keep her talking, to probe for any inconsistencies in her story.

"Early on, did you initiate this defection plan alone, or did you get help?"

"I had help." Roshini wiped tears from her eyes, then perked up. She seemed comfortable talking about her defection plan where she had held control over it. It was only the last-minute theft of the data stick that seemed to have rattled her. Her delicate hand reached up behind her long neck and rubbed it. "After Yasra's death, I discovered Sahir was also an intelligence officer. He worked for my husband, which made sense because I first met Yasra and Sahir at a party my husband had organised. The same party where Yasra introduced me to a partner at the law firm I ended up working for. The last time I saw Sahir, he told me the truth, or at least the truth from his perspective. He told me Fawad was a senior spy in the Pakistani intelligence community and that he had orchestrated Yasra's disappearance and execution. It was Sahir who gave me the video files of my husband and the director-general of the FIA making deals and sharing intelligence with al-Qaeda in the Federated Tribal Areas. He told me Fawad also traded secrets with India's IB, or Intelligence Bureau, allowing him tolerated access into India from time to time. I didn't get any files that corroborate that though. But the details of my defection, I organised myself."

Pierce recalled that the Federally Administered Tribal Areas, also known as FATA, was previously a semi-autonomous tribal region in north-western Pakistan bordering Afghanistan. It existed from 1947 when Pakistan had split away from India as an independent country, until it was merged with the neighbouring province of Khyber Pakhtunkhwa in 2018. The region was the wild, rugged home to about three million Pashto people and riddled with too many Taliban, Islamic State and al-Qaeda hideouts and bases of operations. Roshini was referring to the region by its old name, which again suggested she wasn't really in the spying game, because a real intelligence officer would have known about the change in its name.

"What about the safe? Why did you have to go for that at the last minute and accelerate your defection program? It seems a huge risk when you already had enough to secure your defection."

More tears rolled down her cheeks, and Pierce found himself feeling sorry for her, which was unusual for him after such a short time with an asset. Normally he distrusted everything they said until they proved otherwise.

Roshini said, "Daniella didn't tell me the reasons. She insisted I grab the contents immediately and leave straight away. Domestically, something had changed in the last few days leading up to that request. Fawad was obsessed about something, excited but also scared. Thinking about what might have been going on scares me even now. Have I made my situation worse by taking that data stick?"

"I don't know." Pierce clenched his teeth as his hands clenched the steering wheel. He now sensed this mission would soon turn out to be far more complicated than a simple extraction. "What happened to Sahir?"

"You can guess." She turned away from him and stared blankly at the road ahead lit up in their headlights. "Or maybe not. Sahir shot himself the same night he told me the truth. He never got over what happened to his wife."

For a moment, Roshini couldn't speak, and Pierce wondered if Sahir's death was actually a murder dressed up to resemble a suicide.

Before he could ask more, she cleared her throat and composed herself, then touched him lightly on his arm. "I encrypted Sahir's files and saved them on the Dark Web. That was a year ago, Mark. It took me a long time to position all the pieces before I risked making a deal with the Americans. When we did, we eventually agreed your people would extract me while I was on vacation in my old home here in Patna, and from there the CIA would transport me safely to the US and set me up with a new life and identity. Only when that happened would I decrypt the remaining files, other than the first one I sent to show my offer was genuine. But last week, I had to change my flights, up my timetable, take risks I hadn't been willing to take before, all because whatever it is that's on this data stick I now have was suddenly critical to your CIA."

"What about your family in India? You must have figured the FIA would come after them if they couldn't get to you."

"They are already in the United States, Mark. They left for a vacation last week, but they aren't coming back. My family's safety was part of the deal."

Pierce bit down on his lower lip. He was convinced whatever she had snatched from Fawad Jahandar's safe was the crux of why the FIA were vigorously pursuing her now, and the past al-Qaeda get-togethers with Fawad and his secret trading with India's Intelligence Bureau was nothing more than a distracting nuisance shifting their attention away from a bigger problem brewing elsewhere. She knew everything about her defection, down to the finest detail, except this part. And this lack of knowledge might still cost her her life, and Pierce's too, if he weren't careful...

5

As they drove, the hairs on the back of Pierce's neck suddenly tingled. He checked his rear-view mirror again, but with it being night, and the rain, it was difficult to make out anything other than the headlights of cars behind them. While he sensed they had been found, nothing in his vision suggested this to be true.

Roshini fidgeted in her seat. "If Fawad catches me, I know he will kill me."

Pierce nodded. "Yeah, Roshini, I'd say that's exactly what he's got planned for you."

She nodded as further tears wetted her already damp cheeks. "Was it the data stick that pushed him over the edge?" she said aloud as if this was a question for herself and she was trying to make sense of the many thoughts rushing around inside her mind. "If I'd left only with the video files, might this have been a very different scenario?"

Again, she looked completely vulnerable and stared deep into his eyes every time he looked at her, seeking reassurance this would all work out well, but he wasn't certain it would.

"You love, or at least loved Fawad. And you married him. From an outsider's perspective, regardless of the nature of the intel you took from him, this is a huge betrayal. The data stick might not have changed anything."

"But it was Fawad who betrayed *me*, by lying to me from the start." Roshini shook her head. "He might have loved me once, but if he captures me — us — our ends will be brutal and horrific. I know this with all my heart. I know what kind of man he really is, behind the lies." She touched his arm again. "Promise me, if we are to fail, Mark, you'll shoot me in the heart. I'd rather die than go back to the hell that was my past life."

Pierce considered his answer before voicing it. "It won't come to that. We'll be safely out of India within the next twenty-four hours."

A lightning bolt lit up the sky, casting a fleeting, shadowed glow over rice fields and scrublands that passed them on both sides of the road. Seconds later, another heavy downpour erupted from the dark clouds, and its fresh deluge soon drenched the landscape. In response, the highway traffic slowed, forcing Pierce to do the same. But it wasn't the weather that bothered him. When he glanced in his side and rear-view mirrors, he understood his earlier sense of unease was justified.

Two sets of headlights ducked and weaved through the traffic.

Two enemy targets were closing in.

"Get down!"

"What?" Roshini, busy chewing on her fingernails, hadn't yet seen their pursuers.

"There'll be shooting soon. Get in the back, Roshini. Put on the seatbelt but lie across the seat. Low targets minimise their chance of taking a bullet."

"What did you say? Don't scare me like that."

"You've prepared for this. Do it now."

Pushing the bag with the cash across the seat, she climbed into the back. "How did they find us again so soon?"

"Good question." He too wondered how the FIA had tracked them.

Pierce slowed his speed, matching the traffic to appear inconspicuous, and allowed for new and old trucks, buses and cars to crowd around him, blocking the pursuers from drawing close. He pulled his Glock 19 and held it in his right hand while his left gripped the steering wheel. If the assailants shined a light into his cabin, they would see only one driver and might convince themselves he wasn't their target.

But Pierce realised too late that his ruse served no purpose. Suddenly, the bursts from submachine guns or assault rifles aimed in their general direction drowned out all traffic noises and the rain. Pings of metal on metal were unmistakable as his Maruti Gypsy shuddered from the impacts. He heard, then felt the right front tire lock up.

Roshini screamed.

Two nearby cars collided. Pierce heard the crunching noise of their collapsing chassis. One car flipped; the other ran off the road into the scrub.

With another lethal battle looming, adrenalin pumped through Pierce and heightened his senses as he tried to maintain his grip on the steering wheel with one tire still locked up.

Roshini screamed again, wriggled in the back seat and curled herself into a ball.

Despite his efforts to steer, the locked wheel slowed Pierce like an anchor and kept him on a single course. He downshifted to no effect, then turned the near-unresponsive steering wheel with force until they drifted into the middle of the two lanes. The two pursuing four-by-fours closed in, one on each side as he had hoped, ready to strafe him with bullets.

Together the three vehicles crossed onto a bridge straddling the Ganges River, and then drove in formation. Pierce watched as the lanes narrowed and the distance between their three vehicles decreased until they were almost touching.

Pierce waited until he was parallel with both vehicles at the bridge's middle, when the gap between each pursuing car dropped to less than half a metre. From the glimpsed views offered by oncoming cars' headlights, Pierce identified men in both vehicles armed with Heckler & Koch MP5 submachine guns ready to end his life, but of their numbers he could not yet ascertain.

Using all his strength, Pierce yanked hard on the steering wheel, fighting the locked front tire. Eventually, the Maruti Gypsy responded despite the metal-grinding noises Pierce's efforts had provoked, and he spun them in a circle until inertia took over, the forces of which pressed Pierce heavily against the driver's seat.

The three vehicles collided in the same instant. His central Gypsy impacted with the two outer pursuers and sent them off in random trajectories. The front of his Gypsy hit the enemy vehicle on the left, while the back spun in the opposite direction and hit the pursuing car on the right. The vehicle on his left smashed through the railings and dropped into the Ganges. The one on his right skidded through oncoming traffic until a semi-trailer truck smashed it head-on and crumpled the vehicle.

His body aching from the jarring impact, Pierce tried to control his spin, but there was no further give in the steering wheel. The Gypsy tore along the bridge under its own volition, collected other cars and knocked them aside, but with only enough force to nudge them out of the way. Desperate to control their dangerous drift, Pierce abandoned the steering wheel and instead yanked on the handbrake. The locked-up tire exploded, and the chassis dropped. Sparks flew from the front axle as it scraped across the asphalt. Five seconds later they ground to a halt near the opposite end of the bridge.

Pierce took a moment to recognise he was alive and unharmed. Scratched and bruised, but little more.

"Roshini? Can you move?"

Her screams turned into sobs. Then, realising that they were no longer in motion, she pulled herself together and sat up. "We're alive? What happened?"

"I'll explain later. We need to move."

Taking her hand and helping her out of the car, Pierce spotted throngs of dazed individuals clambering from their own crumpled or pinned cars, lit in random light and shadow arrangements, depending on the angles of the few functional headlights. Horns blasted everywhere. Some people ran at him to express concern, others with abuse and murderous intent.

Not wishing to find himself involved in a riot, Pierce fired his Glock into the air, aimed so the bullet would hit the river when it returned earthwards. In an instant, the mob lost their anger and fled.

Only three men ran not from him, but towards him.

Each slung Heckler & Koch MP5 submachine guns. There must have been a third vehicle he hadn't seen. "Quickly! More assailants. If we jump into the Ganges, the current will sprint us downstream."

"No!" She pressed her hands into his chest and held his stare again with her mournful eyes. "I'll get sick. I can't afford to get sick."

"Better than dying now."

"*NO!*" she screamed. "Find another way!"

Pierce didn't argue, suspecting again that she hid a pregnancy and was worried any infection she caught from diving into the dirty water could affect the health of her child. Meanwhile, the three men closed in for an easier shot. Pierce hesitated only long enough to ensure no civilians stood behind them, then fired six closely arranged bullets at the advancing combatants. One grunted when he took a bullet, fell and dropped his weapon. The other two ducked for cover.

"Time to move!" Without waiting for an answer or capitulation, Pierce dragged Roshini to an abandoned car at the front of the carnage. Keys remained in the ignition, and the motor idled, but no one was inside. Light rain splashed off its windows and panels. It was a hatchback with not much engine power, but in this moment, it was everything he had hoped for. Even better, all the other cars in the wreckage were jammed in and stuck, so there was no way any other vehicle could be commandeered by the enemy and used to chase them. "Get in."

Roshini took the passenger seat and fastened the seatbelt.

Pierce drove.

They heard further weapons fire, but too distant to hit them.

Soon they disappeared down an empty highway and were swallowed by the night.

6

Begusarai, Bihar, India

Deciding that the highway was no longer a safe option after sunlight had crept up over the horizon, Pierce exited into the city of Begusarai on the Ganges and followed the main roads only long enough to divert into the city backstreets. In the narrow and winding lanes, the chances of the FIA finding and attacking them diminished.

Like how Pierce suspected all Indian urban centres were, this city too was crowded and densely packed with people, cars, bicycles, trucks, buses and motorised rickshaws, all of whose ideas of following road rules seemed limited to generally only sticking to the left-hand lane and little more. The weather remained as hot and humid as it had been yesterday, causing his now dry clothes to stick again to his sweaty skin. The rain had also eased since the attack on the bridge, and Pierce was surprised by the odorous fog that hung over the city, because the wet weather should have cleared the haze at least for a few days. The fog probably spoke to how bad industrial pollution was here.

After refuelling at an Indian Oil gas station and feeling confident they weren't being tailed for the moment, Pierce drove until he found a women's clothing store and parked outside.

"What are we doing?" Roshini asked, rubbing her eyes. She had barely slept during their drive, and was disorientated and confused. She stretched her arms up above her head, extending her trim body, and Pierce found himself again transfixed at how stunning she was.

He, however, hadn't slept at all, but unlike her, he had trained and conditioned himself to operate without sleep when he needed to. He focused his thoughts again on this mission's purpose and said, "Your husband is tracking us, Roshini. I don't know how." He looked at what she was wearing. "The clothes you wear, they one hundred per cent from Daniella Estrada's wardrobe?"

Roshini nodded.

"Including your underwear?"

She blushed and said nothing.

Pierce smirked and handed her cash from his wallet. "Go in and buy new underwear, change into it and throw away what you are wearing."

She smiled, and her face lit up, and she said, "Why? Because you think my undergarments could be bugged?"

Pierce nodded and motioned to their gear on the back seat. "I'm also worried about the money, and the data stick. The latter, can you show it to me now?"

Roshini reached into her pocket and withdrew an ordinary-looking data stick, a brand that could be bought at any electronics store anywhere. The print on the disc said it stored 128GB. She clenched her teeth when she said, "Daniella already checked it. She said there are data files on it, but they are locked down with passwords and are highly encrypted."

He glanced around, deciding what to do. The streets were full of pedestrians, but none that caused Pierce to suspect them of being up to anything sinister. Ideally, they would find a safety deposit box and secure the data stick and money in there, and come back for it later, but that defeated the entire purpose of their mission, getting the data out of the country in the first place. Earlier, he'd run a bug sweeper he'd brought with him as part of his standard field kit and found nothing on the money. Now he ran it over the data stick, and similarly nothing pinged.

"You're checking for bugs?" Roshini asked, again using spy lingo.

He looked up at her, and again her eyes fixed on his. "Yes." He clutched the data stick in his hand. "Mind if I hold on to it for now?"

She nodded reluctantly.

He noticed her diamond ring again and motioned to it with his eyes. "Mind if I check it too?"

"Daniella checked multiple times yesterday. I know it's clean, but fine, check again."

She held out her hand and gently rested it on Pierce's arm. He ran the bug sweeper over the ring, and again, nothing pinged. "Go and buy new clothes. I need to make a call anyway, to arrange our extraction. We'll be out of India in twelve hours, twenty-four at the most."

Roshini nodded, took the rupees Pierce offered her, then disappeared into the clothes store.

Pierce waited until she was inside, then dialled the

number of his handler on his burner cell phone maxed out with state-of-the-art CIA encryption software. It took twelve rings before Mitch Hawley answered. His previous handler would have answered immediately.

"Code in," Hawley responded, his monotone voice sounding exactly like an overworked and underpaid customer service officer too long employed with the Internal Revenue Service.

After expressing an exasperated sigh, Pierce proceeded through a series of prearranged code words and responses until they were each satisfied they were who they claimed to be. He didn't like that Hawley went through the process twice, with a different round of questions when only a single cycle was sufficient for identification purposes.

When they were done, Pierce said, "What took you so long to answer?"

Hawley made a snorting noise. "Please, I took your call."

"It's your job to take my calls."

"Don't I know that." He snorted again. "Do you have the asset? Is there a problem? Is that why you are calling me?"

Pierce drew in a deep breath. "That's a yes, Hawley, for all three questions. I'm calling about our extraction point, and I need intel on who is tracking us. I presume you are aware of the shoot-out on the Ganges bridge outside of Patna?"

Hawley whistled loudly, hurting Pierce's ear. "That was you? Of course it was. Trigger Man, you are one crazy motherfucker," he said, using Pierce's code name within the CIA.

"We're being tracked, Hawley. I want to know who they are, the group that attacked us, and how they found us. Names, details, capabilities, etcetera, okay? I suspect FIA, but you need to confirm that."

Hawley made a tutting noise. "We'll get to your request in a minute. First, where are you?"

"Begusarai."

"That's not good. I was expecting you to be a lot further east by now. Your extraction point is in Kolkata." He gave the name and address of an airfield just outside the coastal city. "Be there by sunrise tomorrow."

Pierce gritted his teeth. "Change it; it's too far. Kolkata is five hundred kilometres from my current position, and in this traffic, it's at least twelve hours away."

"I'll see what I can do, but you should have called earlier. I've already made all the arrangements."

"I don't fucking care what you've arranged, Hawley. Change it!"

"Calm down, Trigger Man. I'll get onto it once we hang up, but just in case I can't, head towards Kolkata anyway. Can I ping you on this number if the extraction point changes?"

Pierce couldn't believe what he was hearing and wondered how Mitch Hawley had gotten through the CIA's arduous selection process in the first place. Then he remembered Hawley was fluent in five Asian languages, held a master's degree in Asian geopolitics, and had somehow wooed all the senior heads of the CIA with his insightful analysis of several insurgent groups causing havoc in Southeast Asia. His intel had led to several operations resulting in the dismemberment and reduction in the power and threat capabilities of these groups, lavishing him with high praise all round. The senior powers inside Langley obviously thought Hawley was worth gold to them, but when Pierce had commenced working with him on his first mission three months earlier, he soon realised Hawley was only worried about pleasing those more senior than him. He didn't care who he stepped on to fast-track his career in the agency. Hawley was thirty-two, the same age as Pierce, but that was the only thing they had in common.

"I have other priorities, you know? It's a lot of work for me to change the extraction point again."

Pierce clenched his fists tight and bit down on his lips for a moment. Then he didn't hold back and said what was on his mind. "Hawley, why do you want to be my handler?" When Hawley did not respond, Pierce continued with, "I mean, this isn't really working out between us, is it?"

7

Pierce imagined Hawley smarting from this blunt assessment of their dysfunctional working relationship, but when Mitch Hawley answered, it was not what Pierce had been expecting. "It's not really a question that is appropriate while we're mission active, Trigger Man. We can talk about it when you return stateside if you still feel the need to express your feelings on the matter."

Pierce drew in a second deep breath. "It's not feelings that are on the table. It's professional conduct, but fine, we can talk later."

He had no intention of entering into discussions with Hawley on this subject in the future, but he would have words with his superior, Abdul Ibrahim, when he had a moment. If Hawley fucked up on this mission, as he seemed to be well on track to do, then it was Pierce's life on the line, not his. There were many ways an operator like Pierce could die in the field, and he accepted those risks, but death by incompetence was inexcusable. "Change the extraction point, Hawley, and get back to me ASAP. Meanwhile, tell me who is tracking us."

"No promises on the former. On the latter though, Directorate of Analysis has ascertained that a FIA kill team was tracking you."

"I already said that."

"Yes, but if you let me finish, I have more. Fourteen FIA men flew into Patna two days ago."

"How can so many FIA men fly into India without the IB knowing about it? I mean, Pakistani and Indian intelligence services watch each other as closely as we watch the Russians these days."

Hawley let out a long sigh. "Don't you read briefing reports that cross your desk, Trigger Man, like the rest of us do?"

Pierce growled. "You mean Jahandar trades enough secrets with the IB for them to be happy with him coming and going from India as much as it pleases him."

"Yes, that's our assessment of the situation. The FIA must be in on it and think they are getting the better deal in the intelligence swaps. Otherwise the IB would have done away with him long ago."

Pierce nodded to himself. "Okay, what else?"

"Estrada reported her team eliminated four FIA operatives during the first failed extraction, and satellite imagery as well as our hacks into the local Patna police records showed you wiped out another five on that bridge incident you caused last night."

"I took out an additional two at the Patna safe house."

"Well, good for you, Trigger Man. But getting back to the bridge attack, the other good news for you is it seems the local police have no clue as to who was involved, so they aren't chasing you. So far, the FIA is your only problem. Unless the IB identify and don't like what the FIA are up to on their turf, and then you'll have them to deal with too."

"What about the surviving three FIA operators? Who are they?"

"Yes, I'm getting to that. A little patience, if you don't mind."

Pierce glanced to the clothes store, then read the dials on his watch. Roshini had been inside for four minutes now. He'd give her another four before he went looking for her. "Hawley, just tell me what you know!"

"I'm also getting to that. We've identified that the three survivors are Fawad Jahandar, Roshini's husband as you know, although it seems he took a bullet, which you must have put in him, because we've ascertained he and two others sought out a doctor's surgery after the bridge attack. Probably why they haven't yet recommenced their pursuit of you."

Pierce remembered that he had hit one of the assailants with at least one bullet. "And the others?"

"Yes, the second is Fawad's head of Operational Intelligence, Qusay Vali, who incidentally is also Jahandar's brother-in-law. They are as thick as thieves is what I hear."

Vali was the name spoken by the two assailants Pierce had taken out in the Patna safe house. "You know this, or just speculating?"

Hawley snorted again. "Please, Trigger Man, I'm a professional. Anything I report to you is what I know, and if I'm speculating, then trust that I'll give you odds on the validity of the information I'm providing."

Clenching and unclenching his fists and trying not to let his frustration out, Pierce said, "Fine. Who is the last man?"

"Ah, this is where it gets really interesting. Sergeant Ajmal Mughal, do you know him?"

Pierce couldn't believe that Hawley was taking his time to get to the point. "No, humour me?"

"Weird, I thought you would. He's your type. Thirty-five years old and one hundred and eighty pounds of muscle, he's with the 'Maroon Berets'. That's the Pakistan Army Special Service Group, if you didn't know that. Ruthless motherfucker. For years, he's been engaged in counterinsurgency and counterterrorism operations across Pakistan's former Federal Tribal Areas and now Khyber Pakhtunkhwa in neighbouring Afghanistan, taking out al-Qaeda, ISIS-K and Taliban insurgents. Received training from the US Army Special Forces too. A note here from our Army's dossier on the man reports Mughal as a 'cold, calculating killer, who is scarily efficient at eliminating enemy targets'. Over two hundred confirmed kills. Wow, I hope you don't have to deal with this son of a bitch before your mission is over."

"Well, if the extraction point was closer, I wouldn't have to."

"Come on, Trigger Man, I'm working on it."

Pierce tensed. "Send me photos of all three."

"Of course."

Pierce spotted Roshini walking fast from the store and headed straight to their vehicle. She spotted him looking at her, and broke out in a smile and waved to him. He said into the phone, "Hawley, I need to go. Do as I said, and in the meantime, work out how Jahandar and the other two are tracking us."

"Are you serious? How am I supposed to do that?"

"I don't know how, and I don't care, but it's your job to find out. Oh, and tell me, is Rachel Zang still operational?" He referred to his peer, occasional bedmate and perhaps friend who was also a CIA Ground Branch paramilitary operator like himself. With their different assignment timetables, they hadn't spoken for a month and then only on the phone. Pierce could call Ibrahim, but that would be seen as official communications and definitely breaking protocol. But Pierce's reason for reaching out to Zang was because their relationship was both personal and professional, and she might forgo standard mission protocols and keep it on the low-down. He wanted another contact should Hawley fail to deliver, which Pierce felt could soon be a strong possibility considering Hawley's increasingly problematic working style, and Zang was ideal.

"You know I can't confirm or deny that, Trigger Man. Not while you are operational."

"Just tell her to call me, on this number. And you call me back when you have further information. Got it?"

Pierce disconnected the call before Hawley could complain further.

Meanwhile, Roshini had clambered in and shut the door. She looked at him and smiled once more.

He started up the engine. "Everything okay?" he asked when they were moving with the traffic again.

She nodded, then her demeanour changed completely as if the reality of her situation had been absent from her thoughts for a time, and now she tensed her whole body. "Yes. Just scared out of my mind."

He smiled and squeezed her arm lightly. "Well, things

have progressed. We have an extraction point now, and I have further details on who still follows us."

"My husband?"

"Yes, and two of his close associates. But if we keep moving, we'll be out of here before they reach us."

He realised he was still holding her, so he pulled his arm away, then drove off.

8

Washington, DC, United States of America

When Rachel Zang woke to the morning sun streaming through the fourth-floor window, she realised she was sharing a bed with a man. He draped his muscular arm over her chest as his naked body spooned her equally unclad form. The scenario in which she found herself brought a smile to her face. The lovemaking they had shared the previous night, in a deluxe suite grabbed at the last moment in this upmarket and inner-city Washington, DC, hotel, had been worth the splurge. But it had also been a surprise to Zang that she had "stumbled into" Jay Sanders the previous evening, seemingly by chance. In her profession, "chance" encounters almost never happened by accident.

She had hooked up with Jay before, almost a year ago now for a three-night stand, and then again for a few more planned but brief liaisons after that, all of which had been pleasurable and fun. They regularly crossed paths in CIA headquarters in Langley and had even worked on the same mission assignment for a period of five weeks. Since they were both employees of the Central Intelligence Agency, there was no need for messy investigations into the other potentially being a honeytrap agent from a foreign enemy power, which made their meetings easier. CIA employees, by the nature of their work, were often in and out of the Capitol to brief politicians, so perhaps it wasn't coincidental that they had reunited again after all this time apart and no communication. They did move in the same circles, so statistically speaking, they were destined to run into each other again.

As she further pondered their chance encounter, she rolled over to face him. Like the previous times, it had been a fun night, and Jay was an expert lover. One of the best.

He stirred, then opened his eyes.

Zang mused that he was a handsome man for sure, with closely cropped afro hair, a strong jaw and a gym fit physique that was all sculptured muscle. He was ex-Army intelligence, so military trained like Zang, who was ex-Air Force and a former pilot, but their paths in the CIA had taken very different directions. Jay had become a case officer while she had progressed down the paramilitary operator path. Where they were the same was that they both worked predominately overseas in enemy territories, defending America's safety and security. They were noble public servants, acting for the greater good, and that was a big part of his appeal.

When their stares locked, he smiled, then snuggled close to her. "Good morning, sexy. Last night was fun."

Zang draped her bare arm and leg over him. "Yes. A pleasant surprise all round."

They lay for a moment, with neither speaking. Several

times, they each motioned to talk, but no words came forth from either of them.

Could it be that they had run out of things to say?

Before Zang allowed the moment to become awkward, she asked, "I suppose you can't tell me what you've been up to, Jay? You know, with our lives being all 'need to know' and all that?"

His hand stroked her dark hair, which she'd recently cut short after an assailant she'd fought in a hotel in Taipei had used her own hair against her to swing her around the room, smashing her into walls before she had gotten control of the situation. She still carried bruises on her back and left leg to remind her how close she'd come to not walking away from that encounter at all.

"Actually, Zang, I can tell you what I'm up to. I didn't tell you last night, but I quit the CIA six months ago."

She sat and rolled on top of him, intrigued by this news. "No, you didn't tell me that!"

He smiled and stared into her eyes without blinking. "It really is good to see you again, Rachel. You are incredibly stunning."

She playfully punched him on his chest. "Quit with the smooching, Jay. Tell me, what did you do?"

He grinned again and genuinely seemed pleased with himself. "Got an offer from my old CO. I'm private sector now."

Zang frowned, because she had never imagined Jay Sanders to be the type to take a fat paycheque from a corporation. He was too much the patriot, or at least that was what she had pegged him as until today. "Doing what?"

He laughed. "Doing what pays best for people like you

and me when we quit being public servants. I'm PMC. Private military contractor."

"No way!"

Zang had been about to ask what had prompted him to quit the CIA, a federal government job where they each felt they were best placed to actually make meaningful change for a better, safer, and nicer world. They had discussed this topic before, how the corporate sector was soulless and focused only on making money, and PMCs more so than most. The change seemed uncharacteristic.

Then Zang remembered the story Jay Sanders had told her about his brother the second time they had hooked up. Ben Sanders had formerly been an A-10 Thunderbolt II "Warthog" pilot with the United States Air Force, who had loved flying and had wholeheartedly concluded that a career in the military was just perfect for him. But when it was suspected Ben had motor neurone disease, he was quickly discharged, with his release papers citing ongoing poor performance in his fighter pilot duties as the reason for his dismissal. But it was obvious to everyone who knew Ben, including his wife and two young sons, that this was an action to limit the US military's liability in caring for Ben with the ongoing support he would require to manage his disease.

After that, Jay had never felt the same respect or admiration for their government that he once had, particularly when he watched, heartbroken, as Ben's wife, Sally, had to return to the workforce while their two children had to grow up around a depressed stay-at-home father who was trapped in a body that was slowly succumbing to paralysis.

Thinking upon this, Zang couldn't help herself and

asked, "Did you make this decision because of what happened to Ben?"

Sanders nodded as his face lost its colour and expressiveness. "Yeah. I don't want to end up the same as my brother. I made sure all my health and medical insurance benefits were locked up tight before I joined. I just... I could no longer... Look, Zang, I just don't trust the government anymore. It's that simple."

Not wishing to enter a conversational direction that would only depress them both further, and already having the answers she needed, Zang said, "Well, it's exciting, this new job. I'm happy for you. Who is it with?"

"Executive Believers. Heard of them?"

"No, can't say I have." Zang traced a line with her finger along Jay's firm chest. "Sounds like a religious cult to me."

He laughed lightly. "It's anything but, Zang. Established three years ago by Brad Karson. You know him? Former major with the 1st Special Forces Group, Airborne? The Black Dog of the Hindu Kush?"

Zang had never met the man, but she recalled that Karson had a reputation as a fine tier one operator, with many successful missions in Iraq and Afghanistan, hence his nickname. The men and women under Karson reputedly loved him, while his superiors reputedly gave him a long operating leash, knowing that if they couldn't easily control him, allowing him latitude paid off because he always delivered mission objectives to the letter.

She also remembered that Karson had supposedly lost his wife and child or children to a terror attack on American soil and had blamed the US government for not doing enough to protect his family when they'd needed their support the most. Then he had commenced a series of public attacks against the armed forces, condemning them for not looking after veterans when they no longer had need for them. His personal suffering around this issue had galvanised immense support around him, or so said the rumour networks around Langley and the Capitol.

No wonder Jay and Karson had teamed up. They both felt let down by the government they had each valiantly served, risking their lives in the field while simultaneously feeling they had garnered no respect or support at the conclusion of their working relationships.

"Karson's company is this Executive Believers?"

"Uh-huh."

"I didn't know you two served together?"

"Karson's a great boss. The whole time I was touring Afghanistan, me and all the other men and women serving under him, we always knew he had our backs. I never felt that way with any other CO I served with. Did you know, in his last tour before he retired, Karson never lost a soldier under him in the field? He would never have let Ben down."

Zang frowned. The way Jay spoke of Karson was like he worshipped him, and her joke about Executive Believers being a religious cult now didn't seem that funny. "I also heard he sometimes went by the name 'Special K', and 'K' stood for 'killer'?"

Sanders shrugged. "Some people called him that, I guess, but never to his face. To almost everyone, he is Black Dog."

Not sure what to ask him next, and not ready to get into a deep and meaningful conversation focused on the tragic state of affairs his brother now faced, she reached over and glanced at her cell phone. It was 06:14 hours. "I need to be at Langley soon. But I need a shower first. Join me?"

She jumped out of the king-sized bed and ran to the bathroom.

No sooner had she started up the shower and stood under the steamy hot water, Jay had joined her. He was smiling again and seemed genuinely happy. Perhaps the change to the private sector was exactly what he needed to heal himself and move on with his life.

Winking, he said, "Want me to wash that very slender, very muscular back of yours?"

"Sure."

"A few bruises here. I didn't get too rough with you last night?"

"If you got rough like that, believe me, there wouldn't be another time. Besides, it's nothing, just the perks of my day job dealing with the bad guys of this world."

"I hear you!"

As they washed and flirted with each other, Zang watched as Jay's expression very gradually morphed from playful to serious. Zang had wanted to keep things light, and still did, but in time she admitted to herself she did wish to learn more about Jay's decisions as to why he'd changed sides. "Are Executive Believers based here, in Washington, DC?"

"Near enough. We're in Baltimore so just next door. With over sixty ex-tier one operatives on our books, we're operating pretty much anywhere in the world where there is a war on now. We've had some very lucrative contracts in the Philippines, Iraq and Nigeria, so the cash is rolling in."

Zang nodded as she soaped Jay's chest, feeling and enjoying the solid pectoral muscles beneath his smooth skin. Jay Sanders was in his late thirties, ten years older than her, and still good looking. She wondered why he hadn't settled down with a woman of his own, with the years kicking on, but perhaps he was like her, a wild spirit who never wanted to be tied down to anything or anyone. "That's significant growth in only three years."

Jay smirked as he washed her thighs, then crouched down to wash her long, slender legs. "As I said, Karson is a legend. Everyone wants to work for 'Black Dog'."

"And what exactly do you do for him, this canine pal of yours?" Zang turned away from Jay, not wishing to get turned on as his hands now massaged the inside of her thighs, for she sensed he was ready to go again if she encouraged him. "I think I'll finish up now, thank you." She took the soap and washed herself while Jay, standing out of the stream of cascading water, watched.

"I'm EB's intelligence executive officer. We have so many contracts going down all the time, Karson needs me coordinating his teams and providing them with the intel they need."

"Good for you!" Now that Zang had finished washing herself, she jumped out and dried her skin while Jay finished soaping his body under the still running stream of water.

Suddenly, from nowhere, Zang found herself thinking that their morning conversation seemed more like an interview than the casual banter they had enjoyed at the bar last night. "So why are you in DC and not back at HQ?"

He laughed again as hot water rushed over his impressively chiselled body. "Recruiting, Rachel. Like you said, we're growing fast and need more operators and intelligence specialists on the books."

And there it was, Jay was testing her out, ready to make an offer. "You weren't thinking of recruiting me?"

Jay turned off the water and caught her returned stare,

then frowned. "No, I wasn't, actually. But do you want to go private sector? You could be good with EB."

She shook her head as she finished towelling herself off. Zang was very happy working for the US government, where she felt her work was actually about the greater good. Private military contractors, in her mind, were only about the money. Sure, she'd worked with plenty of PMCs in the past and had found many to be highly competent and decent and got results the CIA needed where they were needed, but it wasn't what she wanted.

Jay took her towel from her hand and used it to dry his own body. "Actually, I was hoping to meet with another operator and offer him a job. Maybe you know him? Mark Pierce?"

Zang did her best to hide her surprise at Jay Sanders's question and because he had overlooked her as a potential recruit. She did indeed know Pierce extremely well, both professionally and intimately. Like with her and Jay, Zang and Pierce maintained an on-again, off-again, casual relationship, and they had worked two missions together, but she hadn't seen Pierce for close to two months now, spoken on the phone only briefly in the last month, so she had no idea where he was or what he had been up to. "No, I don't, I'm afraid."

Jay looked disappointed. "You sure? He goes by the handle Trigger Man."

The question, and how Jay posed it, caused the fine hairs on her forearms to prickle. "You know what, you never asked me what my code name was."

He made a puzzled expression, then said, "I guess not. Never thought about it. What is it?"

"I don't have one. Was never assigned one. Seems to be

something you men need so you can distinguish each other when you hunt in packs."

Her comment confused him. He said, "Am I sensing some kind of resentment here?"

She waved a hand at him. "It doesn't matter. And no. Sorry. Don't know this Trigger Man, Jay."

Jay watched her for a moment, stared intensely with a sudden uncharacteristic coldness, then just as suddenly broke into a grin and smiled, becoming exactly like the man he had been last night, when she had felt excitement at the idea of spending an intimate evening together. "Not to worry, Rachel. I'm sure I'll track down this Pierce character eventually and make my offer."

"You haven't even interviewed him."

"True. I'll interview him first."

Zang nodded, then found her clothes and proceeded to dress in her grey business suit and white blouse, ideal for these warm summer days. Jay did the same.

A minute later, she had all her things and kissed Jay lightly on the mouth in a not-too-subtle gesture to tell him this was goodbye. "This was fun. Maybe we'll do this again, in another year's time."

He touched her gently on the shoulder. "I'd like that. But let's not make it twelve months. That's way too long not to hit that nice bod of yours."

Three minutes later, when Rachel Zang was outside Beacon Hotel, where they had spent the night, on Rhode Island Avenue and less than five minutes' walk from the White House, she marched south. Once out of the line of sight of the Beacon, she took out her cell phone and called Langley.

"Zang?" said Abdul Ibrahim, chief of the CIA's Special

Operations Group and Zang's boss, with ultimate responsibility for all paramilitary clandestine operations occurring anywhere and everywhere in the world, including those that Pierce and Zang participated in. "What's up?"

Zang knew she was contacting the C/SOG only because her instincts were telling her all was not right, and not because she had any hard evidence anything was out of the ordinary. She could have gone to her direct line manager, but her hunch seemed too important not to take it to someone of his seniority. "Sorry to bother you, sir. Something came up. A hunch, really."

"Well then, out with it."

"Does the name Major Brad Karson mean anything to you?"

Ibrahim paused for a very long count of seconds, which gave credence that her suspicions were on the mark. "Funny you should bring up that name, Zang. I'm just on my way to a Senate Select Committee on Intelligence hearing, where Karson is about to testify."

Now Zang paused as she momentarily held her breath. This was news indeed, which immediately shattered any illusion that last night had been a chance encounter.

"Want to tell me what this is about, Zang?" Ibrahim asked, when she hadn't answered him straight away.

"I will, sir. Can I meet you first? Can I sit in on the hearing?"

She waited while he considered her request, then said, "This is highly irregular. But you're cleared, so I don't see why not. The hearing will be at the Hart Senate Office Building at fifteen hundred hours. Get there thirty minutes before that."

9

Deoghar Outskirts, Jharkhand, India

Pierce and Roshini drove for a time, and as the rain eased, she eventually relaxed enough to drift off. Pierce let her be, and by midday they had covered a significant distance and were within India's Jharkhand state. It rained occasionally, but no further heavy downpours followed. The wet roads remained slippery, however, while the traffic grew denser as more people gained the confidence to be out and about when it was not so wet.

The landscape had changed too, become rolling and rocky hills, and they passed many elaborate Hindu temples and bisected large untamed forests. They progressed at a reasonable speed but not at the pace Pierce would have preferred, which led him to calculate they would reach Kolkata by day's end. It irked Pierce that Mitch Hawley hadn't called back with a closer extraction point, but for the moment they seemed to have escaped further detection, suggesting they had thrown their enemy off their scent.

While on a rare, long empty stretch of the road, he turned to look at Roshini better. She didn't seem as distressed as he'd feared she might have become. He noticed her lips and her fluttering eyelids and her long slender neck. Then all too soon, she sensed he was watching her and emerged from her slumber.

Pierce turned away, feeling awkward for staring at her, then gave her a moment to focus on the road ahead while she fully woke. The sunlight on her skin highlighted her attractiveness, but prolonged stress had aged her, with fine wrinkles normally found only on older women. Pierce also sensed her physical discomfort and, judging by her expressions of queasiness, feelings of nausea too. Symptoms explained with a dozen viable reasons, but likely because she carried a child inside her.

She reached over and lightly touched his arm. "Mark! How are we travelling? Sorry, I dozed off there."

"No problem. We're progressing well, and it's always better to sleep when you can."

She nodded, took back her arm and watched the road again.

Knowing that they were not yet in the clear, Pierce decided now was the opportune moment to quiz her about the people who hunted them. "Can we talk about Fawad and his peers?"

"Sure. What do you want to know?"

"The intel I gathered this morning is that your husband is currently travelling with two surviving companions, down from his team of fourteen. The survivors are Qusay Vali and Ajmal Mughal. You know either?"

Roshini shuddered, and Pierce sensed it was because of the fear the names provoked. "Qusay, I know well. He's my husband's second in charge at FIA, and he's also married to Fawad's sister, Hajra. Physically, he's tall and thin. Likes to wear cashmere suits and black dress shirts. Qusay and his wife were always pleasant and nice to me every time we caught up socially."

Pierce was impressed by what he had learnt about their enemy, relayed in a few brief words. "Those are very specific details you've just provided. I've never had a briefing like that from a civilian before."

Roshini shrugged. "When I was planning my escape, I read a lot — and I really mean *a lot* — of spy and espionage novels. I even read them in front of Fawad. He took this as a minor challenge to his authority, but ultimately my act merely amused him. But then he wasn't too subtle about his mistress either. It didn't take me long to learn he hooked up with her every couple of months or so in Goa, India. But to answer your question, I guess a lot of what I read rubbed off, as I hoped it would."

Her answer explained why she knew so much about espionage, but he still felt compelled to test her. "Who are your favourite authors?"

"I don't know. I read so many. Mostly authors who are dead now or have been around for many decades, because those books are easier to come by in Pakistan. Len Deighton, Gerald Seymour, Martin Cruz Smith, Desmond Bagley, and Ian Flemming of course. I could never find female authors in that genre though."

The answer she gave aligned with Pierce's own knowledge of the genre's old greats, so he hadn't caught her out with a lie.

"Mark, what you should know about Qusay is I always knew he was way smarter than my husband. Fawad is impulsive, reactionary, overconfident, and blusters through everything. But my husband is cunning enough to know that he needs someone like Qusay to balance him out, with his calculating mind, perceptiveness, and methodical approach. If anyone was going to catch me out during all those months I planned my defection, I feared it would be Qusay."

"How are they operating with impunity in India? They are high ranking enough so the IB would know if they were in the country."

Roshini shrugged. "I really don't know. I think the FIA and ISI use my husband as an unofficial conduit of intelligence sharing between both countries when it suits them. He likely traded a significant secret with IB in return for looking the other way as he ran an operation to come after me."

They passed a couple of young boys standing next to oxen grazing on the grass at the side of the road. The kids waved as they passed, and Roshini waved back at them, smiling. When she caught Pierce watching her, she laughed, which brought a smile to Pierce's face because their conversations had all been laden with tension until now. "Mark, if I didn't wave, we'd be more memorable. I know the chances of them being questioned are slim, but every little trick applied from the spy playbook betters our chance of survival. Or at least that was what Len Deighton used to say."

Pierce grinned. "Can't agree more. What about Ajmal Mughal? He's a sergeant with Pakistani special forces. What do you know about him?"

Roshini tensed. "I've never met him, but I've heard stories."

"Like what?"

The lighter mood now gone, she tightened her fist

around the passenger hand grip above her passenger window, and her knuckles whitened. "The one that most sticks in my mind was that, if he was coming after you, the best action you could take was to kill yourself, to lessen the pain at your end." She turned to him with tired eyes and said, "Can we stop, take a break? Eat some food?"

Pierce rubbed his eyes, knowing he too was tired. Unlike her, he hadn't slept in the last twenty-four hours, but he also knew from hard-won experience that he had the stamina to keep going for at least two more days before he needed actual sleep. Enough time to see the mission completed.

"Can we?"

Pierce wouldn't stop if he could avoid it, but he was also aware that their hatchback connected them to the Ganges bridge shoot-out, and the police were no doubt searching for it. He had taken a risk driving it for as long as he had. "How about this plan? We stop in the next town, switch cars, then drive for a bit, then grab a bite to eat?"

She expressed shock. "Switch cars? You mean steal one?"

He laughed. "Believe me, if the police catch us, stolen cars will be the most minor charge they lay against us. Didn't your spy novels teach you that?"

Roshini sighed. "I guess so. I know you are right. The car connects us to the shoot-out. But I desperately need to eat. Something cooked though."

He glanced her way. She was pale and listless, and her hand now rested over her belly. He was more convinced than before that Roshini was pregnant. "Okay, let's do this in the reverse order, then."

She touched his arm again, smiled and said, "Thank you."

They soon passed through a large town with faded

concrete apartments, broken tiled roofs, shop stalls built to the road's edge, and electrical wires like spiderwebs cast between buildings and advertising billboards in Hindi. Pierce found a street vendor selling fried bread and curried pastries. He bought a dozen of each and six bottled waters, then drove again.

"Is it cooked?" she asked, draining one of the bottled waters in a few seconds.

"Yes. Straight from the pan."

Pierce devoured a pastry. The curry was strong and burned his mouth, but the flavours were potent. He detected chilli, cumin, coriander, onion, garlic and fennel, and a dozen other spices he couldn't describe. With food in his stomach, his mood lifted. He finished two further pastries and started on the bread, never slowing the car to do so. He often glanced at Roshini, noticing that she didn't eat as fast as he did, but had gained vibrancy with each mouthful.

Later Pierce discovered another parked hatchback of the same make, model, and colour as theirs, in a secluded part of town. Pulling up close and parking, then raising the bonnet to suggest his car had broken down, he took a screwdriver from the tool kit and switched number plates in less than two minutes.

After filling the tank at another Indian Oil gas station, they drove again, perpendicular to their previous route to throw pursuers off their track. So far there had been no sign that anyone was following them, but Pierce knew from training and experience that complacency now could very well cost him the mission and their lives at any moment. He must remain vigilant.

"You think we got away?" she asked, as if reading his

thoughts. On a break from eating, she twirled the diamond ring around her finger.

"It looks that way, but we have to operate as if we didn't."

"I'm not sure I can do this for much longer."

"It might surprise you what people can achieve even when they've given up."

"I haven't given up."

"Exactly."

10

Washington, DC, United States of America

Later in the afternoon, Zang met Abdul Ibrahim
inside the nine-storey Hart Senate Office Building.
Its centrepiece was its towering and asymmetrical
ninety-foot-high atrium, whose skylight brightened all the
interior corridors and offices that looked down on it. She
spotted Ibrahim immediately as she entered, in another of
his signature, tailored grey three-piece suits, a dark shirt and
a charcoal tie, and the shiniest dress shoes she had ever seen
on a man. Ibrahim was in his late forties but looked much
younger, while his neatly trimmed thick black hair and
beard gave him a refined and cultured look. Zang mused
that the C/SOG made an impression wherever he went in
this world.

In the last year, Zang had studied every open-source file
she could find on the man, as she did with anyone who
became a regular fixture in her life. She'd quickly learnt that
prior to joining the CIA, Abdul Ibrahim had reached the

rank of lieutenant commander with the Office of Naval Intelligence, where he had seen action in the Kosovo and Iraq wars.

Of more interest to Zang was his time before his military career, growing up as a teenager in Baghdad, where he was born. His parents were archaeologists from a wealthy family, who later worked with the occupying US forces when they liberated Kuwait from Iraqi president Saddam Hussein's invading military. They had gone on to do their best to preserve Sumerian, Akkadian, Amorite and Hittite sites and artefacts that would have otherwise been destroyed in the bombings that quickly decimated Iraq. Their efforts bought Ibrahim, his parents, and his brothers and sisters permanent resident visas for the United States, and all nine of them had settled quickly in Brooklyn.

This background meant Ibrahim was the perfect Middle Eastern spy for the CIA, with his first-hand knowledge of the region's culture, religions, and his Arabic, spoken as a native because he was one. But Ibrahim had later surprised everyone again when he revealed his perfect fluency in Russian, learnt in college. He had no intention of returning to the land of his birth, and instead had applied for and was granted a senior intelligence role, based in the US Embassy in Moscow, from where he quickly rose to the position of CIA station head.

Years later, after a spectacular intelligence coup he'd pulled off against Russia, Ibrahim then returned to the United States and took up his current role as chief of the Special Operations Group under the CIA's Directorate of Operations. It was when he was the C/SOG that Zang had first met and worked with Ibrahim, during an operation in Venezuela.

As far as Zang knew, Ibrahim was the highest-ranking Muslim operating inside the CIA, and for that, she had to admire him, considering how much distrust there was inside the organisation levelled against this near eastern and often maligned religion.

So when Zang looked at Ibrahim now, she saw all of his past and his string of spectacular successes, and felt glad that she was in the enviable position to learn from this man, with his deep knowledge of the intelligence world, backed with a breadth of experience second to none.

Spotting her, Ibrahim approached with an open hand and shook Zang's outstretched palm. "Good to see you, Zang. How was Taiwan?"

He referred to her latest mission. With fluency in Mandarin, Cantonese and Russian, she was the ideal operative for this otherwise straightforward mission that had gone off without a hitch, other than the beating she had taken, resulting in her short haircut. "Everything went as planned, sir."

He smiled as he walked her to a waiting room just outside the Central Hearing Facility, where the SSCI hearing would occur in a little over half an hour. "I knew it would. Take a seat." He passed her a file in a burn bag. "Read that quickly. You'll need to know its contents before we enter. That gives you" — he looked at his expensive Omega watch — "twenty-five minutes."

Zang nodded. "I'll speed-read it straight away."

"Good. I need to make a phone call. I'll meet you back here."

"Yes, sir."

She sat and ensured her back was to the wall so she could cover all corners for potential threats — not that she expected any — and to safeguard from anyone reading over her shoulder, which she also didn't expect. Only when she felt both contingencies were addressed did she then open the file.

Its content was a dossier on a DARPA employee, one Nigel McMahon. It was also code word classified for a special access program, one that Zang was not privy to and had never heard of. Ibrahim was breaking several federal laws by showing it to her, presumably why it was in a burn bag. As soon as she had finished reading it, she would need to seal it, then hand it off to a cleared official, who would have it destroyed immediately.

But she still had twenty-four minutes to digest it, and Zang was too curious to worry that she might be compromising state secrets and quickly perused the dossier, trusting that Ibrahim had given it to her for a reason.

She read the acronym DARPA again. The Defence Advanced Research Projects Agency was a research and development arm of the Department of Defence responsible for the progress of emerging technologies for use by the military. The dossier detailed that the DARPA mechanical engineer Nigel McMahon was originally from Denver, Colorado, a graduate of the University of California San Francisco, and had long ago settled in San Diego, California. More pertinent to Zang was his area of specialisation. He was a senior engineer who worked on the highly secretive program that designed the propellers used on US Navy submarines.

As the implications of what she was reading hit her, Zang closed the file and took a moment to catch her breath.

Submarine propeller designs were one of the most highly guarded secrets in the entire US defence apparatus.

When Navy submarines entered the dock, Navy divers quickly covered their blades in tarpaulins while still under water. Propellers were only removed or installed inside the submarine workshops, and all ingress and egress points were locked down, all while the tarpaulin remained in place. Any repair or maintenance works performed on a propeller could only occur off base, at a secret location or locations in highly classified facilities spread out across the country, known only to a few cleared individuals, and McMahon was one of the few in the know.

As an operator assigned on dangerous missions inside enemy nations on a regular basis, this meant that if Zang was learning about McMahon's existence, it could only be because he was permanently off the propeller program. This was not a piece of knowledge she could risk taking into the field and have an enemy operator coerce or torture it out of her.

Zang mused that the reason for all this secrecy around the propeller was obvious to anyone who thought about it. Submarines were silent predators, which could be anywhere in the world's ocean at any time. With their nuclear warhead and conventional ballistic missile capabilities, they were the perfect deterrent against any enemy authoritarian regime thinking it might take a shot at America. A submarine could take them out in minutes if they got onto Uncle Sam's bad side in a hurry.

But if these same enemy states knew what those propellers looked like, captured through spy satellite technology or via on-the-ground-based sources such as double agents willing to hand over the schematics, or even through unlawful access to the design specifications themselves, then they could be reversed engineered. Propeller sound and wave propagation characteristics could also be easily modelled, giving those authoritarian regimes in the know every chance of using this information to develop tools to track those submarines, rendering their otherwise invisible and stealthy nature redundant.

Zang quickly flipped through the twenty-page file to ascertain what was important to focus on first. She quickly noticed much of its content was redacted with the obligatory black lines drawn through large swathes of text, but when she examined those blanked sections more closely, they were predominately on the technical side of what McMahon did, and these details she did not need to know. What Ibrahim wanted Zang to see instead were the details on the man himself. He was married with children, didn't seem to have any interesting hobbies, and had never travelled for vacations outside the United States. Other than the nature of his profession, he seemed to be a rather boring and uninteresting individual.

As Zang flipped through the file, she came across a copy of a sealed order signed by the US president himself, authorising McMahon's immediate termination with extreme prejudice.

This asked more questions than it answered.

"Time's up!"

She looked up to find Ibrahim approaching with his hand outstretched. A glance at her wristwatch showed that she'd only been reading for four minutes.

"Can't give you longer, Zang. Since you're not on the original invitee list for today's session, we need to complete more stringent security checks than normal to get you in. That means we need to move now." He took the dossier from Zang, sealed it back in the burn bag, and handed it off to an aide who had been waiting in the background to complete this task. "Destroy it now," he said to the aide.

"Yes, sir." The young man nodded, then disappeared.

As Zang and Ibrahim matched strides, she said, "I hardly got to read any of it."

"You absorbed the gist of it, though?"

She shuddered. "I understood the security implications, that's for sure. And I didn't miss the extreme prejudice bit either."

"Yes, indeed."

Ibrahim straightened his cuffs, then neatened his Windsor-knot tie as they approached the security check with face recognition, body scanners, and sniffer dogs they would have to pass before they would be allowed inside. He placed his cell phone, watch, wallet, and keys on a tray ready to pass through the X-ray scanner, then said to Zang, "In reality, that's all you really need to know. The rest will become immediately apparent to you in the coming hour, I'm sure."

11

After logging their cell phones with the duty officer and clearing security, then getting Zang on the attendees register, she and Ibrahim entered the two-storey Central Hearing Facility several minutes after the session had begun. The room was all brown panelled walling with an impressively large stone backdrop behind the dais, multiple media booths in the side walls that were empty because this was a closed hearing, and many rows of stiff-backed black fabric chairs, arranged to allow viewing of today's topic of discussion.

The facility wasn't overly packed with people, but enough for Zang and Ibrahim to mingle easily enough without being noticeable, and they weren't the only ones turning up late. The fifteen Senate Select Committee on Intelligence members, often referred to in government circles as the SSCI, were all present. Senator Hunter of New York, from the majority party, had just opened with her allotted round of questioning.

The three individuals in today's spotlight comprised two

men and one woman. The men were Jay Sanders and Brad Karson, each dressed in smart suits and ties, leaning forward into their provided microphones. Jay hadn't notice Zang enter because his back was to her, but he also wouldn't be looking out for her because he wouldn't expect her to be here.

The woman under question was a senior operations officer with the CIA, whom Zang recognised as Ryleigh Bresolin. The career-driven public servant was dressed in a long, sky-blue shape-hugging dress and matching jacket. Her hair was styled short and shaved at the back. Shorter than Zang's new style even.

The chairman from Wyoming said, "The session yields the floor to Senator Hunter."

"Thank you, Senator Hostettler," said Kellie Hunter with a nod to the chairman. She leaned forward in her podium seat and looked down upon today's three participants, then gathered her notes, which she had been skimming until now.

Like all elected members of the US Senate and Congress, Hunter looked elegantly put together, but not overstated. Zang noticed her thinness and the lines on her face brought on by age. Her blonde and very straight shoulder-length hair probably took at least half an hour to sit right each morning, but regardless of the effort she put into her appearance, Hunter presented as commanding and authoritative.

"Thanks goes to our participants for joining us today, and thank you too, to the proceeding's chairman, ranking member, and all select senators serving on the SSCI. Mr Karson, Mr Sanders, Ms Bresolin, you've already sworn in, so we will proceed directly to the incident in question that occurred five days ago, on the outskirts of the Pakistani town of Chitral in the Lower Chitral District, Khyber Pakhtunkhwa Province. I think it needs to be said for the record, this region borders Afghanistan and, during the War on Terror, had been the subject of numerous drone strikes by the US Central Intelligence Agency and US Air Force, targeting alleged Taliban, al-Qaeda and other militant groups hiding in the surrounding Hindu Kush mountains. My first question, and I'll start with you, Mr Karson, is what was the purpose of you being in the aforementioned location on the aforementioned date?"

Karson leaned forward, and Zang got her first good look at the "Black Dog" in the flesh, noting his slender but muscular frame, neatly trimmed but thick black beard, immaculate black short-back-and-sides haircut with grey on the temples, and eyes that seemed to narrow and point inwards towards the centre of his face. He was the kind of man she wouldn't have looked twice at in a bar, but his appeal was more to do with the charisma he oozed rather than anything physical. He looked more suited to being a high-powered executive or a cunning lawyer than the military legend that he was.

When Karson spoke, his voice was smooth and soothing. "Thank you, Senator Hunter. I can report that on the day in question, I was leading a mission into an abandoned airfield situated in the region and was engaged under contract with the CIA to extract DARPA engineer Nigel McMahon, who had allegedly defected to the FIA. It was also to my understanding that FIA were allegedly holding McMahon hostage."

"And for everyone in the hearing's benefit, and for the record, who or what is FIA?"

"Pakistan's Federal Investigation Agency, Senator."

"Can you please describe the circumstances of this meeting."

Karson was cool when he answered, "Ms Bresolin organised the details. We were following our mission brief to arrive in this relatively flat field in the outskirts of the Chitral Valley, surrounded by peaks of the Hindu Kush. For the record, this is considered in most US military circles to be open and extremely dangerous terrain. No one in the services goes in there unless they have very good reason to do so."

"And who was there with you?"

The founder of Executive Believers was quiet for a moment before he answered, as if he enjoyed the fact everyone watching this hearing was anticipating every word that he spoke. The pause was for dramatic effect and his benefit alone. "I was leading the mission. I had retired Lieutenant Jay Sanders, who is seated to my right, present as my intelligence executive. There was retired Staff Sergeant Kwang Suwan. She is my team's paramilitary executive. Accompanying us were seven other paramilitary contractors under my command. Employees of Executive Believers."

Karson provided their names and former ranks. "And two pilots in the AgustaWestland AW139 transport helicopter we had rented for the mission. Both pilots were Pakistani." He gave their names and military ranks with equally efficient recall and clarity.

"The last two, they were from the Pakistan Army Aviation Corps?"

"Yes, Senator."

"Not your own pilots or aircraft?"

"No, Senator. They were deployed elsewhere in other

operations my PMC was executing at the time. Or to be clear, is still executing."

Zang noticed that Senator Hunter was making Karson understand she was well read on the operation, asking questions she already knew the answers to. This was a not-so-subtle reminder that she could immediately catch him out in a lie. But Karson didn't seem bothered by her in the slightest. He talked like he was merely placing an order at a fast-food chain.

"You weren't using aircraft assets from our own air force either? For the record, I'm referring to the United States Air Force here."

Karson shook his head. "With Bagram Air Base no longer under US command, we didn't have a lot of choice in air support." He referred to America's primary military base in Afghanistan during the two-decade-plus war that had taken place in that nation. That base was now a failed facility mismanaged by Taliban soldiers who only years earlier had been at war with the United States forces based there.

"Noted. And who was present on the FIA side?"

Karson nodded. "I didn't learn the names and positions of every FIA officer and rank and file present. Most were military, as heavily armed as me and my team, and numbered eighteen. The FIA arrived in a variety of light utility vehicles. Predominately Toyota makes and Chinese Foton Tunland pickups, six vehicles in total. The two individuals I did identify and spoke with were Fawad Jahandar, assistant director of FIA's Technical Wing, and Jahandar's head of Operational Intelligence, Qusay Vali."

"I see," said Senator Hunter as she glanced over her notes again. "What was the nature of this meeting?"

"Our mission brief, presented by our CIA contact officer, Ms Ryleigh Bresolin, who is seated to my right, was that Fawad Jahandar had recently taken Nigel McMahon into his custody, and that we were there to offer Jahandar one million US dollars in cash if he handed McMahon back to us unharmed. We had the option to negotiate to two million if I deemed it necessary."

"And did you, Mr Karson?"

Karson paused deliberately, as if to irritate the senior elected government official. "Did I what, Senator?"

"Deem it necessary?"

He paused again, leaned forward, and said clearly without blinking or breaking eye contact with his interviewer, "No. I didn't deem it necessary."

Zang saw that Karson wasn't fazed in the slightest by any question that Hunter had asked. She'd also noticed that Jay and Bresolin were doing their best to maintain relaxed poses when neither seemed to be in that frame of mind.

"And why not?"

"Because McMahon was not present, Senator. And Jahandar and Vali also went to great lengths to convince me that McMahon was already dead. Cause of death was not specified, but they implied they got a little out of hand when they had questioned him two days prior to our meeting, when the FIA had secured him in their custody."

"Were you convinced that McMahon was dead?"

"No."

"Then you are of the opinion that this DARPA engineer is still alive?"

"No, Senator. I don't think that either."

She looked at her notes, as if puzzled by this contradictory explanation. "It says here, Mr Karson, that Vali presented you with McMahon's cut-up and soiled clothes, drenched in his own blood? And, also, photos of his beaten body?"

"Yes, Senator, that happened as he said. But the quantity of blood present, in my experience, was inconclusive as to whether McMahon had survived the ordeal of his bloodletting or not. The photos could have easily been McMahon while he was unconscious. They weren't conclusive proof either way to his alive or dead status."

Zang touched her finger to her lips, for she sensed Karson was being deliberately obtuse, forcing Hunter to ask multiple questions to get a single answer. And Hunter looked flustered to Zang's eyes. Perhaps the questioning was not going as the senator had hoped.

"I see, Mr Karson. But you say Jahandar told you McMahon was dead?"

"Yes, as I said before."

Senator Hunter sighed, not masking her growing frustration. "Do you know why McMahon defected to Pakistan, suddenly fleeing San Diego where he lived?"

Maintaining his cool, Karson said, "I only know what Ms Bresolin told us during our mission briefing as to what his reasons were. I have no first-hand information on what McMahon's state of mind or intentions might or might not have been."

"And they were?"

"The reasons outlined to me in the briefing?"

Another hint of annoyance escaped the senator's mouth when she said, "Yes, Mr Karson, that is what I am asking."

"We were briefed that Nigel McMahon had accumulated close to eighty thousand dollars in gambling debts to the Mafia. That DOD vetting had not picked up on this until he was well out of the country, attempting to escape justice. It wasn't explicitly said, but what I took from Ms Bresolin's words was that McMahon intended to sell secrets of our nuclear submarine propeller designs to the FIA in return for funds to pay off his Mafia debt and to provide him with permanent immunity and protection inside Pakistan."

Ibrahim turned to Zang and gave her a look that asked if she now understood how all the pieces fitted together. Zang nodded, and they returned their attention to the hearing.

Together they listened through the next hour and a half of testimonials, from Karson, Bresolin and Jay Sanders, as each were scrutinised in greater detail on everything that had happened that day. The narrative was that no agreement had been reached, that the FIA had walked away without the million US dollars they had been offered, and that they were adamant that McMahon was dead. They had killed him. They apologised about that. When a stalemate was reached, Karson and his outfit of private military contractors returned to their helicopter and flew out empty-handed, and that was the end of that.

Mission not accomplished.

And all Rachel Zang could think about during the entire hearing was that Karson and Sanders were lying their asses off.

12

Jharia, Jharkhand, India

Despite Pierce never previously having operated in India, he was familiar with the country's diverse geopolitical, cultural, geographical, insurgent, and military landscape, but he also appreciated there was no substitute for learning about a country than by operating inside its borders.

One aspect Pierce had learnt in the last couple of days, which he would never have picked up in any report on India, regarded its persistent crowds. With a population of well over a billion in a country a third of the size of the United States, the huge numbers of people always surrounding Pierce shouldn't have surprised him, but they did. Men, women, and children who walked or rode mopeds, sat in the back of trucks, worked crop fields even with the heavy rains, were everywhere and a non-stop backdrop to their travels. Clothing was vibrant and diverse in its colours, from saffron to lime green, sky blue and rich orange. It amazed Pierce they all didn't go mad, screaming for a moment of personal space.

When Pierce and Roshini were driving through the countryside again, and the press of human bodies didn't seem so overwhelming, they passed channels cut into the hills that collected and controlled the run-off of monsoonal waters.

Roshini caught him staring. "You curious?"

He nodded.

She smiled as she rested her hand on the back of her long, slender neck. "The monsoon is an annual event, beginning around June or July and ending a few months later. But it is unpredictable both when it starts and how long it lasts, and it's worsened by global warming. If you haven't guessed, we are in the monsoon season now."

"I guessed," said Pierce with a chuckle, pointing to the windscreen wipers he had never turned off.

"Well, these channels are community projects designed to collect or slow run-offs, minimising water seepage back into the earth. Captured water improves crop reliability and allows farmers to plant secondary crops if the wet season lasts long enough. Secondary crops therefore supplement their incomes."

"I've seen artificial embankments everywhere. You sure this isn't a state-sponsored operation?"

"Kind of." She smiled and brushed a loose strand of hair from her eyes. "India is the most culturally diverse country on the planet, so meaningful change only works at the community level. State governments fund individual embankment programs, providing up to eighty per cent of the costs, to ensure they happen."

"And the other twenty per cent?"

"Provided by the benefited community in the form of labour, free of charge — it drives personal ownership in the program."

"Does it work?"

"Actually, it's working well across India."

"How do you know all about it?"

Her face lit up. "I was on advisory committees planning similar projects back when I lived in Patna. And it was those projects that sent me to London, where our NGO supporting the operation was based..." As her voice faded and she looked away, she lost the excitement that had been building in her since the conversation started.

NGO was shorthand for non-government organisation, which were typically non-profit entities active in humanitarianism or the social sciences. "Not the kind of work you did in Pakistan?"

She pressed her elbow against the window and her palm against her chin. "No. Fawad didn't want me to travel unless absolutely necessary, which the communal projects required. Rather rich coming from him when I found out he had a mistress in Goa."

"Infidelity wasn't reason enough to leave him?"

She laughed without humour. "In my mind it was, but in practice... Well, you know my situation."

He nodded, admiring how well she had coped under stress for so long and all the while managing to plan and, so far, successfully execute her defection. "What kind of work did you do in Pakistan?"

"I took a job with a corporate law firm instead, in Islamabad. Helped make rich clients richer."

"You never enjoyed your new life, even before you knew

about your husband's real profession or his ex-marital affairs?"

"No, not really..."

Pierce imagined how drastic the situation must have become for her to run. But was he any different? He'd radically changed his own life's path many years ago, with mixed results. He'd taken risks like she had, and perhaps that was why he had warmed to her so quickly, because they were so similar. He thought about what it would be like to go out to dinner together, have a meal and share a glass of wine, and learn about each other's lives, hopes, dreams and challenges, which seemed to be what normal people did who were not spies or soldiers. He thought about how such an evening was exactly what he needed to feel normal again, and to not always think that he was someone who always had to operate alone.

"So now you are here."

She sighed. "So now I am here."

They were never going to have that night together. And besides, he was certain she was pregnant, and he was exactly not the kind of person she needed in her life right now once this mission was over.

Ahead the sky grew dark and the clouds black.

Roshini switched on the radio and scanned for stations, finding one in English. First, she caught the tail end of a report on the murder from a week ago of a popular human rights lawyer and campaigner against Russian corruption, who, it had now been confirmed, had died by suspected poisoning in a restaurant in Moscow. Then she switched channels and caught a report on the Ganges bridge attack. One car had gone into the river, and the authorities presumed all three occupants were dead. Two occupants of a second car had also been killed when they hit a truck head-on. All other victims caught in the carnage had escaped with minor or non-critical wounds. Pierce felt relief. No civilian casualties — the biggest fear for a man in his line of work. The report continued. Five suspects had fled the scene, a man and a woman who had headed east, and three men who had headed west. Suspect descriptions were vague, which was to their advantage, but the police might know more than they had released to the media.

"Mark, should we swap the car as you said earlier?"

"That's not a bad idea."

He found an old model Hyundai Asta in a village they passed through, which he broke into in under thirty seconds and hot-wired in ten. Then they hit the road again and drove fast. He again noticed the many people, motorbikes, trucks and buses everywhere, but crowds would be to their advantage.

Roshini drank more water and finished a second pastry. "Thank you, for keeping me alive."

Pierce didn't know how to respond to praise, so he kept quiet. He had wanted to say something normal, like the Pierce he imagined himself being in that fantasy dinner he had planned out in his mind, but nothing came to him.

She played with her diamond ring again.

Pierce recognised that despite Estrada's dying assurances, the ring still bothered him. "Roshini, I just had a thought."

She turned to him and stared through tired eyes. "What is that?"

"Is that the only item you brought with you from Islamabad? Other than Fawad's files, money, and the data stick from his safe?"

In the last few minutes, the landscape had grown rugged, preventing roads from taking them in straight lines anymore, and there was a lack of trees and low ground cover. The clouds ahead resembled a dark and brewing storm. He noticed men, women, and children — many only six or seven years of age — walking the roads covered with fine layers of black soot. All appeared exhausted, as if they had worked all day without sustenance.

"The ring." Pierce gestured to the large diamond Roshini had twirled around her finger since their pairing. "Your husband gave it to you?"

She nodded. "He's got his gold Rolex watch. I have this."

"Ever thought he put a tracker in it so he would always know where you are?"

"No, I don't. Estrada tested it. And so did you, remember?"

Another thought occurred that worried Pierce. "What if it only transmitted sporadically? It might not be picked up with conventional sweeping techniques."

Her face lost its colour, and her jaw dropped. "Fawad wouldn't, would he?"

A sophisticated tracker would explain how the FIA's kill team had found them earlier. "Throw it out the window."

She looked horrified. "You're joking?"

"No, I'm not."

"The ring is worth over a hundred thousand US dollars, Mark. It's my insurance in case things don't work out in America."

"It's worthless if they are tracking us."

Pierce's senses heightened. He had thought they had thrown their pursuers off their trail, but not anymore.

Ahead, he spotted a rail bridge crossing their road, then

cutting back into the hills on both sides, creating a natural ravine. A perfect bottleneck and an ideal vantage point for a sniper, and he was driving them straight into it.

Pierce slammed on the brakes, stopping five hundred meters from the bridge. "Get down!"

"What?"

Pierce leaned to the back seat, looking for the bag of money, when the windscreen shattered as a high-velocity round tore into the headrest of his seat, ripping it to pieces.

Instinctively he pulled Roshini down with him, jammed the gears into reverse and floored the accelerator. The crowds on the sides of the road weren't as dense as they had been earlier, maybe forty people in Pierce's line of sight, but it was enough to send flocks of people running for cover in all directions at the sound of shooting.

More bullets slammed into the Hyundai Asta.

Roshini screamed.

Pierce kept flooring the accelerator.

Their erratic backward motion prevented the sniper from achieving an accurate bead, but the killer kept firing, regardless.

Down low, Pierce couldn't see where he was driving.

Soon enough he hit another car that had been approaching, clipping it at an angle. The Hyundai spun one hundred and eighty degrees, and the assassin was behind them now, which was to their advantage.

While changing gears, Pierce noticed the shooting had ceased, which suggested the sniper was reloading. Pierce raised his head a few centimetres but kept it mostly hidden behind what remained of the driver's seat, to see where they were, before the sniper had a chance to start shooting at them again.

To their right the embankment dropped two metres.

Exactly what he needed.

"Brace yourself."

Pierce turned the wheel and drove off the edge. The drop was steeper than he had imagined, and the car was almost vertical when the engine chassis crumpled from the sudden impact, deep within the ditch.

13

Pierce shuddered. The ditch was not only steeper than he'd calculated but the impact was more jarring than he had expected. He felt the bruising across his chest where the seatbelt had caught; then stiffness exploded in his back and neck. Roshini screamed and struggled, distressed in the passenger seat. He realised why his head felt heavy. They were faced downwards, as the car had crashed vertically, and the blood was pooling in his head. But at least they were in a ditch now, out of the sniper's firing line.

Before Pierce could propel himself into action, the cracked windscreen shattered and fell onto the black dirt. This offered a way out. Holding the steering wheel for support, Pierce unclipped his seatbelt, then lowered himself to the ground.

"Come on." He offered a hand to Roshini as he unclasped her seatbelt and caught her when she fell into his arms. He gently lowered her to stand next to him. She doubled over with pain and threw up again.

"You okay?"

She nodded without raising her head.

"I know you're pregnant. I'll do everything I can to protect you and your child."

Her mouth fell open, ready to speak, but no words came forth.

"The assassin is still out there, Roshini. We're behind cover for now, but we need to move."

He checked for his Glock 19 and Beretta APX and that he had plenty of loaded magazines for each weapon in his pockets. But these pistols would be ineffective against the sniper's long-range weapons. Direct confrontation was out of the question. They had to run.

"The car—"

"Will never drive again."

Their immediate surroundings had quickly cleared of people, with no one wanting to take a stray bullet, so they couldn't use crowds as cover while they made their escape. He took her hand as they sprinted through the natural channel. The sheer rock kept them beyond the assassin's line of sight for a few dozen metres, but Pierce knew their advantage wouldn't last. The assailant would switch positions or advance for a more personal kill. There could also be multiple killers, each approaching from different directions. Pierce had no way of knowing, and to remain where they were was the equivalent of suicide.

"Throw the ring away. It's tracking you!"

"You don't know that!"

Deciding that arguing right now wouldn't help their chances of survival, and figuring the enemy knew where they were for the moment with or without a tracking device on them, he decided to move and resolve this problem later.

After they'd covered a hundred metres, the ditch disappeared into flat ground. They stopped, and he said, "I need to reassess our tactical situation." While Roshini crouched low and wiped bile from her mouth, Pierce snuck a glance over the rock.

He spotted the rail bridge he'd seen earlier and a few groups of people and cars still racing for cover. A train crossed the bridge, moving slowly. Pierce followed the curve of the rail and saw the locomotive headed in their direction. He looked to his left, and there was the track, less than fifty metres distant. They had no more than five minutes before the train, pulling at least a hundred empty coal cars, reached them.

Pierce had an idea...

Rocks exploded around his head.

He ducked just fast enough to avoid a successive round of bullets that would have burrowed through his skull. But his mind still registered the muzzle flashes, pinpointing the assassin to a few hundred metres from their current position, sprinting down the road with an M4 carbine assault rifle. The few people still nearby now scattered.

Roshini lay flat on the black sooty earth, covering her ears.

The empty coal-hauling train rattled closer.

He lifted Roshini to a crouching position and brushed her sweat-drenched hair from her face. "When I say go, we'll run to that train and jump on board. Okay?"

Despite her face sweating with fear, she nodded.

Pierce figured the assassin was almost upon them. He raised his Glock while keeping his head down, and fired. The action should cause the foe to duck for cover, so Pierce risked a look over the lip and spotted the man on one knee,

M4 against his shoulder and eyes following the line of the weapon's sights, less than fifty metres from them now.

Pierce fired until he had emptied his magazine. A single bullet hit the assassin, and he went down. It was a lucky shot at this range, but luck had bought them time.

"Go!"

He grabbed Roshini, and they sprinted towards the rail.

The train soon passed them, its surfaces thick with black coal dust and stinking of diesel. The cars were metal buckets each capable of transporting several tons of coal, with tipping mechanisms for easy unloading. Now on a return journey to the mine, they were empty.

With the Beretta APX in his hand, Pierce fired behind him without looking.

The train was moving faster than they were running, but only just.

"Grab that ladder."

Pierce willed Roshini to sprint faster, and she did. Her hands reached out, grabbed a rung, and she pulled herself up.

Pierce dropped behind as the train picked up speed. He caught the ladder on the next car, and he too pulled himself up. Only then did he look back.

The assassin was running too; his M4 hung by its sling around his shoulder while he pumped his legs, closing the distance. The man must have worn body armour to take a direct hit and still function like an Olympic athlete, still able to come after them even now.

Pierce fired the Beretta until the clip emptied.

The assassin ignored the shots, which were wide anyway, then leapt and propelled himself into the air as he caught hold of the lip of a coal bucket. Then with a feat of remarkable strength, he flipped into the bucket, providing him cover, five cars down from Pierce.

Pierce reloaded the last magazine for the Beretta while keeping his head covered. He realised he had left the bag of rupees in the wrecked car, but that was probably for the best considering it too could have been tracked. His more immediate concern was keeping both him and Roshini alive.

"Stay down, Roshini!"

She didn't answer. He supposed she couldn't hear him over the rattling train cars, separated as they were, and with the noise of the clanking rails beneath them.

Before the assassin could line up his weapon, Pierce leapt up and fired down the line of carriages.

The assassin already had Pierce in his sights and in the same moment unloaded a volley of bullets from his M4. Pierce dropped just in time to avoid his head cracking open like a ripe watermelon. This man had just proved himself a professional operator, one Pierce could not afford to underestimate.

The automatic fire continued for several seconds, and Pierce dared not look up again, recognising the assassin would not miss a second time. But to their advantage, neither could bypass their buckets unless they crossed their lips, which would leave them exposed to each other's covering fire.

Pierce then heard a metal object bouncing and rattling inside the bucket adjacent to him.

A grenade?

Guessing that it probably was, he dropped, covered his ears, opened his mouth, and shut his eyes. He felt the blast reverberate through the iron bucket first. Then heard the near deafening noise. The car's metal saved him as the blast energy propelled upwards, firing residual coal dust into the air, which formed a thick black cloud.

Pierce saw his chance, so he sprinted and rolled between one bucket and the next, bringing him closer to the assassin. Then he fired through the vision-impairing cloud so the assassin would think twice about lobbing a second grenade.

He crossed the first damaged coal bucket in seconds. When he reached the next, he fired again. The cloud of dust was drifting backwards as the train maintained its velocity, providing cover along the length of train cars. Pierce repeated the process, shooting and propelling his body forward one car at a time. When he reached the fifth car, the cloud was still too thick to see anything.

Then the assassin's silhouette loomed out of the dust, M4 out in front, ready to shoot.

Pierce fired the last bullet in his Beretta APX, hitting the assassin in the chest again.

The foe staggered backwards, dropping his carbine, but didn't fall. Body armour had saved him a second time.

Pierce closed the distance, grabbed a handful of coal particles and threw them into his opponent's face.

He had hoped the assassin would turn his head to avoid injuring his eyes, but he wore goggles and didn't look away. Pierce charged regardless, knocking the man against the lip of the bucket.

The bullet in the chest had stunned and disorientated the assassin. But he was a professional, trained to ignore his injuries and fight back with punches and kicks.

Now they were close, Pierce recognised him from the file photo Mitch Hawley had sent. This man was Sergeant Ajmal Mughal, of the Pakistan Army Special Service Group, and the killer was as muscular and skilled as Hawley had said he was.

Pierce retaliated with strikes of his own, tearing the man's shirt and causing him to lose his cell phone in the process. Their comparable martial skills soon proved to be equally matched, and ensured each man blocked more strikes than got through, and no impact was effective at debilitating the other.

Then Mughal double feinted, in a pretence to strike from one direction with his right but coming from another with his left fist. Pierce had expected this but failed to see the footwork that tripped him up.

Caught off balance, Pierce stumbled backwards. Mughal took the advantage and advanced, spinning Pierce with a lightning-fast move so Pierce's back was now towards the assailant. He then propelled Pierce forward, throwing him over the lip of the bucket.

Pierce went over, barely catching a guard rail and only just preventing himself from going onto the tracks, where the wheels would have crushed him.

The assassin reached over and punched Pierce in the shoulder. A second blow rattled his head.

Pierce had to take the punishment, for to release his grip was to fall.

He took another blow, blood spraying from his nose, when he saw a release lever.

Letting go with one hand, he grabbed and pulled the lever.

The bucket tipped, shaking the train car as its centre of gravity shifted.

A new cloud of coal dust erupted into the air, obscuring everything except for a momentary glance of Mughal's silhouette as he fell from the bucket and smashed onto the fast-shifting ground beneath them. Pierce couldn't tell if the man had survived his fall or not, for the new dust clouds soon swallowed him.

Pulling back on the lever, the bucket swung back into place.

Exhausted, Pierce pulled himself over the lip and fell into the bucket, breathing hard. He stayed motionless for a minute until he had recovered.

As the dust dissipated, he noticed the assassin's fallen cell phone. It had not dropped out when the bucket had tipped, as Pierce would have expected; it had caught in a dent in the metal.

He grabbed Mughal's phone, then climbed over the buckets again, headed towards the front of the rattling coal train.

He had an idea, but first he needed to find Roshini.

14

As Pierce advanced back across five cars, the coal clouds dissipated, and Roshini came into view. While Pierce and Mughal had fought, she'd climbed across six cars in the opposite direction. A clever move, creating distance between herself and the victor of the battle — there was no guarantee Pierce would have been the only survivor. He yelled her name several times to catch her attention, but she never heard him over the rattling carriages and locomotive up ahead.

As he climbed towards her, the landscape transformed into more rugged hills, covered in soot and coal dust, sparse vegetation and with an air heavy with the stench of ammonia. Hundreds of individuals whom they passed now chipped at coal seams with shovels and pickaxes. Others collected the fragments in woven baskets or hessian bags. Many wore sandals or were shoeless. Children seemed to outnumber adults. These were India's poorest citizens, the lower, uneducated castes, who survived only by working dangerous, manual tasks.

Pierce remembered that Jharkhand state produced most of India's coal reserves, feeding thousands of power-generating plants across the nation. Generations past, these people would have been farmers. When the coal seams had extended into and occupied their homes and plantations, the country's need for electricity forced them to mine the black rocks instead of cultivating crops just to survive.

Pierce checked Mughal's phone while he advanced. Secure encryption locked the device, but the screensaver was a tracking application overlaid on Google Maps. A red light flashed on the rail line as Pierce's own green light closed in on the red. He watched it regularly and soon learnt the tracker refreshed its location only every three minutes. This was how the assassin had located them, and with it only transmitting for short bursts, the likelihood of it being discovered with a sweep was limited.

"Roshini!" he called again.

She turned this time, at first wide-eyed with fear before expressing relief. Soot and dust covered her, just as it covered him.

Pierce caught up with her. "You okay?" He coughed out the dust that had gathered in his mouth.

She nodded.

"Good. Give me your ring."

She held her hand close to her chest. "I can't."

"We'll discuss it first before throwing it away. I promise." He held out his hand. "Please give it to me."

Reluctantly, Roshini removed her ring and placed it in Pierce's palm. "It's also made of carbon. The same compound that surrounds us now."

Pierce nodded. "Don't worry, I've dealt with my fair share of diamonds in my time. A lot more coal in the world though, and nowhere near as valuable." He drew his KAMPO tactical knife from a leg sheath and pried the diamond stone from the platinum band. He then held the ring close to her eyes. "Can you at least give up the band?"

"I guess so. The stone is the real value. Fifteen carats."

Pierce threw the band far from the train, then glanced at Mughal's phone and waited for the tracker to broadcast again. When it did, he watched the green and red dots separating.

Satisfied, he removed the battery and SIM card from the cell phone, dropped its components into the bucket they stood in and smashed the parts under his foot, then threw all the components off the train. "We were being tracked via the band and not the diamond." He handed Roshini's precious stone back. "Keep it safe."

She took the diamond, wrapped it in a silk cloth and tucked it into a pocket in her pants. "Are you saying my husband can no longer track us?"

"Yes, but he and his assassin will figure out where this train terminates soon enough. We need to be far from here before then."

"I can't jump. I've already risked too much stress to my body, and my..."

"Unborn child?" Pierce finished her sentence for her.

She brushed her dirty hair from her face, but even in her dishevelled state, Pierce thought of her as being beautiful.

"You said that before, Mark. How did you guess?"

"Eating only cooked food. Refusing to jump into the Ganges. Throwing up on the road and back in the ditch. All signs you are in the first trimester of pregnancy. It also explains why you are running now, and why you hesitated earlier. This was your last chance, knowing a child would have trapped you in that life you could no longer stomach."

She wiped tears from her eyes. "You think I'm selfish?"

"You shouldn't care what I think. All that matters are your own reasons." It was easier talking to her when they were on a mission, when every word out of his mouth came naturally to him and was precise and focused. "Does your husband know about the child?"

Roshini shook her head. "He'll never know."

"That explains why he's happy to kill you. Children, they change everything between a couple."

"For the worse?"

Pierce laughed and shook his head. "Not that I have much experience in this department, but from what I've seen, for the better."

"I considered he might have loved me again if I told him I was pregnant." She looked to Pierce for confirmation, but he said nothing. She shuddered, then said, "Fawad always wanted children. I was afraid that with a child, he might not need me anymore."

Pierce didn't know how to respond because these were the kinds of conversations that were more suited to a dinner conversation, so he focused again on mission responses. "Well, the plan remains the same. I'll get you out of India, to somewhere he can never reach you."

"What do we do next?"

Pierce pointed to the stackers and stockpiles of coal looming on the horizon. At that distance, excavators and ore-hauling trucks seemed like crawling ants, transferring coal from the stockpiles onto conveyor belts, which fed the coal into stackers loading buckets on another train already parked in the stabling yard.

"We'll arrive in a few minutes. When we do, we need to secure another means of transport and get out fast." Pierce looked back the way they had come. "The assassin was Ajmal Mughal, by the way. He fell from the train, and my guess is he survived the fall."

"I thought you killed him?"

"I might have, but I don't know. But if he's alive, the coalfield is where he'll come for us next."

15

Whedn Jay Sanders stepped into the limo with Brad Karson, he knew immediately his boss was pissed. Most other men would never have noticed this change, with Karson's always immaculately maintained calm exterior, which he had also perfected the whole way through their gruelling hearing, but Sanders had been around the former US Army Special Forces officer long enough to learn how to really read him.

Karson waited until the privacy screen was up, blocking their driver from hearing anything they said, and then ensured their cell phones were inside the Faraday cage he'd especially fitted into most Executive Believers vehicles so they couldn't be hacked into and used as listening devices. He watched Sanders with a cold stare until they merged with traffic on the I-395 highway, taking the tunnel under Constitution Ave and the Ulysses S Grant Memorial, exiting them from downtown Washington, DC, and directing them into the outer suburbs of their country's capital.

There was no audible malice in Karson's voice when he spoke, but it was there, nonetheless. "Want to explain to me, Sanders, why Rachel Zang was at the hearing?"

Sanders swallowed against the uncomfortable lump forming in his throat. He had seen her too, but only towards the end of the hearing, so had no idea how much she had witnessed of their testimonials delivered under oath. "Her being there was just as much a surprise to me, sir."

"That makes it worse and still doesn't explain her presence."

"I agree, sir."

"Not good enough. You honeytrap her the previous night on my orders, yet you don't learn anything from her about Mark Pierce and what his plans with Roshini Jahandar are, and instead we're suddenly on her radar? That means we are on the CIA's radar too."

"Yes, sir."

"Don't 'yes, sir' me like that. Explain yourself."

Sanders didn't have an immediate response ready that Karson would like, but one of the many important lessons he had learnt from his commanding officer over the years was, when faced with no other options in a conflict situation except desperation, you attacked with everything you had. "I warned you, sir, that Zang would see right through any ruse we tried on her. She caught on, and this is the consequence."

Not moving, Karson was quiet for a few seconds before he spoke. "You are my executive intelligence officer, Sanders. You and Suwan and Captain Gang Keng in our base in

Indonesia are my most senior personnel, and your salaries are far above generous. That means I expect far more from you three than I do from anyone else in my organisation."

"Yes, sir. I appreciate that."

"Do you, though, Sanders?" When he didn't answer, Karson said, "I've started a bidding war. The Iranians, the Chinese, the North Koreans, the Syrian government and most especially the Russians are all willing to pay upwards of one hundred million dollars each for the submarine propeller data we are so close to getting our hands on. We even have a terrorist organisation calling itself the Dekaract that is also offering serious money for the schematics. And the number they are all offering is growing every day as these groups start to realise what it is really worth to them. With stakes like that, I expect more from you."

Sanders tensed, tried to be like Karson and keep his emotions hidden and in check. He was never certain how well he could achieve this though, especially in the presence of a man as perceptive as his boss. He had long suspected Karson could read him as well as a python could read the intentions of a mouse it was about to eat. "I advised you not to do it, sir. You didn't take the advice of your intelligence officer."

"Then you should have offered a better, alternative route to the same information. One that would have worked so I wouldn't have to resort to your clumsy honeytrap attempt."

Sanders sighed, knowing that he was getting nowhere. Once Karson felt that he was right about something, even when it was obvious to everyone else that he was wrong, the only option was to capitulate and agree to it too. So he decided to deflect and pick up on a point Karson had made earlier that had nothing to do with Sanders's perceived fuck-up.

"Why are the Russians so interested?"

Karson paused for a moment, as if deciding whether to answer Sanders or not. Then he said, "Do you know of Rurik Izmaylov and Daniil Pavlenko?"

Sanders nodded. "Two human rights lawyers, and members of the Russian opposition who have called out the corruption of the Russian president and his oligarchs and their failures in the war in the Ukraine. Is that who we are talking about?"

"Yes, well, Izmaylov is dead. Poisoned in a restaurant in Moscow two days ago."

Sanders shrugged. This wasn't news. The entire world knew that the Russian president often assassinated Russians and others who spoke up against him or challenged him, commonly through poisoning or feeding them radioactive elements that caused painful deaths over days or weeks, but also through bullets, blades, bombings and shooting their planes out of the sky. Izmaylov and Pavlenko had done well to draw the world's attention to the president's corruption and abuse of human rights within his authoritarian regime, and Sanders had been amazed that they had not been silenced until now. "I'm not surprised, but how does this factor into our problems?"

"Because the Russians have told me Daniil Pavlenko and his family are now in hiding in the Russian city of Sochi on the Black Sea, with plans to defect to America before the Russian president can assassinate them. A CIA extraction team has the family semi-secure in Sochi, hiding them until a nuclear US Navy submarine can extract them and bring them to the west. But if the Russians have the propeller designs, they can use this data to catch the submarine red-handed in Russian territorial waters... You get where this is headed, Sanders?"

Reluctantly, Sanders nodded. "Yes, sir."

"We can maximise this sale only for as long as it takes the US Navy to extract Pavlenko and his family from Russia, or until the Russians find and execute them in Sochi."

Sanders nodded as it hit him how desperately Karson wanted to punish his own nation for what the US government had allowed to happen to his own wife and two sons. That was why Sanders had joined his boss in Executive Believers, because they both suffered with the same pain, and that had made them kin of a kind.

"Sanders, we need to sell the propeller data to the Russians before Jahandar does. That doesn't give us a lot of time, so we can't afford any further fuck-ups. You hear me?"

"Then what do you want from me, sir? An apology? A promise that I won't fuck up again? You don't want either. I've known you long enough to know that."

Again, Karson was quiet for a moment, and he allowed it to stretch out until only Sanders became uncomfortable with the silence.

Soon they were out of the tunnel and turning left onto the Southeast Freeway, headed for the Welsh Memorial Bridge. It was a pleasant sunny day in downtown Washington, DC, but the mood inside the limo was nothing like it.

Sanders realised then that Karson was waiting to hear how he was going to fix this situation.

His mind unwillingly flashed back to a recent operation he wished he could forget. Last year, the Philippine government had hired Executive Believers to take out an insurgent cell of Marxist-Leninists causing havoc with a profitable copper mine on the island of Mindoro. Sanders's local contact and fixer for the region, a former intelligence officer with the Philippine Army, had worked his way onto EB's payroll in return for providing ready and daily actionable intelligence on the insurgents' movements. Sanders remembered the intelligence officer's name had been Isagani, and he was a joker by nature, so completely misread what kind of operator Karson had expected him to work with. So when their team came under attack in a surprise ambush, and Karson lost two soldiers under his command, Karson set his eyes on Isagani as the man at fault. The Filipino had not lived up to their bargain and needed punishing.

Sanders expected retribution, but not for Karson to slice Isagani open with a knife, wrench his intestines from his gut and string them over a barbed-wire fence.

Sanders still had nightmares, remembering when they were driving away from the scene, watching the poor man in the rear-view mirror, barely standing as they drove away in a rice plantation in the middle of nowhere, his insides on the outside and spread everywhere, knowing this was the spot he was going to bleed out and die.

Then, as if a cold vice had just squeezed his heart, Sanders understood what Karson was asking of him. "You want me to deal with Zang? Scare her off?"

Karson nodded. "Get it done tonight. But with nothing linking back to us. No, scratch that. I have contacts you can use. Leave it to me since you weren't able to deal with her."

Again, Sanders swallowed against the uncomfortable itch growing in his throat. If he fucked up a second time, it would be his own guts next on the line.

He reflected that Karson was a difficult man to understand. Early on in their working relationship, Karson had seemed to be nothing more than a charismatic, driven and honest human being. Sanders didn't believe this to be true anymore.

During their tour together in Afghanistan, Karson had often put himself in the line of fire when under attack from Taliban, Mujahedeen, and al-Qaeda forces, risking his own life to save the men and women who served under him. Sanders had once believed they were almost like brothers because they shared the same pain, Karson from losing his family to an al-Qaeda attack on American soil that the US government should have prevented, and him because of how that same government had treated his own veteran brother, Ben, in diminishing his very real disability. But they weren't alike at all. In fact, Sanders was starting to wonder if Karson ever experienced any real emotional connections with anyone but himself, including his family. Where it had once seemed they were friends, now it appeared that Karson gave Sanders no thought or care because he no longer served a purpose. His dead wife and children, he never talked or express feelings about them either.

In groups, Karson commanded presence like a powerful, charismatic leader, and everyone soon fell in love with him. Sanders had too, in the early days, but as he had understood the truth behind his boss's outwardly projected and fake personas of being caring and empathic, it had become too late for him to get out. He was now complicit in a treasonous operation against the interests of the United States.

When you were alone with Karson and he didn't like what you had done, the veil went down, and the true nature of the Black Dog of the Hindu Kush revealed itself. Just like how Sanders was experiencing Karson now.

Sanders nodded, looked away and tried not to let the

numbness spreading across his body affect him. "Okay, I have an idea how I can get this done."

"Good. I have a man in mind who can do the job with Zang. His methods are... unconventional." Karson leaned forward. "Now on to other matters. Your recent trip to Sante Fe, was it fruitful?"

16

This time there was no lump in Sanders's throat when he answered Karson because the situation in Sante Fe he did have under control. "Yes, sir. My hunch was correct. McMahon did mail the submarine propeller data to his brother in Arizona. I managed to intercept the post box before anyone noticed it had arrived." Sanders pulled a data stick from his pocket, knowing that it was unusual in its appearance, parallelepiped-shaped with a matt black outer shell. One end carried four slots to allow the insertion of data cables, but it was not like any conventional physical data storage device available on the commercial market.

"Good," said Karson, taking the stick from Sanders. "Have you managed to get the files off it? I'm presuming it's encrypted?"

Sanders chose his next words carefully because he needed a positive spin on the many problems this device presented, all of which would hinder their conspiratorial scheme further. "It's a little more complicated than that."

Again, Karson was silent for a few seconds longer. "Explain?"

"This data stick is a prototype of the CIA's Directorate of Science and Technology. I mean, it's only been available for a few months now, and being tested on a few select operations. It's called a carried interlocked encrypted data device, or CIED device. Pronounced 'see-ed'. Holds eight terabytes of data, is immune to almost all electromagnetic spectrum radiation, isn't affected by submersion in water even when it is boiling, and you can drop it from twelve storeys without damaging it. You'd need to unleash a fragmentation or thermite grenade within three feet of it to destroy it, or an entire building to come crashing down on it. But the real problem is the encryption and the steps you need to access it."

"Which are?"

"It comes in two parts. This is only one half of this particular CIED device. You need the other half for it to work. When they are physically locked together, only when a voice-activated code is spoken into it does the data become accessible."

The slightest hint of a smile spread across the Black Dog's face. "So this means Jahandar has the other half, but like us, he too can't access the propeller schematics. He was lying to us in Chitral, claiming he had the propeller data all to himself. Correct?"

Taking a deep breath, Sanders nodded.

While Karson processed this new information, Sanders looked out the speeding limo's window, saw they had crossed over the Anacostia River and had taken the exit onto the two-lane highway to Baltimore. At least they were headed home and not to some remote industrial wasteland complex where Karson might beat him to within an inch of his life or execute him, as he had with other members of Executive Believers who had failed him. "Yes, sir. That's how I read it too."

"This suggests Jahandar has nothing of value on his own because these CIED devices are useless unless we have both."

"Correct, sir. And I'm guessing the voice required to unlock it will be McMahon's own. If he was clever enough to put the data on the CIED device before he ran, he was smart enough to make himself the only voice able to unlock it."

The smile on Karson's face was slight, but it was wider than before, and enough for Sanders to realise he was no longer in his boss's bad books. "Then we still have a chance with this, presuming McMahon is still alive and still in Jahandar's custody. Looks like we are finally able to negotiate with our FIA friend. Where is Jahandar now?"

"Still in India, pursuing his wife and Mark Pierce in Jharkhand state, was the latest report I received. It was bad timing that she ran when she did."

"Actually, I don't think it was. From what I hear, Jahandar's FIA masters aren't happy with him disappearing suddenly to India. They'll be worried if it comes out how deeply Jahandar is entangled with al-Qaeda in the Hindu Kush, because it will put severe and unwanted strain on the US-Pakistani relationships no one wants right now." Karson turned to Sanders and stared at him with a stone-cold face and without blinking. "Did it occur to you, Sanders, that Roshini Jahandar might have stolen the other half of this CIED device, and that is why her husband is chasing her with such zest?"

Finally, Sanders felt he was one step ahead of his boss because he too had already guessed this.

But the next words out of Karson's mouth still surprised the former CIA officer.

"That's why, Sanders, I secured us the contract with the CIA to fly Roshini Jahandar and Pierce out of India when they reach the extraction point. Do you remember CIA officer Mitch Hawley?"

Sanders nodded. "Didn't he get himself into trouble with inappropriate behaviour towards an officer under your command?"

"He did. And I got him off facing criminal charges of sexual misconduct. In his undying gratitude, he does favours for me here and there. Securing this contract for EB was one of them."

Sanders nodded and looked away, hoping that he never did anything stupid enough for Karson to end up "owning" him in the same way, though he felt he was well progressed down this path already.

"Don't look so worried, Sanders. We should have both Roshini and Pierce by the day's end. We'll have the other half of this CIED device then, and once we secure McMahon, we'll all be stupidly rich beyond our wildest dreams. Doesn't that sound like heaven to you?"

17

Sochi, Southern Federal District, Russia

Karen Dwyer, chief of the CIA's Eastern Europe office, had thought her days of operating under a non-official cover were well behind her now, but instead, here she was, in Russia's premier seaside resort town of Sochi, risking her very life deep inside enemy territory on a mission whose only tangible outcome was a good news story, and then only if she pulled it off.

At least the weather during the summer months here in southern Russia was pleasant, enough to get out and about in a blouse and jeans, and the cityscape was as cosmopolitan as any refined European city, but she still needed to apply "Moscow Rules". The people on the streets, dressed in normal clothes and drinking normal coffee in normal cafés and driving normal cars and shopping in normal shops, could have easily persuaded her that the situation was not as dangerous as she believed it was. But the risks she was taking were near insurmountable, and she couldn't assume she was safe even for a few seconds if she let her guard down. Karen Dwyer, C/ED, and therefore supposedly too senior for fieldwork, had to assume nothing. She had to operate as if the Russian Federal Security Service or FSB secret police were already onto her, and that everyone she dealt with was under opposition control and planning her downfall every waking second of her days while trapped inside this enemy's home-ground territory.

At fifty years of age, Dwyer felt she was too old to be involved in cold face cloak-and-dagger ops, but when Abdul Ibrahim had asked her to undertake this delicate extraction mission as a personal favour to him, she couldn't refuse. Why the hell had she fallen in love with Abdul all those years ago? Why did she still love him now, even though they weren't anything more than a casual and occasional item of passing interest for each other, and allow herself to be manipulated into this dangerous mission?

Then she remembered the risks he had taken for her, multiple times in the past, because she had asked the same of him. She realised again that she owed this mission to him. It was the only reason she was here.

Checking that her shoulder-length grey hair remained secured in her hair tie, she used the burner phone she had purchased only minutes earlier, and called on an encrypted line to Langley, Virginia.

To his credit, Abdul Ibrahim answered straight away. They proceeded through a series of code and distress identification words, then spoke as normal people would, despite the stress they were both under.

"I can't thank you enough, Karen, for getting Pavlenko and his family out of Moscow."

Dwyer tried not to clench her teeth. "We're all still in Russia, my old friend. We are still far from being safe!"

"I appreciate that. Where are the family now?"

"In a safe house. Wilks is watching over them while I stepped out to call you and to secure us groceries." Chad Wilks was the Ground Branch paramilitary operator assigned to Dwyer for this mission. As an ex-Navy SEAL, he was proficient in water extraction missions, so ideal for securing them out of Russia when it came time for them to move again. He had proven competent already, many times over, and Dwyer was glad to have him on the team. "What's the delay? Why can't we secure the family on the submarine already?"

Ibrahim didn't answer immediately, and Dwyer used the moment to scan the crowds, looking for anyone who might stand out and who might be a tail. She saw no one who alarmed her, but that didn't mean they weren't there.

"Abdul, the wife and especially the kids are out of their minds with fear. What is it you're not telling me?"

Ibrahim finally answered her. "We don't know if we are compromised, Karen."

Her stomach involuntarily tightened. "What do you mean?"

In a quiet tone so his voice wouldn't carry in this public space, Ibrahim answered her. "We are having problems getting a submarine to you."

"What?" She then asked in a whisper of her own, "I thought it was all arranged with the Turkish government, to allow a sub through the Bosphorus Strait to collect us?"

"That's not the problem."

Trying not to tense her whole body and project to the

people around her that she was overly stressed, Dwyer said as calmly as she could, "Then what is the problem?"

Ibrahim cleared his throat, which he only did when he was about to tell her unwanted news. She braced herself. "Karen, the Russians might have a means of tracking our subs."

"*WHAT?*"

"Stay cool. I have the situation under control, but the risk is still there. Until we can confirm the Russians won't be able to track us, you need to sit tight. If an American military submarine is caught in Russian territorial waters, Russia might use that as an excuse to bomb us with tactical warheads or, worse, go nuclear. Particularly considering how close you are to the war in Ukraine right now. The Russians might see a sub outside of Sochi as confirmation of America's direct involvement in the war, even though we are not."

"You can't be serious?"

"Unfortunately, I am."

"For how much longer must we wait?"

Dwyer knew from hard-learnt lessons from past operatives lost in the field that the longer they remained in Russia, the greater their chance of getting caught. If the FSB found them, their future was grim and would end only in humiliation, torture and execution. It would be the same for all of them, even the children, the Russian president was that ruthless. These people they were rescuing were human rights lawyers, campaigners against the corruption and dictatorial practices of the government hunting them, and innocent children. None of them deserved to go down and die in the most horrific means possible.

"A few more days."

Dwyer wished to stamp her feet but resisted the urge. "Abdul, you know we won't last that long. The FSB are already in Sochi looking for us. You've told me as much already."

"I know, Karen, and I'm sorry. But you understand as much as I do how important this mission is. When you secure Daniil Pavlenko and his family out of Russia, this will embarrass the Russian president to no end and help turn public Russian support away from their leader. We need to erode this strong-man persona he has built around himself, especially now while he is at war with the West in Ukraine, and this is a great way to do it."

Dwyer had a thousand arguments as to why this mission was pure folly. But then she remembered the looks of fear and terror in the eyes of Katerina, Daniil's wife, and their two children, the eight-year-old boy Anatoliy and his eleven-year-old sister Emiliya, waiting it out in the safe house, knowing that the Russian secret police could come for them at any minute. The Russian president was a brute of the worst kind if he thought it was acceptable to torture and murder innocent women and children, and Dwyer realised she wasn't about to let that happen on her watch.

"Don't take too long, my friend, or you might not see any of us, me included, ever again."

"I know," said her former lover, expressing genuine concern, which she'd never heard in the rhetoric of anyone else senior with whom she had worked with in all her long, twenty-seven-year career at the Central Intelligence Agency. "All I can tell you, Karen, is that I have my best operatives working on it."

"The best?" she asked, not quite believing him.

"For you, Karen, I wouldn't do anything less."

18

Jharia, Jharkhand, India

Pierce and Roshini jumped from the train as soon as it pulled into the stockpile yard. Large excavators with car-sized buckets and mining trucks with house-sized trays moved through the yard and around them at various speeds. The air was thick with dust, and the oranges, reds and purples in the sky resembled a permanent sunset. Pierce started coughing on the ammonia and methane fumes wafting from the earth, and realised he was deep inside what he could only describe as a new definition of hell.

"We need to move."

"I know... I just can't run... as fast as you." Out of breath, Roshini struggled to articulate her words. Pierce slowed his pace, and she pointed. "Mark, apartment blocks. We'll find transport there."

Pierce followed the line of her finger. Huge, dirty concrete apartment towers, each eight stories high and lined up in rows, must have housed residents evicted from their pastoral homes that had vanished into the encroaching coal mines. People ambled everywhere amongst these buildings, but all moved lethargically. Many carried wares on their heads, and the women wore colourful saris despite the grimness of the scene. Everyone was thin.

Pierce took Roshini's hand, and together they jogged down the rise to the settlement. Street vendors sold beverages and food scented with cumin and paprika that looked undercooked. Some residents begged for money. Pierce noticed many citizens were inflicted with horrific burns, both old and new.

"This is Jharia," Roshini explained as she caught her breath. "India's coal-producing region since before independence in 1947 and operating well into the era of British reign. These mines caught on fire more than a hundred years ago, and they've burned ever since."

"A coal mine that's on fire?"

She pointed further down the sloping valley to the coalfields with many operating mining trucks and excavators.

Pierce looked with her. Between the heavy mining equipment, men, women and children dug their own coal and collected the black rocks in baskets and blankets. Flames erupted from many orange-hot sinkholes resembling lava craters in a volcano. He counted at least thirty burning fires.

Coughing, Roshini said, "Be careful, Mark, the wrong step could open a hole in the ground, and you'll fall into a burning pit."

Pierce nodded and wiped the soot away that had gathered on his face. He recognised the fumes in the air would affect the health of Roshini's child, as it would affect any pregnant woman in the region. "We need a car, and fast."

They rushed through streets of compacted earth with dirty puddles everywhere. Women cleaned clothes in brown water and laid them out to dry on patches of broken concrete. Thin gangly dogs roamed between litter pits, keeping their distance from the humans.

"These people are poor. No cars."

Pierce searched for options. If Sergeant Mughal had survived his fall, he'd be here any minute. And Fawad Jahandar and Qusay Vali would not be far behind him.

He heard a car as it screeched around a decrepit apartment block, a red Skoda hatchback. The driver slammed on the brakes when a group of young children ran onto the road in front of it. The vehicle stopped abruptly, and Pierce recognised the driver immediately as the very man he expected it to be, Mughal. In response, Pierce pulled his Glock and fired into the windshield, shattering it, then fired at the front wheels, deflating both tires. Pierce then turned his aim again onto the sergeant whom he had missed with his earlier bullets, but the assassin was faster, as he had already dropped out of his side door and secured cover behind the bullet-riddled chassis.

"Run!" Pierce yelled, realising they were both exposed, and that Mughal now had sufficient cover to return deadly fire.

Roshini and he sprinted inside an apartment block with no doors in the frames as the concrete structure around them chipped and exploded from impacting rounds.

Together they raced through the apartment block, past women cooking meagre meals on tiny fires while infants played around them. A man with a broom, who pushed dirt through the corridors, watched them pass with vacant eyes. The shooting didn't seem to bother him, or he didn't hear it.

Out the opposite side, they crossed the compacted roads from one apartment block to the next. "Keep running!" Pierce yelled. "Find an apartment. Choose a room and hide. I'll come back for you."

Roshini nodded and sprinted off.

Pierce stopped once he was inside the doorframe of the next apartment block. He twisted to see the assassin appearing in the exit of the previous apartment. He fired his Glock until the magazine emptied.

Residents meanwhile fled in all directions around him. The assassin returned fire while Pierce ducked behind the concrete wall and reloaded. He was down to his last magazine for the Glock and six rounds left in the remaining magazine for the Beretta APX.

When the lull in the shooting came, Pierce leaned out and fired again. He couldn't see Mughal, but his intention at this point was not to kill but to keep his opponent pinned down. A tactic they could both play only until one of them ran out of ammunition.

Pierce saw the airborne grenade almost too late, with only enough time to throw himself to the ground behind a fallen concrete block and cover his head with his hands.

The grenade detonated, and the ground shuddered. His ears rang from the noise as the air filled with smoke. Dust and fine rubble rained down around him.

After counting to three, he looked up, recognising that he was unharmed. The concrete block had saved him from disintegration in a flash of rendered flesh and bone.

Then the concrete wall at the front of the apartment shifted and dropped, shearing off the side of the building.

Pierce sprinted through the ground floor to the other side while several stories of the apartment fell away and toppled towards the adjacent apartment block where the assassin hid. The carnage would force Mughal to flee and escape through the other side or die from the rubble crashing down upon him.

The destruction might also kill many innocent people. Pierce concluded he needed to move the action away from civilians.

He ran on, reaching the second apartment block, and then was on the streets again. He looked for Roshini, but she was nowhere in his line of sight. She must have found cover, but before he could find her, Pierce needed to determine if the assassin lived. He gripped his Glock with five bullets remaining and raced around the damaged apartment block. Residents fled as fast as their weak legs could carry them before the remainder of the building collapsed around them.

Pierce turned a corner and spotted the assassin covered in concrete dust, appearing as white as a ghost, but otherwise unharmed. Pierce had an easy shot, and the assassin hadn't seen him yet. But if Pierce missed, he'd hit civilians who had gathered in the street behind him, who were trying to understand, in their shock, what had just happened.

Pierce approached with his Glock raised to get a closer, cleaner shot.

Then Mughal saw him and fired, not caring about civilian casualties.

Pierce ducked as a bullet hit an old man next to him, who fell dead to the earth. Pierce fired two shots, high so as not to hit anyone, and then ducked behind a concrete pillar. Too many dead people already because of their gunplay.

Three bullets remained in the Glock.

Mughal fired again, then blended with the panicked crowds so Pierce couldn't shoot back.

Pierce waited until the firing stopped.

He then glanced around the pillar and spotted Mughal searching for his next magazine.

The man was out of bullets.

Pierce raced at him with his Glock out in front. Once there was an absence of civilians in his line of fire, he repeatedly squeezed the trigger. One bullet. Two. Then three and they were gone.

But the special forces sergeant moved with lightning-fast and limber motions. Pierce had missed him each time.

Unable to find a fresh magazine, the assassin sprinted, taking off towards the burning coalfields as he lobbed an object at Pierce.

Another grenade.

It fell short, then exploded. Its concussion wave propelled Pierce backwards. He landed hard on his back, with the wind knocked out of him and his hearing damaged. The only sound he could hear was a whistling whine.

The grenade blast had been sudden and felt like a volley of bricks thrown at his chest.

He pulled himself to his feet as fast as he could, but slower than was prudent, because of the pain that shot through all his muscles.

Pierce realised that his hands now shook violently. This was an old infliction that often bothered him at the worst possible moments. His jacket and shirt were torn in many places. The Glock was empty, and the Beretta had vanished.

He couldn't properly hear the screams because of his damaged hearing, but he saw victims' mouths expressing the same fear. Bloody arms reached into the air, seeking help.

Bodies and dismembered limbs and organs lay everywhere. A few of the wounded or stunned staggered and stumbled through the devastation.

Survivors ran into the carnage, offering first aid.

Mughal had cared nothing for the lives of innocents.

Pierce spotted his foe several hundred metres distant, disappearing into the burning coalfields.

Ignoring his aching body, the ringing ears and shaking hands, Pierce took chase.

19

Roshini followed Mark's instructions and ran towards the closest apartment block. She almost entered, then realised it would be the first building the assassin would check, so she ran to the next. She'd heard an explosion earlier and hoped that this was Mark eliminating Mughal while she also feared it had been Mughal assassinating Mark instead. But she couldn't worry about that, she had to get away, with or without the CIA man to help her.

As she turned a corner, a speeding black Land Rover tore up the dirt and almost hit her. The driver slammed on the brakes the moment she stopped running to avoid a collision. Instantly her muscles tensed, and her senses heightened ready for action, but then she froze where she stood. Even knowing that her position left her exposed, and willing herself to act, she couldn't. The circumstances felt all wrong, and it mostly had to do with her perception of the driver and the passenger.

The Land Rover's doors flung open, and unsurprisingly,

Qusay Vali and her husband, Fawad, stepped out. Qusay raised a submachine gun and lined her up in his sights. Today he was nothing like the intelligent and considerate man she had known for years in benign social settings, with piercing eyes that seemed to penetrate her very soul and a lack of acknowledgement that she might be a thinking, feeling being, and this scared her.

"Don't resist, Roshini!" he yelled.

Only when Qusay advanced did Roshini will herself to move. As she sprinted, the concrete wall behind her chipped and shattered as bullets burst from the weapon's barrel and impacted around her.

She ran into the closest apartment block and took the stairs, three steps at a time.

Glancing back, it was Qusay who came after her.

Roshini remembered how they had laughed together at parties, shared conversations at restaurants, and how she'd enjoyed day trips with Fawad, Qusay and his wife, Hajra. The man was always friendly, polite, helpful, and never sleazy.

But now his only goal was to kill her. Qusay and her husband had no intention of bringing her back alive.

Her heart pounded as she sprinted to the top floor while she could hear Qusay and Fawad sprinting up the stairs behind her. People of all ages and genders were everywhere, getting in the way, and she had to push past them roughly, knocking them aside. An old woman cooked rice in the hall, burning garbage as fuel. A blind teenager sat on a stool, his hearing alert to the shooting, but frozen to his spot because he couldn't identify its source.

"There she is! The whore!"

It was Fawad, coming up behind her.

More bullets flew up the stairwell.

Roshini suppressed a scream and battered down the door to the nearest apartment. The rusted hinges collapsed, allowing her access. Dozens of children inside, covered in soot and dirt, looked up at her. There was no furniture, but scraps of litter were everywhere, as was the stench of human sweat and urine. Three boys leaned the door back into its place, then crouched low with the others. Nobody made a noise. None of the children wanted the gunmen to enter their abode and start shooting.

She heard Qusay and Fawad outside as they reached the top of the stairs, eight stories up.

"Where are you! You bitch!" Qusay yelled.

Roshini had never witnessed her brother-in-law lose control before, but then the stakes had never been so high. If she escaped with the intelligence in her possession, Fawad and Qusay could soon find themselves in very precarious positions with their FIA masters and with whomever they were trying to provide the information on the data stick to. She was not surprised they hunted her to kill her, because it was now either her or them, but it still hurt after so long being friends, couples and lovers.

"Come out now!" grunted Fawad with laboured breaths. "I'll forgive you, wife, if you show yourself."

Her first thought was that they didn't know which apartment she had run into. That gave her time to act.

Several boys took her hands and pulled her to the window. Roshini realised now, when it was too late, that running up the stairs had been a mistake, for there were no exits here. What could they show her that might help?

Then she saw the long wooden plank that stretched

between this apartment block and the next, three metres long and forty metres above the road.

A small boy, about six years of age, crawled across to the other side with the dexterity of a monkey. He beckoned her to follow.

When she hesitated, a larger child crossed the plank so he could also show her it was safe, but he was nowhere near Roshini's weight.

The two boys beckoned her to cross, with urgency in their stares. Roshini understood their fear. The men in the hall had come for her. The boys didn't wish to be complicit in her protection, but they weren't callous enough to betray her either.

Roshini shuddered. She had questions, but the room was silent, and it seemed suicidal to make a noise. She wondered how many times other unwanted visitors had raided this dwelling before. Most likely these boys were threatened by the criminal syndicates that ran the poor neighbourhoods, demanding a cut of their coal collection earnings in return for their "protection". Her heart went out to these children, sickened by their plight and hopeless situation. She remembered the diamond in her pocket and vowed if she were able, she'd sell the precious stone to support charities serving these children's needs.

She heard shooting from the streets below. Then screams of fear and pain.

The boys behind her pushed her towards the plank.

Roshini realised she had no choice. If she stayed, Qusay and Fawad would find her and kill her. With the fighting below, she couldn't assume Mark Pierce had survived to save her. She had to save herself.

With controlled movements, she climbed out onto the

plank, telling herself the boys must have crossed it dozens of times a day. Thirty centimetres in width, it creaked as she put her weight on it.

She crawled out and looked down.

The earthen road seemed so far away.

Vertigo overcame her, and the world seemed to spin. People fleeing from the battle below didn't notice her. She spotted Mark chasing a man into the coalfields and so far away from her now. She wanted to call out, but again her fear of being heard stopped her. What could Mark do anyway?

She crawled until she reached the halfway point. So far, and despite its creaking, the wood had supported her weight.

"Roshini!"

She turned with careful movements so as not to overbalance and fall.

Qusay waited at the window. His weapon pointed at her. "You ruined my fucking life! Why weren't you a good fucking wife for Farad and just kept that mouth of yours shut?"

Roshini leapt onto her feet and ran the last metre and a half, diving into the window as bullets rattled around her. She rolled onto the dirty concrete floor with the children, covering her head as chunks of concrete exploded around her.

Then the firing stopped.

Everyone was uninjured.

"Fucking weapon!"

She looked up. Qusay had abandoned his assault rifle and now sprinted across the wooden plank.

On instinct and reacting because of her fear, she stood and pushed the plank away, felt it wobble, then tip and fall.

Qusay expressed surprise and locked eyes with her as he fell with it. He screamed for a few seconds. Then... nothing.

Roshini looked down. His oddly angled body lay broken and still in the mud.

"Roshini."

She looked up to find her husband watching her from across the three-metre gap.

"Roshini, why?" He wasn't threatening her with a weapon, his outstretched hands instead beckoned to embrace her. She noticed bandages under his T-shirt and around his lower ribs and spots of blood where the wound had leaked. This must have been where Mark had shot him, back at the bridge. His eyes expressed the physical pain the wound had caused him. "I loved you, and I thought you loved me?"

She remembered their first dates in London when everything had been a dream, and how charming and considerate Fawad had been, how he had made her believe there was no one else in the world but her. She remembered the first time he had told her he loved her, and how she once believed it.

"Come back to me, you *bitch!*"

Roshini shuddered. For too long she had doubted herself and her motives, questioned constantly if she had misinterpreted her husband's actions.

Not anymore.

"You're done with me, *husband!* You would have murdered me soon enough if I hadn't acted first."

She caught his stare, recognised in his returned expression that she was correct. He no longer loved her. How could a man betray a woman he'd promised to love, adore, protect and worship? He was not a man.

His face momentarily softened. "I realise... I was wrong."

"I realised that too." She reached into her pocket, to take out the real data stick she had taken from Fawad's safe and not the decoy she had given to Mark, to show her husband just how deeply she had extracted her revenge upon him.

But the matt black data stick was gone!

Blood draining from her face, she looked down, fearing the data stick had fallen from her pocket while crossing the wooden plank. She didn't see it, it was too far down for her to make it out anyway if she had dropped it here, but she saw Qusay again, and he hadn't moved. He was dead.

"Roshini?"

She looked up again. Fawad winced every time he moved because of his wounds. She realised in his incapacitated state, it would be no competition to race him to the base of this building.

She glanced back at him and saw that he had guessed her intention.

He pulled a pistol and fired.

She was already running.

20

Pierce crossed the coalfields at full speed, his ears ringing and his limbs trembling.

The assassin, three hundred metres ahead, raced along a coalface ridge. Nearby, giant excavators dug at the seams, drawing tonnes of fossilised fuel up in their buckets each time their teeth tore into the black earth.

Loose coal shards underfoot caused Pierce to slip often. When he reached the coalface, it was a four-metre drop to the base, so he slowed his pace so as not to slip and fall. With a shaking hand he drew his KAMPO tactical knife in his left hand and readied it for battle, then sprinted on.

A jet of flame rushed past him.

Pierce jumped as the earth opened. Black smoke and the red-orange glow of burning coal heated his skin. He'd almost stepped into a burning sinkhole.

He looked back. Mughal had seen the fire hole too, and Pierce next to it. The assassin drew his own fighting knife and held it in his right hand, then sprinted towards Pierce.

Pierce ran from the burning hole, not away from but

towards his foe. The air, thick with coal dust, reduced visibility to less than a hundred metres and hurt his eyes with the quantities of ammonia in the atmosphere. The coal crumpled under his feet whenever he moved, a disadvantage that would impede them both. When Pierce found stable ground, he stopped and waited for Mughal to reach him, allowing Pierce time to hold the higher ground. The ringing in his ears became more noticeable now he had stopped moving.

His foe slowed, switched his weapon to his left hand. Mughal was the same height as Pierce, with thick black hair and a close-cropped beard, but was far more muscular. His face was handsomely proportioned, but his eyes behind the goggles were dead. Despite his bulk, his movements seemed limber and precise. This assassin would fight with dexterity as well as brawn.

Mughal climbed the rise until he was at the same elevation as Pierce and never broke eye contact. When he spotted that Pierce's hands and legs trembled, he grinned.

For many seconds, neither man moved. They were both panting hard from the exertion and the toxic compounds in the air, and each waited for the other to make the first move, to learn their foe's fighting technique before they parried. Knife wounds were fatal more often than bullet wounds. The first man stabbed would be the first to die.

Pierce heard an approaching excavator. He resisted the urge to split his attention, but sensed that with the poor visibility, the operator hadn't yet seen Mughal and Pierce in their standoff.

Then its teeth tore away the coal near where they stood.

The ground collapsed under their feet.

They both struggled up the rise.

Pierce advanced as he stumbled and thrust with his KAMPO knife in the same motion.

The assassin had expected this, parried, then struck with his own blade.

Pierce ducked, avoiding a strike that would have taken his ear.

The ground kept crumbling.

Each man fought to keep his footing while striking and parrying, blocking arms with arms, feet with feet, and blades against blades. Pierce's ringing ears affected his balance, and moves that would have been instinctual often became clumsy without a sense of orientation and unresponsive muscles.

After several minutes of intense combat, when neither side had struck with anything that equated to a successful injury inflicted on the other, they separated. Each struggled for breath, and now Pierce's unprotected eyes watered from the unwanted chemicals building in them, which was a problem Mughal didn't have with his goggles.

Then Pierce slipped again on the collapsing ground at the same moment the assassin did. He steadied himself with a hand on a block of coal, but released it suddenly because of its heat.

His hands and legs trembled and threatened to give out from under him. He willed his shakes to disappear, but they didn't.

Then a jet of fire shot from the ground between them.

The men separated as the excavator bucket tore into the surrounding earth. The ground crumbled, and they slipped further down the coalface. Pierce saw the ore-carrying truck loom out of the dust cloud. From the coalface, the truck was still at a lower elevation, so he threw himself onto the roof and landed hard on his side, his breath knocked out of him.

A few seconds later, the assassin thudded onto the roof next to Pierce.

While coughing and expelling phlegm from their throats, the two men sprang to their feet and squared off. With shaking hands, Pierce searched for his knife, not finding it. He looked to Mughal and noticed he was also bladeless and no longer wore his goggles.

The assassin came at Pierce. He punched and kicked with nimble skill and a flexibility Pierce had never encountered. His foe was in full control of his body's precise actions.

The excavator tore at another seam of coal, clawing at the burning pocket that had caused the earlier ignition of flames. Fire and smoke exploded from the tear in the earth, smothering both fighting men with soot.

Pierce rushed his opponent, tackled him for a close-quarter brawl. The two men punched, elbowed, kneed, and kicked, but with no space to gain momentum on the constrained truck roof, their strikes were ineffective.

But Pierce wasn't fighting for a battle-winning blow. His tremors held him back from engaging at full capacity. He couldn't hear the machinery with his ringing ears, but in his peripheral vision, he watched the excavator bucket swing again, so when it released its load, Pierce timed his action to push the assassin into the falling coal.

Black rock rattled around them. Flames danced in the dropping coal. Mughal screamed as fire raced along the length of his back.

The truck lurched to the left and drove on.

Both men slipped with the sudden movement and tripped into the coal bucket.

Pierce landed on his back. The uneven coal twisted his muscles and bones to near-breaking point, and the heat from the coal burned his skin. The injuries already sustained during the grenade detonation compounded the jolt of the fall, and the pain almost caused him to black out. When he did recover his senses, it took him far too long to gather his breath, suppress the pain and climb to his knees.

He was too slow.

Mughal was faster, which allowed him to take Pierce in a headlock, crushing his neck as his other hand pushed back on Pierce's head.

The CIA operator fought back, using all his strength to repel the opposing arm from crushing his windpipe.

The air was thick with soot and smoke. Pierce could barely see anything. And he felt he was burning up. This was a hell on earth indeed. If he didn't do something smart soon, the choke hold would drive him into unwanted unconsciousness.

Then flames shot from the burning coal collected in the truck's tray.

Mughal reacted by crawling away, but to do so he had to release his grip on Pierce's head. He punched Pierce several times in the left kidney to distract him, giving Mughal time to clamber away.

With the intense pain, Pierce almost blacked out again.

Then the hand was back on Pierce's head, pressing his neck forward into the choke hold again.

Struggling to breathe, Pierce remembered the assassin had lost his goggles.

He gathered up a handful of hot coal dust and threw it into his foe's face.

The coal burned his hands.

It burned the assassin's eyes too.

Mughal screamed as he released Pierce.

The truck hit a rut, and the coal shifted.

Orange-hot coal rattled to the top layer.

Pierce scrambled from the bucket before it ignited with fire.

Blinded, the assassin slipped and fell backwards, landing on the hot coal. He screamed further and contorted every limb in near-impossible angles as the heat bubbled underneath him. His flesh singed, then caught with dancing flames. Even over the ammonia stench, Pierce could smell the assassin's burning flesh. The truck lurched again, and the hot coal opened a hole in the tray. The assassin disappeared inside as the hot coals quickly silenced his screams.

Coughing and spitting out black phlegm, Pierce paused for a moment and gathered his breath. His ears rang with an annoying whine. His hands shook.

When the air cleared, and he'd gathered his breath, Pierce climbed into the cabin, surprising the driver and ordering him to stop. The driver obeyed.

Pierce descended the truck's external ladder, then raced to the decrepit apartment buildings. He spotted a black Land Rover with the doors open. It looked too expensive to belong in such a desolate place. Senses on alert, Pierce approached the abandoned vehicle.

No one was inside, and he was surprised to find a pair of binoculars and a Heckler & Koch MP5 submachine gun and several spare magazines on the back seat. Pierce grabbed the weapon and pocketed the magazines.

He checked his surroundings. The streets were empty, which was not surprising considering the carnage that had occurred.

"Roshini!" he called out.

Silence.

He called her name again.

From nowhere, she sprinted around an apartment block, running straight at him.

A man followed, then stopped dead when he saw Pierce, who now had the MP5 pointed at his centre mass. The man raised his hands, and Pierce recognised Fawad Jahandar from his CIA file, but also from the sunlight reflecting off his gold wristwatch. He had nowhere he could run to before Pierce could shoot him multiple times.

"Just fucking die, you bitch!"

Roshini raced to Pierce and hid behind him.

"Is that your husband?"

"Ex-husband," she growled.

Fawad's fear evaporated, and his face transformed into a sneer. He marched towards them.

"Don't kill him," she begged. "He isn't long for this world, but I don't want you to be the one to cause his parting."

Pierce nodded. He fired a short burst into the ground around Fawad, forcing him to halt in his brave advances towards them. "Get in the car, and keep your head down," he said to Roshini while maintaining eye contact with Fawad. He watched from the corner of his eye as she climbed into the passenger seat and crouched down low, out of both their visual range of sight.

"You can take her!" Fawad screamed as he dropped to his knees, which sank into the coal-smeared earth that was all around them. "I don't need her anymore." He laughed manically.

Pierce noticed that Fawad held a matt black metallic stick in his hand. It stirred a memory in Pierce that he couldn't quite place in any context that made sense. Instinctively Pierce patted his own pocket, still with the data stick Roshini had given him, so he had not lost the CIA-requested intel she had worked so hard to escape with.

He screamed again. "If you're going to kill me, just do it."

"I'm not going to kill you because she asked me not to."

He sniggered again. "Don't you get it? Roshini still loves me, even if she has convinced herself she does not. She won't let you take her away from me. She'll come to her senses soon enough."

Pierce shook his head. "My promise is only for today. If I see you again, Fawad Jahandar, it will be for the last time."

"I'll make the same promise to you, American."

Pierce lowered his weapon and returned to the driver's seat, seeing Roshini with her hands in her head and rocking back and forth to combat the fear from consuming her. He started the engine and tore off, leaving Fawad Jahandar stranded on his knees. "It's all okay." He spoke to her in the most soothing voice he could muster. "He can't harm you anymore."

It was only when they were far away from Jharia that Pierce realised what Jahandar had held in his hand, and now he regretted not taking it from him when he had had the chance despite whatever the cost to Roshini might have been in that harrowing moment.

21

Rachel Zang sat opposite Abdul Ibrahim in his seventh-floor office within the CIA's original headquarters building and looked out over the sea of car parks servicing the majority of the agency's twenty thousand plus employees. This was not Zang's first time in her superior's office, but with each visit she was always in awe of the framed American flag that hung on the wall behind Ibrahim, juxtaposed against the copy of the Qur'an on a podium next to Ibrahim's flatscreen. But what could have been more American than this scene, as her country was one of the most multicultural and diverse nations on the planet? Then she pondered that her ancestry was Hong Kong and Cantonese only one generation back on her father's side, so it made the scene even more poignant with her being there.

A recent addition was a framed photograph of Ibrahim shaking hands with Britain's prime minister. She wanted to ask how that recent photo op had come about but suspected that was a story for another time.

Instead, Zang listened closely as Ibrahim briefed her on recent tech released from the CIA's Directorate of Science and Technology, the prototype CIED device used for the physical transportation of terabytes of highly sensitive information. Then he turned to the matter regarding the rogue DARPA engineer, Nigel McMahon, who had used a CIED taken from DARPA's logged registry to steal detailed schematics of US Navy submarine propellers.

"There are three components to this situation, Zang, which we need to contain immediately. Unfortunately, the schematics are outside of the US now on McMahon's CIED device, and we need to neutralise all three threat vectors that have influence over its de-encryption. I don't need to tell you that the Russians, the North Koreans and the Chinese will pay hundreds of millions in hard currencies for this information. If any of these enemy nations find a way to track our submarines, well, you know where this all leads to."

"Yes, sir."

"But it's worse than that. I'm concurrently running an operation in Russia, to extract several high-value assets from that rogue nation who can potentially embarrass the Russian president and weaken his position internally. But we can only get those assets out of Russia via a submarine entering Russian territorial waters. If it is discovered... Well, I need not tell you what the implications are here. And we can't keep these defectors hidden indefinitely either. The clock is ticking."

"I completely understand, sir."

The chief of the Special Operations Group nodded.

"Sir, can't we swap out propeller types on our subs? I know it's a logistical nightmare, but it eliminates the risks."

"It would be nice if we could. The problem is, our DARPA engineers have spent decades perfecting propeller designs that minimise sonar signal generation, and to throw all that research out now puts us decades behind our enemies. Plus, it's highly likely McMahon took all our designs — existing, experimental and abandoned — to the enemy."

Zang nodded, conceding her boss's point. "Of course."

"Let's get back to what we can do to fix this. We know McMahon abandoned his wife and three kids nine days ago, when he flew out of San Diego to Tokyo, then booked another flight to Kuala Lumpur and then on to Peshawar, Pakistan. It was at Bacha Khan International Airport outside Peshawar that FIA's assistant director of their Technical Wing, Fawad Jahandar, and his head of Operational Intelligence, Qusay Vali, collected McMahon together. After that our trail on McMahon's movements gets sketchy. We believe McMahon took one half of the CIED device with him to Pakistan, hid the other half somewhere here in the United States, and used his own voice as the only code that could unlock it. That gives him a convincing bargaining chip with Pakistani intelligence to keep him alive and to receive payment. But you and I both know the FIA and their sister organisation, the ISI, have an abysmal track record of keeping their word, even to traitors who are coming over to their side."

Zang nodded, as she had guessed this much already. "I presume McMahon mailed the other half of the CIED to someone he trusted or to a mailbox?"

"Yes, that's our working assumption. We're investigating

all options there, including tearing apart his house looking for it. We're also leaning on the FBI to help, without telling them anything as to the 'whys', as we usually do. I feel sorry for McMahon's wife and children. From what our investigating team on the ground is telling me, Annabell McMahon is utterly distraught. She believed her husband worked for a private shipbuilder, had no idea he worked for DARPA and held one of the highest security clearances in the nation. She also had no idea he was a gambling addict with insurmountable debts to the Mafia either. Still refuses to believe it, in fact, despite the evidence we have shown her."

"Yes, it's awful."

While Ibrahim had described Annabell's situation, Zang mused upon her own family upbringing and how her father had destroyed her family with similar lies and deceits. She could empathise with the poor woman, perhaps too much. She felt an anger building inside her that was akin to how Annabell must be feeling.

Ibrahim made a cage with his fingers and rested them on his desk. "Because the data is on a CIED device, it gives us some hope that we can still contain this."

"So, following your line of logic, sir, this suggests Jahandar is in possession of one half of the CIED and that he also has McMahon locked away somewhere."

"Yes, except this is where it gets complicated."

"How so?"

"I had a team in India and Pakistan ready to orchestrate the defection of Fawad Jahandar's wife, Roshini, to the United States. Totally unconnected to what happened with the propeller data breach, and I suspect this unintended mix-up might have thrown all Fawad's schemes into chaos."

This was an unexpected revelation, and Zang didn't know what to say.

"I can tell by your look this news doesn't impress you."

"Perhaps more, it shocks me."

Ibrahim nodded. "Months ago, Roshini Jahandar contacted our Islamabad embassy. She had evidence proving that her husband and his boss, the director-general of the FIA, maintained an ongoing and profitable working relationship with al-Qaeda in the province of Khyber Pakhtunkhwa, formerly the Federated Tribal Lands, in the Hindu Kush regions of Pakistan. They were essentially on-selling intelligence to them that we, the CIA, provided to the FIA and ISI in our ongoing efforts to curb global terrorism."

"Wow, that's quite an intelligence coup if you could pull that off, even though we've known this for decades. I know that's why we didn't tell the ISI we were sending Navy SEAL teams into Abbottabad to kill Osama Bin Laden. So if we have evidence the FIA is in bed with al-Qaeda, we can use this to coerce them into cooperating with us? Was that the plan?"

"Exactly. But when I realised Fawad Jahandar likely had one half of the CIED device, we decided to move up the timetable on Roshini's defection to days rather than weeks. I had my team in India and Pakistan already coordinating the defection, led by Daniella Estrada. Do you know her?"

Zang shook her head.

"Well, she didn't make it, unfortunately, and neither did the rest of her team."

"I'm sorry to hear that."

"You can read the details in the report I'll make available to you after this meeting. But the long and the short of it is, I instructed Estrada to instruct Roshini to fast-track her defection schedule and to steal everything her husband kept in their family safe in the process. We knew she had the passcode. She had told us this already. It made her defection riskier, of course, but there was a good chance he'd left the CIED device there for safekeeping. Well, it paid off. Estrada reported that they had secured Roshini and her intel and were making their way to the extraction point when Jahandar and his team of FIA and Pakistan Army Special Forces operators loyal to him ambushed Estrada's team, killing and mortally wounding them all except for Roshini. That's when I sent the Trigger Man in, to secure Roshini away from danger and to get her out of India in one piece."

Zang stiffened as two thoughts struck, first that she had never been given a code name like Pierce had and that this still bothered her, but the other was more pertinent to the mission, so she focused on that point. "That explains why Jay Sanders asked me for details on Pierce. He wasn't trying to recruit him into Executive Believers. He and Karson wanted intel on Pierce to help them track him in India."

Ibrahim nodded. "Yes. Exactly."

"So, sir, I'm now thinking that the exchange Karson, Sanders, Jahandar and Vali conducted in the Chitral region wasn't to negotiate McMahon's return, but to negotiate a deal to sell the submarine propeller data together?"

"Yes, I agree. I highly suspect Karson is operating way beyond sanction here."

Suddenly several elements of this mystery were now making sense to Zang. "That would suggest Karson has the other half of the CIED device."

"That's our working scenario, yes."

Zang shuddered as she came to understand that Sanders had essentially honeytrapped her, or almost had, into giving away sensitive information that could have cost Pierce his and, in association, Roshini Jahandar's lives. She was furious towards her casual lover, knowing that he had consciously and unscrupulously used her. Tactics that all CIA operatives used against targets and assets in their day-to-day work, but now when it was one of her peers and a bedroom mate using this tactic on a supposed ally, it made the hurt more visceral and unfair.

Zang had several questions buzzing in her mind that she needed answers to, but one was more important to her above all others, for personal reasons because she considered Mark Pierce her friend, and he had never betrayed her. "Is Pierce okay?"

Ibrahim nodded. "Last time he reported in, he was driving Roshini to their extraction point in Kolkata. We'll know his situation by this evening, when he is expected to report in again. And whether he has the CIED device or not."

Zang couldn't help herself and sighed with relief. But she also found herself at odds with this emotional response because she and Pierce were both paramilitary operators and always in the field on dangerous missions. Injury, torture, and death were real possibilities for each of them. That was why Zang had always kept her relationships casual. If something happened to her or one of her other "bedroom friends", the pain of loss wouldn't cut deep. "Does Pierce know any of this background that you're briefing me on now?"

"Not yet. I didn't want to tell him about the CIED device unless absolutely necessary and regret not doing so now. I'll brief him when he gets back stateside. Roshini's safe return and securing the data she carries is his number one priority for now, and we'll leave it that way."

The intercom on Ibrahim's desk buzzed. His personal assistant seated in the smaller adjoining office just outside his own said, "Abdul, Ryleigh Bresolin is here to see you now."

Zang suppressed a smile. Ibrahim's personal assistant Roxy Long was the only CIA employee of lesser rank than him who had gained the right to call him by his first name. This infuriated many CIA employees who felt they deserved that right too, but not Zang. Ibrahim had earned her respect, not demanded it.

"Thank you, Roxy. Send her in." With the exchange concluded, the C/SOG looked up at Rachel Zang and said, "I want you to sit in on this meeting. Should be rather interesting."

22

When Senior Operations Officer Ryleigh Bresolin stepped into Abdul Ibrahim's office, she first expressed surprise, then pinched her lips. "Sir." She directed her attention only to the C/SOG while smoothly avoiding the other woman in the room — Zang. "I understood that what I was here to discuss was for your ears only?"

Ibrahim directed Bresolin to a seat next to Zang with a wave of his hand. "Paramilitary Operations Officer Zang is read in, and she needs to hear this."

Resisting a sneer, Bresolin instead nodded, straightened out her sky-blue dress, then sat without looking at Zang. "Very well."

Zang guessed Bresolin to be in her late thirties, so ten years older than herself. She looked good, probably ran ten miles or swam fifty laps every day, as Zang did, and her short hair suited her. But she carried an air of arrogance about her that Zang didn't like and, more importantly, didn't trust. She knew that whatever she was about to hear would be informative and, dare she think it, entertaining, but also likely not that helpful towards resolving their current crisis. Knowing that expressing an opinion would only aggravate the situation, Zang would say nothing and watch as the discussion progressed.

Ibrahim leaned back in his chair and seemed relaxed. "I'd like you to brief me and Zang on what really happened in Chitral five days ago."

Bresolin stiffened, then sat taller. "With all due respect, sir, I wasn't physically there, nor was I listening in."

"That doesn't answer my question."

"Sir, you heard the testimony given by Karson and Sanders yourself. You were at the hearing. I saw you." She turned to Zang, acknowledging her for the first time. "And so were you."

Zang said nothing and kept her facial expression neutral. This was Ibrahim's meeting, and she wanted to see how he would run it, and learn from the experience.

Bresolin turned her attention back to Ibrahim. "Very well. Prior to the Chitral meeting, myself, Karson and Sanders did know about McMahon's data stick containing the stolen submarine propeller schematics, if you were wondering? That's what Karson and Sanders were really trying to get back, although we didn't know it was a CIED device at the time. Nigel McMahon is not the real security risk here." She returned her attention to Zang. "I still don't understand, sir, why she is here. The fewer who know about this scandal, the better."

Ibrahim made another cage with his fingers as he leaned further back in his plush chair, projecting his naturally oozed sophistication and coolness. "It's not a scandal yet, and it's our job to make sure it remains so. But it was *your*

PMC contact, Bresolin, who involved Zang in the first place."

Bresolin frowned. "How so?"

Ibrahim then proceeded to brief Bresolin on how Sanders had contacted Zang and asked about Pierce, but to his credit, left out the details that Sanders and Zang's relationship was an intimate one. "Zang's one of my top operators. She quickly ascertained something iffy was going on and put most of the pieces together herself before she came to me with her suspicions."

Bresolin didn't acknowledge the comment with words or even a nod, but Zang felt secretly pleased that her boss had this much faith in her. She was obviously doing something right, considering where she had stood with Ibrahim when they had first met, when his first words spoken to her were to question her motives in an operation that had gone wrong, which he believed she had handled poorly.

"And, Bresolin, I should point out that the CIED device was never mentioned in the hearing, by you, Karson or Sanders. Lying to a senatorial committee has serious criminal implications."

The senior operations officer shifted in her seat, licked her lips, then said, "I didn't lie, and neither did my colleagues. We weren't asked about the CIED device, or any type of data stick for that matter, so we didn't bring it up. There was no reason to."

Ibrahim leaned forward and held Bresolin's stare. "Are you sure that was wise? It sounds to me like you're playing a dangerous game here."

Bresolin adjusted the hem of her dress, then said to Ibrahim, "With all due respect, sir, the problem lies with you. You compromised my mission with the Roshini Jahandar defection. We should have been talking weeks ago, coordinating our efforts because we were both working the same target. Both our operations are now severely compromised as a result."

Ibrahim nodded as his face lost some of the tension building in his muscles. "On that point, I agree, Bresolin. That wasn't very professional, of either of us. Where is Fawad Jahandar now? Do you know?"

"Sir." Bresolin cleared her throat and stiffened again. She no longer hid in her body language that this debriefing made her uncomfortable and unwanted. "He's in Jharkhand, India, chasing your operative Trigger Man and your asset Roshini Jahandar across that state. And making matters worse, the FIA and the ISI have now learnt that Fawad Jahandar has long been selling state secrets to both al-Qaeda and India's IB, which has put him on their kill-with-extreme-prejudice list."

This was news to Zang, but judging by Ibrahim's calm response, not news to him. He said in his usual refined and cultured voice, "Would it be news to you, Bresolin, that the director-general of the FIA was killed less than an hour ago in Islamabad, with a car bomb?" He pulled a file from his top drawer and passed it over, opening it to a photograph of a sedan gutted with flames. Bresolin couldn't suppress her shock at hearing this news and seeing the photos, and neither could Zang.

"Oh, shit!" said Bresolin.

"Indeed," said Ibrahim. "It's either al-Qaeda, FIA or ISI cleaning house. Maybe IB, but I doubt it was them."

Bresolin raised her voice when she answered, "It won't be al-Qaeda. The news I was bringing to you was, we've got good intel that Fawad Jahandar handed off Nigel McMahon to al-Qaeda regional commander Kaajal Khan shortly after Jahandar secured him, and this occurred before Karson and Jahandar's meeting in Chitral."

Zang knew the name. Kaajal Khan was typical of most Islamic militant al-Qaeda insurgents in that he was unwaveringly anti-American, anti-Jewish, and dogmatic in his belief in the restoration of fundamentalist Islamist ideals of Salafism, achieved through jihad and the ongoing war of terrorism aimed at the West. Khan reputedly maintained a stronghold inside an elaborate cave network in the Pakistani region of the Hindu Kush mountains, near Pakistan's border with Afghanistan, where he maintained a small army of battle-hardened warriors, itching at the bit to do battle with non-believers and the unholy. Despite the years of effort and dollars the CIA had expended in attempting to locate Khan's secret mountain hideout so they could permanently shut it down, no one in the West had gotten anywhere close to locating it. And now one man who could unlock the secret of America's classified nuclear submarine propeller designs was hidden away inside that stronghold, which was as far away from the CIA's reach as it was possible to get in this world.

"It's not good," said Bresolin, overstating the fact. "But to clarify the situation, Khan will be on the deal with Jahandar to sell McMahon's data. And Jahandar will want to move on this quickly now that he is out of favour with the FIA and ISI. He'll need the money made on the sale to fund his going into hiding. Probably in India because of his connections with India's intelligence services."

Ibrahim nodded. "Yes, this just gets worse and worse the more we know."

"Sir," said Bresolin, "to be clear, the director-general's

death will be one hundred per cent the result of actions taken by the ISI or FIA. No one else was involved, not even us. They are merely cleaning house before this embarrasses them further."

Zang decided to ask her first question since Bresolin's arrival. "Do the ISI or FIA know about the CIED device and the nature of the data on it?"

"God, I hope not. This is a mess as it is."

Ibrahim cleared his throat, drawing both women's attention back to him. "What about Karson and Sanders? Surely, Bresolin, it must have crossed your mind that the two of them could be complicit with Fawad Jahandar and Qusay Vali in selling on the CIED device data? You must have observed, as I did, that they both lied multiple times during the Senate committee interview?"

From Bresolin's shocked expression, it was clear to Zang that she had not considered this possibility at all, but now that she had, her face had turned a very pale shade. "You can't be serious, sir?"

Ibrahim frowned but said nothing.

"Major Karson is one of the most patriotic men I've ever had the fortune to work with, even when he turned mercenary. Do you know how loved he is by the men and women who have served under him?" Her body tensing, Bresolin now spoke with anger. "Sir, do you also know that Karson lost his wife and two twin five-year-old sons to a terrorist attack five years ago? Their car was deliberately run off the road. It crashed thirty feet down the side of a steep cliff, or did you forget that detail when you made that accusation? Al-Qaeda were taking out revenge on him, and we did nothing to prevent that attack. The man has been through enough already, having paid too high a price for his service, and now you accuse him of being a traitor?"

"If I remember correctly, Bresolin, it was Karson who claimed it was a terrorist attack, and nothing was ever substantiated in that line of investigation."

Bresolin glared at Ibrahim; she clearly could not believe the accusation he had just voiced was anything more than an insult to her and Karson.

"Isn't it also true, Bresolin, that you've spoken up recently against DARPA programs that provide soldiers in the field with anti-psychotic drugs? Drugs that Karson has also gone on the record as saying are detrimental to the health of active service men and women?"

"So what if I have? Our government, regardless of which party controls Congress, is a mess." Her face turned bright red. "No one is looking out for the rights of people like us, who put our lives on the line daily to protect this country. Our representatives only care about maintaining the military-industrial complex and lining their own pockets. It's my democratic right and my duty to both stand up to injustices like this *and* be patriotic to my country! I hope, *sir*, that you do too. But from what I'm hearing now, I don't think you are."

Ibrahim nodded, as if agreeing with her, but then he said, "It's a point well made, and I support your stance. But why is it that I sense, Bresolin, that when you tell me where Karson and Sanders are right now, I'm not going to like it?"

"No, I don't think you will." Bresolin stiffened again. "Because I just sent them to India, to extract Jahandar if Trigger Man doesn't get to him first. Do you believe I have acted inappropriately in your eyes, because I don't?"

23

Kolkata, West Bengal, India

It was late into the night when Pierce and Roshini reached the private airfield on the outskirts of Kolkata, chosen for the thick semi-tropical scrub that grew around the strip, offering seclusion from prying eyes. They had just made it on time, as Mitch Hawley had messaged Pierce hours earlier to tell him that the Antonov AN-32 turboprop twin-engine military transport aircraft would only be on the tarmac for another hour before it departed.

Pierce had driven non-stop for six hours and still hadn't slept since collecting Roshini in Patna a day and a half ago. Exhausted, his body hurt everywhere from the beating he had taken from Sergeant Mughal. His ears still rang like church bells pounding in his head, and he couldn't fully control the tremors in his hands or legs.

Roshini and Pierce had barely spoken during the drive, both in the comedown shock often experienced after a battle. She jittered and bit her nails, and he knew why. The trauma of the last twenty-four hours presented a strong chance of causing a termination. Even though he wanted to, he didn't know how to comfort her, so he said nothing.

Now, when they parked just outside the airfield where they remained hidden by the trees, they saw the lights illuminating the runway. He used binoculars he'd found in the Land Rover to get a better assessment of the site, not yet trusting that they were safely away from Jahandar and the FIA. Several men and one short, toned and muscular woman, all in black combat fatigues with M4 carbines and body armour, secured the plane. They moved and behaved as American operators should, but the hairs on the back of Pierce's neck were tingling, and he didn't know why.

"What happens now?" Roshini asked, wiping her wet eyes with a tissue. Her fingers bled where she had torn at her nails.

Pierce lowered the binoculars and turned to her. He grabbed her hand in his and squeezed it affectionately. "In theory, you walk to that plane and get on board. It takes off and delivers you safely to the United States."

"That's it?"

"That's it."

She caught his stare. "You're not coming with me?"

Pierce looked away. His mission brief was to join Roshini on the aircraft, but something about the data stick Jahandar had held in his hand during their encounter in the Jharia coal mines still bothered him. He remembered the other data stick Roshini had shown him, and wondered if this was a decoy. Deciding to test a hunch, he turned to Roshini and passed her the data stick. "Make sure you take this with you."

She took it reluctantly. "You still haven't answered my question?"

Pierce sensed that Roshini was not telling him everything, but those same senses told him that she was not consciously acting against his interests either. "Let me make a phone call first."

"To whom?"

"The CIA. I won't be a minute, and if I hear what I need to hear, I'll walk over and get on that plane with you."

She nodded as her eyes wetted. He sensed that she didn't want him out of her sight. He wondered what it was that she wasn't trusting.

"Give me a moment."

He called Mitch Hawley, who answered after eleven rings. "Code in."

Pierce rushed through the confirmation protocols confirming it was him and that he wasn't under duress.

"Okay, let's do that again, Trigger Man."

"No fucking way. I'm on a timetable."

Hawley made a snorting noise. "If you insist, but I'm not happy about it. Are you at the extraction point? They are waiting for you."

"I am. Confirm the plane make and model that you sent, and the tail number."

Hawley told him, and it matched what Pierce had already observed.

"You sent paramilitary support. How many?"

"I don't know that information, Trigger Man. I don't need to."

"Why not? No, don't bother answering that. What are they armed with?"

"I don't know that either, Trigger Man. Those kinds of operational details aren't important to me."

Pierce involuntarily clenched his fists and bit down on his lips. Then he said in the calmest voice he could muster, "Listen to me very carefully, Hawley, if you want to stay being my handler, those details will be important to remember in the future. You understand me?"

Hawley made a dismissive clicking noise with his teeth. "I don't think so. From what I hear, you can't hold down any handler for any length of time. It sounds as if the problem is not with me, but you."

Pierce bit down on his lips again. There was some truth to what Hawley had said, but there had been one handler whom he had worked with successfully for years, Mackenzie Summerfield, and he missed her now that she was gone. He would have done anything to get her back on the team again rather than deal with idiots like Mitch Hawley and his predecessors before Mackenzie. She was the only one who had cared about her job and about doing it well. For everyone else, it was a mere stepping stone towards more senior and glamorous positions.

Roshini made a face at Pierce, suggesting that he hurry along, so he said to Hawley, "Hold a minute." He put his ineffective handler on mute.

"What's going on, Mark?"

"It's all good. The flight out is confirmed clean and ready to go. But just give me a minute." He unmuted the call. "Hawley?"

"Rather than put me on mute, why don't you call back? It's not like I'm not busy here, and I don't wait all day in hope that you—"

"Give me a break, Hawley! Zang, have you spoken to her? Passed on my message?"

"No."

Pierce waited several seconds for Hawley to explain his actions, but only frustrating silence followed. "Are you going to elaborate on why not?"

"I told you before, Trigger Man, you are operational. Protocol dictates that all comms go through me and only me. You can talk to Zang all you like when you are back in the States and not before."

"Fuck!" Pierce did his best to control his rising anger, but it was difficult. "I'll tell you who'll have words when I get back, Hawley. You and me. Now put me through!"

"Is that a threat? Are you threatening a fellow CIA officer?"

"Take it however you want, Hawley. I don't give a fuck." Pierce had a number he could call Zang on and another number to contact the S/COG, Abdul Ibrahim, should he need to, but hadn't yet because it was against mission protocols to break cover, as Hawley had said. But he figured when he handed Roshini off in the next few minutes, the mission was done, and the call was warranted. He needed that call because something about this entire mission stank of a set-up he couldn't yet understand.

"This is highly inappropriate, Trigger Man."

"If you think any of our conversations to date have been appropriate, Hawley, then you don't fucking understand what being a part of the CIA team actually means. Roshini Jahandar is walking to the plane now. I'm making you accountable for her safe return."

Pierce ended the call and growled.

When he looked up, Roshini was staring back at him

with her eyes wide and her stunned expression frozen on her face. "That didn't sound good."

"It's all fine." Pierce knew he had answered her too quickly and too abruptly, but he didn't know what else he was supposed to do. "It's just that me and Hawley, well, we just don't like each other."

"Your contact, who you were just talking to?"

Pierce nodded.

"That, I understand. Happens everywhere, in offices and workplaces the world over."

"Well, you are all cleared. Get out of the car and walk to the plane."

A tear rolled down the side of her face, and she lost the strength she had been carrying in her only moments earlier. "Please, Mark, I'd feel so much more comfortable if you were joining me."

"No. Sorry, I can't."

She touched his arm again, and Pierce noticed that he liked it when she did. "Why?"

He knew he should be getting on that plane with her, but the data stick seemed more critical, that the consequences of not going after it would be worse than abandoning Roshini. He also considered keeping her with him so he would "know" she was protected, but that would put her in far more danger than putting her on the plane. There were no good solutions here. "Because this hasn't ended, Roshini, not yet."

"For you, or for me?"

"Me... I'm sorry. My words mustn't offer you any comfort."

"You're going after Fawad. I asked you not to kill him."

He did have a plan for Fawad, but that required Pierce

communicating that plan with Ibrahim first and reaching the Pakistani intelligence operator before the FIA, ISI or IB did. As he thought through his plan, Pierce massaged his forehead and willed his headache and ringing ears to desist. At least his shakes were now subsiding. "I won't kill him. I promise." When he said it, he knew he meant it because Fawad Jahandar's termination was not his intention.

Roshini nodded.

Pierce didn't know why, but he found himself explaining himself to her. "There is more I need to uncover behind what the FIA are up to. I'm a lone operator. That's how I work best and how I need to work now."

"Somehow, I don't think that's true." Then she squirmed in her seat before looking Pierce in the eye and said, "Tell me something about yourself? Something personal? Something real?"

He frowned. "Why?"

She shook her head, then looked away. "I don't know why, Mark. I feel like I'm never going to see you again, or if we do, it will be under impossible circumstances. You're a good man, and I just want to know something about you. The real you, that I can hold on to, so that I know this all makes sense, on a deeper level..." She bit down on her lower lip for a moment before massaging her forehead with the palm of her left hand. "Don't worry about it. I'm just being silly."

She went to open the door, when he grabbed her arm. "You're not, Roshini. Unfortunately, I understand what you are saying too well."

Roshini relaxed and fell back into her seat. "You don't have to tell me anything."

"But I will." He thought upon what he could reveal about

himself that would give her the comfort she needed, but also not compromise him in the future. Then he found himself saying, "Sixteen years ago, my parents were murdered. It was a political crime. They were gunned down. I didn't witness it, but I heard..." His voice became croaky, so he cleared his throat. "I don't know why they were killed, even to this day. But I can tell you it sent me down a very long and arduous path full of darkness and pain, but one that eventually brought me to this very moment with you, Roshini. I'm glad we met. You've given me new perspectives on life that make the darkness and pain not so dark and not so painful anymore."

She took a moment to compose herself, then sat in silence for a minute. "Thank you. I'm sorry to hear that, but perhaps it will help that this is exactly what I needed to hear." She reached over and kissed him on the mouth.

Pierce was too shocked to respond with words, and she had drawn away before he could respond with a kiss of his own. But he wasn't sure he wanted to either. He made it a rule never to get intimately involved with civilians, because in his profession where he constantly faced danger and death on a regular basis, civilians could be used against him, and mostly they would suffer unnecessarily as a result.

But the kiss had been nice.

It also seemed jarring when only seconds before he had revealed a deep and traumatic secret about himself to her.

Before he could say a word or reflect upon this moment further, she was out of the car and walking towards the AN-32 transport.

He watched as the stocky female paramilitary soldier met with her, and they exchanged words.

Once, during the conversation, Roshini looked into the

darkness, searching for Pierce, but not seeing him. Then she followed the extraction team as they returned inside the jet. It taxied for a few minutes, then took off.

Steeling himself against his vulnerable emotional state, Pierce stiffened and stared unblinking into the night. He drove away only when the aircraft's lights were no longer visible in the night sky.

24

After Roshini was gone, Pierce drove into the heart of Kolkata, the former capital of India during the early period of the British Raj and the current capital of the West Bengal state. A gigantic urban sprawl, Kolkata was a city with an urban population of fifteen million people, and it showed in the density of foot traffic, men running barefoot transporting passengers in rickshaws, cars and buses everywhere, and thousands of stalls hawking bright clothing, fruit and vegetables, and kitchen utensils hung in plastic bags high above their shop owners, even during this late hour of the night.

After an hour of driving in the densely arranged streets to ensure he wasn't being followed, Pierce found a cheap hotel in the Khidirpur neighbourhood. He parked his car three blocks from the hotel, wiped it down and removed everything that could associate Pierce or Roshini with the vehicle, then returned to the hotel.

He grabbed street food and bottled water and ate it on the walk back, then paid cash from his operational funds for a room on the third floor, with a view out over the dirty and wide Hooghly River that flowed through the centre of Kolkata. It was the ideal view. Any potential sniper positions visible from his window were too far away to achieve a realistic or workable bead on him.

Outside, on the streets below, the noise of persistent traffic droned on, but not loud enough to bother him. The air smelled stale and of petrol fumes, which was common in all large metropolises he had worked in across the developing world.

After dragging the wardrobe over and securing it in front of the door to slow any intruders who might surprise him during the night, Pierce sat on the lumpy bed, rehydrated, then called Abdul Ibrahim using the CIA encrypted app he'd installed on his cell phone.

"Trigger Man?" said Ibrahim when he answered, sounding not at all surprised that it was Pierce who had called him. They rushed through identity-confirmation protocols; then he said, "I have Rachel Zang in my office with me, but no one else. I'm putting you on speaker."

"Sure."

"Pierce," said Zang, by way of greeting.

"Zang," said Pierce, acknowledging her.

Several seconds of awkward silence passed without either speaking another word. The last time they had seen each other was during a night together in a hotel in Baltimore, after a meal out at a Thai restaurant, followed by a few beers at a local bar. That meeting had been pleasant and fun, but had been two months ago, and they had spoken only a couple of times on the phone since. Pierce mused that their relationship was contradictorily both intimate and distant, and right now it was leaning closer to the latter.

Ibrahim interrupted the silence. "Tell me, Pierce, why aren't you going through Mitch Hawley?"

Pierce sighed, not ready to have this conversation, but aware that he must. "Did you get my message that I needed to speak? Either of you?"

They both said no.

"Then that's why I'm not going through Hawley."

Ibrahim chuckled. "You need to figure out how to work with him."

"Why? He's useless."

"Come on, Pierce. You know why."

Pierce smarted. The unfortunate truth was that Mitch Hawley was connected to old money and to his uncle, a senior congressman with significant sway in the halls of government. It was an often-voiced rumour in Langley that Hawley was only using the CIA to progress his career, positioning himself for politics like his uncle had, and was likely to run as a congressman himself in a few years. After Pierce's success during a recent mission in London, Hawley got it into his mind that having a stint at being Pierce's handler could only look good on his résumé, so had orchestrated for it to happen. And when Pierce learnt that his former handler Mackenzie Summerfield wasn't returning after her grave injuries, he had found he had no argument to prevent this pairing.

Pierce snorted. "Hawley's going to fuck up big time, and when he does, unnecessary lives will be lost."

"Let's talk about that later. In the meantime, he's still your, and now also Zang's, handler. But back to the mission. Where are you?"

"Kolkata."

"What?"

"I'll explain—"

"Pierce," interrupted Ibrahim, "where do you think Roshini Jahandar is?"

"I dropped her at the extraction point. She got on the extraction point aircraft, and I watched her fly out three hours ago."

"Good. Well done, Trigger Man." The way Ibrahim answered left the paramilitary operator wondering if his boss was holding back a key piece of information from him. "But why wasn't I told about it, and why weren't you on the plane with her?"

"Sir," said Pierce, wanting to move on to what he considered the most important piece of intel he needed to report. He had only just remembered where he'd seen images of the data stick model Fawad Jahandar was holding. "There is a lot more going on here. I don't know why you weren't informed about her extraction, but I don't believe that is the most critical item here, since she's safe now. But her data might not be."

"What do you mean?"

"Are you aware of a new Directorate of Science and Technology tech currently being tested in the field? A carried interlocked encrypted data device? A CIED device for short?"

Zang laughed derisively and without humour, and this worried Pierce. He sensed he was about to hear intel that would hinder his current mission — because he didn't believe this mission was anywhere near to being completed yet.

"I take it from your snigger, Zang, you know about it too? You both do?"

"Yeah, unfortunately, we do."

Ibrahim asked, "Did Roshini have it on her when you put her on that plane?"

Pierce paused as he realised Ibrahim had long known about the CIED device and had chosen not to brief Pierce on this before sending him to India. If he had, they might not have been in the mess he suspected they were in right now. "No, sir. I didn't realise what it was at the time, but when I last saw Fawad Jahandar, in Jharia, Jharkhand, he held it in his hand." He also realised that Roshini must have lost the data stick during their escape across India, but she had not mentioned this to him. Perhaps she had feared that revealing she was without the data, his country might have reneged on their deal to take her to America. He found that he didn't blame her either if this was the choice she had made. "I take it there was a reason you didn't want me to know about the CIED device?"

"My mistake, Trigger Man. I thought this was to be a simple operation, and the fewer field operatives who know about this new tech, the better it is for its operational effectiveness. But now things have changed, I regret not telling you earlier." Ibrahim's voice grew louder and more direct. "But let's get back to what you have just told me, Pierce. Is Fawad Jahandar still in the wind, and does he still have the CIED device on him?"

"Only one half of it. And yes, I didn't kill him because I would have lost Roshini's trust if I had."

"That's... not the news I hoped to hear."

"My mission objective was very clear, sir, that I was to get Roshini safely out of the country. I achieved that, but I also accept Jahandar's escape and his still having the CIED device are still my responsibility, and why I'm still in India. I have a plan to rectify all this, by the way, if you are willing to hear it?"

"Very well, Trigger Man. Tell us."

As the overhead fan pushed the hot humid air around his tiny abode, Pierce proceeded to debrief Ibrahim and Zang on his mission to date, reporting the confirmed deaths of Qusay Vali and Sergeant Ajmal Mughal, the slaughter of Daniella Estrada and her team in Patna, and describing Jahandar and Vali's connection to al-Qaeda in Pakistan.

Before he got to his plan, Ibrahim and Zang provided a returned brief on their last twenty-four hours, covering the topics of Brad Karson, Jay Sanders, Nigel McMahon and the stolen nuclear submarine propeller data and McMahon's presumed incarceration in the al-Qaeda Hindu Kush stronghold operated by terrorist Kaajal Khan, and the likely deal being cooked up between Karson and Jahandar to sell this secret to the Russians or the Chinese for a stupidly ridiculous amount of money.

"I'll send you encrypted dossiers on all the players involved in this mess thus far, Pierce. Of critical importance are several other assets not related to your mission, who we have in play in Russia, that we are trying to extract via a nuclear submarine lying in wait just outside Russian territorial waters. But until we are certain the Russians can't track our subs, they must wait in hiding. I shouldn't be telling you this, Trigger Man, but I will. The assets are civilian politicians who can embarrass the Russian president if we get them out, and two of them are children."

Pierce bit down on his lips and wished he hadn't learnt this news. Children should never become involved in the awful world of spies, mercenaries, terrorists and dictators that were the bread and butter of CIA operations, for they only suffered when they did. Now Pierce had the extra burden of knowing that if he failed in his already half-botched operation, children could die as a result.

"Okay," was all he could say in response.

When Ibrahim and Zang finished their briefing, much of what Pierce had experienced since arriving in India now made more sense to him, and his first question was, "So Karson's turned traitor? I never read him as the type."

Zang asked, "You knew him?"

"No. But a man like Karson, his reputation gets around. From what I understand, the men and women who served under him loved him too much, like they were all suckered into the cult of Major Brad Karson. But he had some good ideas too, on how to reform the military and improve veterans' lives. I'll give him credit for that."

Ibrahim laughed lightly. "I'd say the truth is somewhere in the middle. There seems to be two sides to the man. Pierce, perhaps you only know his public persona? There are many accusations that he's a cruel asshole when he's speaking privately to someone, especially when they've disappointed him."

Pierce recalled that Karson was a tier one operator, a member of 1st Special Forces Group (Airborne), therefore trained as an elite soldier of the United States government, with multiple tours of duty in Iraq and Afghanistan and a low body count of men and women working under him in the field. He also knew Karson's tragic story of how al-Qaeda sleeper terrorists operating inside the United States had murdered his wife and sons as revenge against his attacks on their strongholds in Afghanistan, and how that horrific event had transformed the man into a colder, more efficient killer. A worthy foe indeed, backed by bucketloads of charisma, a powerful motivation for revenge, and now it seemed Pierce and Zang were about to go head-to-head with him.

"Sir, you won't make any friends if you are wrong about Karson. This could cost all of us our careers if we go after him and we are mistaken about him turning traitor."

"I agree, but I've delved deeper into Karson's past. Anecdotal intel suggests his wife and he fought constantly in the years before her death. She wanted him to quit, get a normal job, and be more at home and be a proper dad like he had promised her. Even threatened to leave him and take their sons away if he didn't."

Pierce nodded and considered the implications of what Ibrahim had said. In the United States, three women were killed by an intimate partner every day, and domestic violence was rampant across the nation. Was this what Ibrahim was suggesting here, that Karson had murdered his own family because they were holding him back, then covered up his murderous ways with an al-Qaeda revenge story? This seemed a stretch, even for Ibrahim, who was normally exceptional at extrapolating from known intelligence and accurately guessing their enemy's intentions.

Knowing that speculation without any real evidence was pointless, Pierce was about to ask another question on a topic that troubled him when Ibrahim spoke again.

"Pierce, if FIA and ISI are coming after Jahandar with his termination on the agenda, he won't be returning to Pakistan any time soon, if ever. Especially now when he is the only survivor of his team of fourteen who entered India in the first place, in his botched attempt to snatch Roshini back. You mentioned you had a plan?"

Zang spoke before Pierce could. "Keep in mind, Pierce, it

also looks suspicious that Jahandar was the only survivor, so the FIA and ISI will now also wonder if he was in on his wife's defection."

"True," said Ibrahim. "Pierce, you were saying?"

Pierce nodded to himself. "Yes, sir. I have a mission plan. Roshini mentioned a few times during the last two days that her husband keeps a mistress in Goa, one he visits regularly. My instincts are he'll run to her now, especially with Qusay Vali out of the picture, who would otherwise be advising him not to take such risks. Also, I understand he traded secrets with India's Intelligence Bureau, so he might be looking to defect to them, and hiding out with his mistress is a good place for him to be until he can make a deal with them. With your permission, I was planning on tracking him down there. If I'm correct, I can recover the CIED device if he still has it and, knowing what you have just briefed me on, extract Kaajal Khan's stronghold location from him as well."

"Good," said Ibrahim. "That's exactly what I want you to do. I'll send Zang to assist you, but only after she completes an equally important and related mission that I have tasked her with first. She might get delayed, so I'll have another operator in India meet you in Goa to assist you in the meantime."

Pierce raised an eyebrow. "And what mission is that?"

"Two years ago, Brad Karson purchased an island in the Indonesian archipelago. It's called Kadal Beracun, and it's wedged between the much larger islands of West and East Nusa Tenggara. Of interest, during the Second World War, the island was a forward operating air base for the Imperial Japanese Navy. We have substantive intel that Karson has re-established its eighty-year-old ruins as his own forward operating base, with a new camp, training ranges, inventories, workshops, a refurbished runway, and munition and supply stores to support Executive Believers operations in the Asia Pacific region."

"That sounds like quite the investment."

"It does. Karson has been careful to cover his expenditure here, through various shelf companies in Panama, Luxembourg and the Cayman Islands, as Hawley pointed out, to ensure the location of this base is a highly guarded secret. But he doesn't know we know. And I'm sending Zang there to investigate."

This was all very interesting to Pierce, but he still didn't understand its relevance to their current crisis. "What do you both hope to learn, sir?"

Ibrahim cleared his throat, then said matter-of-factly, "Because the Antonov An-32 you put Roshini Jahandar on three hours ago just happened to be an Executive Believers–owned aircraft. We don't know how that fuck-up occurred, but we are looking into it. Just to be clear, we didn't expect you to know this. Zang and I are only just learning this ourselves."

Pierce felt his gut tighten and his skin go cold all over despite the heat of his subtropical hotel room. He'd known something had been off at the extraction point, and again during this conversation with his boss and his peer, and now he understood why that was, and regretted not trusting his gut at the time.

He knew why he had failed today. After a recent protracted operation unsanctioned by the CIA, where Pierce had been fighting for his life and to clear his name as a wrongfully accused traitor, where he'd been tortured and had almost died multiple times, Pierce had come close to becoming a beaten man. Luckily, he had survived through that trauma, but it had cost him, and one of those costs was his ability to trust himself. He needed to get that self-belief back again; otherwise fuck-ups like this would soon become his norm. And no operator could last long in the field if they couldn't resolve this problem.

"Fuck!" he said out loud.

"I have been told Karson just reported to his CIA handler, Ryleigh Bresolin, that you and Roshini never showed at the extraction point. That his team had to leave India empty-handed."

Ibrahim had been holding back from telling Pierce everything, and Pierce didn't like this minor manipulation of his trust. "Then the fucker's lying."

"We know that, Pierce. The question is, what are we going to do about it?"

25

Java Sea, Indonesian Airspace

Roshini Jahandar woke suddenly and found herself disorientated and sickly. Opening her eyes, she saw she was inside the rattling cargo hold of a transport aircraft, on a passenger seat, one of many aligned along the fuselage. She became aware of the propeller-engine drone around her, and the view through the windows was of a pitch-black night. She also noticed the many strapped-down cargo crates spread through the central axis of the aircraft.

"Ah, the wife awakens."

Roshini looked up and across at the female soldier opposite her who had spoken, then at the dozen other soldiers like her who were also strapped into their flight seats. She remembered them now, from the airfield in Kolkata. All wore identical black military fatigues, and each held a military rifle over their laps. Roshini remembered the stocky, muscular woman too. She had been in charge and had led her on board and now watched with an amused expression as Roshini fully emerged from her slumber. This worried Roshini because she didn't remember falling asleep.

"Where...? What is happening?"

The woman, with her short haircut and limbs all muscle and no fat, said in an American accent, "You picked a rather unfortunate time to flee your husband, Roshini Jahandar."

Roshini felt confused about the statement. She looked at the other men and one other woman, but they were all cold of expression, and none of them would look at her. "I don't understand. You asked me to defect now, said I couldn't wait any longer?"

The woman cracked her knuckles, then said, "You're talking about the CIA? They asked you to move quickly?"

Again, Roshini was confused. "Isn't that who you are?" She noticed her clothes then and how dishevelled and unaligned they were on her frame. One button on her blouse was in the wrong buttonhole. She was immediately horrified by the thought these soldiers might have undressed then redressed her while she had been unconscious. Had they drugged her? Was that why she couldn't remember falling asleep, and woke suddenly and feeling disorientated?

"What's going on?" Her voice came out croaky, almost as a whisper, but she made herself ask the first of several questions on her mind, ones she knew she wouldn't like the answers to. "Why was I asleep for so long? Did you...? Did you drug me?"

The woman smiled, then said in a cold voice, "Rohypnol, yes. The date-rape drug."

Roshini shuddered and shrank back into her seat.

The woman laughed. "We didn't do anything like that.

We just searched you, for the data that you stole from your husband. Disappointingly, all we found was this." She held up the decoy data stick Roshini had given to Pierce. "It isn't the data stick we are looking for."

Roshini didn't know what to say, or if she should answer anyway.

The woman nodded to the soldier seated next to her, whom Roshini now noticed had a laptop open on his lap. "McFarlane here hacked it. Nice video files of your husband hanging out with al-Qaeda goons. I particularly like the ones of him with Kaajal Khan, but again not what I'm looking for."

Roshini felt in her pocket for the data stick she had snatched from Fawad's safe, but it was empty. A memory suddenly came back to her, of it falling while she had crossed the plank between the two apartment towers. Then of Fawad holding that same data stick in his hand in Jharia while Pierce pointed his weapon at her defeated husband. He had not killed Fawad out of mercy and because she had asked this of him. She'd been afraid to tell Pierce she had lost the real data stick in Jharia during their escape, and with its loss, she feared the CIA might not honour their deal in extracting her to the United States. They would find out eventually, she knew, but had hoped the truth came out after she had touched down in America.

"I can see in your eyes, Roshini, that you do know where it is?"

She shuddered, feeling violated and betrayed, but still not fully understanding what was happening here. "Who are you? Are you taking me to the United States? Back to the CIA in Washington, DC?"

The woman shook her head. "My name is Staff Sergeant

Kwang Suwan, not that it will matter to you. We do work for the CIA, but when we arrived in Kolkata to collect you, you never showed."

"What do you mean? I'm right here."

Suwan laughed without humour. "I can see that. My men can see that too. So can you, Roshini. But as far as the rest of the world is concerned, including your beloved saviour Mark Pierce and his boss Abdul Ibrahim and everyone else in the CIA you trusted your life with, you never arrived."

"But—?"

"But nothing!" With a finger pointed like a gun at Roshini's left eyeball, Suwan interrupted her in a firmer tone. "I don't care about anything else. Do you or do you not know where the data stick that I speak of is? And before you answer, know this, if you lie, I'll order my men to beat you. Just a little, but enough for you to know I am serious."

Roshini felt as if thousands of spiders were crawling across her cold skin.

"Where is the data stick? I'm waiting."

"My husband has it. He took it from me in Jharia. So please don't hurt me. And now can you please tell me what is going on here?"

Suwan stiffened, then drew in a long, centring breath. She reminded Roshini of a prize fighting bull about to charge.

"The thing is, Roshini," said Suwan, returning to her calm and now emotionless tone, "if you never got on this plane when it took off, then you can't get off it when we land in Singapore. And since you no longer have the only thing me and my boss needed from you, I've run out of reasons to keep you alive."

Roshini had no words.

"Where is your husband now?"

"Please, I beg you, I don't know. He's in India. Or was yesterday. That's all I know. You have to believe me!"

Suwan unbuckled her seatbelt, then hooked a cable hanging from a rail in the ceiling to her belt. She motioned for the other soldiers to belt up or harness themselves as she had. Suwan's eyes then turned to the load ramp at the rear of the aircraft.

Roshini noticed that she alone wasn't wearing a seatbelt.

"Anything else you want to tell me?"

Roshini felt like her entire world was receding, and her skin prickled. As she watched the soldier called McFarlane secure his laptop in his pack, she felt tears stream down her face, and still she couldn't understand why horrible things were happening to her. "You can't...? I mean...?" She glanced out a window, but all she could still see was darkness. "Please, Fawad might be in Goa, with his mistress. But that's all I know. Please?"

The cabin was silent. Nobody moved or looked at her.

Suwan turned to McFarlane and said, "You're closest, Corporal. We've dropped to a low enough cruising altitude, so the pressure differentials aren't a problem."

"Please? You can't! It's inhumane." Roshini sobbed audibly.

Suwan acted as if Roshini were not there as she talked to McFarlane again. "Open the load ramp and throw her out. I'll make the call to Karson and tell him what we've learnt."

26

Langley, Virginia, United States of America

I t was after 21:00 hours when Rachel Zang finally exited CIA headquarters in Langley, feeling both tired and stressed after her long day. She'd changed into her tight-fitting leather pants and matching jacket, black helmet and ankle-high boots, kicked her Kawasaki Ninja 250 sports bike into gear, then sped out the security gates onto the George Washington Memorial Parkway exit. Once free of the CIA's secure compound, she turned onto one of six routes she took at random each night to return to her apartment in nearby Reston Town Centre, chosen by the roll of a die.

Tonight's random selection was a three, which equated to a longer route through Georgetown Pike comprising thickly vegetated forests and single-lane roads where most of the houses were worth well upwards of several million dollars. If Zang didn't know which direction she was taking home each night, no one who wished her harm would know either. Basic tradecraft, but a constant adherence to the rules

of being a spy was what would keep her alive and operational.

A longer route, however, did have the added advantage
of clearing her mind, as motorcycling, as she had discovered
in the last few years, relaxed her. Speed focused her
thoughts only on her driving, and for the next twenty
minutes or so, her mind didn't drift to mission-related problems. She focused on potential tails, challenging road conditions, and traffic density, the latter of which was light given
the late hour.

As the early signs of a migraine started to fade, Zang
came up to an intersection and immediately sensed all was
not right.

A Ford Bronco SUV pulled out onto the road in front of
her. Zang pressed down hard on the rear brake pedal,
burning rubber on the tarmac, and slowed just in time to not
hit the idiot.

What happened next occurred in an instant.

Zang was about to hurl abuse the driver when a black,
football-sized metallic object zipped past her at near bullet
speed and collided with the Bronco. There was an explosion,
and the interior of the SUV ignited with flames, instantly
incinerating whoever was inside.

The blast catapulted Zang from her Ninja and sent her
rolling into the undergrowth.

She tumbled several times before getting caught in vines
and a cluster of oak and maple trees. The impact hurt like
she'd just been beaten up by a dozen angry men. It had all
happened so fast, she only registered the sequence of events
when it was over.

Then she saw flashes in her eyes, and blood trickled
from her nose. Nothing felt broken, so she tried to get to her

feet, but it hurt to move. And now her migraine, which she had kept at bay so well during the day, was well on its way to crippling her.

Fighting her growing discomfort, Zang tried to make sense of what had happened. The only thought that came to her was a recent report circulated by the CIA's Directorate of Analysis, centred on how the Ukrainian military fighting against invading Russian soldiers were using drones packed with explosives, guided by AI technology, to take out their enemy. Zang had a sneaking suspicion that this same tactic had almost taken her out tonight. The Bronco, pulling out at the last minute, had unintentionally made itself the target instead of her.

As Zang tried to get to her feet again, she heard a car pull up and park close to where she had separated from her sports bike. She heard two doors open, then slam shut. Then the sound of boots grinding in the roadside gravel filled her ears.

Whoever these individuals were, they weren't expressing shock at what had just happened or calling out to ascertain if everything and everyone was okay. That was what normal people would do right now. Instead, they were near silent and moved with purpose.

Zang heard the cocking of guns. Two of them.

She ceased struggling because they were close. If she ran now, she would make herself an easy target. It hurt too much to move with speed or conviction anyway, and her migraine made that course of action almost impossible.

Zang decided to unholster the SIG Sauer P227 semi-automatic pistol from her hip holster instead. She pulled back the slide, chambering a round in the breach, then waited, playing dead.

"Did she survive?" one of the assailants asked the other as they both approached. "There's no point complicating the scene by shooting the infidel if she is already dead."

They both spoke English with Middle Eastern accents.

"Keep your mouth shut," said the second.

There was no longer any doubt in Zang's mind that they were here to finish the job.

When Zang heard them get to within ten feet of her, she suddenly rolled onto her back, ignoring the pain and flashing lights in her peripheral vision, and in two quick shots spaced only a second apart gave the two killers each third eyes as she blew skull, blood and brain matter out the backs of their heads.

27

An hour later, Zang found herself seated in the back of an ambulance, wrapped in a blanket while red, blue, and white flashing lights from police, fire and medical vehicles lit up the night. The medic had already examined her, saying she had only suffered minor bruises and cuts, but still insisted they take her to hospital for X-rays and other checks. Zang had told the young man that she was good. Migraine tablets had diminished most of her pain, and she'd suffered worse injuries in the field and recovered fine without medical attention. This would be no different.

The two bodies Zang had shot and were now covered in blankets, however, were not fine. Neither of them was the man in the Bronco, and while the firefighters had doused the inferno the vehicle had become, there was almost nothing left of the occupant. The driver thankfully had been alone, the only innocent victim in this violent encounter. Still, a family was about to receive the tragic news that their husband, father or son was never coming home again.

Feeling a mild tingling numbness in her fingers and face, Zang watched the many emergency service personnel work the scene. The local Virginia police had been first to arrive, but when the CIA's own police officer from Langley's Security Protective Service had showed up minutes later, the SPS had taken over. This was an intelligence matter. They held jurisdiction when it was one of their own involved in a crime. The two killers would soon be chilling in a CIA morgue, ready for subjection to a CIA-led forensic autopsy and a CIA-led background check, and that was the end of the discussion.

While wondering if she would get any sleep this night, and knowing she needed it, Zang gave up on that idea when she spotted Abdul Ibrahim approach. He handed her a cup of hot coffee. She thanked him for it and noticed he had brought two, the second one for himself. He wasn't getting any sleep either.

"I heard your Ninja didn't make it," Ibrahim said with a grin.

Zang made a snorting noise and felt the blood congealing in her nostrils shift. "The CIA going to buy me a new one?"

"We pay you good salaries so you can take out insurance so we don't have to."

She shook her head, knowing that she did indeed have insurance; otherwise Ibrahim's quip wouldn't have been funny in the slightest. "Have the bodies been identified yet, sir?"

Ibrahim took a long sip of his coffee before he answered, "Yeah. Two Iraqi citizens. We're investigating their backgrounds, and it's looking likely they have links back to al-Qaeda."

Zang was already calculating in her mind how Karson or Sanders might have orchestrated this assassination attempt, but it was a stretch to say that Executive Believers were the likely culprits, considering that she'd run several unconnected operations against al-Qaeda in the last few years, providing this terrorist organisation with sufficient motivation to come after her on a revenge attack. But on the flip side, there had been no overt threats made against her by al-Qaeda-linked groups until tonight, and this would be seen as an unlikely coincidence in light of everything else that had gone down today.

"Sir, I could have been a random target. Just a CIA employee these two spotted exiting Langley who they decided to take a shot at."

"We found the drone's control pad in the vehicle of the two dead Iraqis, so there's no doubt it was them. They'll be thoroughly investigated, of course, and when we find or confirm more, I'll let you know."

Zang nodded, noticing the stiffness encroaching her muscles now that she was well past the surge of adrenaline induced by the attack. "I'm presuming I'm still investigating Karson in Indonesia?"

Ibrahim gave her a long hard stare she couldn't interpret.

"Unless there is something you're not telling me, sir?"

"I'm still sending you, yes. It's just that there's an aspect of Karson you may not have considered, and which I didn't until tonight."

Zang frowned. "What do you mean?"

"Did you know Karson's a vocal public advocate for better veteran disability pensions? He lobbies for better research into post-traumatic stress disorder and its causes, and also demands more accountability by the armed services towards veterans with mental health needs. Supports charities and research into chronic traumatic encephalopathy, or CTE, a disorder that causes the death of nerve cells in the brain, which might be connected to grenade blasts as a physiological cause of PTSD. He runs Facebook and Twitter accounts with tens of thousands of followers, where he regularly posts videos on all these topics. Got more vocal when he retired from the army. Half of Congress hate him. The other half love him. I hadn't realised how vocal and widespread his attacks against our government were until tonight."

Zang bit her lower lip as she considered this new information. "They are all noble causes, and all ones worth fighting. But Karson could also be duplicitous, and it wouldn't be the first time something like this has happened. I hope he's a good guy, but when you hear stories where he's absolutely and thoroughly destroyed individuals who cross him, emotionally without laying a finger upon them, you've got to wonder."

Ibrahim glanced over his shoulder, to ensure no one assessing the crime scene was close enough to overhear them. "I only started thinking about this after you left. When I learnt of your assassination attempt, my immediate thought was that Karson was behind it. And I asked myself why."

Zang nodded. "Me too. Same thoughts."

"Be very careful with him, Zang. Karson is charismatic, super-confident and self-assured, and one of the best tier one operators the United States government has ever trained. He'll now come after you on all fronts, physical, psychological, emotional, financial. He'll be relentless."

Feeling compelled to take action, Zang shrugged the

blanket off. She wasn't going to the hospital. She was hardly hurt at all. Remembering how calm and unperturbed Karson had been at the Senate Select Committee on Intelligence, she had wondered how much of his performance as a cold and unemotional alpha male had been an act, and how easy it had been for him, because deep down he was nothing but a cold and emotionless human being?

She'd soon find out.

"I'll sneak onto the island and observe. See if Roshini Jahandar and the CIED device is there. I'll stay out of sight, and when I have working intel, I'll report in. We can go from there."

"Yes, we'll stick with that plan. I'll have a Ground Branch team on standby to assist you should you need them."

"Thank you, sir."

Ibrahim nodded. "Good luck, Zang. Just don't get yourself killed."

28

Sochi, Southern Federal District, Russia

I t was tradecraft 101 that, when operating inside hostile territory, a spy should always minimise one's chance of being identified by the enemy, and one of the best ways Karen Dwyer could have achieved this was by staying put in the safe house. But the young boy under her care, Anatoliy, was running a fever. He needed children's paracetamol, and to her annoyance, the safe house didn't have any, not even the adult's version. So in the early hours of the morning, when few people were up and about, Dwyer stepped out and headed for the closest drugstore, or pharmacy as they were called in Russia.

Her Ground Branch operator, Wilks, had offered to go instead, but he'd been out on the streets more often than she had since the Pavlenko family had come into their care. The risk of being spotted was less if she went alone, and someone needed to stay with the defecting family at all times anyway.

The pharmacy was four blocks from the safe house, and

Dwyer ran a surveillance detection route to check for tails. Not spotting any, she arrived at 08:00 hours and found it closed. Most pharmacies in Sochi opened at this time, so she hoped this was only a case of the proprietor running late.

A tall thin man also waited outside. His hair and beard were scraggly and overgrown, and his leather jacket looked too sizes too big for him while his skinny jeans made his legs look like thin twigs. The boots he wore were black leather and worn, reached high up over his ankles and were ideal footwear for a surveillance operation. He smoked a cigarette and danced from one foot to the other, as if agitated, which made him seem like a crazy person anyone would notice. Dwyer couldn't read him, but her immediate thought was to keep walking. The next pharmacy was another five blocks away from the safe house, and if the scraggy man was an FSB operative, then the game was already up. It was already too late to run.

"Morning," he said when he noticed her also standing by the pharmacy door.

"Morning," she answered in Russian. She tried not to catch his eyes in the hope that he wouldn't look at her either.

He blew out smoke, then smiled. Looking back at him, she noticed that his teeth were crooked, yellow and full of decay, signs that he was poor if he couldn't afford dental care. "At least the weather is better here, hey, than in Moscow?"

She nodded and again looked away, not wishing to engage in conversation because that would make her memorable. But perhaps it was already too late for that.

He was about to say more when a middle-aged man in a nice suit and with a wide gut approached and unlocked the door. "Sorry I'm late," he said as he ushered them inside.

The proprietor quickly entered, and Dwyer sensed his agitation. This caused the hairs on the back of her neck to tingle, but knowing the paracetamol was important, she decided she would get in and out as fast as she could. They couldn't afford to have a sick child in their midst with everything else threatening them from the shadows.

Inside, the leather-jacketed scraggy man went straight to a shelf and grabbed bandages and antiseptics, then rushed to the counter, clearly in a hurry to get served and get out again. This came as a mild relief because if he were an FSB operative, he would have lingered.

As Dwyer found the paracetamol in another aisle, her hand reached out to grab a pack for children just as she heard a police siren and then saw the flashing lights of a marked squad car screech to a halt outside.

Dwyer tensed her whole body and closed her eyes tight as two officers ran inside.

She expected to be cuffed in seconds, then led outside to be scooted away for rapid delivery to the local FSB headquarters, where the interrogations, humiliations and tortures would begin. Suffering would stretch for hours, days, and weeks until they killed her and dumped her body somewhere where it would never be found.

She was not ready for this. This was not how she'd planned to go out. It wasn't fair, not after surviving so long in Russia without once physically coming to harm.

Then she heard the officers scuffling behind her, and the smoker arguing with them.

"You can't beat your wife like that, Dmitri," said the first officer.

Dwyer looked over her shoulder.

The police had the skinny man in cuffs. He was half

pleading, half insulting them as they dragged him outside and locked him in the back of their squad car. He was complaining that his wife deserved his rough treatment of her. Then they were driving off, and Dwyer was alone in the pharmacy.

"Are you okay?" asked the proprietor.

In her fear, Dwyer had forgotten about the owner of the pharmacy. She turned to him and composed herself. "Yes. What happened?"

The proprietor leaned forward and said in a quiet voice, "Best not to ask questions like that, wouldn't you say?"

Dwyer nodded and paid for the children's paracetamol. She'd wanted to buy more packets to stock up, but knew to do so would be unusual and therefore memorable. Dropping the packet into her pocket, she disappeared and returned as quickly as possible to the safe house, masking her frantic state.

29

Goa International Airport, Goa, India

The next day at midday, when Pierce arrived at Goa International Airport after a three-hour flight across India, he found himself surrounded by bustling international tourists transitioning in and out of the country's premier beach resort destination. Everyone was smiling, relaxed and excited. Pierce was the opposite.

Feeling responsible for her fate, he had wanted to go after Roshini Jahandar, fearing for her safety now that she was in Brad Karson's clutches. Ibrahim had insisted Rachel Zang follow that lead instead, asserting that Pierce was already in the country and had a better chance of finding Roshini's husband because he'd already met the man. While the logic made sense and while Pierce had not liked it, he had accepted it, hence why he was still in India. As backup for Pierce, Ibrahim had arranged for a technical operations officer with working knowledge of the subcontinent to meet with Pierce in Goa, and together they could work up a plan to find Fawad Jahandar.

Outside in the taxi pickup area beyond the confines of the air-conditioned terminal, Pierce immediately felt the heat of the hot tropics blast his face again. At least the air here in Goa didn't stink of human waste and diesel as it had in Kolkata, and it wasn't raining for a change, but that only meant his shirt fabric clung to his skin because of his sweat rather than rainwater.

He scanned the taxis and Ubers until he spotted the olive green Nexa Jimny four-wheel drive parked exactly where Ibrahim had said the officer would present himself. A thin, lanky man in his mid-twenties wearing a short-sleeve T-shirt and loose black pants leaned against the car, checking his cell phone while he typed furiously into its digital keyboard. The individual fitted Ibrahim's description of his contact, so Pierce approached. "Hello, I'm hoping to see a rave in Goa. I heard Yotto was playing?"

The man looked up, smiled and replied with, "Sorry, Yotto isn't in town. But I heard Fernanda Pistelli might be."

The contact had given the correct coded response, so Pierce put out his hand, and the man vigorously shook it. His accent was Indian, but his mannerisms were American. "Pleased to meet you. I'm Akash Parab, a technical operations officer with the Directorate of Operations. That means I do all the geeky computer and surveillance tech wizardry, but I'm also familiar with India and speak three local languages, as I grew up here."

Pierce grinned. "Great to meet you, Parab. Mark Pierce is my name." He looked to the four-wheel drive, noting its many scratches and dents, yet it appeared to be in good working order. "How long have you been in the country for your vehicle to look like that?"

"I drove down from Mumbai yesterday, where I've been based the last three months. If I only half look after it, it blends in better."

"I'm sure it does. You have equipment?" He whispered close to Parab so only he heard, "Weapons?"

Parab gave a sly grin. "All the equipment you requested is packed nicely in the rear compartment." He leaned in close to Pierce and spoke in a softer voice. "The very special equipment is inside the second spare wheel, if you know what I mean?"

Pierce nodded. "Well, shall we get going?"

"Sure. Would you like to drive, or shall I?"

Pierce considered his options. Driving meant he had control of the vehicle, particularly important if they came under attack, as he was likely better trained in defensive driving than Parab would be, but as a passenger Pierce could observe and learn more. "How familiar are you with Goa?"

"Very."

"Then you drive. Let's go somewhere not so conspicuous, where I can assess the gear."

"Then let's get moving."

Once Pierce was strapped into the passenger seat of the Nexa Jimny, Parab was back behind the steering wheel and took off at speed. They first drove through streets comprising modern houses surrounded by an abundance of tall palms, then turned onto a divided two-lane road dominated by mopeds. The urban sprawl reminded Pierce of a half dozen other Asian tropical resort towns he had operated and recuperated in in his past.

As the four-wheel drive bounced over the undulating roads, Pierce asked, "Parab, what have you been briefed on?"

"You're looking for Fawad Jahandar. FIA assistant director of their Technical Wing, who, it is reported, is on the run from FIA and ISI, who have a kill or capture bounty on his head. He might also be trying to defect to the IB. You're in Goa because you have intel Jahandar has a mistress here, and suspect he might run to her while he goes into hiding, but that sounds like a long shot to me."

Pierce noticed the grin plastered on Parab's smug face. "Something tells me you know something I don't?"

The CIA technical operations officer laughed loudly. "I did some digging last night, in the hotel I stayed at on the drive down. Trawled a few data packs my pals at the NSA sent me," he said, referring to the National Security Agency, the United States' premier signal intelligence organisation. "I now have three call transcripts with a fifty-eight per cent probability of being from Jahandar to Goa in the last fourteen hours."

"And?"

"Whoever he was talking to, who we are yet to identify, has a one hundred per cent chance of being in northern Goa, and she is a yoga instructor."

Pierce grinned. "That narrows our search parameters considerably." Subconsciously, he touched the small of his back where he would normally carry a pistol, finding nothing and remembering he was unarmed. "What about that weapon we talked about?" His eyes motioned to the back where the spare tyre was kept.

Parab beamed triumphantly. "Yes, indeed. I heard that your weapon of choice is a Glock 19 semi-automatic pistol with 9mm rounds, with a standard fifteen-mag capacity. Is that correct?"

Pierce raised an eyebrow. The Glock indeed was his favoured weapon, and he couldn't believe his luck that he would be using one on this mission, when more often than not in the field he had to settle for inferior locally produced handguns. "Yes, that's right."

"Then this is great news, Pierce. I have for you India's version of the Glock 19, a Pistol Auto 9mm 1A. This one is not so old either, only a 2012 version. It was formerly a West Bengal police-issue weapon, so you know it has been fired many times, and therefore is reliable."

Pierce shook his head, but he was also chuckling. Parab had overplayed his hand, trying to impress Pierce, and he had been doing spectacularly until he had tried to sell the handgun he had secured, which was a far more inferior weapon to his preferred Glock.

When they passed a stretch of natural tropical scrub outside of the urban areas, they stopped and stepped out to remove the two 1A pistols from the tyre, one for Pierce and the other for Parab, each with two spare magazines. The weapons were indeed worn and didn't slide or click open as easily as Pierce would have liked, but they were functional. Once Pierce's pistol was safely tucked into his belt at the small of his back, they got back inside the vehicle and drove again. Parab seemed to know where he was headed, so Pierce asked, "What strategy do you have in mind to find Jahandar?"

"That's easy," said Parab, another big smile erupting. "We speak to the street children. They know more than anyone who comes and who goes in Goa. They will direct us to the yoga instructor we seek."

30

Seletar Airport, Singapore

Four mercenaries gathered on the tarmac, positioned midway between Executive Believers' two aircraft. The mercenaries and the aircraft were within the confines of Singapore's Seletar Airport, which catered to mid-sized businesses and individuals who owned planes, so they were not out of place here. Jay Sanders was one of those mercenaries, and he found himself wiping sweat from his forehead now that he had stood under the sun and in the humidity for more than a few minutes. Major Brad Karson stood next to him. They had travelled together from Washington, DC, on the company's HA-420 HondaJet now parked behind them, a six-seater business jet that was Karson's pride and joy.

The two soldiers who had met them stood before their more practical Antonov AN-32 turboprop twin-engine military transport, also purchased by Karson, but unlike the HondaJet, it had been secured at a bargain price the previous year from the Indian Air Force. The HondaJet was ideal for moving Karson quickly around the world to attend to meetings with clients in executive-level comfort, while the AN-32 was ideal for managing mercenary logistics and soldier transport into and out of military zones. The two Executive Believers soldiers they were meeting were Staff Sergeant Kwang Suwan, the company's paramilitary executive, and her offsider and communications expert Corporal Mike McFarlane, a signaller formerly with the United States Army Signal Corps.

After proceeding through salutes and greetings, Suwan gave Sanders a sly smile. He never knew whether these grins were flirty or expressions of disdain, but whatever her intention, he had zero interest in her other than on a professional level. But the truth was that she scared him. Suwan was all muscle, and while not visible at the moment, he knew her toned body was covered in multiple tattoos comprising Chinese-style dragons. Her hair was shaved at the sides while long on top to create a quiff-style haircut. All warning signals that she was not an individual to be messed with, and for good reason. Kwang Suwan had secured seventh place in the Muay Thai or Thai kickboxing world championship two years earlier. She was a world-class hand-to-hand specialist, and very few individuals who had challenged her physically ever walked away without a broken bone or two for their efforts.

Sanders knew this because he'd witnessed Suwan in action on the field, beating to death numerous male opponents who were foolish enough to engage with her in a melee fight. Only Karson was her equal, and only because as a man he was twice her mass and a highly efficient hand-to-hand combatant himself.

"What's wrong with you, Sanders?" she said as she strutted over. "Your man card expired?"

Sanders avoided getting on Suwan's wrong side, so when they provoked each other with words, he held back from telling her what he really thought about her. Yet when he smiled, he showed teeth. He needed to antagonise her a little; otherwise she would never respect him at any level. "Nice to see you too, Suwan."

"Sweating a lot there, old man?"

He couldn't help himself and replied with his own taunt. "I notice you aren't sweating, but then reptiles never do."

Suwan tensed, readying herself for a fight.

Karson raised a hand to silence them both. "Cut the chatter, we have work to do." He held Suwan's stare. "Master Sergeant, do you have the other half of the CIED device? And remember, your answer had better be what I want to hear."

Suwan lost her bravado and seemed to shrink a little. Major Karson was the only individual Sanders had ever witnessed Suwan fearing. "No, sir. Roshini Jahandar didn't have it on her when we collected her."

The Black Dog of the Hindu Kush growled like his namesake. "That's... not good. What about Pierce?"

"He never showed. Roshini told us he had dropped her off. We went looking for him, but couldn't find him."

"So you left without him?"

Suwan swallowed. "Yes, sir."

Sanders watched Karson tense, and knew his boss was close to giving one or all of them a serving, and his verbal beratings were the cruellest Sanders had ever experienced in his long career in covert operations. Karson could expertly cut down any man or woman who crossed his path using words alone, somehow seeing into their souls and immediately understanding and leveraging their greatest fears. And when Karson turned to violence, his cruelty was off the scales. Thankfully he kept his cool and said instead, "That's... fucking not good, Suwan. Does Pierce have the CIED?"

Suwan quickly shook her head. "I don't believe so." She glanced at McFarlane, who was doing his best to avoid being noticed by averting his eyes and not engaging with anyone involved in this conversation. "McFarlane and I interrogated Roshini on the flight here. She says her husband has the device and believes he's still in India, running free with it."

Karson nodded and relaxed marginally. "That's a better outcome than if the Americans had it, Suwan. This means we can still secure it. We need both halves if we are to get stupidly rich from this. Each half on its own is forever useless."

The kickboxer regained her composure. "Sir, we didn't waste our time on the flight. Roshini told us much about her husband and his habits."

"Meaning?"

"Fawad Jahandar has a mistress in Goa, India. Varsha Pandya is her name." Suwan opened her cell phone and showed them all a photo taken off the internet of an attractive woman in her thirties with long dark hair, posing for the camera. "Pandya's a former Bollywood star. She's featured in many Mumbai-produced movies but retired from acting about five years ago and moved back to her home in Goa to open a yoga studio. Her social profiles make her easy to track, and her business draws many celebrities to her from all over India, and Jahandar too, apparently. We know exactly where she is."

Karson raised an eyebrow. "You know this, how?"

Suwan shrugged. "McFarlane and I called in some favours from our Syrian clients whom we are currently doing business with." Sanders knew she was referring to the Syrian government's secret police, the Mukhabarat, who had hired Executive Believers to decimate Kurdish military outposts in the warring country's eastern regions. "The Mukhabarat hacked Pandya's cell phone for us last night as we flew. Pandya took a call from Fawad Jahandar yesterday, arranging to meet up last night at Goa International Airport." Suwan's face broke into a smile as she gave Sanders another nod. "It's not only your intelligence executive, sir, who can find people."

Sanders couldn't help himself and said, "I hope your intelligence is reliable, Suwan, and not just something the Mukhabarat made up so you would pay them."

"Oh, it's good, Sanders." The master sergeant played an audio file of a phone conversation between Jahandar and Pandya saved on her cell phone, making arrangements for him to hide at her Goan home.

There was no doubt in Sanders's mind then that the male voice was their target's, and Sanders felt a sinking feeling grip his gut. He worried that Karson might now wonder if he really needed Sanders on his payroll if Suwan could pull off intelligence coups like this without him.

"Okay, let's focus," said Karson. "I'm glad for all your sakes the two halves of the CIED device are still in play. We have one, and Jahandar has the other. We still need McMahon's voice activation to unlock it, but Jahandar will know where our al-Qaeda friend Kaajal Khan has him hidden, so we can focus on the DARPA engineer later. The objective right now is to take Jahandar."

"How do we do that?" said Sanders, immediately regretting the question because the solution was obvious. Fly the team already prepped on board on the AN-32 to Goa and snatch Jahandar there. A simple mission compared to some of the contracts Executive Believers were currently leading in many of the world's worst countries, including in Syria. "Okay, scratch that. I know how."

Karson shook his head, expressing his disappointment. "Except, Sanders, you're not coming with us."

"What do you mean?"

Karson turned to Suwan and nodded toward his military transport plane. "Jahandar's wife, she on board?"

"Yes, sir. When she refused to cooperate, I threatened to throw her from the plane at an altitude of six thousand feet, and that got her spilling all the beans. Therefore, I didn't need to carry out my threat. She's on board. I did take the liberty of drugging her while we are on the ground, though, so she couldn't cause trouble."

"Good. If we have the wife, she serves as leverage we can use against Jahandar should we need it." Karson turned to Sanders. "You take the HondaJet and fly Roshini to our base in Kadal Beracun. Secure her in the cells, then lean on every intelligence source you have to, to geolocate Kaajal Khan's hideout. Do I have to remind you, Sanders, we guessed during our meeting in Chitral that our FIA friend had handed McMahon off to Khan for safekeeping in his al-Qaeda stronghold?"

"No, sir, I remember."

"Good, then move fast because once we have Jahandar, Pakistan is where we'll move to next."

"Yes, sir," said Sanders, but this time his voice sounded flat to his ears and probably did to everyone else present.

Karson snarled, "What's your problem, Sanders?"

Sanders swallowed, then quickly formulated a response that lessened the chances of him aggravating his boss further. "Nothing, sir. I'm just thinking through how we can minimise our exposure here. Because the risks..."

"What do you mean?"

"Sir, so far, no one in the US military or intelligence circles has any real suspicion that we could be behind the sale of the submarine propeller information. But if it gets out that we are, it doesn't matter how much money we make, our countrymen will throw every resource they have at us to bring us down. And I mean they'll use every 'terminate with extreme prejudice' resource in their arsenal. I have no wish to 'retire' to somewhere like Russia, Iran, or North Korea, because they are the only nations that can keep me alive."

"Grow some balls, Sanders!" said Suwan with a frown. "No operation is without risk."

Karson nodded. "The master sergeant is correct. That's why we also need to eliminate Pierce. He's spent too much time with the wife, so who knows what he knows. And Fawad Jahandar, his wife and McMahon, we also deep-six when this is all over. And let's not forget Rachel Zang. She too needs to permanently leave this world."

Sanders felt his jaw drop as he drew in a sharp breath. "Rachel? You can't be serious? She doesn't know anything. And I thought the attack on her before was to scare her off?"

"You wish that were the case." Karson pointed his finger at Sanders's chest and stepped forward, as if challenging him to a physical brawl. "I know you fucked her, Sanders, and have feelings for her. But I don't care, as this is bigger than some fling you had. You said it yourself, we can't have this coming back to any of us. Loose ends, wherever they occur, need tying off, permanently."

Sanders felt sick as he comprehended how much his already dubious relationship with Karson was costing him. He was now being asked to murder individuals who were close and dear to him, and was further regretting coming over to Executive Believers in the first place, tempted at the time by Karson's overly generous salary, bonus and benefits package. But Sanders also realised he had no choice in their current predicament, for Karson was correct, they were not going to survive this daring scheme unless they were diligent in eliminating all vectors that pointed towards them as being behind the sale of the stolen US nuclear submarine propeller data.

"Get it together, Sanders. When this is all over, we'll frame Jahandar as the culprit, and he won't be around to contradict us. It will all be good for all of us. But right now, we are on a timetable, and recovering the other half of the CIED device is our priority. Now, unless there are any other questions, we all know what we have to do." He looked at them all, holding their eyes for many seconds, but no one responded. "No questions? Good. Then get to fucking work."

31

Mandrem, Goa, India

Through an afternoon of clear skies and tropical breezes, Mark Pierce and Akash Parab drove from one Goan beach to the next in search of Fawad Jahandar and his as yet unidentified secret lover. They focused on the northern beaches, where most of the state's yoga retreats and luxury resorts were situated. Their journey took them from the towns of Candolim to Baga and Anjuna; then they crossed the Chapora River to explore Ashvem and Mandrem Beaches, all of them picturesque and alive with tourists visiting from all over the world and just as many local Indians out and about enjoying the vacation vibe evident everywhere.

In each location, Akash Parab proved he had an instinct for identifying and engaging with local street children, getting them to open up to him and share their knowledge. Pierce learnt that street children was a term for homeless youngsters prevalent across India who were orphaned. They survived in gangs comprising other youths by begging, stealing and scrounging for food and shelter on a daily basis while staying out of the way of criminals and the police.

With each group, Parab entered into easy banter using a language or languages Pierce could not identify, but was presumably either Konkani or Marathi, the local tongues spoken by the majority of Goa's citizens. Eventually Parab would show the children Fawad Jahandar's photograph, tell them about the man's expensive gold watch, and then offer six thousand rupees for any real evidence of the man's location. Each group claimed they had seen Jahandar, but insisted Pierce and Parab return tomorrow when they would prove their claim.

By the time Pierce and Parab had walked Mandrem Beach, where they had engaged with three different gangs of boys in this location alone, the sun was setting, and both men were beat. Western tourists in their bikinis and swim trunks now dressed in sarongs, dresses, shorts and T-shirts, then wandered back to their beach bungalows and holiday resorts. Locals were as numerous, and they too packed up their belongings and moved on for the day.

Pierce and Parab found a café bar overlooking the sea, where they ordered beers and a meal. The establishment called itself "Synchronicity", not out of place with the lively names of other local bars, restaurants, clubs and venues Pierce had spotted since his arrival in Goa, such as the Boomerang Bar, SinQ, Leopard Valley and Mr Tof Tof. With fairy lights and potted palms everywhere, the establishment catered to eight couples and a group of a dozen young ravers discussing the possibility of seeing a DJ set later at Anjuna Beach. The setting sun had almost disappeared into the Arabian Sea, and the palm-lined coast was a spectacular sight, far more pleasurable than most of the regions Pierce had operated in during his career. But postcard-picture views weren't drawing them any closer to their target. Roshini was still in danger and possibly dead, and the submarine propeller data could still end up in enemy hands, so after they had eaten, they would find a hotel and from there use electronic means to hunt their target.

"Don't look so down, Pierce," said Parab, drinking his beer with gusto. "We did good today. Street children all over India are cunning and smart, and all those we spoke to will now be spreading the word amongst their friends. By morning, one of them will know something, and we'll have our man."

Pierce chinked beer bottles and drank from his own. "Yes, we did."

He noticed two men enter and grab a table positioned so they could watch anyone and everyone who entered and left the bar with ease, as Pierce and Parab had done. They ordered beers, then sat without talking.

Keeping an eye on them in his peripheral vision, he said to Parab, "What language were you speaking today?"

"Marathi. My family originates from Mumbai. It's a common language there, as it is in Goa. I also speak English of course, and Hindi. And my Urdu is pretty good."

Pierce raised his bottle. "Four languages. Impressive."

"Yes, maybe. But my skills are only useful in India and Pakistan."

"But still useful."

He shrugged as he simultaneously frowned and pouted. "I guess so. They say join the CIA, see the world. It's one big adventure. But since joining, my only overseas assignments have been back here in India, where I grew up."

Pierce chuckled. "That's because we blend best with what is familiar to us. Every intelligence operative needs to be able to do that. Not many can blend into multiple locations."

A pretty young female server brought them food, their order of green chicken curries complemented by potatoes, lemon wedges and salads. She smiled at Pierce, then blushed when he smiled back and thanked her.

When the two men were alone again, Pierce devoured his food. He continued to watch the other two men without directly glancing at them, aware that they had barely touched their beers and were not conversing.

"Pierce, can I ask you a question?"

"Sure," said Pierce, returning a portion of his attention back to his colleague. "Ask whatever you want, but I can't guarantee I can always answer."

The technical operations officer shook his head vigorously. "No, no, this is nothing about your past or state secrets. I just..." He hesitated, then bit his lower lip. "It's just, that waitress. She was flirting with you, with her eyes. Wasn't she?"

Pierce raised an eyebrow and leaned back in his chair. He had not expected this line of questioning, so drank more of his beer, providing him with a moment to decide how to frame his response. "She's not my type, and we're working."

"She's attractive though. And she was flirting with you. Why not?"

Pierce paused as he considered if this conversation was appropriate. But he did sense that Parab was merely seeking to learn from Pierce, that there was nothing sleazy in anything he had said or suggested so far.

"I don't know why I'm telling you this, Parab, but I keep

relationships casual. I only sleep with women who are in the same business that we are." Only once the words were out of his mouth did Pierce realise this wasn't strictly true, for he had developed growing feelings for Rachel Zang. Despite wishing that he didn't carry such feelings, he knew he would have taken an opportunity to explore a more in-depth relationship if she had allowed their pairing to be anything more than casual. How had he fallen for her so easily, when so many women before her had never captivated him in the same way?

And then there was also the familiar connection he had felt with Roshini, and how easy it had been to exist in her presence, even though they had barely known each other across a twenty-four-hour period.

"What do you mean?" Parab asked.

Pierce shrugged, then ate more of his curry, which was proving to be one of the tastiest dishes he had eaten since the samosas he had shared with Roshini in Jharkhand. He noticed again that the men who had arrived after them hadn't ordered any food and had still barely touched their beers. "Our work is risky. We have a much higher chance of getting killed on the job than almost any other profession in the world. Plus, the people we deal with are often sociopathic assholes who'll use our loved ones against us if given the opportunity. Anyone I've hooked up with, I want to know that if I die, they've understood and respected the risks I choose to face, and that they are as skilled as I am at looking after themselves and know the risks of our profession as I do. That said, when I'm on downtime between missions, I might occasionally hook up with a civilian, but I won't get close to them."

Pierce watched, amused, as Parab proceeded through a

variety of facial expressions while he digested everything Pierce had told him. He opened his mouth to speak several times, but each time stopped himself. It was only on the fourth attempt that he spoke. "I never thought about any of this like that."

"I can't say my choices are ideal, or that they are fulfilling my emotional needs, but I only go for women who are also seeking casual one-night encounters to keep things simple." Pierce shrugged, then ate more of his curry and drank more of his beer. He was hungry and thirsty. "Why do you ask?"

Parab shrugged as his smile revealed the embarrassment he felt. "I... have a girlfriend, back in Maryland. We've been dating since college. I don't know why I'm telling you this, but she's the only woman I've ever really known... intimately. Her name is—"

"Don't tell me!" Pierce cut him off. "I don't need to know anything about her that can be used against her should I be compromised. You understand me?"

Parab looked down at his curry, then reacted as if he were surprised to discover it there, even though he had eaten from the dish many times already. He shovelled more of the chicken and potatoes into his mouth, chewed, then swallowed. "See, again, I'm not thinking about my situation in any way that aligns with the job I do. What's wrong with me?"

Pierce waited until the young man held his stare. "Why are you asking, Parab? You have a strong relationship, which is something to be proud of. The longest girlfriend I ever had was three years, and that was a long time ago and never very stable. You're doing far better than me."

"But I'm not. You see, I can't tell my girlfriend what I do. Because of the contracts we signed when we joined up. She thinks I work for the Treasury. Has no idea I'm with the CIA, and the NSA before that. Lying to her all the time, to protect state secrets, it's too much pressure on a serious relationship. I wish sometimes I could just be cavalier in my girlfriends like you are."

Except that I'm not, Pierce was about to say.

Instead, Pierce wondered how he had found himself providing relationship advice to a peer. This wasn't a conversation style he was accustomed to, and not with someone he barely knew. Part of him wanted to shut down this talk before it got personal for him, but another part of him was intrigued by the inner emotional thinking of another man only half a decade his junior. Pierce was about to repeat that this was why he kept his relationships casual and only with women already operating in the intelligence and military circles, but realised this would only make Parab feel worse about himself, not better.

Instead, he asked, "When did you join the CIA?"

"A year ago."

"Direct from the NSA?"

Parab nodded. "It was stupid. When I was with the NSA, I never travelled anywhere except to my desk at headquarters in Maryland, every single workday. I was bored stupid, but lying to my girlfriend was easier in that job. But with the CIA — which I enjoy so much more than the NSA, by the way — I'm overseas in this part of the world so much, my girlfriend can't stand it. She doesn't understand why I am away so often, and I don't have answers for her."

Pierce finished his curry and beer, while he noticed that Parab had slowed in his eating. He wondered again why Parab had opened up to him, then realised that, like himself, Parab was likely mostly operating on assignments like this one. He worked with short-term CIA operators or case officers flown in for brief and very specific missions, who then left. He had no time to build strong relationships with peers or even friendships. Parab was also young; at least five years separated them, which could feel like a lifetime in their profession. He hadn't had the time to work out his self-identity to the depth Pierce had.

"I don't know how to answer any of your questions. It sounds to me that joining the CIA perhaps wasn't the best choice for you or your girlfriend."

"But I love this work so much more," he said, repeating himself. "I was dying in the 'No Such Agency'. Fieldwork is exciting. I love it."

Pierce watched one of the newcomers reach into his jacket pocket, and wondered for a moment if he might be going for a weapon. He tensed and prepared himself for violent action.

"What's bothering you, Pierce?"

"That we're being followed."

To his credit, Parab responded with a smile and didn't react outwardly. "You mean the two men seated at the back to my left, five metres from us, and their friend in the Suzuki Jimny outside?"

Pierce nodded, impressed that Parab was more situationally aware than he was, because Pierce hadn't spotted the SUV. The men resembled Indian locals at a casual glance, but they barely talked to each other, and their demeanours were all wrong. "From what I can tell, Parab, they're both carrying semi-automatic pistols under their jackets."

"I can tell you the Suzuki followed us across the Chapora Bridge. What should we do about them?"

Pierce rested his hands on the table while keeping the

two operatives in his peripheral vision. "I guess it depends on who they are."

"They could be Indian intelligence, but I don't recognise any of them. I don't think that is likely, though."

"Why?"

"Firstly, because I heard them speaking Urdu. Urdu, of course, is spoken in many parts of India, and it holds many similarities to Hindi. It is not uncommon to hear that language here. But they don't speak it with an accent I recognise."

"And secondly?"

"When one of them opened his wallet just before, I noticed Pakistani rupees inside."

Pierce nodded, impressed. "FIA? ISI?"

"That's my guess. One of them for sure."

One of the watchers now not very subtly kept his eye on Pierce, then made a call on his cell phone. He had been reaching into his pocket not for a weapon, but a communications device.

Pierce said quietly, "The one on the left is making a call. Reinforcements?"

Parab played with his curry, stirring it with his fork, expertly acting if nothing untoward was going down behind him where the Pakistani operatives waited. "If this encounter leads to a physical confrontation, word will spread quickly through Goa. Jahandar will hear about it and then disappear."

"Then I suggest we finish up, walk out of here like we know nothing, then try to lose them on the streets. I'm taking a chance our Pakistani friends are letting us do the legwork in finding Jahandar, to snatch him from us when we have him in our custody."

Parab pretended to drink his beer, but now that they needed their senses about them, he wouldn't put any more alcohol into his system tonight.

Pierce knew from experience a single beer wouldn't affect his abilities, but he wouldn't drink any more tonight either.

"We should finish our meals, Pierce. Not rush them. Anything out of the ordinary would look suspicious."

Pierce was about to say he agreed, when a dozen young boys raced into the restaurant and rushed straight at Parab. Pierce didn't understand what they were yelling, but he heard the name "Jahandar" multiple times. They were excited, holding out their hands for money.

But Pierce wasn't concerned about the boys anymore.

He was reacting to the first Pakistani operative now drawing a pistol from where he had concealed it under his table.

It was always best to be the first to start shooting in a firefight.

32

"Weapons free!" Pierce yelled at the same moment Parab and he dived from their table and away from the congregation of boys. He heard a single gunshot and hoped the Pakistanis weren't fools enough to shoot children, and that the shot was fired into the air to cause chaos. But chaos it did cause, and instantly the restaurant transformed into a cacophony of screams, with fleeing and scrambling patrons, overturning tables and more gunshots.

Pierce rolled behind the bar as he withdrew his Pistol Auto, then waited for a lull in the shooting before responding. He glanced around the side of the bar, searching for foes, but all he could see were the legs of men, women and the children rushing to escape.

When he turned back the other way, he noticed too late that the second Pakistani operator, who hadn't pulled a weapon, had thrown himself over the bar and now came crashing down upon Pierce. The impact winded him and gave the foe the advantage, pinning Pierce's gun arm against his thigh and pressing his weight down on him.

Soon they were wrestling, but Pierce couldn't fight effectively, as he was too low to the ground and wedged up against the back of the bar. Plus, his attacker carried at least twenty more kilograms of muscle, providing him with brute-strength superiority.

Pierce struggled, but all too soon the Pakistani's free arm was pressing down on Pierce's throat, ready to crush his windpipe. Pierce responded with repeated punches to his foe's kidney while angling his chin downwards to protect his throat.

Around them, he heard further screams, trampling feet, and gunplay presumably between Parab and the Pakistani with the gun.

Pierce punched again despite his growing difficulty in breathing. At first the foe resisted, but then the blows seemed to weaken him. Pierce attempted to slip out from under his foe's weight, which was pressing on him. His attacker realised what Pierce intended, so lifted his central mass to a higher vantage point over Pierce's chest.

Giving up on the kidney punches, Pierce's hand dropped and felt around for another weapon to use. The pistol in his other hand was useless. He couldn't angle it to fire without risking shooting himself too. And he was running out of time, for his attacker had found a better angle to use both hands to press harder on Pierce's throat.

His lungs fought for oxygen.

Then his free hand found what he had hoped to find, a fallen spirit bottle.

He smashed the glass across the foe's head, shattering it

and cascading gushes of blood from multiple cuts across the man's scalp and face.

The Pakistani screamed and rolled backwards.

Pierce spun the Pistol Auto around, brought it up fast and blew out half the man's skull with a single 9mm round through the forehead.

After he rolled the dead weight of the corpse off him, Pierce could still hear shooting. He ducked around the other side of the bar, where he spotted the Pakistani shooter and a new companion at his side — presumably the operative who had been waiting in the Suzuki.

They hadn't seen Pierce, so he shot them both multiple times in their chests until they both dropped dead.

Pierce ducked back behind the bar as he reloaded. "Parab?"

"Yes, Pierce?"

"Three targets down."

"Roger that!"

They waited a few seconds to assess their situation until they were both certain the restaurant had emptied, and no one was still shooting.

"You okay, Parab?"

"Yes. All good. I think so..."

"What's up?" With his gun out in front, Pierce checked all corners until he felt satisfied that they were alone. A quick check of the ruined establishment identified the Pakistani men were the only casualties. Pierce had been mentally preparing himself for the sight of dead children, but luck had been on his side today, so he wouldn't have to deal with that emotional burden.

Then he saw Parab trembling in his corner where he'd been shooting from. "You're just standing there? What's up?"

Parab nodded, but otherwise remained motionless as he stared unfocused at the scene and barely blinked. "I've... never had anyone shoot at me before." He cleared his throat as a single tear escaped his left eye. "I've never shot at anyone, either, intending to kill them."

Pierce stepped up to Parab, gripped his shoulder and held his stare. "Parab. Akash, listen to me?"

"Yes?"

"Remember your training. This is going to hit you, hard. Harder than it has already. You're going to feel numb, disconnected, as shock takes you, but you've got to compartmentalise. That's what the Farm taught you," Pierce said, referring to the CIA training facility where all new recruits learnt all kinds of tradecraft, fighting and escape and evade techniques, and intelligence, gathering methods for months and months on end. "Can you do that for me, and we'll talk about this later?"

Parab nodded. "This is a very big mess!"

"I know." Pierce grabbed a fallen pistol, a modern Russian SR-2 Udav 9x21mm semi-automatic. Deciding he could never have enough weapons, he pocketed it, then snatched two spare magazines from the dead shooter. Then he searched all three corpses' pockets, finding wallets with only cash and, in one, an unmistakable photograph of Fawad Jahandar. Pierce slipped the print into his pocket. "We need to get out of here."

Parab nodded, then sprang into action.

Out on the streets, they heard the distant sirens of police cars responding to the chaos.

A cell phone rang somewhere in the carnage, buried under a fallen table or the spilt food.

"That will be the Pakistanis' backup," said Parab as he

wiped down the cutlery and bowls they had been eating from, removing fingerprints. "You are correct. We need to leave immediately."

Pierce nodded and made for the exit, when he noticed a scuba tank, masks, goggles and flippers next to one table where a couple had been seated earlier. It gave him an idea. He grabbed the mask and tank, finding its weight to be at least half full.

"What's that for, Pierce?"

"I'll explain later. You drive."

Within ten seconds they were inside the olive green Nexa Jimny and speeding down the narrow streets crowded with mopeds, street stalls, parked cars, more cafés and bars. Parab honked at a boy leading a white Tharparkar cow by a rope until he got out of the way; then they sped on. The sirens grew louder, but no police cars were visible yet.

Pierce placed the scuba tank between his feet, then looked up to see where Parab was driving them to. He was headed north. "No. Take the main road, back to Panaji."

"I disagree. Or at least, not yet." Parab expertly took a narrow turn down a dirt track barely wide enough to drive between the walls of the houses on each side. Then they were out on the beach, churning up sand as they sprinted south, with the waves crashing mere metres from them. People still out on the sands enjoying the moon and starlight jumped out of their way as they sped past. "We can bypass the police this way."

"Good thinking," Pierce said, meaning it, while he checked over his new Udav semi-automatic pistol, concluding it was well maintained and functional. He reloaded it with a fresh magazine, pocketed it, then passed the Pistol Auto over to Parab. "That was a lot of shooting back there. Need a fresh weapon?"

Parab nodded and took the pistol, which he secured between his left thigh and the seat. Soon he spotted a road leading off the beach and followed it through more throngs of crowds milling at a night-time market. He used his horn to get the slower, unaware pedestrians out of their way, and while they all complied, many abused them for his efforts.

Pierce listened for the sirens and heard them far behind them now. Parab's plan had been a good one. "Well done."

Parab readjusted the rear-view mirror for a better view behind them. "It's not over, I'm afraid. We still have company."

Pierce looked back, spotting two black Suzuki Jimny four-wheel drives pursuing them. "Our Pakistani friends called for backup after all." He readied his weapon, not wanting to shoot first in case they weren't enemy combatants, regardless of how unlikely that scenario was. "Jahandar will hear about this. We need to shut this down quickly, get everyone off our trail so we can pursue our target unhindered and accelerate our mission."

Parab grinned, enjoying himself now despite almost dying earlier and their current pursuers still threatening them with an early death. "The man called Pierce has a cunning plan. I can tell."

"I do. Drive to the Chapora River bridge."

Parab momentarily lost his enthusiasm as he glanced at the scuba tank resting between Pierce's legs. "Now that I think about it, I'm not sure I'll like what you have in mind."

"I'll tell you later. Just make sure you are wearing your seatbelt."

Parab strapped himself in as Pierce had done earlier,

then accelerated once they were past the dense houses and street stalls of an urban centre, before driving onto a two-lane country road surrounded by low-growing lush vegetation.

Then they heard gunshots.

Pierce glanced back, noticing muzzle flashes from the first Suzuki Jimny.

Pierce returned a few shots of his own, missing as he knew he would with the distance separating them, the bumpy road and the lack of visibility at night. But the returned gunfire had the desired effect, scaring the driver, who braked suddenly. Then it fishtailed as the second vehicle crashed into the back of it.

Pierce watched in the moonlight, hoping to see both vehicles lose control and crash. But both drivers recovered, corrected and pursued again.

"Fuck!"

Pierce returned fire.

The enemy shooter returned a fresh volley of shots, and a lucky hit shattered their back window.

Pierce ducked, then checked for bullet holes in his flesh, finding none.

He looked to Parab. "You hit?"

"No. At least I don't think so." He pointed at the yellow-painted concrete bridge ahead of them now. The structure was about half a kilometre in length and crossed the Chapora River.

The Pakistani operatives were gaining on them now the road was straight, and with the railings of the bridge boxing them in and funnelling them into a single course of action, they were running out of options to escape their pursuers.

Except for the escape method Pierce had planned out earlier.

Ahead, coming at them from the other side of the bridge, Pierce spotted at least three police cars with their lights flashing.

"Brace yourself!" Pierce warned as he grabbed the steering wheel and turned it sharply.

They hit the concrete railing, smashed it into rubble and torn rebar, then careened through the newly created gap and dropped ten metres into the slow-flowing river below them.

33

As the river rushed towards them, Pierce wrapped his arms around his head only seconds before the four-wheel drive smashed into the water. Airbags exploded, protecting them from serious injury, but the jolt of the sudden stop still rattled Pierce. He grunted as his eyes filled with white flashes, and his ribs ached as if a vice compressed them.

Then water rushed into the cabin.

Before they went under, with the headlights still shining in the otherwise near absolute blackness of the night's river, he looked to Akash Parab, discovering the technical operations officer remained conscious. As realisation hit Parab as to what Pierce had done, he panicked as he clambered to unlatch his seatbelt and fling open his side door.

Pierce gripped his arm. "Wait!"

The cool water was up to their waists and rising fast.

Parab thrashed and convulsed. He couldn't get his fear responses under control.

"Buddy, we have the scuba tank. We're fine."

"Fine?"

"Yeah! If we sink, everyone will think we're dead. No one will come looking for us."

As the water passed up around their shoulders, Pierce turned on the tank, then passed Parab the mask, which he slipped over his face just as the water came up around their chins.

Pierce hyperventilated, and then they were underwater.

The headlights shorted, and then everything was pitch black.

Still holding his breath, Pierce felt in his pockets until he found his Maglite and switched it on. It illuminated the cabin, and he could see they were still sinking. They dropped perhaps five or six metres before they settled on the marine sediment.

Pierce gave the thumbs up to Parab, who returned the gesture. They swapped over the mask and took it in turns to breathe.

In the few minutes it took to get their shared breathing procedure under control, Parab had calmed his nerves. Pierce pointed to the doors, then made hand signals they should swim out.

Parab nodded, then unbuckled his seatbelt.

Together, they swam out of the ruined four-wheel drive. Pierce strapped the scuba tank over his back. Taking it in turns to breathe from the mask, the two men allowed the currents to carry them downstream.

After what Pierce guessed was ten minutes of swimming, they surfaced on the northern bank of the Chapora River, discovering a road with only light traffic. On the opposite side was a resort comprising many bungalow huts. Pierce abandoned the scuba tank; then the two men sprinted across the road and entered the resort.

"Fucking hell!" said Parab. "That was reckless."

"We survived, and no one will be looking for us."

"You partake in these kinds of dangerous antics often?"

Pierce grinned.

"Fuck! Perhaps I'm not cut out for fieldwork after all."

"You're doing fine. Better, in fact, than I expected."

Parab shook his head and looked as if he were about to be sick, but then recovered. "If only I could tell my girlfriend about this. She might be impressed."

"Sorry to disappoint, friend, but I don't think that's a good idea."

"You're right. What's the plan now?"

"Find an empty bungalow, steal any clothes we find so we can get out of these wet ones, then get ourselves to Panaji."

Akash nodded. "I guess that makes sense."

Ten minutes later, Pierce was dressed in khaki cargo pants and a black T-shirt, while Parab had donned a floral-patterned shirt and denim jeans. They took to the streets in a brisk walk until they found the liveliest part of town, where bars, nightclubs and restaurants were still open. Their cell phones were dead after immersion in water for too long, so they bought new ones at a late-night vendor with the wet rupees in their pockets, then exchanged phone numbers.

Back outside, they stood on a street corner, ready to hail down the first taxi they spotted.

"Pierce, news of the café and bridge attack will spread like wildfire now. Jahandar will hear about it and run."

Pierce considered Parab's warning for a few seconds, then

said, "I tend to agree, but our target's got to be even more careful now than we do. The Pakistani operatives had Jahandar's photo on them." He pulled the water-soaked photo of the disgraced Pakistani intelligence officer from his pocket and showed it to Parab. "This was in one of their wallets. It's likely it wasn't the only one, so we can presume the local police will have his photo now too and will be looking for him as well."

Parab wiped sweat off his brow. "That suggests he'll stay put tonight."

"And thanks to the street children who crashed our dinner, we know roughly where he is."

"And we know his girlfriend is a yoga instructor. That narrows it down even further."

Pierce nodded. "Exactly! We need to get moving. Again!"

34

Sumbawa, West Nusa Tenggara, Indonesia

Rachel Zang travelled almost non-stop for twenty-four hours, first on a CIA jet, which took her on a direct flight to Sultan Muhammad Salahuddin Airport situated on the Indonesian island of Sumbawa, from where she hired a four-wheel drive. She then drove this vehicle deep into the tropical dry forests until she reached a remote location identified only by the GPS coordinates provided to her by Mitch Hawley. She waited there patiently until night fell and then a little longer until a package parachuted out of the skies, delivering an assortment of otherwise locally unavailable and mostly illegal equipment comprising an M4 carbine, a SIG Sauer P227 semi-automatic pistol, body armour, two oxygen tanks, scuba gear and associated wetsuit, a torpedo-shaped waterproof canister, a matt black Seabob F5 underwater scooter, solar recharging cells, and a whole host of other gear she would need if she were to successfully complete her impending covert mission.

After loading everything into her vehicle, she drove east again through a now rocky and sparsely treed landscape until she reached the far eastern coast of the island. Even in the dark this new location seemed idyllic, with a view of the sea from an isolated beach. Here at least the trees were denser and more jungle-like again, so she drove into a thick portion of the undergrowth and parked. After she covered her vehicle with branches cut down from nearby trees to camouflage it, she clambered back inside, locked all the doors and slept with the P227 resting in her lap.

That had all happened yesterday.

Now that it was morning, Zang stirred. She opened her eyes as the sun crept up over the horizon. The empty beach was indeed spectacular. She munched on rations and drank from her water bottle as sunrise morphed into morning, and her food and the tranquil scene refreshed her.

Stepping out of the vehicle, and knowing this was an isolated part of Indonesia, she changed into her black one-piece swimsuit, strode down to the beach and swam in the warm subtropical water for several minutes, revitalising her further and loosening the cramping muscles in her back and neck. She didn't need a migraine today, and saltwater swimming always seemed to fix that problem.

Enjoying the warm water and feeling bold, Zang swam further out, testing the currents to identify that they pushed to the south. This was all she needed to know for her next steps in her plan, so she swam back to shore and walked back up the beach.

Zang towelled herself off as she stared across the ocean until she found Kadal Beracun Island about two miles out. About three miles long north to south and half that east to west, the island was mostly covered in thick subtropical dry broadleaf foliage. Zang knew from the National Reconnaissance Office–provided maps she had studied on the flight over that Karson's airfield and base of operations was on the other side of the island. Anyone based there wouldn't see potential visitors approaching from the west, as Zang intended to do, but that didn't mean there wouldn't be sensors watching for intruders.

While formulating her plan, Zang examined her black Seabob F5, which was a recent addition to CIA field kits and a novelty to her. The underwater scooter was shaped like a torpedo that was about three feet long, one and a half feet wide and a foot in height, with handlebars for its user to hold on to. Its jets would propel her through the water at speeds of up to twelve miles per hour while keeping her submerged to depths of up to one hundred feet, but she didn't need to go that deep. Twenty feet would be sufficient, low enough not to be obvious to any surveillance drones that might be in the area, and this would deliver her to the island in less than half an hour, hopefully unnoticed.

She slipped into her wetsuit, then stored all her weapons, military fatigues, field kits, and provisions for a least a week of operations behind enemy lines into the torpedo canister. Then she checked over her scuba tank, fins, goggles and breathing apparatus.

When she was ready, she called in on her sat phone, knowing that it would be prudent to maintain communications silence while on Kadal Beracun Island, as Major Karson, Sanders and his other goons would likely be monitoring for such signals. This was her last realistic check-in opportunity.

Mitch Hawley answered almost immediately; then they quickly proceeded through identification and non-distress reporting protocols.

"You in position, Zang?"

"Yes, thank you, Hawley. The maps, briefing files, and the supply drop had everything I needed. You are too good."

"Glad to be of service. Do you want the latest intel?"

"Sure."

"No problem. An NRO optical imaging surveillance satellite passed over the island ninety-six minutes ago, and we coordinated another two pass-overs yesterday. Karson's HondaJet is there, but it's the only aircraft present. We've identified at least twelve soldiers on the island, mostly staying in the huts near the airfield. Those twelve include two groups of two who take it in turn to patrol the island. Both groups have been seen on the eastern side, so you know."

"Thank you," Zang said, meaning it and wondering why Mark Pierce found Hawley difficult to work with, because that was not her experience at all with this helpful man. "Have you identified Karson or Sanders?"

"Negative, I'm afraid."

Zang felt a lump rising in her throat as she prepared herself for her next question. "What about Roshini Jahandar? Any positive identification on her?"

Zang didn't know Roshini, had never met her or had any personal connection with her, but that didn't stop her feeling partially responsible for allowing Executive Believers to have snatched her so easily, after Roshini's bravery in acquiring secrets that could soon determine whether America retained a formidable nuclear submarine force or not. She was on the side of good, and Zang planned to honour her conviction by doing whatever she could to protect and rescue Roshini. That was, presuming she was still alive.

"No sign, I'm afraid. No positive ID on anyone on the island. If I get intel to the contrary before you enter the island, I'll contact you."

"Thank you."

As a pause grew in the conversation while Hawley presumably checked his files, Zang held herself still and stared out across the subtropical sea. She was about to infiltrate a heavily weaponised and protected private military base, so she would have to keep her wits about her. The mission was purely reconnaissance, for Ibrahim had insisted she was not to engage, only to observe. If she received confirmation Roshini or the CIED device was in Karson's possession, then Zang was to call it in. Ibrahim would then send in a CIA Ground Branch team currently stationed with the Marine Rotational Force in Darwin, Australia, to swoop in and contain the situation. Proof of Roshini's capture was all the evidence they needed that Karson had turned bad, and it was Zang's duty to secure that intel. But Zang was worried that if she confirmed that Roshini was alive and Karson's prisoner, she would not be able to help herself and would do everything in her power to rescue Roshini and get her off the island, with or without support.

"Zang?"

"Sorry, missed that. What did you say?" She realised she had let her mind wander, not something she could afford to do in the coming hours and days.

"I was just seeing if any other intel had come in, but nothing new, I'm afraid."

"That's okay. Thank you, Hawley. Deploying now."

She ended the call, tied the torpedo canister to a belt

hooked around her waist, then walked into the ocean with the Seabob in hand. Once in the water, she affixed her mask, flippers and breathing apparatus, powered up the Seabob, then dived and powered out into the ocean, destined for the mysterious Kadal Beracun Island.

35

Mandrem, Goa, India

Pierce and Parab spent the next few hours driving and walking the late-night streets and back alleys of Mandrem, eventually locating the dozen boys who had stormed the café, now hiding out in a crumbling lean-to behind several grouped bars and restaurants closed for the night. They slept rough, mostly on lengths of cardboard or tattered cloth. They were immediately alert upon Parab and Pierce's approach.

Parab kept his cool and his movements non-threatening by holding his arms out wide to indicate he had no weapon in hand that he might plan on using. He asked the boys where they had seen Fawad Jahandar.

Pierce couldn't follow the rest of the conversation because it was spoken in a language he didn't understand, and it proceeded for many minutes. Eventually, Parab seemed satisfied with their answers, then paid them for their information. They then left and headed down to the beach less than a hundred meters distant.

With the warm sea breeze and morning sun on their faces, Pierce asked, "What did they say?"

Parab ran his hand through his hair and forced a smile. Pierce saw that he still carried residual stress from the earlier shoot-out and car crash into the river, and didn't blame him for his jitters. "Jahandar is on a yacht, anchored off the coast here. I know the boat, for it belongs to Varsha Pandya. I should have guessed this earlier."

"Who?"

"Varsha Pandya is a famous Bollywood star. Or once was. She was very popular for a time, featured in many movies made in Mumbai, but retired about five years ago and moved back to Goa. Do you watch much Bollywood?"

"Not enough to know intricacies like that."

"Well, she opened a yoga studio here, which attracts celebrities from all over India. You'll like her, Pierce. She is a rather stunning woman."

Pierce shrugged, not fully understanding why a successful actress and business owner would want to tie herself into an intimate relationship with a sadistic intelligence officer from a foreign power. But then again, this wouldn't have been the strangest relationship he had encountered in his time.

"Jahandar is her boyfriend?"

"It seems they have some kind of intimate relationship, yes. But this could be good news." Parab scanned the horizon, presumably searching for boat lights bobbing on the Arabian Sea, as Pierce now did. "Jahandar and Pandya might still not know about the Pakistani intelligence attack today.

They might still be anchored out there, too far away to hear or see the shooting."

Pierce nodded. "I've got an idea. What's the model of her yacht, do you know?"

Parab pulled his cell phone from his pocket and, after a few minutes of searching, found his answer. "A Fairline Squadron 42 super yacht, according to registration data I just hacked."

Raising an eyebrow, Pierce said, "You found that in three minutes, on the fly, using only a burner cell phone?"

The other man shrugged. "I'm better behind the scenes with a proper laptop and a decent internet connection, but not from all the way back at Langley. I like being in the field, but, you know, not directly in the firing line like you are. Somewhere in the middle is ideal."

"I get what you mean. Thanks, by the way! That's very helpful. Much better intel than I've been relying on recently. Give me a minute."

Pierce then called Mitch Hawley on his new cell phone. This time his support officer answered immediately, but his tone of voice lost its enthusiasm on hearing Pierce's voice. After they proceeded through their coded identifiers, Hawley said, "You know it's the middle of the night over here?"

Ignoring his question, Pierce said, "I'm in Mandra, Goa, India. I need the most recent satellite imagery from the region. I'm looking for a Fairline Squadron 42 yacht anchored in the Arabian Sea near my current position."

"Really?" He made an exaggerated groaning noise down the phone line.

"Yes, really."

"Is it mission related?"

Pierce didn't answer him.

"Well, if you insist, Trigger Man, I'll get the signals intel for you first thing in the morning."

"No! Get it now."

"What's the urgency?"

Pierce couldn't believe Hawley was even asking him this question. "Just get it done. Call me back in five minutes with your answer. You can always take it as read, anything I request from you is time critical."

Biting down on his fury, Pierce disconnected.

"What was that about?" asked Parab.

"Nothing. Well, I'm obtaining SIGINT. At least I hope I secure it in the next five minutes. If it is any good, I should be able to pinpoint which boat out there Jahandar is hiding on."

"And how do you plan to get out there when you do?"

The sun had risen high now in the east. They weren't far from the surf, so Pierce and Parab walked in that direction along the beach on Pierce's signal. "If I remember correctly, there was a shop just down here that hired out jet skis."

36

Kadal Beracun Island, West Nusa Tenggara, Indonesia

The swim through the perpendicular ocean current flowing between West and East Nuse Tenggara islands was easier than Rachel Zang had expected, for the Seabob effortlessly sped her through the water. She passed several schools of tropical fish, arrays of sponges and occasional starfish on the sandy bottoms. At one point she caught the attention of a curious but otherwise shy grey reef shark that decided she wasn't worth the risk of a confrontation and moved on before Zang needed to formulate a plan on how to deal with it. Zang mused that many tourists paid good money for vacations to see sights like this, and she was doing it all on a government paycheque.

The Seabob allowed her to maintain a consistent depth of twenty feet below the surface, significantly reducing the chance of someone spotting her from the air, yet shallow enough so she could bypass decompression stops should she need to surface suddenly. The speed she achieved was impressive, even when slowed by the torpedo-shaped canister dragging behind her with her gear inside.

Once Zang surfaced on the western shore of Kadal Beracun Island, she quickly dragged her Seabob and equipment canister along the sandy beach until she reached the subtropical foliage, where she hid her belongings out of sight from aerial view. Then she noticed the battery icon on the Seabob was almost flat. Not what she expected, as the device was supposed to bring her both to and from the island, and she wondered who back in Langley was responsible for that oversight.

Deciding to deal with the Seabob problem later, with her Benchmade 275 Adamas fold-out knife, she sliced off a large palm frond and, using it like a broom, dragged it along the beach to cover her tracks. It wasn't a perfect erasure of her presence, but better than the obvious footprints that she had left behind after first exiting the water.

Back undercover, Zang stripped out of her wetsuit, then opened the torpedo canister and laid out her equipment. She checked over her SIG Sauer P227 semi-automatic pistol first, her small arm of choice, then did the same with her M4 carbine, a select-fire, gas-operated, magazine-fed assault rifle used extensively by the US military and also favoured by her. Both weapons passed her preliminary checks and seemed to be in good working order, so she gathered up her dappled green combat fatigues from the canister in preparation to slip into them.

It was in that moment she sensed, then heard, movement in the nearby undergrowth.

Snatching up her pistol, Zang aimed the muzzle into the dense green vegetation. She saw nothing, but the grasses and leaves shuddered. Then entire bushes shook violently as a creature distinctively not human now shuffled fast towards her.

Zang's skin prickled as she tensed and stepped backwards. It could be a deer or a banded pig, in which case it would not be a threat to her, but it could also be a wild dog or a saltwater crocodile, which she would need to deal with immediately.

Before she could speculate further, the grass and bushes parted less than six feet from her. A gigantic lizard six feet long rushed at her, its clawed feet churning up the earth as it sprinted energetically and with focus. Its dinosaur-like mouth opened wide and salivated, ready to bite down on her.

Instinctively, Zang fired twice, killing it.

The noise blasted her ears as she realised she had not yet fitted the suppressor that would have otherwise muffled the shots. The sound would carry across the island, and Karson's people had a good chance of hearing the shots.

Zang blinked and stared disbelievingly at the motionless creature.

Dead now, she recognised it as a member of the world's largest living lizard family, a Komodo dragon. An apex predator in this part of Indonesia but only found in four nearby islands, for Komodo dragons weren't supposed to be on this one. Mitch Hawley should have known this and informed her of the dangers these reptiles potentially presented to her during this mission.

Then the bushes rustled again as a second, larger Komodo appeared, then lunged at its dead brethren. In seconds it had the dead Komodo's head in its jaw and commenced the process of gulping it down.

Horrified by what she witnessed, Zang fired again. It

took three shots to kill this larger specimen, and when it was dead, she found her breathing to be erratic and her heart pounding against her chest. The monstrous predators had rattled her.

The forests were unsafe. These lizards could sneak up on her unannounced and take her without warning. The first Komodo dragon was about the same size as her, and the second one was bigger, so she couldn't discount the possibility these predators would snack on her too, if given the chance. Plus, they had forced her to use her weapon five times, and the decibels her pistol had created now likely signalled her presence on the island to her enemies.

Slinging her M4 and throwing the P227 back into the canister, she dragged her gear back down onto the beach. She was in the open again, but here at least she had the opportunity to spot a Komodo dragon rushing her. The speed at which they had both moved had both shocked and startled her, and this was a complication she didn't need.

Then she heard a motorised noise in the air behind her.

She spun around, spotting a Chinese CW-30E surveillance drone hovering above the ocean swells, about a hundred yards from her.

Gritting her teeth and unleashing her frustration, Zang fired a burst from her M4 carbine into the drone, shattering it instantly. She watched as its wreckage dropped into the crashing waves and vanished, but its destruction brought her no inner satisfaction.

So much for subtlety, Karson and his Executive Believers mercenaries would know she was on the island now and would come for her. She could swim back to West Nusa Tenggara, but with the Seabob's battery already almost depleted, she'd have to swim under her own power, and that would place her on the water surface and easily identifiable if another drone investigated. When Zang concluded her only option was to hide out on the island, she quickly dressed in her green combat fatigues, tactical boots, plate carrier and chest rig, fitted suppressors to both weapons, then slung her pack with rations, medical kit, radio and satellite comms, and other field tools. She concluded there was no point concealing her other equipment; the enemy already knew she was here.

Then she spotted another Komodo dragon casually strolling along the beach towards her. This was a large specimen too and seemed to be eyeing her. Then it took off in a sprint towards her.

Zang raised her M4, ready to kill it. She didn't want to, knowing they were an endangered species, and killing two of them already didn't sit well with her. But if it attacked, she had no choice. She lined it up in her sights, readying herself for the kill.

Then it swerved right and disappeared into the foliage where Zang had sprinted from earlier. She soon saw why. It had picked up on the scent of its dead brethren, and now it would feed on their readily available corpses.

Zang wasted not a second more and sprinted into the jungle.

37

Zang chose speed over stealth to make her escape. With a coastline of less than eight miles, Karson's paramilitary teams could reach her in a patrol boat or by foot in less than fifteen minutes, which gave her that long to vanish and find somewhere to hide until nightfall, by which point she would decide whether to continue with her mission to determine if Roshini Jahandar was here, or swim back to West Nusa Tenggara. But with either option, her first priority was survival.

As she ran, crashing through the subtropical undergrowth of thick bushes and grasses, she knew the path she flattened behind her was an easy follow. To counter her pursuers' efforts, she headed in a direction that continuously lowered her elevation until she found what she hoped to encounter, a stream with flowing water she could use to cover her boot prints.

Only it was dry.

Zang cursed, remembering it was the dry season in this part of the world. Kadal Beracun was a subtropical dry forest, so despite its hot and humid conditions, it didn't constantly rain here as it did in other more luscious rainforests.

Thinking quickly, Zang noticed the many smooth rocks jutting from the dry bed. She stepped on these, jumped from one to the other, and followed its path further inland.

The island proved to be rather rugged in its deeper interior, and at the higher elevations of three hundred feet or more, she spotted this was where the vegetation thickened, so that was the direction Zang took.

After she had danced across a hundred yards of smooth rock, Zang took a path across a sloping grassy plain while taking care to step on rock or firmer ground where she was less likely to leave tracks.

As she ran, she spotted another Komodo dragon resting under scrub a dozen yards from her.

When it spotted her, it took off in a fast-running gait and came for her.

Zang could have shot it, but knew she needed to conserve ammunition for use against Karson's paramilitary teams when they finally came after her. She recalled reptiles were cold-blooded and could only sustain short sprints in their pursuit. She had to risk outrunning it, so sprinted swiftly from the galloping creature.

Zang ran for two minutes, pumping her legs as fast as she could and burning energy. When she'd reached a rise, Zang turned, ready to shoot the predator if it still followed, but it had given up and now rested in the sun fifty yards behind her.

Panting, sweating, and silently cursing, Zang glanced around and noticed she was in a wide-open grassy area.

Then she heard and spotted another CW-30E

surveillance drone, but this one circled much higher than the previous aerial tracker, ensuring it was well out of her effective firing range. It must have seen her though, because it hovered in a stationary position above her, no doubt alerting paramilitary teams to her location.

Deciding that engaging with it was pointless, Zang sprinted again and headed for higher ground and into thicker foliage and rockier terrain.

Rock chips shattered around her as she heard gunfire. She recognised the noise as controlled bursts from an assault rifle and knew these bullets were intended for her. Zang didn't look back and sprinted onwards until she found cover behind a rock and flattened herself against it.

She waited for a lull in the shooting, then turned and fired off a controlled burst from her M4 towards where she calculated the shooters had positioned themselves. Her efforts paid off, as she spotted three enemy combatants in military fatigues and body armour wielding M4 carbines where she expected them to be.

They returned fire. Zang ducked behind the rock again, then scrambled further up the rise for a better and, more importantly, unexpected firing position from her attackers' point of view. As she crawled, she heard more shots, knowing that the enemy were laying covering fire while they advanced on her position.

The drone passed overhead, again out of reach, relaying Zang's exact position.

Cursing, she aimed her carbine around the corner of the covering rock and fired several bursts towards the combatants closing in on her. She hit one, shattering his skull. Then she turned to the next target, shooting out the legs of this female paramilitary combatant. Blood hosed from the wound in her legs, and she hit the grass and dirt screaming and cursing.

Two more combatants fired at her, chipping the rocks mere inches from her position.

Zang ducked back as she realised there were at least three more enemy combatants advancing on her. She switched out magazines, moved, then when she heard a lull in the shooting, fired again.

This time, her covering shots hit nothing.

Her enemies were learning, keeping better cover as they moved in on her. She kept up the firepower, for pinning them down was better than letting them get close.

She heard more bullet fire, and in the same instant her M4 was ripped violently from her hand, almost breaking her finger in the trigger guard as it was wrenched away from her. Zang's gut tightened as she realised someone had shot her weapon from her, and that shot could have only come from behind.

She turned fast, her back pressed up against the rock as she pulled her P227, ready to engage.

More gunfire shattered lines of chipped rock around her.

Three more paramilitary goons, two men and a woman, had advanced up behind her. All three soon had their weapons aimed at her head and were unable to miss at the close range they had managed to acquire by sneaking up behind her unawares. They also had the sun behind them, providing additional cover.

"Drop your weapon!" ordered the centre man.

Zang paused, recognising the speaker immediately. "Sanders?"

"Drop it, Zang, or the next bullet will be your last one."

Knowing she was out of options, Zang lifted her hands in

surrender and allowed the SIG Sauer P227 to fall into the bushes.

Jay Sanders approached, and when he was close to her, she saw immediately that he was also surprised to see her. He kept his M4 trained on her head, a shot that wouldn't miss should he choose to take it.

"Fucking hell, Zang!" he shouted through a tightened jaw. "Why the fuck are you here?"

Zang forced a grin as his two armed companions stepped up to flank him on each side. Their weapons were firmly aimed at her, ready for a kill shot should they need to take it.

"Jay, you wouldn't shoot an old flame, would you? Not after everything we've been through together."

He shook his head, but his expression she couldn't read, with the sun shining behind him. She noticed the barrel of his M4 was still pointing at her head. "I can't protect you. Whatever happens, Rachel, you have to understand, you made the choice to be here. Not me."

38

Arabian Sea, Goa, India

Mark Pierce powered the jet ski through the tranquil water situated far off the Mandrem shores and searched with the only tool available to him, his eyes. Mitch Hawley had not secured the satellite imagery Pierce required, so Pierce took a risk and headed out to where several boats moored about a kilometre offshore. But not before he'd downloaded the specifications of a Fairline Squadron 42 yacht from the internet, a slick thirteen-metre flybridge motor luxury yacht, and memorised images of it. He figured if he powered around the water until he spotted it, this tactic would be faster than waiting for Hawley to provide him with its exact location.

Thankfully Pierce's tactic paid off, and after an hour of cruising past many boats loaded with partygoers and fishing crews, a Fairline came into view.

Cutting the power, Pierce coasted up to the anchored luxury yacht until he was close enough to hook a mooring line between his jet ski and its forward railing. Drawing his SR-2 Udav pistol, Pierce listened until he heard a couple at the aft laughing and joking. They spoke in a language he couldn't understand or identify, but which sounded similar to tongues he'd heard spoken in India since his arrival.

He climbed on board, then snuck forward until he discovered a man in board shorts and a woman in a bikini lying together on the main deck. The man was Fawad Jahandar, and he wore bandages around his midsection and bruises caused by the bullet he had taken in Patna. The woman appeared to be the Bollywood star Varsha Pandya, who was even more stunning in real life than she appeared in her online photos. The couple drank sparkling white wine from glass flutes while she decadently fed him slices of mango, and they laughed casually like nothing in the world outside of each other existed. When Pierce thought of the many fates that could have befallen Roshini, he felt his body tense and his face redden. Jahandar cared nothing for her.

He lifted his Udav into a firing position and advanced, surprised that they were still unaware of his presence.

When Pierce pressed his pistol into the top of Fawad Jahandar's head, the Pakistani spy and Pandya lost their smiles as their expressions turned cold and their bodies became rigid with fear. Jahandar turned his head to stare up at Pierce, and it took him several seconds to recognise who it was who now threatened his life.

Pierce pushed the weapon hard into the centre of his face, next to his nose. "Did you forget the first rule of tradecraft, Jahandar? When you need to run, go somewhere where nothing that is connected to your past exists."

Pandya sat taller and stiffened as she subconsciously wrapped a towel around her. "Manish? What's going on?"

Jahandar ignored her, shook his wrist where he still wore his exorbitant gold-plated watch as if it irritated the skin underneath, and stared coolly at Pierce. "I don't know who you are or what you want. But if it is money, I have lots of it. Please don't hurt me or my fiancée."

Pierce raised an eyebrow. "Fiancée?" Then he noticed the diamond ring on Pandya's finger, not too dissimilar to the one Roshini had worn. "How many lovers do you have, exactly, Jahandar?"

The man said nothing, but his eyes immediately gave away that there could still be other women in his life, other than Roshini and this former Bollywood star turned yoga instructor.

Pierce turned to Pandya. "What did Fawad tell you that he did? Oh, you do know him as Fawad Jahandar? Right?"

The woman shook her head as realisation that her lover might not be who she imagined was now dawning on her.

"The man you share your yacht with, his real name is Fawad Jahandar, if that's not yet clear. He's a senior spy with Pakistani domestic intelligence, and two days ago, I was rescuing Fawad's wife from being murdered by him."

Pandya drew in a sharp breath and tensed again.

"Yeah, that's right. Jahandar here was trying to kill Roshini because of secrets she had that could have compromised him."

With colour draining fast from her face, Pandya turned to Jahandar and said, "Manish, please, tell me none of this is true?"

"Lies! All of it lies!" Jahandar exclaimed loudly. In his flamboyant outburst he tried to knock the pistol from Pierce's grip and snatch it. But Pierce was ready for this, and he missed. For his insurrection, Pierce smashed the pistol grip across Jahandar's head, drawing blood and momentarily stunning him.

As Jahandar recovered, Pierce turned to the now distraught woman. "I hold nothing against you, Varsha Pandya, and I promise I will not harm you. But I do need you to sit quietly and say and do nothing until your lover here and I have finished talking. Can you do that?"

Pierce felt for her, she was processing more information than any civilian could ever imagine having to come to terms with in only a few minutes, but there was nothing he could do about that. He would have sent her off if he had that choice, to get away from the violence that could soon erupt between Pierce and Fawad Jahandar, but he couldn't risk her using a radio or cell phone and calling in the police or coast guard.

She nodded and tensed again with fear as she drew her towel more tightly around her.

"Good."

Jahandar sat upright and touched his head where a trickle of blood had now formed. When he looked up at Pierce, his eyes were like daggers aimed right at Pierce's heart. "I'm not who you say I am. I'm a movie producer. Manish is my name, and I'm an innocent man." He turned to Pandya. "Please, Varsha, you have to believe this is all some horrible joke perpetrated by this violent stranger."

Pierce shook his head. "Would it trouble you to know Roshini is alive and now in your pal's custody." When Jahandar expressed surprise at this revelation, Pierce said, "Yes, Major Brad Karson has her. Who knows what she's told him." He nodded to the still tense Pandya. "She certainly knew about your lover here in Goa. If I can figure it out, so can he."

Now the colour drained from Jahandar's face.

Pandya seemed to notice this, and she spoke up. "Manish, is this true?" As a tiny tear escaped her left eye, Pierce sensed Pandya was now piecing together other oddities she was remembering from her past encounters with Jahandar. Perhaps not everything that he had said under his cover as a Bollywood movie producer had ever properly added up in her mind, but now she was starting to understand why. Jahandar was about to lose her forever, when she reached that moment when she realised just how thoroughly and completely he had betrayed her.

Pierce turned again to Jahandar and pressed his advantage. "I should also tell you ISI and FIA were in Mandrem yesterday, looking for you too. Didn't you hear about the shoot-out last night and the police arresting them?"

Again, judging by Jahandar's shocked expression, this was news to him and now worried him further.

"I guess it's true what they said about Qusay Vali, your head of Operational Intelligence. You were the hothead, and he was the cool, controlled brains behind all your actions. But with him gone, your lack of self-control has no checks and balances. No wonder you ran to your lover here, because if Vali were still alive, he would have told you what a stupid idea that was. He would have told you to run to IB straight away." When Jahandar's eyes grew wider still, Pierce added, "So that was the plan?"

Now Jahandar fumed as he tightened his fists, readying himself for a fistfight he must know was never going to happen.

Pierce pressed his pistol forward. "And what about Kaajal Khan, the al-Qaeda regional commander you instructed to hide and secure McMahon in his Pakistani mountainous hideout? He won't be too pleased either, to learn that you're not keeping up with your end of the bargain."

Tense and also trembling, Pandya said in a small voice, "What deal is he talking about, Manish?" She sobbed then. "Is your name really Manish? Is the injury around your waist really from coral? Do you really love me? Is this all a farce?"

This time Jahandar ignored her questions as his stare locked onto Pierce's returned gaze. "You...!"

Pierce spoke over him. "Everyone's coming for you. Karson, ISI, FIA, IB, al-Qaeda and me, the CIA. How long do you think you can survive with so many enemies now?"

"You going to kill us, justifying your actions with these despicable lies?"

Pierce fired a shot past Jahandar's head, ensuring the round disappeared out across the ocean and wouldn't hit Pandya by accident. They both flinched at this sudden act of aggression and cowered lower onto the deck. "That's your first warning, Jahandar. The second one is in your left foot. The third in your right. Then I start with your hands."

Jahandar convulsed and gagged for a moment but didn't bring up any of his stomach's contents. "Okay! Okay! What do you want?"

"The CIED device I know you have hidden here. And Kaajal Khan's exact location." Pierce smirked as an idea came to him. "Tell you what, give me both of those right now, and I won't kill you. I'll let you both go, unharmed."

Pandya was hysterical now. "Tell him, please, Manish. I don't want to die."

Pierce aimed his pistol at Jahandar's foot. "I'll count to three. One... Two..."

"Okay. I'll tell you! But you promise you'll let us live?"

Pierce was surprised at the desperation in Jahandar's

returned stare, but admired that he'd considered both his and his girlfriend's well-being in this moment. He wasn't purely just out for himself, so Pierce nodded.

Pandya let out a long breath and pressed her hand to her chest, deflating.

Jahandar nodded furiously as his eyes grew wide. "Kaajal Khan's cavernous hideout is in Pakistan's Lower Chitral District, at the base of the Hindu Kush where the Solangi and Jakhro Rivers meet. He never leaves. That is where McMahon is too."

"And the CIED device?"

Nobody got a chance to speak next. The air around them erupted with bullet fire as Varsha Pandya's chest opened with multiple meaty holes where several metal projectiles destroyed her.

39

A s bullets zipped around him, Pierce dived behind the built-in lounge Jahandar and Pandya had sat upon. From the corner of his eye, Pierce watched Jahandar dive down the stairs to the lower decks, but he couldn't worry about him for the moment. More machine-gun fire raked the main deck and flybridge above him, splintering wood and pinging off metal. If Pierce remained on board any longer, he knew one of those bullets would eventually hit him, so he dived over the opposite side and swam deep.

Most bullets lost their power after a metre or so of trajectory underwater, so Pierce kept himself this far beneath the surface. He kicked hard and, with his pistol still in his hand, propelled himself through the clear water using a rapid breaststroke.

Pierce could hold his breath underwater for about two minutes, but he hadn't had time to consume a deep lungful of air before diving, so rose to the surface after an approximate count of ninety seconds.

When he surfaced, after gulping oxygen, he turned in a full circle, taking in three speedboats that now circled Pandya's mostly shattered and now probably sinking yacht. No one had yet noticed Pierce, for the men in the speedboats were watching the yacht, holding Uzi and Heckler & Koch MP5 submachine guns with smoking barrels aimed in its direction. Perhaps they hadn't seen Pierce go over and weren't looking for him in the water yet.

He dived again and swam towards the closest speedboat, only surfacing near the underside of its hull where he knew he couldn't be seen by anyone on board. He'd counted three men on that boat, so he was prepared when he pulled himself up on the side positioned away from the yacht and started firing.

Two of the attackers went down immediately.

The third turned and fired his Uzi where Pierce had been only seconds before, for Pierce had dived again and waited just under the water's surface. When the boat rocked, and the weight shifted so the hull was angled towards where Pierce had clambered up seconds earlier, he fired upward through the fibreglass hull until the SR-2 Udav pistol clicked empty.

A second later the third assailant dropped into the clear blue water, blood trailing from multiple holes in his feet, legs and groin.

Pierce swam to the dead body, relieved him of his Uzi and a spare magazine in his belt, then swam to the surface. When he exited the water, he clambered up and into the speedboat with the decimated crew.

No sooner was he on board than he was being strafed with bullet fire again.

Leveraging one of the two remaining corpses into a

sitting position as a shield, Pierce started up the motor and sped off, not caring which direction he headed in, only caring that he was creating distance between himself and his attackers.

But when he had powered the speedboat for a minute, he realised how much water the vessel had taken on. All the shooting it had endured, including his shots through the hull from below, had wrecked the boat, and it was sinking fast.

Cutting the engine because it wasn't propelling him anywhere, Pierce looked up and noticed two speedboats pursued him, while two more in the distance he had not seen before had encircled Pandya's also slowly sinking yacht, and men were boarding it. No doubt their intention was to capture or kill Jahandar and secure the CIED device from him, but again, Pierce had more pressing problems to deal with than trying to secure these targets himself.

The two pursuing speedboats were almost upon him now.

He looked around, and luck had it, he spotted a scuba tank, goggles, mask and flippers.

Pierce dropped the tank over the protected side as the men in the approaching speedboats filled his vessel with further metal projectiles. Grabbing the accessories, Pierce dived back into the water.

Once submerged, he fitted the goggles and flippers, then searched for the scuba tank.

It was dropping and was well over fifteen metres below him now. In another ten metres it would disappear inside a vast field of seagrass spread out beneath him.

Pierce dived and swam fast after it.

He felt the pressure build in his ears and sinuses as the depth increased.

Kicking fast, he just managed to snatch the scuba tank less than a metre from the dancing tips of the tallest seagrass.

Several shapes suddenly moved around him.

Pierce momentarily panicked, but still managed to hold his breath when he realised he'd disturbed a group of bluespotted stingrays that darted fast around him and then away from him. Stingrays weren't by nature aggressive towards humans, but Pierce knew that when cornered they could lash out with the poisoned barbs at the ends of their tails, and the venom they injected could severely incapacitate and perhaps kill Pierce. He kept still and non-threatening until they were far from him, then realised his lungs were burning.

Pierce swam fast towards the surface, not wishing to breathe compressed air at this depth. He didn't know how much oxygen mix remained in the tank, and there might be insufficient quantities should he need to decompress in stages on the way up. But when he was less than five metres from the surface, he couldn't hold his breath any longer. He slipped on the mouthpiece, turned on the tank and sucked in a lungful of soothing oxygen.

Then he noticed a team of four new divers swimming towards him.

They'd all donned black wetsuits and rebreathers so their expelled carbon dioxide bubbles were contained and wouldn't give away their positions on the surface. But more importantly to Pierce, they carried spearguns.

Pierce knew in his gut these divers were not from the

same team that had disintegrated the yacht with their chaotic and uncoordinated acts of violence. These foes were something else. Precise. Focused. Coordinated.

One fired his speargun, aimed at Pierce.

40

Pierce kicked hard to propel himself through the ocean water. The fired spear shot past, coming within half a metre of hitting him, its cord trailing behind. He knew it should have hit him with less than fifty metres separating him from the team of four, who were now closing in. Perhaps their intention was not to kill but to capture, and it had been a warning shot.

Pierce had no intention of allowing them either option, but preventing him from making his escape was the open water. There were no obstacles in sight to hide behind, so he'd have to fight them all eventually.

As Pierce kicked, creating propulsion through his flippers and burning energy in his leg muscles, he glanced at his tank gauge for the first time. It showed less than ten minutes of air remaining. Diving into the seagrass for cover was no longer an option, because at that depth he'd burn through the remaining oxygen in less than a minute and would have nothing left to decompress with on the way up.

He glanced back.

The divers had split into two groups, and they were gaining, ready to flank him on two sides. If they'd wanted to spear him, they would not have missed a second time.

Pierce looked up, spotting what he'd hoped would be there, the hull of a blue wooden boat chugging through the water. It wasn't one of the speedboats, but a larger vessel that might belong to the divers chasing him, or an innocent crew passing through this scene of carnage unawares. But a boat provided options regardless of who piloted it.

He glanced back again. Two of the divers were almost upon him. A man and a woman.

Pierce ceased swimming and turned to fight.

The man lunged forward with a knife. Pierce grab the arm, but the foe had power behind his muscular arms and expertly forced forward the blade until it cut Pierce's air hose.

Struggling for breath again now that oxygen was denied to him, Pierce wrestled the man. He soon felt his lungs burn and knew he would drown if he didn't disengage and swim to the surface.

Despite knowing he was running out of options, Pierce glanced at the woman, who was treading water two metres to his left and holding her armed speargun casually. She presumed her companion had control of the situation, and with two more divers closing in, the four would either force him to the surface as their captive or hold him down to drown him.

Then Pierce acted and pushed the man off, releasing his grip on his arm and kicking off him so he shot through the water towards the woman. She hadn't expected this and, in her shock, didn't resist as he wrestled the speargun from her.

Fighting his instincts to breathe despite his complaining

lungs, Pierce turned the speargun and fired it at the boat passing overhead. The spear shot through the water, and a second later its barbed tip buried into the wooden hull.

Pierce held on tight to the speargun, knowing that the connecting line would go taut any second. When it did, the tension catapulted him through the water, speeding him away from the divers at about three times their top speed.

Desperate for breath, Pierce kicked until he broke the surface, not daring to release the speargun for fear of dropping back to where the military-trained divers would find and capture him. He breathed in sweet air for many seconds and just allowed himself to be pulled, knowing that each second took him further from danger.

Until he realised the fishing trawler had slowed and was now lazily turning in a circle.

Pierce was drifting in the current towards the slowing boat.

A muscular and stocky woman in a tank top and shorts, wearing a cap and sunglasses, looked over the railing and spotted him. "Are you okay, friend?"

Pierce couldn't place the accent. She wasn't Indian, but also didn't sound European or American.

"Let me throw you a rope."

Pierce raised his arm and gave her the thumbs up. The woman could be part of either crew that had come for Jahandar and him, but Pierce figured if she was, he had better odds fighting on a deck than in the ocean to ensure his own survival.

She threw out a lifebuoy, which Pierce caught and gripped tight.

A minute later, she had a rope ladder over the side for him to climb, which Pierce did.

On the deck, he collapsed, exhausted. He just needed a few seconds to recover his breath.

He didn't get them.

The woman performed the most perfectly executed roundhouse kick Pierce had ever witnessed, before her foot smashed him hard in the face, rattling his jaw and sending blood spraying from his mouth.

Now he was on the deck, sprawled on his front with his face pressed uncomfortably against the wet deck.

She kicked him again, twice in the left kidney. The pain was like being pummelled by falling rocks. His vision spun, and tears exploded from his eyes. When Pierce rolled over, then tried to get to his feet, he noticed four other figures gathering on the deck around him.

They all wore black wetsuits and diving equipment.

They all carried spearguns except for one woman.

The closest man tore off his mask.

His dark unblinking eyes seemed to focus with the same lack of emotion that a shark expresses. But it was the short-cropped black beard and carefully trimmed short black hair with greying temples that immediately identified the foe as Major Brad "Black Dog" Karson.

"You fought well," Karson said as he stood over Pierce with the tip of his speargun aimed at Pierce's right temple.

Beaten and exhausted, Pierce couldn't respond.

The woman who had given him a thorough beating stepped up behind Karson. Pierce recognised her now from her file photo as Staff Sergeant Kwang Suwan with her quiff-style haircut. She was muscular and stocky but also compact. He noticed the many Chinese-style dragon tattoos that, in his pain delirium, seemed to fly along the flesh of her arms, legs and exposed midsection. She said through a sly upturned mouth, "I would disagree, sir. He gave me no resistance at all."

Pierce thought he was about to pass out. He willed himself not to, but also recognised the choice might not be his.

Karson crouched down on his haunches, then positioned the speargun so that it pressed into Pierce's exposed throat. "I came for Fawad Jahandar and the CIED device. They got away, snatched by whom I can only presume were FIA, ISI or al-Qaeda. Instead, I get you, Trigger Man."

Pierce snorted a laugh, which merely resulted in spraying a sizeable glob of blood from his nostrils. "You know, I heard a joke about you once, and the nicknames you like to be called. It was rather funny."

Karson pressed the tip further, drawing a line of blood across Pierce's jaw. "The only reason I'm keeping you alive is because I know you and Jahandar talked. Believe me, that's the only reason."

The Black Dog lifted the speargun away from Pierce, then suddenly brought its grip down hard onto Pierce's skull before everything went black.

41

Waiting with nothing to do stoked the worst kind of fear that Karen Dwyer could imagine, and now she was experiencing it, she knew her fears were founded.

The three-bedroom safe house she shared with Wilks, Daniil Pavlenko and his wife, daughter and son was exactly on the right side of "too small" for them not to get antsy with each other at the most minor of insurrections. No one could go out. No one could stand anywhere close to the windows in the third-storey apartment because to draw the curtains with such nice weather outside was another way of drawing attention to themselves. The family couldn't use phones or log in into social media accounts or browse the internet. To do so would bring the FSB straight to their doorstep. There was television and the radio, but with the Russians' paranoid control over state media, there was nothing worth watching or listening to either. There was a backgammon set that had been played to death, and a board game called Arkham Horror where the aim of the game was to prevent a sleepy New England town from being consumed by alien horrors from other dimensions, with what seemed to be a third of the cards and pieces missing. There was a deck of cards, which the children, Anatoliy and Emiliya, were using to play poker with, using dried pasta shells as chips. The food in the refrigerator was uninspiring, and there was nothing to drink. The latter suited Dwyer and Wilks but left Daniil and his wife, Katerina, on edge. At least the boy's fever was better now that he'd taken several of the children's paracetamol tablets Dwyer had brought back from her dangerous outing.

Taking a break from sitting on the tired, sagging sofa, Dwyer stepped into the kitchen and leaned over the sink. She stared for a few minutes at nothing. Her mind was blank. Everything felt numb and pointless.

When she heard the wife, Katerina, enter behind her, Dwyer sprang into action as if nothing were wrong, and filled her empty glass with tap water. Then on a whim, splashed more of that water on her face, refreshing her tired eyes.

"Thank you for the medicine. I was worried about my son."

"No problem."

Katerina stood for a moment, biting down on her lower lip as her eyes rolled over every corner of the kitchen. "Any news?" she asked as she leaned against the refrigerator with her arms crossed.

Dwyer shook her head. "I'm sorry, nothing."

"Can you call your CIA masters and ask?"

She shook her head again. "Every call I make increases

the risk of the FSB finding us. My people won't call until they have news."

Katerina nodded as her bloodshot eyes again looked to every part of the kitchen except to where Dwyer stood. "How do you do this? Waiting, knowing that they could come for us at any moment?"

Dwyer counted to five in her head before answering, "I don't know is the truthful answer."

The Russian frowned. "What do you mean?"

"Katerina, you and your family must have lived in fear for years. You can't go against your president and not fear for your life and the lives of your family at some level? So I could ask the same question; how did you do that?"

Katerina tensed as her back stiffened. "You're right. We have, but this is somehow different. Today, I 'know' rather than 'speculate' that the secret police are coming for us. We're trapped here, and that makes it worse. When we were moving, there was hope. Now I just feel as if we are all just... decaying where we stand."

Dwyer sipped more of her water, her mind agreeing with everything this woman said. She felt as if the walls were closing in on them too, but until Ibrahim could confirm that their exfil submarine route couldn't be tracked, there was no other option. And there were no other known routes to whisk them away from this maniacal authoritarian state that she would risk either.

"I don't know if it helps, but I once had an asset inside the Russian military who operated for five years feeling like this, as though the walls were constantly closing in on him, and that the FSB were only a hair's breadth away from discovering he was a double agent."

Finally, Katerina looked at Dwyer. "What happened to him?"

Dwyer shook her head. "He got out. He's safely away from Russia now."

"What? That's not an answer!"

"It is, I'm afraid. All I'm trying to tell you is that fear is just a moment, and it doesn't last. Right now, this is horrible. For you, your husband, your children. It's horrible for me and Wilks too. But it will pass. We won't be here forever. It will end."

"But it could end with us all incarcerated in an FSB torture cell. I don't want to watch while brutal men torture my children in front of me. I just won't." She turned suddenly when she realised that she had raised her voice and that Anatoliy and Emiliya might have overheard her. But when she glanced back into the lounge area, they were now both preoccupied with a television show about a private investigator bear. With her eyes focused on Dwyer again, she said, "I just can't go through that. I just can't."

"You won't have to."

"How can you be so sure?"

Dwyer opened her jacket to show where she holstered her MP-443 Grach pistol, positioned for easy reach and a quick draw. "I couldn't go through that either. This option is better, and there are plenty of bullets for all of us. If it comes to that, I won't hesitate."

Katerina stared at her without blinking and her mouth wide open.

Dwyer said, "You agree, don't you?"

Slowly, the Russian wife and mother, fully dedicated to her family and willing to give everything in her power to "save" them, nodded.

42

Kadal Beracun Island, West Nusa Tenggara, Indonesia

Rachel Zang spent the next twenty-four hours in a cage. Karson's soldiers had removed her weapons and kit, then marched her back to their base, on the eastern side of the island. They had threatened her with violence when they realised she had killed two of their team, for the woman she had shot multiple times in the leg had bled out. Zang had no sympathy for them because they were all professional soldiers and knew the risks of the profession they had chosen, but she sensed several of her enemy were of opposing opinions, for the dead had been wrapped and slung onto hastily constructed stretchers, and the soldiers carrying them had grumbled the whole way back.

When they approached Karson's paramilitary base, she'd had a chance to further ascertain its layout beyond what she had seen on satellite maps. It comprised many bungalow huts, multiple transportable containers, equipment stores, bunded fuel tanks, satellite dishes, radio communications towers, a four-thousand-foot runway taking up about a quarter of the length of the island, several hangars, a workshop, a large field of solar panels, and oddest of all, three crumbling and ancient circular concrete pits about ten feet deep and one hundred feet across. She had no idea what the latter were for, but had noticed the rusting metal poles in the centre of each circle. She knew this facility had formerly been a Japanese base from World War Two, but other than the three concrete holes, little remained that spoke of its historical origins.

Of the soldiers, she counted ten, not including the two dead. Listening to them talk and judging by their accents, they were mostly Americans, but she also heard German, Mexican and Spanish accents. She couldn't fault any of them their military prowess and feared that if she had to fight them again, she would lose. Her instructors were their instructors and were counted as amongst the best in the world.

The airfield included a light business HondaJet, but as for the Antonov AN-32 military transport in Karson's arsenal and the leader himself, there was no sign.

Zang also searched for Roshini Jahandar, but to no avail. At least there were no signs of freshly dug graves.

When they stepped next to a transportable container with several tiny, barred windows, Sanders ordered the surviving female soldier to strip Zang of her clothes except for her combat pants and T-shirt. Then Sanders had her handcuffed again and locked her in a barred cell, one of four within the transportable. It was not unlike mobile prisoner cells Zang had seen in Bagram Airfield the few times she had passed through that Afghan airbase when the United

States had been an occupying force there. Each cell contained a tiny bunk, a crate with several bottled waters, and a bucket for toiletries.

The rest of the day and the night had been uneventful other than the incessant infestations of mosquitos that had fed on her blood while she tried to sleep. So, in the late morning, when Jay Sanders came to visit her again, Zang felt irritable, tired, hungry and generally pissed off.

"I brought you food." He passed her a meal ready to eat, or an MRE as they were commonly known as in the military.

She took the pack through the bars and opened it. This one featured a beef taco, so she devoured it quickly. "About fucking time!"

Sanders stood back from the cell bars. He had guessed correctly that if he stood within grasping distance, she would have struck out to forcibly remove the cell's keys from him and, if she could, break both his arms at the same time.

He watched her eat for at least a minute, saying nothing.

Zang ignored him, next devouring the chocolate bar, then the crackers and cheese. When she searched for the matchbook and the flameless ration heater normally included with the pack that could be used to rapidly boil water, she noticed Sanders had already removed both. Those items were a potential weapon in an operator's hands, and he knew this.

Once the food was consumed, Zang opened another bottled water and guzzled its contents. She caught Sanders admiring her with the same look in his eyes that had been present in their hotel room in Washington, DC, less than a week ago now. In response she rattled her still cuffed hands in his face. "Why the fuck do I need these?"

"You and I both know, Rachel—"

"It's Zang to you now! You've lost the right to call me by my first name anymore, Sanders!"

Her now very ex-lover nodded. "You shouldn't have come, Zang. You should have left this well alone."

Zang let out a humourless chuckle. "I'm not the traitor selling state secrets to the Russians or the Chinese or whoever the fuck it is paying you for submarine propeller schematics."

The colour drained from Sanders's face. "So you know, then? I wish you hadn't said that. I could have gotten you out alive if you didn't know, but now..."

Zang shook her head and stared at him through narrowing eyes. "You can still get me out. Uncuff me, open the cell and give me a weapon. You and I can shoot our way out of this mess, and then, and only then, might Langley forgive you."

The next words out of Sanders's mouth were aggressive and loud. "You've got no fucking idea, Zang! I didn't just choose this overnight. It just happened slowly, one small decision after another that all seemed innocuous, that all seemed to be the right choice at the time. Unfortunately, it all added up to create this mess that came out of nowhere, now when I'm in too deep to ever get out."

"Bullshit!"

"Bullshit, yourself, Zang! You won't be so smug years from now when you're burned out and non-operational, when the CIA wants nothing to do with you and discards you like yesterday's trash. If you survive to experience that moment, because it will come if you live that long, I hope you remember this conversation and the choice you could have made!"

Zang was about to yell a counterargument back at the

man she had stupidly slept with, but then she properly heard what he had said. "Choice? What choice?"

Sanders took a step forward and ran his sweaty hand through his already sweat-drenched hair. "I thought about it all last night. There is a way out. It's a long shot, and I doubt the Black Dog will believe me. But it's worth a try."

"What's worth a try?"

He paused, then said, "We tell Karson that you came here with the sole purpose of joining Executive Believers?"

"WHAT? No way!"

Sanders stepped closer still. "It will work. Killing two of our team won't help, but we have to try. I thought it through and fabricated intel that shows you've just been disavowed from the CIA. You had to run, and you chose to run to me."

Zang squirmed and moved backwards from the bars and the man whom she had once believed was a decent human being. "You've got to be fucking joking?"

"I'm not, Zang. Karson will kill you, and he won't be pretty about it. I've seen what he can be like. Once, in Kandahar, he had two Tallies held captive while we were out in the field. We knew they knew the location of a hidden Taliban stronghold. Karson figured he only needed one prisoner to tell him where it was, so he picked one at random and took his head off with a fighting knife, one brutal cut at a time. Then he kicked the severed head around like a football, all the while telling the other Tallie he was next unless..."

Zang felt like she would be physically sick just listening to this story. "You chose to work for this man, even knowing he was like that back when you both served in Afghanistan? You're worse than I thought."

"No, it was during a mission with EB that I'm talking about. By then, Zang, I didn't have a choice."

Zang shook her head again as her nostrils flared. "This is all bullshit, Sanders. You're not doing this because you're afraid. You're doing this because of the money Karson's promised you. You think he'll make you stupidly rich, and that will make up for all the hurt and frustration the US government has thrust upon you and your family. And I'm guessing he's told everyone else in EB the same story. You think Suwan doesn't have her own demons with the US Army? I know she does, because I checked. Your so-called beloved leader is using you and your pain. All of you!"

Sanders waited until Zang left a long enough pause in her rant before answering, "So, your answer is no, then?"

"Of course it's fucking no!" She rattled her handcuffs again. "Now it's your last chance. Get me out of these and get me a gun, and I might, just might decide not to shoot you in your sorry arse too when I shoot my way out of here!"

"What's going on?"

A tall, late-middle-aged man entered wearing combat fatigues, tactile boots and a Makarov semi-automatic pistol holstered on his belt. His dark hair was peppered with many greys, but his style was militaristic, and his face was immaculately clean shaven. By his stance, Zang could tell he was former military and officer class.

Sanders saluted him. "Sir!"

"At ease, Lieutenant. What are you doing with the prisoner?"

"Captain, I was providing the prisoner with a meal."

The officer's approving nod was slight. "Well, that might have been a waste."

Sanders frowned. "Why, sir? If you don't mind me asking?"

"The major has radioed ahead. He'll be landing in the

hour, and he has a prisoner with him called Pierce. You know him?"

Zang's heart sank when she heard the name. Pierce was a good man, the only decent man she had dated in years. She still didn't understand why she didn't want a more permanent and emotional relationship with her fellow Ground Branch operator, because on paper he was perfect. But whatever the reason she insisted on keeping him at arm's length, she still felt affection towards him. And now that he was about to join her as another of Karson's prisoners, their situation might soon end up in the same place the two Taliban soldiers had found themselves in; one butchered in front of the other because Karson only needed one of them to spill the beans. That just didn't seem fair.

"Yes, sir," answered Sanders. "Well, we haven't met, but I know of him."

"This is going to be interesting, then." The captain nodded to Zang. "Prepare her and the other prisoner. Karson wants all three of them present when he lands."

43

A naked Pierce struggled against the ropes that bound him by his wrists and ankles to a wooden chair. Men in balaclavas speaking in Australian accents covered his face in a wet towel, then dropped a bucket of water over him.

Pierce screamed. They wanted his bank account details. All of them.

He woke suddenly, realising he'd experienced a nightmare.

Only that nightmare had been real, from a time in Central Africa when he had endured ongoing tortures for months on end.

But he wasn't there now. He was inside the fuselage of a military cargo aircraft, surrounded by Karson, Suwan and a dozen paramilitary Executive Believers mercenaries who had captured him in Goa. He was handcuffed, but at least he had clothes on him this time, even if they only comprised a T-shirt and the black cargo pants he had stolen in Mandrem. But he had nothing else, not even his belt, boots or socks. His head hurt too, and he remembered this was because Karson had rendered him unconscious with a strike from the grip of his speargun.

He also knew he was about to face further nightmarish tortures, but this time, he wouldn't be able to wake from it. When the aircraft came to a standstill, two of the PMC soldiers manhandled him out of the rear cargo bay. The air outside was as humid and sticky as it had been in India, but the vegetation had changed to a dry tropical scrub. A quick scan of the airfield, hangars, solar arrays and many huts and transportable buildings told Pierce that this was Kadal Bercun, Karson's supervillain hideaway.

Karson stepped up to Pierce and stared him down, but his intimidation wasn't as effective as he might have liked. Karson was slightly shorter, so when he menaced, he had to do so from a position of disadvantage.

Pierce said with a grin, "Was I too short with you earlier?"

The major's response was to punch Pierce hard in the gut.

Pierce had been ready, tensing his stomach muscles, but the blow still hurt and sent him down on one knee.

"I'll have what I need from you in time, Pierce. I've thought it through. You won't be able to resist."

Soon Pierce was shaking, and he couldn't get his convulsions under control. This infliction that often came from nowhere when he least expected it had caught him out before, and here it was betraying him again. He knew why. It was because he feared the tortures Karson was about to subject him to. With all the horrors Pierce had endured in the last year, from waterboarding to starvation and forced dehydration, to stress positions and a lengthy period incarcerated inside a coffin, Pierce didn't believe he would hold out for long this time. In fact, rather than face torture, Pierce was ready to kill himself if given the chance.

Then he spotted Rachel Zang and Roshini Jahandar, both handcuffed and on a forced march directed towards him. Zang wore a T-shirt and army pants, while Roshini still wore the same blouse and suit pants she had purchased in Begusarai. Like him, neither woman wore shoes, their expressions were near lifeless, and they both appeared exhausted. Thankfully, Pierce could see no signs that either woman had been tortured.

Yet.

"Zang!"

"Pierce!"

"Roshini! Did they hurt you?"

The lawyer burst into tears and would have fallen to her knees if the PMC soldier manhandling her hadn't kept her on her feet.

"How very romantic!" said Karson with a sneer. "But it suits my purposes. Where is Captain Keng?"

"Here, sir!"

A tall, older male soldier in combat fatigues holstering a Makarov pistol stepped forward. Pierce noticed he was standing next to Jay Sanders, and although Pierce had never met the man personally, he knew him from his file photo. With Sergeant Suwan coming up behind Pierce to stand next to him, it seemed Karson had all his key people in one location.

Karson said to Keng, "We need to be wheels up ASAP. Do a full maintenance check on the AN-32, refuel her and pack her with long-range tanks."

"Yes, sir. When is ASAP, exactly, if you don't mind me asking?"

Karson turned to Pierce. "When the so-called Trigger Man tells me exactly what I need to know."

Pierce snorted. "Everyone in the CIA already knows, Karson, that you plan on selling the propeller schematics to the Russians and the Chinese. Killing us and no amount of money will now keep the CIA and the full force of Uncle Sam's military from hunting you down, to whatever end of the Earth you think you can retire to."

"True, but lots of money is better than no money when the situation is what it is."

Pierce felt the tremors in his legs and hands. His infliction had worsened not because of the tortures Karson was about to inflict on just him, but on all three of them. Who would Karson start with? He suspected the order would be Roshini, then Zang, and finally him. He wasn't mentally ready for this, and he feared Karson could sense this too.

Karson pulled his Glock 22 from his holster, then nodded that Roshini and Zang be brought forward until they stood before him. The scene behind them, just off the tarmac, was tropical scrub and pristine beach, and its serenity all looked wrong with what Pierce knew was about to come. The weather was nice, the air clear, and a flock of birds passed lazily overhead, with no idea what was about to go down.

"We didn't get to snatch Fawad Jahandar in Goa as we planned to, which means we don't have the other half of the CIED device. And we also don't know where Nigel McMahon is either, whose voice we need to activate the two halves when brought together."

Zang spoke up. "Well, then you are fucked, aren't you, Karson?"

The former special forces major remained calm and in control and didn't react with any emotion to Zang's outburst. "Not exactly. You see, Zang, I know Pierce had a conversation with Jahandar just before we showed up." He turned to Pierce. "We know because we spotted you with one of our drones, jumping off his yacht just before Jahandar's kidnappers shot the boat to pieces."

"He didn't tell me anything, Karson."

The major raised an eyebrow, then raised his Glock and pointed it at Pierce. "You sure about that? You willing to bet a life on that?"

Pierce felt his gut tighten and the world shrink around him. He couldn't speak.

"You don't think I'm serious. I'm very serious, and to prove it to you, I'm going to kill one of these very lovely ladies right now, right in front of your eyes."

For a long count of seconds, nobody moved, and nobody said anything. The only noise was Roshini Jahandar quietly sobbing, and the distance sea waves crashing on a nearby beach.

"I don't need both of them."

Pierce had no time to think or react.

Karson lifted his pistol and, with a casual, aimed shot, blew out Roshini's brain and skull matter.

44

Pierce was overcome with dizziness and almost collapsed onto his knees, for he was not prepared for Roshini's sudden and brutal execution, and he only remained upright because Suwan and another of Karson's Executive Believers kept Pierce immobile on his feet. Somewhere, off to his right, Pierce heard a soldier throw up. He must have also been shocked at the raw display of the unjustified killing. Then Pierce realised that the vomiting man was Jay Sanders.

Pierce glanced at Zang. She too had lost her colour and could only stare at the scene with a vacant, detached demeanour that suggested she was losing her mind as fast as he was.

As Roshini's lifeless and crumpled body bled out in the crimson-soaked patch of grass where she had fallen, Karson stepped over her and approached Zang. While Captain Keng and another soldier kept the CIA operator immobile, Karson forcibly lifted her bound hands and pressed the muzzle of his pistol into her left palm. "Pierce, I won't kill this one so quickly. It will take time. Hours, probably."

"Wait!" Pierce called out.

"For fuck's sake!" Zang shouted too as she wrestled her minders and tried to strike Karson across the head with her bound hands. The major ducked easily, but then Zang rushed him a second time, which forced him to press his pistol against her chest.

A kill shot.

"Do it, you asshole!"

Pierce fought the soldiers holding him, which now numbered four and still included Suwan. He was powerless to resist their combined strength, which far outpowered his own capabilities.

Calm still, despite the chaos and tension erupting around him, Karson now played with his weapon, tracing a line with its muzzle across Zang's restrained body, passing over her collarbone, then a breast and finally drawing an invisible line along her right arm. "By all means, Pierce, keep saying nothing, and I will eventually shoot her somewhere where it hurts, bad."

"Okay!" shouted Pierce, knowing that he was beat. There was no part of him that would allow Rachel Zang to be tortured while he could do something about it. "Al-Qaeda have Jahandar. I'd already dealt with Pakistani intelligence before you showed up."

Karson didn't look at Pierce. He kept tracing the path of the pistol along Zang's struggling body. Now he pointed the lethal end at Zang's hip, where Pierce knew she carried scars from an old bullet wound. "That still doesn't tell me where they took Fawad Jahandar and the CIED device."

"Don't tell him, Pierce!" Zang screamed. "If you don't tell him, he loses."

The weapon fired, and for a second, Pierce thought Karson had shattered Zang's hip.

But she remained standing, and the blankness on her face and listlessness in her eyes suggested she was now fighting her body to avoid going into shock. He realised she had lost the ability to speak.

But Pierce hadn't.

Knowing that what he was about to say would cost them both their lives in the coming minutes, but this was a better alternative to suffering the brutal tortures neither of them had the will to resist, Pierce blurted out what he knew. "Kaajal Khan has him."

"I already know that, Pierce!" Karson pointed the weapon at Zang again, now covering her lower belly, where a bullet would rupture her intestines and result in a painful and protracted death.

"Karson! Listen to me. Jahandar only told me that Kaajal's stronghold is within the Lower Chitral District. In the Hindu Kush mountains at the juncture of the Solangi and Jakhro Rivers. That's it, that's all I know. But it's enough for you to find him."

Karson paused as he considered this information, then turned casually towards Jay Sanders, who was only just recovering from puking up his last meal, and said, "Did you hear that, Sanders?"

Sanders made a gurgling noise, then replied more cohesively with, "Yes, sir."

"Then get onto it. You're my intelligence executive. Confirm what Pierce just said is the truth."

Sanders nodded, then marched with haste towards one of the transportable huts near the satellite dishes. All Pierce cared about for the moment was that Karson no longer chillingly caressed Zang with his Glock.

When Karson noticed all his mercenaries were silently standing to attention, many of them pale faced and profusely sweating, he waved them into action. "Take the prisoners to the pits. Tie them together."

"Yes, sir!" said Staff Sergeant Kwang Suwan with an enthusiasm Pierce didn't sense in anyone else. She pointed to Roshini's corpse, unmoving in the sun where she had fallen. "What about her, sir?"

Karson scanned the island until he spotted something of interest to him. Pierce followed his eyes until he too spied what the Black Dog saw, a gigantic lizard lumbering across the runway, legs swaying from side to side as its powerful tail swished effortlessly behind it. Pierce recognised it immediately as a Komodo dragon.

As it got closer, it seemed unperturbed by the humans as its forked tongue tasted the air. Perhaps it had smelled blood, because it moved in a direct line towards Roshini's corpse. With a sickening knot in his stomach and his throat constricting, Pierce knew that Karson was about to allow this reptile to feed upon the dead woman's flesh.

Karson caught Pierce staring. "You've guessed correctly. The Komodo dragons will eat her. There will be more than just this one soon, and they will fight over her as they tear her flesh to pieces. It's quite a sight to watch, and when it is over, there will be nothing left of her."

Pierce shook his head. "You know, Karson, I'm starting to think you are a lot like the Komodo dragons in that you don't have any real feelings at all. That they never existed in the first place."

Karson said nothing, staring not at Pierce but through him, like he didn't exist. "Take them away. We have work to do."

45

Twenty minutes later, Pierce and Zang were bound together by a three-metre chain threaded at the ends through their respective handcuffs. The chain itself passed through a metallic O-shaped ring on top of a rusted metal pole two and a half metres tall. The pole was positioned in the centre of a large circular concrete pit, about thirty metres across, encircled by three-metre-high concrete walls. They had entered the pit via a ladder, which still rested against the concrete wall. The only entry points were culverts equally spaced in four corners that were each half a metre high by a metre wide. Pierce didn't think these were for drainage anymore, as what they were originally designed for. They were now there to allow Komodo dragons free access in and out of these death pits. The various masses of squished horns, hair and teeth known as gastric pellets discarded throughout the pit confirmed Pierce's fears, and the horns suggested that these reptiles thankfully fed on goats and deer more often than they did upon humans who displeased Karson.

Four of Karson's mercenaries had watched over Pierce and Zang during the lengthy period it had taken to get them both secure in this elaborate prison, and their well-aimed M4 carbines meant there had been no chance to fight back. Their efficiency in the process suggested this was not the first time human prisoners had been left here to die, and when the mercenaries were done with their work, each man climbed out of the pit and disappeared to undertake other duties. Or perhaps they didn't have the stomach to watch Zang and Pierce's slow demises as they were eaten alive by prehistoric-appearing reptiles, judging by their earlier sickened expressions when Roshini had been snacked up; they just wanted to get away.

Only Staff Sergeant Suwan stayed. She now stood three metres beyond Zang and Pierce's reach. When Pierce re-examined the dragon tattoos covering her exposed arms, he started to see them not as Chinese mythological symbols of power, good luck and strength, but as stylised representations of the Komodo dragons themselves.

Zang sneered at the kickboxing champion. "Turns you on, does it, Suwan? Watching like this?"

Suwan shrugged. "I don't really care what happens to either of you. Both of you represent the worst of what our government has become. You deserve to die like this."

Pierce interjected before Zang could reply, "I take it the US military did you wrong too?"

"You could say that."

"Like everyone else here? You've all been broken by the system. What are the odds of, hey, all you misfits all ending up here together?"

This comment caused her to pause and consider his words.

"What was it? Bullying? PTSD? So-called vitamin supplements they gave you that drove you mad? A dishonourable discharge?"

"It doesn't matter what happened to me. All you have to know is that Karson looks after us when no one else will. That's why we're a family, and why you two will forever be nothing more than clone troopers."

Zang laughed. "Suwan, you're all insane. This is not a family. It's a cult, and Karson is the psychopathic pseudo guru who's got you all believing his fucked-up bullshit!"

"You wouldn't understand!"

"No, you're right there."

Suwan was about to retort when Karson and Sanders appeared at the lip of the concrete ledge, near where the ladder remained in position. First Karson, then Sanders descended and joined Suwan, to admire their handiwork, the two barefooted CIA paramilitary operators stripped down to pants and a T-shirt each, chained together and about to die, as if they were gladiators preparing to do battle in an ancient Roman colosseum merely to entertain mad emperors and their subjugated cohorts.

As Pierce watched his three enemies stand together in a row, he realised he didn't have a plan on how to get out of this one. With criminals and terrorists, often they were never smart enough to think through everything that could go wrong in a scenario, allowing Pierce the opportunity to chip away until he found a flaw in their schemes he could exploit. But Karson, Sanders and Suwan were all US military trained as he and Zang were, and by design, none of them made idiotic decisions.

Except that Karson was a psychopath who enjoyed watching other humans suffer, and that was an aspect of this fucked-up scenario Pierce might be able to leverage. Karson should have just shot Pierce and Zang in the back of their heads and been done with them, because while they still lived, they still had a chance to escape. Instead, he would torture them first in the most elaborate means his mind could imagine, just for the kick he'd get out of it.

Pierce said, "You know, I've been thinking about you lately, Karson, and now I think I understand you."

Karson was impassive as he said, "Your intel checks out. We hacked into viable satellite feeds and leveraged our contact networks. It does seem Kaajal Khan is where you said he would be. Which means I'll find McMahon, Jahandar and the CIED device all in this one location, when the last two arrive."

"I'm happy for you."

"That also means I don't need you anymore."

"Well, to be fair, Karson, I never needed you."

From behind Pierce, Zang laughed at his joke, genuinely amused.

Pierce talked on. "I think your problem, Karson, is you don't understand how to fit in with normal people, and it bothers you. It's a problem because you pathologically constantly need people around you who express their love and adoration of you, whom you can manipulate to do the craziest of things, because it's the only aspect of your miserable life that gets you off."

Karson drew his Glock and pointed it at Pierce's head, aimed right between Pierce's eyeballs.

Despite the sweat rushing off Pierce and the trembles in his legs and hands, he kept his cool and kept talking. "I think the only way you believe you can relate to other people is through shared trauma. It wasn't an al-Qaeda terror cell that killed your wife and kid, was it? I'm almost one hundred per cent certain now that you murdered them yourself, because it was the story you needed to unite you with all these other misfits you've surrounded yourself with. Because genuine emotional connectivity just doesn't cut it with you, not with your long list of mental failings."

Finally, a crack appeared in Karson's expression as rage simmered just beneath the surface of his quaking skin. Without conscious thought, Karson marched fast towards Pierce until he was almost close enough to press the barrel of his pistol into Pierce's forehead.

Then he stopped, paused, and recovered himself. "A clever play, tricking me into wanting to kill you quickly, Pierce, but one that ultimately failed." A smile spread across his lips, but never reached his eyes. "Do you know the origins of these concrete pits?"

Pierce shrugged.

"The Japanese used them during the Second World War to torture their prisoners. They had a rather ingenious trick whereby those who displeased them would be bound and knotted in ropes in such a manner that, every time they struggled, the cords would gradually tighten. Some prisoners would take days to die as the ropes slowly strangled them."

"Only you would relish a fact like that, Karson."

Karson held Pierce's stare. "I thought about roping you. But I went to a lot of effort to populate this island with Komodo dragons stolen from nearby Komodo Island. So I think I'll leave you to my dragons after all, as that will be less pleasant for you both. I'd hang around to watch if I could, of course, but I've got a huge paycheque I need to collect." He holstered the weapon, and then in a surprisingly fast strike, he pulled a knife and slashed the blade across Pierce's forearm.

Pierce stepped back, more from shock than because of the wound. It was a superficial cut and not at all life threatening or in need of serious treatment, but it still bled.

"Now let me tell you what your problem is, Pierce, and hers too," he said as he nodded towards Zang still standing just behind Pierce and to his left. "Komodo dragons can smell blood from the other side of the island. There are hundreds of these critters on Kadal Beracun, and they'll all now be converging on you. Only a few were lucky enough to feast upon Jahandar's wife because Komodo dragons don't share, they fight over the spoils. Most of my dragons are still very hungry."

"You got a point there?" Zang said, speaking up from behind Pierce.

"I do, Zang, and the point is this. These dragons, when they bite you, they'll inject their own brand of poison into your flesh. The first bite won't kill you, and neither will the second or third or fourth or even the twentieth bite. That's because they know their poison stops your blood from clotting, so any wound they inflict upon you as they tear your flesh to pieces won't ever stop bleeding. Second, the poison causes your flesh to rot while you are still alive. Rotting flesh is easier for them to digest. Think about that in the coming hours, because that's all the time I estimate you both have left to you, as my dragons play with their food before they eat it." When neither Pierce nor Zang answered him, his eyes became colder still. "Don't think I won't enjoy this. I have cameras everywhere, so I can watch your demise on live stream."

Pierce forced a laugh. "See, I was right, you're a

psychopath who gets off on all the wrong things in this world."

Karson shrugged, then turned to his two senior operators. "Master Sergeant, stay here and keep an eye on them. They are trouble, so if they look like they might escape, shoot them. Otherwise, let our cold-blooded island friends do their work."

The former Thai kickboxer snapped off a smart salute. "Yes, sir."

Now Karson turned to Sanders. "You, Lieutenant, on the other hand, are coming with me, as are alpha and beta squads. I can't trust you with Zang. I've seen how you've watched her."

Pierce noticed the redness around Sanders's eyes and how puffy his face had become. When he answered Karson, there was a croak in his voice. "Yes, sir. I understand."

"Good. I'll give you your one minute with Zang to say your goodbyes; then get your arse onto that plane. Wheels up within the next ten minutes."

46

W ith blood still dripping from the cut in his arm, Pierce watched with interest as Jay Sanders ignored him and marched up close to Rachel Zang. They locked eyes, both pairs of which were bloodshot as if they had each cried earlier. Then Pierce saw the pain they both expressed, and understood they were close, likely lovers.

Pierce didn't know how he felt about this revelation in the moment. Zang and he were by no means exclusive, and they had each certainly slept with other individuals during the last six months they had known each other, but that didn't mean Pierce's emotional responses weren't flaring right now; they were. He just didn't understand what exactly he felt in the moment.

But he did know he was curious, so he watched as Zang and Sanders stood less than half a metre apart and stared deeply into each other's eyes.

Then Sanders rushed her, grabbed Zang by the waist with one hand as the other slapped her hard across the face.

Zang recoiled only for a second, expressing surprise and shock at his violent outburst. Then she punched him, harder than he had hit her, and the force of her blow sent him staggering backwards.

When Sanders recovered his footing, he touched his mouth to discover blood on his lips. He shook his head as he looked to his former lover again. "Rachel Zang. I thought you were smarter than this. You could have been standing at my side, getting rich like the rest of us. Instead..." He didn't say any more. He spat the blood pooling in his mouth at her, missed and instead hit the dirt and concrete near Zang's feet.

Zang tugged on the chain as she rushed at Sanders again. The other end, however, was looped through the metal pole and remained attached to Pierce, and he felt the force pulling him back. So he stepped backwards, giving Zang more of the chain and more room to manoeuvre. But the distance wasn't enough, even with his offering, for she still couldn't reach Sanders.

"I don't know what I ever saw in you, Sanders. Once I thought it was a 'good man', but that doesn't exist in you anymore, does it? Or it never did."

Sanders didn't answer.

Brad Karson, who watched and expressed amusement at the spectacle, made a helicopter motion with his hand. "Okay, lovers' tiff is over. Time to move out."

Pierce watched Zang as she watched Sanders and Karson climb up out of the concrete pit and then disappear.

Only Suwan remained behind, to stand on the lip of the concrete wall with her M4 carbine at the ready, watching Pierce and Zang tug at the handcuffs and linking chain binding them together and to the metal pole. Perhaps she watched to ensure they couldn't break free of it. Or she might be waiting for the Komodo dragons to appear in the concrete culverts, ready to tear chunks of flesh off Pierce and Zang, to eat them slowly, thereby offering a protracted and painful death.

"What are you looking at?" Zang shouted up at Suwan when she had stood there for several minutes without moving. "You into torture porn like your sick boss?"

Suwan didn't answer, because they all heard the noise of an aircraft taxiing, then lifting off from the runway.

A minute later, they all saw the AN-32 turning in a wide circle in the air above them. Then it disappeared, headed northwest and destined for Pakistan.

When the air was empty of aircraft again, Suwan turned her attention back to Pierce and Zang. "Seems you have a reprieve for the moment. The only Komodos I can see in the vicinity are snacking on your dead girlfriend. But some of them are going hungry. Like the boss said, bigger Komodos don't like to share with the smaller ones."

Pierce tensed as his nostrils flared, but he kept his cool and didn't respond to her verbal taunts. He needed to focus on his current predicament and how to escape, but so far, he had no ideas on how to achieve this.

But Zang wasn't so restrained. "Suwan, you bitch! I promise you I will kill you. You hear me?"

Suwan laughed, then turned to leave. "I'll come back later, when the Komodos sniff out where you are." Then she disappeared.

Pierce moved immediately. He gripped the metal pole embedded firmly in the concrete slab under their feet and pulled on it with all his strength. But the engineering was too good, for the pole gave no sway, no matter how fast Pierce pulled at it.

As more blood dripped from his open wound, he turned to Zang. Her eyes were darting everywhere, searching for a tool or weapon they could use.

Pierce asked, "What's the story with you and Sanders?"

Zang shrugged but wouldn't turn to look at Pierce, not even fleetingly. "It's none of your business."

"Maybe, except where it affects your and my chances of getting out of here alive."

Now she did turn to Pierce, and he looked at her properly. Pierce considered Zang one of the most beautiful people he had ever seen, with long slender but muscular limbs, a lithe body with the grace of a cat, and emerald-green eyes that sometimes didn't look real. But now, with her covered in dirt and her few remaining clothes tattered and scuffed like his own, her eyes bloodshot and her skin lined with the bruises and cuts from recent wounds, all he saw in her was a friend and a peer whom he needed to work with so they could both walk away from this situation unharmed.

Zang said, "You should have let Karson kill me. He would have. I was baiting him into doing it."

Pierce shook his head. "Karson's a psychopath. He wanted to hurt you, badly. And he wanted to hurt me too, knowing..."

"That's not good enough, Pierce. We can't let the data on the CIED device get out, and you told him exactly where it is!"

Pierce opened his mouth to answer. He wanted to tell her he had done what he had done because he cared too much about her to let her suffer through horrendous tortures.

"You could have baited him into killing you too."

Pierce stiffened and stood taller. "I disagree. He's in too much control to allow that. We would have both been tortured, and I would have given up Kaajal Khan's location eventually. I wasn't willing—"

Zang interrupted, "Well, I would have let you die horribly if our positions were reversed."

Pierce nodded. "I know, but you weren't tortured for seven months straight in an African warlord camp. Have you ever been tortured in the field before, by the enemy, Zang?"

He saw that she was about to argue, when her face softened. Zang had been there for him after Pierce had escaped his African torturers. She had seen first-hand the damage his captors had caused him. "Pierce, I'm sorry. You're right, I haven't been through anything like what you have suffered. I'm just angry that Sanders got the better of me."

Pierce nodded. "Understandable. But right now, we need to get out of here." He pointed to the culvert behind Zang's back, where he spotted the approach of a lumbering Komodo dragon, its fork tongue tasting the air. Pierce remembered the cut on his arm where Karson had sliced him. It still oozed blood. The Komodo dragon was tasting him. "Do you have a plan, because I don't have anything good?"

Zang nodded and stepped next to him. When they were closer together, she revealed a hacksaw blade hidden under her T-shirt. She showed him at close proximity because of the cameras Karson had mentioned he had installed to watch the spectacle.

"How did you get that?"

"Sanders slipped it to me, just before."

Pierce felt his eyebrows rise. "So he's not all bad?"

"Maybe, but we're no longer friends. And never again one with benefits. Make yourself useful, Pierce, and hold off that Komodo while I get us out of this chain."

47

Pierce spotted not one but two Komodo dragons exiting the culverts and approaching him and Zang. They weren't moving fast, rather they were taking their time to assess their surroundings, taste the air and otherwise bask in the hot sun. But their lethargy could change at any moment.

Pierce attempted to get a measure of them both. One was about a metre and a half in length and perhaps sixty kilograms, the other two metres and perhaps eighty kilograms. The larger one was the same size as him, but it had sharp claws on four feet, a large powerful mouth full of teeth perfected for both tearing to shreds and poisoning its prey, and these creatures weren't chained and immobile like Zang and he were.

Behind him, he heard Zang cutting at the chain. If she could break just one link, they could uncouple themselves from the pole and each other, allowing them to flee this pit, but he didn't believe she'd get through before one or both of the Komodo dragons struck at him.

Zang grunted.

"How are you going back there?"

"It's not working. The chain's metal is too strong for the hacksaw. I'm just blunting it."

Pierce scanned for the cameras hidden in the semi-tropical scrub above the lip of the encircling concrete walls, not seeing them but knowing they were there. It was only a matter of time before Suwan or anyone else in Karson's team spotted what Zang was up to, before sending men to take the blade from her. "What about the pole? Does the blade cut it?"

"Are you crazy? How does that help?"

"If you take it down, we can at least move." He pointed to a rubbish pile about eight metres beyond his reach. Even with Zang giving up all her length of chain to him, he knew he still couldn't reach what his eyes had just spotted there that might help them. "There is a long stick in that trash pile, about two metres long."

"Feet, Pierce! Tell me in feet. We're fucking Americans!"

Pierce nodded, realising that he always thought in metric, but that was not surprising considering where he had operated for almost all of his childhood and adult life: countries that weren't the United States. "Okay, six feet. It's cut with a Y-shape at the end. I'm guessing it's used to keep these dragons at a safe distance."

"How is that helpful?"

"If you cut down that pole, it will be!"

With each of their voices rising in response to the mounting tension they both felt, Zang spoke her next words at speed. "In the meantime, I see gastric pellets close enough to grab. You might find a weapon in one?"

"Roger that!"

His eyes searched until he spotted the nearest desiccated remains of a Komodo dragon's regurgitated stomach contents. It looked to include the horn of a goat, perhaps fifteen or twenty centimetres in length, so useful for attacking the dragons with strikes to their eyes and ears.

"Zang?"

"What is it?" She didn't cease her efforts to hack at the metal bar while she conversed, which Pierce was grateful for. "This is working, by the way."

"How long do you need?"

"Don't know. Fifteen, maybe twenty minutes."

"Great!" he said sarcastically. "Can you speed it up a bit?"

"If you are complaining, then you come and cut!"

"Fine by me, but that means you fight off the Komodos!"

Zang paused for a moment, then said, "No, you win in the awful jobs category. I'll cut faster."

Even ten minutes seemed too long, with the first dragon now strutting across the concrete towards Pierce, its flicking tongue tasting the scent of blood oozing from his still open wound. "Well, I need some slack on the chain if you want those fifteen minutes."

Zang turned to him; then her eyes widened when she saw how close the Komodo dragon had come in just a few minutes.

"There are two more entering from that culvert." Pierce pointed to the concrete structure that had been empty only seconds earlier. "Come on, give me some slack."

"Okay! Okay!" Zang shimmied up the pole until her chained wrist was close to the O-shaped ring, allowing the maximum extent of reach for their linking chain.

With more room to manoeuvre, Pierce stretched out for

the horn in the gastric pellet, but it was still thirty centimetres beyond his reach.

"Use your feet, Pierce!"

"You think I didn't think about that?" Pierce answered at the same time he switched tactics and stretched out his foot to hook the desiccated lump. The closest dragon, the one he estimated to be one and a half metres in length, was a mere two metres from him now. If it charged, Pierce was both too close and too low to the ground to feel that he had any chance of beating it off. He didn't want to suffer a bite, knowing that the poison would be horrific to his body even if he survived the attack.

"Pierce! You're running out of time."

He wanted to tell her to be quiet so he could concentrate. Instead, he blurted out, "Just give me a minute!"

The dragon had paused, watching him with its dead, black eyes. Its tongue kept flicking and flicking.

"Fuck!" Pierce exclaimed as he kicked out his left, bare foot, hooked a toe into the dried stomach contents and dragged it closer to him.

Then with no warning, the dragon took off, sprinting towards Pierce, its clawed legs flicking from side to side as its body wobbled and its mouth gaped open ready to consume him.

When the dragon was less than a metre from Pierce, his left hand was close enough to grab the horn. He snatched it up just as the dragon was upon him.

Pierce struck the creature multiple times in and around the head. Thankfully the many attempts made by the creature to bite Pierce had missed, while the horn mostly bounced off its chainmail-like hide. Then Pierce hit its eye, and the creature recoiled and lumbered backwards.

Pierce scrambled to his feet and moved backwards towards Zang.

With the pressure released on the chain, she dropped back to her feet and commenced with her cutting.

Pierce saw her act in his peripheral vision, but he was more interested in the four dragons, all of them out in the open, and all of them circling himself and Zang. At least he had the horn as a dagger, and the Komodo dragon he had attacked now bled from a hole where its eye had once been. Wounded, at least now he wasn't the only one giving off the scent of fresh blood. But Pierce also knew it had been as much luck as it had been skill that the dinosaur-like creature hadn't bitten him.

"Zang? Where are we at?"

"Working on it."

"Work on it faster. They're ganging up on me now!"

The three healthy dragons now circled near the edge of the concrete walls. Pierce couldn't sense if they were interested in him, the dragon he had wounded, or both. But whatever their intentions, there wasn't a lot he could do about it until they lunged at him.

"What do you know about Komodos that I don't?"

Zang made a snorting noise but, to her credit, didn't halt with her sawing as she answered him. "Sanders told me their poison prevents our blood from congealing. You get bitten, you'll just keep bleeding and bleeding."

"How does that help?"

"It helps by not letting them bite you."

"Wonderful!"

With the half-blinded dragon no longer seemingly interested in snacking on the humans because of its wound, Pierce chose to circle Zang, watching the other Komodos in turn as they lumbered closer, and tried to guess which one would come for them first. "Did your boyfriend tell you this before or after you broke up?"

"For fuck's sake, Pierce, get a grip."

"Me get a grip? You're not facing down what I'm dealing with here, Zang!"

"What the hell do you mean?"

"I just want to know if he was motivated in protecting or scaring you?"

"I was in a prison cell and handcuffed at the time, if that makes a difference?"

Pierce felt a tug on the chain, and when he glanced back at Zang, he noticed that she had dropped to one knee to get a better angle for hacksawing. He had thought of lunging again at the injured dragon, hoping to turn it into the preferable meal option instead of Zang and him, but now she was close to the ground, he didn't have enough length left in the chain to reach it.

"Zang!"

"Working on it! Okay?"

Then one of the four Komodo dragons rushed Pierce.

48

Pierce stood his ground, held the goat horn as he would a fighting knife, and waited until the creature was close enough to strike. He hoped to pull off the same trick twice, by blinding it, but this creature, which resembled some kind of dinosaur from prehistoric times, seemed bigger and more powerful than him, and it wouldn't be a fair fight.

And then by lucky chance, the wounded Komodo wandered into its bigger brethren's path.

The two reptiles collided, and soon they were fighting, with jaws snapping and claws flailing everywhere. The bigger beast was winning, as it tore a chunk of flesh from the smaller Komodo's shoulder.

"Fuck!" said Pierce to no one, appreciating that instead of the half-blinded Komodo, it could have easily been him that was the bigger creature's snack in that moment.

"What's going on?"

"Just keep sawing. You'll know when this becomes a

problem you'll have to deal with, because the chain will go slack."

Zang didn't answer, and he hoped she didn't see what happened next, because the larger Komodo had its mouth around the head of the half-blinded creature, pinning it down. Then the smaller head disappeared inside the wide, gaping mouth of the larger predator. To Pierce's disgust, he realised the larger Komodo dragon was trying to eat the second creature whole.

This caused a flurry of action from the two remaining dragons, not as large as the first two. They descended upon the tail and back legs of the presumably suffocating dragon now swallowed up to its throat.

Pierce then heard the noise of bones breaking. Presumably, the larger dragon's jawbones crushed the vertebrae of the partially eaten reptile, and the latter creature ceased struggling.

But this didn't soften the fury erupting around the creatures. The jaw of one smaller dragon now tore off a leg, while another opened the skin around the lower intestines and dragged the long organs out, then into its throat.

Pierce felt queasy at the thought this was still a possible end for him and Zang, but for the moment, the animals seemed more interested in feasting on a lifeless meal than on them, so they had a second reprieve.

The scent of the blood and faecal matter became overwhelming, ejected from the dead animal, and Pierce knew those smells would now be drawing further dragons to this location.

He turned to Zang, to find her still furiously hacking through the metal pole.

"Hold on!" Pierce said as he stepped up to her. "I have an idea."

"Yeah, it'd better be a good one."

"It is."

Zang had cut halfway through the pole, so Pierce climbed up it, then yanked on it several times until the pole snapped and came crashing down onto the concrete with him.

"Pierce!" Zang screamed behind him.

He turned just in time to see a new Komodo dragon rushing him.

Pierce swung the pole, collecting the creature in the head with enough force to snap its neck and kill it.

"You know these are an endangered species, right?"

"So are we, Zang, if we don't get out of here right now!"

Finally, they had a weapon that was effective against these predatory reptiles, but it was heavy, and their ability to use it was limited by the length of the three-metre chain still linking him and Zang and the pole into a single connected unit. He looked at the concrete wall encircling them, and knew they weren't free yet. "Zang, we've got to get out of this pit!"

"I have an idea. Follow me, and swing that at anything that gets too close."

"Didn't you just say you wanted to protect these cute little animals?"

"Can't you tell when I'm being sarcastic?"

"No. But a phrase related to pot, kettle, kettle, pot springs to mind."

Pierce and Zang moved with haste to the concrete wall. With it being three metres high, Pierce could potentially make a run up the wall and pull himself up the length under normal circumstances, but not while encumbered with the pole, chain and Zang. Then he had an idea. "I'll lift you up; then you take up the pole."

"Okay!"

Pierce linked his hands together, making a step, which Zang then used to catapult herself up and over the lip.

"Any threats up there?"

She glanced around, then shook her head. "Negative. Pass me the pole."

Pierce slid it up the chain at the same time he noticed that the two smaller Komodo dragons had given up fighting the largest creature, which by now had swallowed most of the dead dragon. Therefore, it seemed the smaller dragons had decided Pierce was their next best option as a target, and now advanced on him.

"I can make a run up! You pull me up."

Zang shook her head. "I can't, not with the lack of give in the chain. Oh fuck, Pierce! Behind you."

The first of the two Komodo dragons rushed at Pierce. He only had a second to spare to get out of its way as its head crashed into the concrete wall.

Without conscious thought, Pierce leapt onto its back, then used its height to propel him further up the concrete wall. His fingers caught on the lip, and with a skill and power he never knew he possessed, Pierce was up and out of the pit in seconds.

49

Mark Pierce counted until he had sucked in ten deep and desperately needed lungfuls of air, and then he was on his feet.

A second later, an equally out of breath Zang also clambered to her feet to stand next to him.

Together, they scanned the semi-tropical scrub that grew close to the three concrete pits on the side they had scrambled up, and then across the pit to where the camp and runway lay.

Zang shielded her eyes as she scanned the facility. "I can't see anyone. You think they all left for the Hindu Kush?"

Pierce did a quick mental calculation. "If I remember correctly, an Antonov AN-32 can carry up to forty fully equipped troops, and with four crew to pilot it, that could mean everyone is gone."

Zang nodded. "Well, we know Suwan at least is here, and my guess is so is Captain Gang Keng."

"Who is Keng?"

"Ex-Republic of Singapore Air Force. I'll tell you more later."

Pierce nodded. "We should keep moving, get this chain and pole removed, and find kit and weapons."

"Best plan you've come up with yet."

Pierce shook his head and said nothing.

Still chained together, they stealthily advanced on the rows of transportable containers, with Pierce carrying the length of pole.

The first container they looked inside was a mechanical workshop.

Before either of them stepped inside, Pierce glanced around the rest of the camp, wondering why no one had come for them yet. Perhaps Suwan, Keng and any others still here had no appetite for watching two humans be torn into meaty pieces by the roaming dragons, so weren't watching the video feeds while assuming Pierce and Zang would not escape their fate. This suited Pierce, but he didn't like how quiet everything was. He couldn't even see Komodo dragons sauntering around the camp. "Hey, Zang, you go in and look while I'll wait out here."

"Why?"

"Because these containers lock from the outside. One of us needs to protect the exit, and I'm holding the pole."

She chuckled. "Makes sense."

Zang was only inside a minute when she spoke back in the same quiet voice they had been using, "There's a vice here. We could use that to snap off the ring at the end of the pole."

"Okay!" Pierce passed her the pole, and she tightened the vice grip around the ring. Then Pierce turned the pole from side to side, loosening the metal. "Who is Keng?"

Zang now kept watch from the door of the container while Pierce worked. "I didn't recognise him until Karson said his name earlier. Captain Gang Keng is ex-Republic of Singapore Air Force. RSAF. If I remember correctly, he was the former base logistics and maintenance leader of their Tengah Air Base."

"So now he's running logistics here on Kadal Beracun for Executive Believers?"

"Makes sense. More so when I remembered a file that I'd seen on him. He was kicked out of the RSAF after thirty years of exemplary service, when he got into gambling debts with the Singaporean Triads and then almost beat to death three teenage enforcers sent to collect his debt."

"Fits the profile. Another disenfranchised soldier drawn to the Karson cause." Pierce felt the O-ring weaken, then snap. The three-metre chain still linked them together, but at least the unwieldy pole was no longer a hinderance. Lowering it carefully to the floor so it wouldn't make a sound, he searched the tool inventories until he found a crowbar about half a metre in length.

"What's your weapon of choice?" he said, calling back to Zang as he tested the weight of the makeshift fighting stick in his hand.

"Let me look."

They changed places, and she soon found a wooden pole about three centimetres thick and two metres long. Pierce gave her a quizzical look when she stepped out carrying a weapon he had not expected.

"It's my makeshift version of a bō fighting stick." When he didn't answer her, she said, "I've trained in Bojutsu. You heard of that?"

He nodded. "Just, not what I expected."

She frowned. "What did you expect, then? A samurai sword? A ray gun?"

He shrugged. "I don't really know."

"Women aren't as physically strong as men, no matter how hard I train or perfect my martial skills. Therefore, I choose weapons that give me an advantage over big, muscular men like you."

"Not arguing with you." Now he grinned. "But part of me wants to see you fight with that."

Her frown deepened. "Keep your mind on the mission, Pierce. We aren't out of this one yet."

Pierce smirked before they both moved off again at stealth, sneakily looking into each container before moving on to the next.

Suddenly, at the eighth container, the metal around them pinged as dozens of bullets ricocheted off the steel fabricated walls.

In response, Pierce ducked, inadvertently yanking Zang back with him because of the chain still connecting them.

"Be careful!" she exclaimed as she ducked down close to him, behind the side of the container and out of the line of sight of their attackers.

"Yeah? I might have just saved your life?"

"Then it's business as usual all over again. I'll no doubt save yours in a minute. Shall we start counting?" She waited for a lull in the shooting, then sprinted for the adjacent container to the one they hid behind. But she didn't get far before the chain pulled on her, and with Pierce carrying far more bulk and muscle mass than she did in her slender figure, despite her toned physique, it was Zang who landed on her arse, not him. "Fucking hell!" she exclaimed as she scampered back to Pierce while he dragged her closer.

The shooting started up again, and they were back where they started.

"Why didn't you follow?"

"Why didn't you tell me you were moving?"

"My God! You should have anticipated that!"

"That's settled! One of us is team leader, and—"

More intense shooting drowned out their arguing. Pierce sensed it was coming from two directions now, as Karson's mercenaries must have moved into new positions to flank them.

"And that's me, Pierce. You follow my orders, soldier!"

Pierce was about to argue with her, but figured she had as much right to that title as he did. "On your count, then, we move."

All the muscles in Zang's face tightened. "Yes! Exactly! Now shut your mouth and on the count of—"

"Three!"

They sprinted together at the same moment several Executive Believers mercenaries turned the corner behind them and opened fire. Zang and Pierce barely evaded the next volley of projectiles set on butchering their bodies with meaty holes.

At the next container, Pierce halted and readied his crowbar to smash the first soldier to come around the corner. "What are you waiting for, Zang? Open it! Look inside!"

"That's what I'm damn well doing!"

Pierce glanced back at her momentarily, saw her struggling with the lever mechanism. "Swap?" he said, holding the crowbar out to her.

She glanced at it only momentarily before she snatched the crowbar and flung the bō stick to Pierce. He caught it nimbly at the same moment she shouted, "Behind you!"

Pierce turned and smashed the first mercenary across the head, breaking the man's jaw and sending blood and teeth flying. In less than a second, he switched direction and whacked the stick into his foe's grip on his M4, breaking finger bones.

A second merc was racing behind the first, raising his weapon to shoot Pierce.

Pierce pivoted the stunned and wounded first foe in front of him to act as a shield. The mercenary took about five bullets in his chest rig, but a few got through the gaps because he was instantly spewing up a bucket's worth of blood. In the same second, Pierce slipped his finger into the trigger guard of the dead man's M4 and returned fire, cutting a crimson line of five-five-six bullets through his neck that half severed it.

The foe acting as Pierce's body shield struggled, but weakly. He was bleeding out, but Pierce twisted his neck sharply anyway until it snapped, thereby putting him out of his misery.

"I have weapons," he said casually without looking back at Zang, knowing that more mercs could be coming around the corner of the container at any moment.

"So do I."

She stepped around him with a Mk 153 shoulder-launched multipurpose assault weapon, more often referred to as a SMAW. It was a rocket launcher used to destroy bunkers and other fortifications. Pierce turned the corner with her and watched as she fired the 4.5-kilogram rocket into a group of mercs advancing towards them. They were too late to escape her fury, as the rocket burned past their congregation and hit a container behind them.

While Pierce had been careful not to stand in the back-blast of the SMAW, the power of the rocket was devastatingly impressive, disintegrating the container it hit, then engulfing the mercenaries in an outrushing of hellish flames. The shock front then hit Zang and Pierce, throwing them from their feet and sending them tumbling together across the grass and lower subtropical scrub encroaching upon the base.

As they tumbled and rolled, Pierce marvelled that they didn't break wrists or arms with their still linking chain pulling them in unnatural directions.

Seconds later, when they came to a standstill, Pierce and Zang sat in the grass and dirt as dust and ashes settled on and around them. They both turned and examined the field of devastation. The rocket had destroyed at least four containers, if not more. The fireball generated by the explosives still burned like a rocket flame from the container it had directly hit, and also sent a thick black trail of smoke into the otherwise clear sky. They were lucky the munitions store they had stumbled upon hadn't fuelled the flames and destructed with it.

"Fuck, Zang! I think that might have been a thermobaric rocket. The type our marines used in Afghanistan to collapse entire buildings."

She was already clambering to her feet and then scooped up their two fallen M4s and threw one to Pierce, which he snatched from the air.

When she noticed he was still on his haunches, she frowned again. "Are you hurt? I mean, I only care if you are badly hurt."

He snorted a laugh. "Well, in that case, no."

Pierce leapt to his feet and ensured his M4 was locked and loaded.

"Come on, Trigger Man. I still haven't seen Suwan and Keng. This day isn't yet over."

"First, let me arm up further."

50

The munitions container included a variety of weapons and gear that brought a smile to Pierce's face. First, he used a bolt cutter he found to shear the chain from both their manacles. Then, while taking it in turns with Zang to cover the entrance, they each slipped on tactical boots, plate carriers and combat rigs, armed themselves with fresh M4 carbines and Beretta M9 semi-automatic pistols, and Ka-Bar fighting knives. Zang looked over the SMAW positioned by the door where she had dropped it, biting on her lower lip as she presumably considered how she could still use it.

Pierce laughed at her. "If you take it, you're carrying your own rockets." He passed her a box of fragmentation grenades. "These are just as good."

"Thanks." She slipped four into independent grenade slots on her chest rig.

Pierce did the same.

When he didn't move because his mind was wandering, she frowned again. "What's up?"

"Nothing. You're team leader. I'm following your instructions."

"Smart arse."

She was out the door of the container, and Pierce followed her, gripping her shoulder each time he came up behind her to let her know he was there. He kept checking their rear while she concentrated on forward threats. They'd passed through the container array and into the bungalow huts, but still hadn't encountered any further resistance.

"We'll head for the communications room and call in," said Zang. "If we can get word to Langley before Karson lands in Pakistan, a US Navy cruiser or sub might be able to shoot them down. Or a fighter jet out of Guam's Andersen Air Force Base would be just as effective." She moved again, M4 carbine out in front and covering all corners as they advanced. "We only need to take out one half of the CIED device to end this once and for all. And you and I both know Karson has his half with him on the AN-32."

When Pierce caught up to her, he placed his hand again on her shoulder. "What about Jay Sanders?"

"What about him?" she answered with a snarl.

"You were...?"

"Lovers?"

"Yeah? I just thought it would be a difficult choice for me to make if I had to. To take him out like that."

Zang made a snorting noise as she moved again. "You mean, like if it were me up there, you'd hesitate? Like you hesitated earlier, trying to convince Karson not to kill me outright?"

Still not seeing any threats, Pierce said, "Yeah. If it were you, I'd be having second thoughts about shooting you down right about now."

"I'm not a traitor, Pierce, so it's not something you'll ever need to worry about. But if for some bizarre reason I become one, I give you permission to kill me however you see fit to do so."

Now Pierce frowned. He remembered an intimate conversation they'd shared back in Florida, where she had opened up to him about her troubled relationship with her father and the sadness that she had felt at the loss of her mother to suicide. There had been tears and hugs and expressions of real emotions, but that version of Rachel Zang was non-existent in the woman he followed now.

"Noted, Zang. Just so we're clear, that's all."

"We don't need this conver—"

She didn't have time to finish her sentence as another shock front threw them off their feet and sent them tumbling across the dust and green patches of vegetation again. The satellite dishes, radio communication towers and the fuel tanks had simultaneously detonated, transforming the landscape into further rubble and debris with a second furious fireball.

When Pierce ceased rolling in the billowing dust clouds, with his ears ringing and one side of his face hot from where the blast had hit him head-on, he finally regathered his strength and coordination, stood, then helped pull Zang up onto her feet as well.

In the distance, they spotted the HondaJet accelerating for take-off on the twelve-hundred-metre runway.

Screwing her face tight and clenching down on her teeth, Zang fired her M4 until she emptied the magazine. Her efforts were futile, as the business jet was already too far beyond effective range and getting further from them by the second.

"Fuck!" Zang exclaimed. "I could have flown us out on that!"

Pierce shrugged. "That's got to be Captain Keng in the pilot's seat, and I'd put money that Sergeant Suwan is with him."

"Why would they run and destroy their base? Their odds of taking us out two on two, if that is what their number had reduced to, weren't insurmountable?"

As the HondaJet got smaller on the horizon and was now rising above the clear blue tropical seas, Pierce shielded his eyes and looked for other aircraft. "Perhaps the US Air Force or Navy is already on its way here, and Keng knows it."

"They'll be headed for the Hindu Kush, no doubt."

Pierce nodded. "That's where the money is."

Zang stormed in a circle. Her anger was written over every centimetre of her body, and Pierce could guess why. Regardless of what she had said about Jay Sanders, his betrayal had cut her deep, whereas the only emotions Pierce was grappling with in this situation were Roshini Jahandar's unnecessary and tragic death and his inner reconciliation with the fact that he had liked Rachel Zang far more than she had ever liked him. He accepted that they could remain friends and colleagues, and this would not be difficult for him, but he'd start stepping back from her emotionally now. He didn't need unwanted complications in his life when there was no commitment in the first place, and he'd still need time to process and grieve for Roshini, which he would be better off doing alone anyway.

Across the base, towards the wreckage where Zang had shot off her thermobaric rocket, several Komodo dragons loitered. Pierce watched until he understood what a group of them were up to, feeding on the remains of the mercenaries they had killed earlier. Pierce laughed as he cynically reflected that only the reptiles were winning out this day.

Pierce dusted himself off. "We need to find a boat and get off this island."

"Yeah, you're right there, Pierce. And then we need to haul arse and get ourselves to Pakistan."

51

Embassy of the United States, Islamabad, Pakistan

Thirty-six hours later, Mark Pierce and Rachel Zang found themselves in a secure meeting room inside the CIA cordoned-off section of the United States' embassy in Islamabad, after an arduous journey from one side of Asia to the middle of it. The US Marines out of Darwin had shown up a short time later after Keng and Suwan had made their escape, and on Ibrahim's prearranged orders, had quickly flown Pierce and Zang to Singapore while ensuring they received medical care during transit, and from there they had caught another flight to Islamabad.

When Pierce and Zang had been flying, they slept, and the rest of the time they barely spoke to each other. This seeming aloofness at first had surprised Pierce, but then he understood that Zang was very comfortable in his presence. She wasn't talking because she had nothing to say, but because they didn't need to in order to understand and respect each other.

She was a complicated woman, but to be fair, so was he. No surprise, then, that they hadn't worked it out as a couple.

A little over twenty-four hours later they arrived at the embassy and were shown to this meeting room and told to wait. Pierce made them both coffees from a machine in a small kitchenette area off to one side. They both drank it black, so he didn't ask what she wanted and just handed it to her in its full steamy darkness. She took it gracefully, looked up at him with her expressive, emerald-green eyes, and smiled with warmth. "Thank you."

He made a toast with his own mug, then sat diagonally across from her at the conference table.

"What's eating you up, Trigger Man?"

He shrugged. "I realised I never asked. Do you have a code name?"

Her laughter expressed her sarcasm better than any words could. "No. Never assigned one. Nothing that stuck, anyway. But that's not what I asked you."

Pierce drank his coffee. It was late into the night, but he didn't expect to be getting any further sleep soon, so caffeine could only help with the briefing that Zang and he were about to partake in. "If you must know, I was thinking about Mackenzie Summerfield."

"Your previous handler when you were a two-person outfit in West Africa?"

He nodded. "I was thinking if she were here instead of Mitch Hawley, she would never have let Roshini Jahandar onto that Executive Believers flight, and Roshini would be safely inside the US by now."

"You miss her, don't you?"

For a moment, Pierce wasn't certain if Zang was referring to Roshini or Mackenzie. He decided she meant the latter.

"We were friends. I trusted her completely. She knew what she was doing, and she was good at her job."

Zang nodded as she drank her own cup of liquid caffeine. "I only properly worked with her once, in the United Kingdom. But I know what you mean."

The double doors to the meeting room sprang open, and two men entered. The first was the C/SOG Abdul Ibrahim with his signature crisp suit, sharp tie and pressed white business shirt. He carried a laptop under his arm and ushered the second individual, whom Pierce immediately recognised as Mitch Hawley, to take a seat. The younger man's suit was also expensive and tailored, but his was navy and his tie a dull red. His hairstyle was that of a foppish schoolboy, short on the back and sides, and long and side blown on the top. His wire-framed glasses gave him some-what of an air of authority he might have otherwise lacked. He carried a leather briefcase, and when he took a seat, his back was as straight as a rod, and his stares were icy. That was until he turned to Zang, and then he was all smiles and charm. Pierce saw it immediately; he was infatuated with her.

Zang and he were both exact opposites to the two suits in their dress styles. Zang wore an oatmeal woollen jumper and denim jeans, while Pierce had settled on dark brown cargo pants and a fleece jacket. They both wore desert boots covered in dust and dried mud.

Ibrahim nodded to them all individually. "Pierce, Zang, glad to see you are both in one piece. You both know Hawley, of course."

Zang's return nod was curt.

Pierce leaned back in his chair and made himself big. "We do indeed." For a moment, Pierce thought to call out

Hawley's incompetence for letting Roshini Jahandar onto the Executive Believers flight. But that would only antagonise Hawley and Ibrahim too, and the mission was more important than any unaired grievances that could wait until this was all over.

Ibrahim fired up his laptop. "By the way, Pierce, Akash Parab, how did you find him?"

Pierce couldn't help but turn to Hawley at that moment and hold the handler's returned stare when he answered, "Parab is excellent. I presume he's okay, after I left him suddenly in Goa?"

"He is. And your comment is noted. But back to more pressing matters." Ibrahim plugged a cable into his laptop, which linked to a wall monitor that now flashed up with satellite imagery of Pakistan's Lower Chitral District, specifically the fork in the river where the Solangi and Jakhro Rivers met, and the large, sheer cliff mountain that loomed over it.

"Every tango on our hit list is at this location right now," said Ibrahim as his stare turned cold. "Karson, Sanders, Suwan, Keng and the rest of the surviving Executive Believers outfit. There is also Kaajal Khan and his al-Qaeda forces. And hidden in Khan's cavernous network buried beneath that impressive outcrop are Nigel McMahon and Fawad Jahandar. Our drones and our satellites haven't actually seen any of them yet, but they are there, and so are the CIED devices. Both sides are about to go to war with each other, and we're going to insert ourselves in the middle of it all. With that said, are you all with me so far?"

52

Hindu Kush, Lower Chitral District, Pakistan

As dawn peeked from the eastern skies, Jay Sanders spied the meeting of two rivers from a natural ledge halfway up the side of a steep and rocky mountain, seen through the scope of his M110 semi-automatic sniper rifle.

He waited to initiate death.

With the chill of the Hindu Kush winds gradually seeping into his flesh and burrowing mercilessly down into his very bones, Sanders had seen no sign of movement yet in Kaajal Khan's stronghold, even as it became easier to see as night transformed into day. The Mark 5HD 3.6-18x44 riflescope, even when set to eighteen times magnification, had failed to spot the caravan of horse-backed riders presumably bringing Fawad Jahandar to this location, but they couldn't be far off. His intel on the matter was good, and he should know because he had sourced it. There were still officers inside the ISI who owed him, who weren't averse to taking a bribe here and there when the returned favour was easy for them.

Sanders knew they were in the correct spot because of the same intel, but also because the even taller mountain with its sheer cliff edges, half a mile away across the fast-flowing glacial-melt rivers separating Khan's mountain from his own, was dotted with goat paths, cut stone steps, and multiple cavernous entrances leading deep into the al-Qaeda stronghold. Somewhere inside the maze of caverns there was the other half of the CIED device, which if recovered, translated into several hundred million dollars split between the team. Karson would walk away with the lion's share, of course, but even a few cool millions would suit Sanders. He needed the money, to hide, because there was no doubt in his mind all the military and law enforcement powers of the United States government would be on their tail when they sold the CIED device's traitorous secrets. What other choice did he have?

He thought about Zang in that moment and how he cared for her and how small he had felt when she could only look at him with disgust in her eyes. Perhaps slipping her the hacksaw blade had been a mistake, but he couldn't just stand by and let her die like so many others who had crossed Karson's path in the recent past. He owed his lover that much, an opportunity to escape and to live. But if she had survived, he hoped she was also smart enough not to come after him and Karson.

Clearing his head of his morose thoughts, Sanders concentrated again on what was in front of him. Further beyond Kaajal Khan's mountain was a range of the steepest and highest mountains Sanders had ever laid eyes on, resembling shark's teeth covered in the purest white snow overlaying stark rocks of the darkest greys and browns, and stretching from one horizon to the next. No one was coming from that direction, for nothing survived out there.

The path leading to the rope bridge that crossed up the side of Kaajal Khan's mountain was the only way in and the only way out for humans arriving on foot. It was from this approach that Karson and his platoon of the remaining twenty-four soldiers would assault the enemy, but only when they were certain al-Qaeda had delivered Fawad Jahandar to his final destination.

Sanders heard two individuals approaching, scrambling up the rock from the cave where Karson had established their base. He wasn't laid out here to terminate a target, so Sanders took his eye off his scope and turned. The figures were who he expected, Major Brad Karson donned in the same black military fatigues they all wore, and Corporal Johnson Garry, their team's best sniper.

Sanders snapped off a salute. "Sir."

"Lieutenant," said Karson before he turned to Garry. "Take over from Sanders, will you, Corporal. This man and I need to talk."

"Yes, sir."

They swapped positions. Sanders was ready to return with Karson to their cave when his leader said, "Walk with me."

"Yes, sir."

They followed the steep goat track further up the mountain while staying low to avoid being spotted by al-Qaeda sentries and lookouts potentially positioned anywhere in this vast and breathtaking scenery. When they were out of Corporal Garry's earshot and at a valley between two peaks that led to the other side of the mountain upon a path that had brought them here during the night, Karson crouched low and scanned the landscape with his binoculars. "I have good news and bad news."

Sanders squinted against the sun. Despite the below-freezing temperatures, the sunlight was bright in the thin air at ten thousand feet, where the air pressure was two-thirds what it was at ground level, so it burned hard. "I'm happy to hear it in whatever order you want to tell me, sir."

"I'll tell you the good news first, since it won't take long."

"Very well, sir."

The Black Dog nodded. He caught Sanders's returned stare, but there was as much warmth in those eyes as there was in the high mountain air. "The Russians are desperate for the submarine propeller data and will pay far more than anyone else for it. The high-value target they are seeking, Daniil Pavlenko, is still hiding out in Sochi on the Black Sea. The Russian president is adamant on making an example of him and his family. The American's intended to smuggle them out on one of their nuclear subs, but the Navy won't move until they can be absolutely sure the CIED data hasn't been compromised."

Karson paused, so Sanders asked, "How does that change the situation, sir?"

"Nothing tactically, but they have doubled their price if we can get it to them within three days."

Sanders performed a quick calculation in his mind. If his percentage estimates were correct, the new offer would see him walk away with his share of just over nine million dollars. With that kind of cash, he could both hide effectively while still living in comfort. He tried not to allow his excitement to show at finally receiving a break that was worth fighting for. "The only thing that could prevent us from achieving our plan is if Jahandar doesn't arrive in the next forty-eight hours."

"But you said he would?"

"What I actually said, sir, was that elements of the Pakistani Army on al-Qaeda's payroll flew in an al-Qaeda team from Goa to a spot thirty miles downstream of the Solangi River where it meets the Chitral River, into the closest flat spot in this location. That was two days ago."

Karson nodded as he likely calculated the speeds at which Taliban, Mujahedeen, Pashtun and other ethnical and tribal groups in Afghanistan could move through this type of terrain, learnt from when Karson had operated in that neighbouring country when he served with US military forces. Some of those mountains they could see now were in Afghanistan, so the terrain was not that different here. Sanders had guessed they would arrive in two to four days, and Karson would come up with a similar calculation.

But Karson didn't speak those numbers; instead he said, "I haven't told you the bad news yet."

Jay Sanders took in a deep lungful of the cool, thin, mountainous air and feared that the news Karson was about to tell him was that he knew Sanders had slipped Zang a hacksaw blade back in the Komodo dragon pit. If that were so, then Karson wouldn't keep Sanders alive any longer than he needed him to be around, and from where Sanders saw the situation, his worthiness as an asset lay in the past.

"The facilities at Kadal Beracun are destroyed. US Marines have swarmed the island and shut it down."

Sanders felt both relief and fear as a cold wind picked up and blew across the valley where they sat and strategised. "How did that happen, sir?"

"You tell me, Lieutenant?"

Sanders opened his mouth to provide a lame answer, but all he could think about was Rachel Zang. If the Marines were there, then she might be okay. The thought of her being dead chilled him more than the iciness of the Hindu Kush ever could. Then his answer came to him, one that would put him on the attack again. "Sir, I go back to what I said nearly a week ago. Bringing in Zang was a mistake. She and Pierce might have escaped and caused the carnage, and surely you knew the risks of not just killing them outright?"

"They did cause the carnage. Somehow, they escaped, and when I found out, I watched the recording to learn how. I had not watched the live stream as I had promised Zang and Pierce I would."

Sanders felt his gut grumble as deep fear permeated his abdominal regions, and only just managed to hold himself from expelling his bowels. Karson might have seen him pass over the blade in the video and was about to reveal this fact, and if he had not, he still might do so in the future with the video evidence he still had access to, and decided to watch the sequence of events with a closer eye on the details. "What did you see?"

"Zang had a hacksaw blade. She cut the pole until Pierce could snap it, and that allowed them to escape. I don't know where she got it from."

Sanders pretended to consider possibilities and was about to offer several lame explanations when Karson spoke again.

"It doesn't matter. As you said, Sanders, the CIA are already onto us. We just need to wrap this up quick, and to do that, I brought in reinforcements."

"You did? Who? How?"

"Sergeant Suwan and Captain Keng survived. They are

about to join us, coming in on the same path we took to get here, and before that as guests on a UN World Food Program mission flight out of Karachi."

"When are they getting here?"

Karson looked at his wristwatch. "About now."

Sanders looked down the valley path and understood now why Karson had brought him here. Suwan and Keng, camouflaged in their black military fatigues and tactical boots, rucksacks and body armour, and each carrying an M4 carbine, marched up the less steep side of the mountain now, on the opposite side to Kaajal Khan's stronghold. The UN helo drop-off point was ten miles behind them. They must have walked all night to reach this point by sun-up.

"Anything you want to tell me, Lieutenant, before they reach us?"

Sanders felt his throat tighten. For a second, he thought of reaching for his holstered M9 and blasting Karson's brains out the back of his smug head, but two things stopped him.

Nine million dollars.

And no one outdrew Brad Karson in a fast draw.

53

Sochi, Southern Federal District, Russia

It had been twelve hours since Karen Dwyer had last seen or heard from Chad Wilks after sending him out to purchase groceries, as they were running low on supplies, and she now suspected the FSB had her paramilitary officer in their custody and were subjugating him to an extreme and brutal interrogation. Conversely, and just as likely, he might also be injured somewhere and unable to move, or hiding out because he'd been spotted, or dead from a shoot-out, but her worst fear remained her first thought on this troubling matter, that Wilks was alive and had already given up Dwyer's and the Pavlenko family's safe house location.

Therefore, the dilemma facing Dwyer now was whether to stay or move. Either option was fraught with danger.

Katerina sat on the musty lounge with her two children, cuddling them. Her eyes were red and streaked with tears. She'd guessed that their situation had worsened dramatically. Perhaps she feared this would be the last time she would be with her son and daughter. And Dwyer knew she could well be right.

Daniil Pavlenko came up to Dwyer and asked if he could speak in private.

She nodded, and they stepped into the bedroom Wilks and she had bunked in while the Pavlenko family had crammed into the second of the two remaining bedrooms.

Pavlenko was a handsome man in his mid-forties, with thinning blond hair, a strong jaw and a tall stature. While his suit was crumpled from living in it for days on end, he still looked smart, and Dwyer could understand his charismatic appeal that had prompted millions of Russians to support him. But today he was as exhausted as the rest of them, and when he leaned against the doorframe and crossed his arms, he looked ready to fall over.

"Wilks's not coming back by now is not good, is it?"

Dwyer ran her hands through her grey hair, which was starting to feel oily from lack of a wash, but she had been too scared to shower in the last few days. When the FSB came and stormed their safe house, she didn't want to be undressed. "No, Daniil, it's not."

The Russian activist's face contorted into a series of unnatural expressions while his fists clenched and unclenched, and he alternated from crossing his arms to raising them above his head while his palms pressed into his temples. "This is all my fault. I should never have spoken out against the president and his corruption and program of assassinating dissidents like me. My family is about to suffer... Is already suffering, and it's all my fault."

Dwyer took in a deep breath before she answered, to control her own frustration that she felt towards their current circumstances. "It's not your fault, sir. Your president has destroyed your country, turned it into another authoritarian dictatorship like the Soviets did, but run like a criminal organisation, which uses detention, interrogation, torture and assassination to silence anyone who speaks up against him. The International Criminal Court is investigating his complicity in war crimes during the invasion of Ukraine that has killed hundreds of thousands of your own citizens and fifty thousand Ukrainians unnecessarily. Meanwhile, with all your country's oil money going into the war effort, the health and the living conditions of the average Russian is declining, even though he and his inner circle of oligarchs are only getting richer by the minute. You have done a commendable job, sir, for calling all this out. Don't feel bad about anything you have done."

Pavlenko nodded, but he didn't look any less miserable than he had a minute ago. "They're all fine words, Dwyer, but you and I know nothing that I have done will amount to anything. The president won't suffer, he'll still maintain his power, and he will still die of old age in his role. All I've done is bring myself and my family a world of pain, and a short-lived one at that, because of my self-outspokenness."

"You can't think like that. We'll get out of here, soon. You'll be in America within the week, and then he'll never be able to touch you or your family again."

Pavlenko stared at her with eyes that looked as if they were dying slowly. "But that's the problem, isn't it? And what I wanted to talk to you about. Wilks has been gone too long. The FSB is onto us."

"We don't know—"

"But we have to presume they are coming for us. Isn't that your training as a spy? If you detect something out of the ordinary, you have to assume you are compromised. Right?"

Dwyer nodded. What Pavlenko said was the truth, and realistically, moving now was their only option.

A better option was just going it alone. That was the truth of her training, as assets never held the same value as an operative in the field in the CIA's eyes. Dwyer should just run and get out of Russia on her own, and she had a much better chance of succeeding if she did take this course of action. That was okay when assets were Chechen terrorists who wanted to switch sides because suddenly they had let their masters down and now their own side wanted them dead, or when it was a former SVR or FSB operative who, after years of torturing and murdering dissidents, decided a cushy life in the west was their optimal retirement plan. But Daniil and Katerina Pavlenko weren't the morally corrupt individuals she normally dealt with in the game of espionage and counterespionage, they were decent and ethical and brave, and they deserved a second chance. And then there were their children, Anatoliy and Emiliya. There was no power on this Earth that could convince Dwyer to abandon these children to a horrific fate. No, if they were to run, then they would all run together.

"Dwyer?"

She nodded again. "Pack your bags. We leave in ten minutes. But remember, sir, we will be on the move constantly until we can be extracted. We'll be living in a van, all five of us. And we'll risk being spotted, more so than if we remain put."

"But if the FSB have Wilks, it's only a matter of time before he gives us up?"

Dwyer shuddered as she imagined the tortures the FSB

could be subjecting the CIA operator to right now. Water-boarding, electrocutions, burns, pulled fingernails, or even power drills forced through the hands and feet were all possibilities, and she knew from studied first-hand intelligence that too often crossed her desk, the Russians were not beneath this kind of torture to get what they wanted.

"Yes, sir. We have no choice. But also, be aware there is no other safe house we can run to. We must keep on the move, for days still until the Navy has a window of opportunity to get us out. Are you ready to commit to that course of action?"

54

PAF Base Peshawar, Peshawar District, Pakistan

Sixty kilometres from the Pakistan-Afghanistan border, with the afternoon sun low on the horizon, Mark Pierce and Rachel Zang drove up to the security boom gates of Pakistan Air Force Base Peshawar in a Land Rover Defender. When they showed their US military identity cards, they were allowed inside under escort, as US forces regularly transitioned through this facility between executions of the agency's various covert missions undertaken inside the Central Asian sphere. They were led into a compound hired out by the CIA, not that this information was available on any record, public or secret, but the soldiers who ran this base knew all about it and grinned when Pierce asked to be taken there.

The interior of the compound was exactly like dozens of others Pierce and Zang had operated from in the past, with equipment stores, live-in facilities comprising basic bunks, kitchenettes and washrooms, and various closed rooms for mission planning and operations support.

When Zang and Pierce were ushered into the briefing room, inside there waited six other individuals who immediately stood out as special forces types, with their muscular frames, casual attitudes and "fuck you" stares. Pierce presumed this was a CIA Ground Branch paramilitary team, all ex-Army Green Berets or ex-Navy SEALs. The closest of them, a man with a barrel chest, arms like tree trunks, and a bushy beard, stepped up and pumped Pierce's hand. "You must be Trigger Man?"

Pierce nodded. "I am."

"Welcome to Team Lima X-ray. We're your boots on the ground, Af-Pak ass-kickers and all-round terrorist neutralisers. I'm code-named Killefer, and this is Sledge Man, Toxic, Bragger, Waxer and Random. But I'm also Lima X-ray One, and the team are respectively Lima X-ray Two, Lima X-ray Three, etcetera."

The team gave Pierce as series of nods, waves and grunted greetings.

Pierce nodded and said, "This is..." He was about to introduce her as "Zang", but remembering Ground Branch tended to only use call signs on a mission, and realising that he still didn't know hers, he looked to her for guidance, but all he got in return was an icy stare full of fury. "She'll tell you her call sign."

Zang said nothing.

Killefer didn't acknowledge her. "No offence, Trigger Man, but our impending briefing is for operators only. Analysts belong down the corridor."

Zang tensed, and her face brightened. "Fuck you, Killefer. I'm Ground Branch, just like you."

Killefer raised an eyebrow, then returned a smug grin. "No offence, lady, but where we're going is no place for a woman."

"Fuck you again!"

The men all laughed, then said nothing.

Pierce felt his anger rising now, but he kept it squashed down inside him. "Killefer, she is on the team. She's as good as anyone here."

"Yeah!" said Sledge Man, who was a large, bulked individual with close-shaved hair and a thick but neatly trimmed beard. He had been cleaning his HK416 assault rifle until this moment, but now looked like he was itching for a fight, perhaps to relieve the tension of sitting around and doing nothing while they had waited for Zang and Pierce to show. "Then she'd better prove it."

Zang snapped back, "You prove it!" She found a seat, kicked it back and fell into it, and firmly planted her boots up on the table. "Go on. Hundred push-ups. No offence, but where we're going, those muscles don't look to have the agility I need for them to deliver on this job."

Stunned, Sledge Man halted in his cleaning, placed his carbine on the table, then leaned forward in a seated position with his legs wide apart. "Believe me, miss, these muscles can do anything."

Zang shrugged. "Like I said, prove it."

Sledge Man opened his mouth, but no words came forth, and the rest of the team shifted uncomfortably where they sat or stood. Pierce mused that perhaps they had considered getting all crass and threatening, then had changed their minds because Zang was a woman.

Eventually Killefer massaged his chin under his beard

and said, "You've got spirit about you, miss. I'll give you that. But you're not coming."

"Yeah?" said Zang. "But I am."

She stared down Killefer, and the two refused to break eye contact.

Eventually Killefer turned to Pierce, shrugged and made googly-eyes at him.

Pierce shrugged back. "She's told you she's coming, so she's coming, Killefer. Arguing further doesn't serve any of us."

Killefer opened his mouth to say more but was interrupted when the door sprang open and in stepped a woman Pierce had never previously met, but her file was one he had studied recently. Ryleigh Bresolin looked exasperated in this moment, but she was also very much playing her part as a senior CIA operations officer and appeared comfortable in her field kit comprising well-worn cargo pants, desert boots, and a khaki shirt. When Zang and she crossed glances, Bresolin made the slightest snorting sound, which suggested to Pierce the two women had crossed paths in the past and that encounter had not gone well.

Bresolin seemed to count everyone off in her head. "Good, you've all made it. Zang, bring your team into the ops room, where you'll be briefed."

Zang smiled, then turned to a smarting Killefer. "After you, Lima X-ray One."

He shook his head. "It's your funeral."

"It'd better not be! You'd better ensure every one of your team gets back in one piece, soldier. Including me and the Trigger Man. Are we clear?"

"Yes, ma'am." He moved to walk out, but then paused. "You never did tell me your code name, though?"

Zang was about to respond, when suddenly she seemed lost for words.

Pierce had never seen her speechless before, and this brought the tiniest smile to his face.

When she caught him grinning, Zang straightened and said, "Since you find it so funny, Trigger Man, why don't you tell him what my code name is?"

Pierce nodded, knowing that she had trapped him. He didn't know her code name, and perhaps she'd never had one. She was likely testing him now, to see if he could come up with a handle that wasn't sexist or inappropriate or not worthy of her.

"After you... *Ronin.*"

It was the first code name Pierce could make up for her that wasn't purely based on gender, which he knew she would have hated, such as "Huntress" or "Dryad" had he used either of those. He had seen too many other men give their female team members code names like that in the past, resulting in most of those women then hating them for years to come. In feudal Japan, a ronin was a samurai who had no lord or master, and in some cases, had also severed all links with his family or clan. Historically, the name only applied to men. He thought it was an appropriate name for her. He hoped she did too.

They exchanged glances.

She eventually smiled, then bit her lip, and finally nodded appreciatively. "Yeah, got my ancestry wrong with that one, Pierce, since Zang is Chinese, not Japanese. But it's mine, and that's all that matters."

Pierce and Zang were the last out of the room, and as she passed him, she whispered into his ear, "Thank you."

55

The operations room was keypad locked and enterable only through steel reinforced doors, suggesting the CIA's presence here was more than just a passing interest.

Once inside, Pierce discovered Abdul Ibrahim and Mitch Hawley tapping away at keyboards and studying digital maps of satellite and drone paths as they crossed over Pakistani Hindu Kush. There were no windows, and all the air-ventilation ducts were covered over with noise-disrupting shields. What did surprise Pierce was Akash Parab seated at another monitor, running facial-recognition software over a series of male faces that flicked too fast across the screen for Pierce to remember any of them.

"Akash Parab!" Pierce said with a smile.

"Mark Pierce!" Parab was out of his seat and pumping Pierce's outstretched hand. Then they were patting each other on the shoulders. "When you didn't return from your ocean outing, I thought you were dead until the chief told me otherwise. So glad to see you are okay."

"Yeah, I'm good, thanks. Great to see you on the team, Parab." He turned to Ibrahim. "I presume Parab's on the team?"

Abdul Ibrahim, the formidable chief of the CIA's Special Operations Group, nodded. "Of course." Today, he'd dressed in a tan suit and white shirt and was uncharacteristically without a tie. "Now that you and Zang are here, we need to get down to business. Parab has checked for listening devices, and our encryption is good." He held out a bag. "Cell phones and other listening devices off and placed in here first, though, before we proceed. The Pakistanis can't help themselves but listen in if they can, and we don't want them alerting our enemies to what we are up to."

Everyone complied, and then Ibrahim deposited the bag in a Faraday cage, preventing electromagnetic radiation from getting in and out of the metallic box.

Killefer stepped forward until he stood before Pierce. "You ever HAHO jumped before, Trigger Man?" Then remembering that Zang was coming with them whether he liked it or not, he said to her, "Have you?"

Zang smirked. "High-altitude high-opening jump? Of course. What height are we deploying at? Thirty thousand feet at night will allow us to travel under canopy for a distance of, what, forty miles, say, to insert ourselves silently into Kaajal Khan's hideout?"

Killefer nodded. "Very good. Except that it won't be forty miles. Khan's hideout is at an elevation of fifteen thousand feet, so we only have about ten maybe fifteen miles of lateral play depending on the wind, but you are essentially correct."

"Then no problem."

Killefer turned to Pierce.

Pierce hesitated before he answered with a lie. "Yes,

multiple times." He didn't tell them specifically where he had learnt parachuting techniques, knowing that if they knew the truth behind this fact, then no one on the team would trust him to come with them, not even Zang. The highest altitude he'd ever jumped from was six thousand metres, but he'd read up on HAHO jumps to know the differences, mostly comprising the need for air masks and specialist suits at higher elevations so they didn't suffocate or freeze to death during the descent. He could pull this deceit off.

Killefer nodded. "That's good, because it is the simplest means of getting us in. The C-17 will be too far away to be seen or heard, and no one will see us deploy. You and Ronin will be Lima X-ray Seven and Eight respectively for this mission."

Ibrahim switched on a projector, creating a replication of Hawley's laptop screen projected upon a clean wall. It was a satellite image of Kaajal Khan's al-Qaeda stronghold, forged inside a mighty mountainous peak overlooking the fork of two rivers. "We still don't know if Fawad Jahandar has been brought here yet. We're hoping we spot him before he arrives, because a Predator drone can then take him out immediately. That will neutralise one half of the CIED device. Destroying one half, as you all know, results in the data in both being rendered useless, and then the mission is over. But we have to prepare as if both halves are in play and need recovery. Zoom in here, will you, Hawley?"

The handler did as he was instructed, enlarging a position on the mountain on the opposite side of the Solangi River.

Ibrahim continued with his briefing. "Earlier this morning, one of our satellites spotted four individuals in this location. We've identified them as Brad Karson, Jay Sanders, Gang Keng and Kwang Suwan, or put it another way, all of Karson's remaining senior operators all in the one location. We believe Karson holds the other half of the CIED device, and if we'd been able to get a drone into position this morning, we could have taken them out already. Any questions so far?"

"I do," said Ryleigh Bresolin, with her arms crossed and her expression sour. She'd kept to the back of the room, and judging by her snarly tone, Pierce could guess why. "How can you be so certain Karson is the enemy? He's a good man. He's served his country, and the hero has suffered for it. I can't believe we are going to just execute one of our own." She looked around the room, seeking returned stares that indicated they agreed with her, but finding none. "Am I the only one here who sees what a terrible mistake this all is?"

Ibrahim nodded solemnly. "I'm sorry you feel that way, Bresolin. On the surface, I agree, Karson did a lot of good. But he's also done lots of horrific things too, such as horrendous tortures, beheadings and disembowelments, which is a brutality we only expect from our enemies, such as Islamic State. Not our own soldiers."

Bresolin tensed. "If you put it like that, it suggests you don't, or won't, appreciate the horrible realities of war. *Sir!*" She spoke his title like it was a bad taste in her mouth.

"Bresolin, everyone in this room has operated in a war zone. Everyone appreciates the chaos of battle and the horrible things we need to do to keep America and the world safe, but none of us resort to torture and killing as a sadistic pastime. Regardless of all that, Karson plans on selling submarine schematics to our most dangerous enemies, and that makes him a terrorist and a traitor operating way beyond sanction—"

"But that still doesn't justify—!"

"Bresolin!" Ibrahim raised his voice at her, expressing an uncharacteristic frustration towards one of his underlings in an open forum. "Let me tell you what I learnt two days ago. With Karson turned terrorist, we have sanction to unlock his personal files. Karson's wife was seeing a psychologist for a year before she and their children died, and I've seen all the session notes. She feared for her life *and* those of her two boys. Karson beat her regularly, and she kept photos of her bruises hidden on her cell phone should she ever need to use them. Do you know what horrible thing happened next?"

Bresolin didn't answer and only stared at Ibrahim with steely eyes.

"Bresolin, the week after she decided to move out and take her children with her, to run from Karson, was the week 'al-Qaeda' killed them. Want to watch the traffic footage of Karson following his wife and children as they drove out of town that day?"

Again, Bresolin gave no response. She clearly couldn't believe him or didn't want to.

Pierce could empathise, for Karson did carry a certain charisma and a magnetic personality that some people would find difficult to resist, which he'd seen first-hand, even when Karson had been about to feed him and Zang to Komodo dragons. But that didn't change facts, that on the inside, Karson was a cold-hearted psychopath who cared for no one, not even his own wife and children.

"It's all fake intelligence. Set up by his enemies to frame him!"

Ibrahim shook his head. "Okay, Bresolin, I've made up my mind. You're off the team."

"What—?"

"It's too late. I see there is no going back. Step out of this room, and I want you on the first flight back to Langley. You are stood down until you and I have had a chance to have a good talk about all of this. Am I clear?"

"Sir?" All colour had drained from her face, for she had not seen this coming.

Ibrahim silently stared her down until she turned and walked out of the briefing room, smarting the entire way out.

After she was gone, Pierce watched the room. The mood quickly moved away from the tension of the last moment and refocused again on the satellite image projected on the wall. It seemed everyone else here had studied the intelligence and seen it for what it was, facts, and that Karson was indeed a clear and present danger worthy of termination with extreme prejudice.

"Getting back to the mission," said Ibrahim, "is everyone here clear on the situation thus far?"

The team now nodded.

"Good," said Ibrahim. "Look at this crate Suwan and Keng are carrying. We believe they brought in dozens of Black Hornet nano surveillance drones. Only six inches by one inch, and weighing less than an ounce, Karson will be using these to map out the interior of Kaajal Khan's cave network before they strike. That gives them an advantage, as they might already know Nigel McMahon's exact location inside the stronghold, but they'll definitely have a better map of the caves than we've been able to secure."

"But an opportunity," said Killefer, "if we get our hands on their feed. Can we hack it?"

All eyes turned to Parab.

When he realised everyone was looking at him, he said in a quiet voice, "I'm trying, sir. Their cyber security is state of the art. These are professionals we're talking about. Karson and his team are from the same military schools that all of you attended."

Killefer nodded. "That's very true, and many of us here have trained under him. What about Karson's team numbers? Any update on his troop force size?"

Ibrahim turned to Pierce's handler analyst. "What's the latest, Hawley?"

The young Ivy League college educated man cleared his throat as he opened a new file on his laptop, then read it as he spoke. "The few surviving Executive Believers mercs that our US Marines captured on Kadal Beracun Island are still undergoing interrogation. They are still reporting that eighteen troops were on the flight to Pakistan, not including Karson, Sanders, Keng and Suwan."

Killefer was quick to respond with, "Why haven't they gone into Khan's hideout yet and hit it? They definitely have a clear head start on us." When he received no answer, he spoke more tersely. "Hawley?"

Hawley shrugged. "I'm not a mind reader, sir. I don't know what they are thinking."

"But your background is that of a targeting analyst as well as a field operative handler. Analyse!"

Pierce spoke up, interrupting the heated conversation, because a thought pertinent to the mission had just occurred. "They're not moving in, Killefer, for the same reason we're not. They're waiting for Jahandar to show. They need the other half of the CIED device and Nigel McMahon in order to get what they want, so they won't go in until they know both are there."

Killefer nodded. "Of course." He turned to Parab. "Do we know Karson's mercs' exact positions right now?"

"No, sir. They are too well hidden and spread out across the opposite mountain. We suspect that, apart from this morning's meetup, they will remain hidden under rock cover or in caves, or are covering themselves with thermal blankets."

As Parab talked, Pierce noticed an image saved in the corner of Hawley's screen. It was of what appeared to be a group of farmers following the goat trail that snaked along the Solangi River. It was the easiest route to follow from the Chitral River to reach Kaajal Khan's stronghold. The group of twenty-odd men included many pack-carrying donkeys. They looked to be Pashtun people because of their choice of clothing comprising perahan upper garments with their wide and loose sleeves, baggy pants and turbans.

"Anyway," said Ibrahim, "as I was saying—"

"Wait a second, sir!" Pierce interrupted as he pointed to the image on the screen. "Hawley, what's this group here?"

"Nothing," the young man said with a snarl. "Farmers."

"Put it up on the screen. Zoom in."

Hawley looked to Ibrahim, his expression sour as he shrugged his shoulders in a questioning gesture while his eyes rolled.

Ibrahim nodded that Hawley should do as Pierce instructed.

"This is a waste of time," Hawley grumbled as he pulled up the image for everyone to see. "They're just farmers. They moved through this morning and kept going. I'm not an imbecile, I ran facial recognition on everyone I could scan, and nothing came up."

Pierce pointed to a farmer in the centre of the group with his face obscured by his turban, holding his hand up as a shield against the sun. "Zoom in on him."

"Why?"

Pierce couldn't believe he needed to argue with this man to get him to just do his job, when Zang said, "Hawley, Trigger Man has a point. I see it now, and you all will too, in a minute."

Hawley fussed for several minutes until he deemed to zoom in on the farmer. What soon became obvious to everyone in that next moment was that the man wore a shiny, golden watch about his wrist.

Zang shook her head, then crossed her arms. "Wow! Jahandar's Rolex."

When Pierce had arrived in Islamabad, he had been very careful to prepare a detailed report on his actions so far, which he had sent to Ibrahim, who in turn would have distributed it to everyone on this team. Pierce's notes had made special mention of Jahandar's expensive gold wristwatch, which might have been sold off along his journey to the Hindu Kush, offering a potential lead to track their target's movements. Instead, here it was, either still on Jahandar's wrist or taken by one of the men in the group and worn by them now.

Hawley growled, "That's not Jahandar. I ran facial recognition on him earlier, when I had a clear image of him. This is all a waste of time."

Pierce said, "Doesn't matter. Jahandar was with them, and they would have passed him off to Kaajal Khan's men as they passed through. How long ago did this happen?"

"Earlier this morning, around eleven hundred hours."

Pierce clenched his fists tight. "Fuck, Hawley! You can't afford to make basic mistakes like that! This is not fucking amateur hour!" Shaking his head, he turned to the team and said, "Jahandar is already in the caves. We have no choice now but to engage them on the ground."

Hawley stood and pointed at Pierce. "You have no right to speak to me like that!"

"Fuck you, Hawley! I do."

"Well, fuck you too! You son of a bitch!"

Ibrahim spoke up. "Quieten down, Hawley. Trigger Man is right, you failed on your watch, so you and I will have words later." Ibrahim returned his attention to Pierce.

"This isn't right!" said Hawley. "You don't have the right to talk to me like that. None of you do."

"Shut the fuck up, Hawley." Raising his finger at the man, Ibrahim again turned his attention to Pierce and the others. "But right now, getting back to the mission, Karson will also know Jahandar is there and will be moving in too."

"But Karson and his mercs won't move until nightfall," said Zang. "They'll be spotted otherwise, so we still have time to prepare and go in with a hope of still salvaging this mission."

"Only a couple of hours until nightfall, and we need to be wheels up by then," said Killefer as he turned to his team of elite special forces operators known collectively as Team Lima X-ray. "Okay, men and lady, we're mission go! Many of us know Karson personally, have served under him, but make no mistake, he is a son-of-a-bitch traitor and the enemy now. So pack your kits and up the attitudes, and let's go kick some traitorous assholes all the way back down to the lowest levels of hell where they belong."

56

Hindu Kush, Lower Chitral District, Pakistan

Four hours later, in the cargo bay of a C-17 Globemaster military transport cruising at thirty thousand feet or nine thousand metres above the Hindu Kush, Pierce sat quietly and breathed from his bottle of pure oxygen and wondered if he could pull off a HAHO jump he'd never trained for or previously attempted.

He'd been breathing from his tank, as had the rest of Team Lima X-ray, since take-off from Bacha Khan International Airport, where all PAF Base Peshawar flights arrived and departed. They flew north towards Afghanistan, to support a ruse that they were taking out a Taliban terror cell in the Afghan portion of the Hindu Kush mountains that Parab had allowed the ISI to hack, so Pakistani intelligence had no notion that the CIA was again conducting a secret capture or kill mission inside their own sovereign territory. If they got wind of it, there was no doubt in Ibrahim's mind that someone in the ISI would leak this information to

Kaajal Khan, allowing the al-Qaeda terrorist to relocate McMahon, Jahandar and the CIED device to another location before they could get there.

As the aircraft rattled and shook around them, Pierce turned to Zang. She was seated next to him. Dressed in black Gore-Tex waterproof layers, thermal undergarments and chest rigs with ceramic plates, she carried two parachutes, with the main one at her back and a reserve at her front. Like Pierce and the rest of Lima X-ray, she slung a Heckler & Koch HK416 assault rifle and breathed pure oxygen behind her rubber mask. The layers were to protect against the frigid cold they would experience when they jumped from a height of nine kilometres above mean sea level, the oxygen because the air outside was too thin at this altitude to sustain them on the way down, and the lack of nitrogen in the mix was to ensure that gas didn't build up in their bloodstream as the air pressure increased during their descent. Other equipment that they all carried included ropes, pitons and carabiners, should they need to conduct mountaineering insertions or transfers during the raid.

When she spotted him watching her, Zang gave him the thumbs up and smiled at him through her mask, so Pierce returned the gesture.

As the roar of the C-17's four turboprop propellers drowned out all noise, the loadmaster stepped forward and raised a fist before Lima X-ray One, then held up two fingers. Two minutes until they jumped.

Lima X-ray One, or Killefer, turned to his team and repeated the same gesture.

Everyone switched out their oxygen bottles and reattached their air hoses to fresh tanks, which would provide them with enough oxygen for the descent. When Pierce saw how the rest of the team performed this task, he mimicked their actions.

"Forward to ramp!" Lima X-ray One shouted over the rattling noise, made worse as the loadmaster strapped himself to the bulkhead railing and lowered the cargo ramp. Suddenly the cargo fuselage interior was filled with a chilled wind that roared louder than the engines.

The load master held up another fist, but with only one finger extended now.

Then Team Lima X-ray lined up, counted off from one to eight, with Pierce and Zang at the rear. With their thirty kilos of gear each, they trudged to the ramp and waited. Then, when the loadmaster held up his fist with no fingers extended, they each stepped off into the night and fell into the screaming, churning darkness.

They were in freefall for only fifteen seconds before they deployed chutes. Pierce felt the jolt as his chute caught, and then they drifted in the starlit night towards a landscape dominated by the most rugged and desolate snow-capped mountain ranges Pierce had ever laid eyes on, and he had seen plenty of snow and mountains in his career.

They dropped for many minutes, following a line resembling a snake as they descended. Lima X-ray One as team leader guided them in, for it was his responsibility they hit the target, still some twelve kilometres from them, with pinpoint accuracy.

As they descended, Pierce concentrated on adjusting the pull on his chute to ensure he remained directly behind Lima X-ray Six, aka "Random", some thirty metres below him. Pierce had only performed a few low- and mid-altitude air-drop missions in his career, and all of them for military units that were nowhere near as professional as the Navy

SEALs, US Army Special Forces or other special force branches of the United States military, and Pierce had witnessed too many unnecessary deaths on those jumps caused through incompetence and mismanagement. This, he hoped, would be his first jump where everyone in the team, including himself, made it to the surface in one piece and unharmed.

After eighteen minutes of flight, Kaajal Khan's mountainous stronghold came into focus. They planned to drop at a flat section of rock approximately two hundred metres from the highest identified cave entrance. Through his night optical devices that lit up the world in shades of green, Pierce identified paths cut into the sheer rock faces of the mountain, where he spotted occasional al-Qaeda troops moving from one cave entrance to the next. The drops from those ledges were hundreds of metres, and he would soon find himself fighting the enemy on those precipices and inside those caves.

The other risks they had gone over during the rushed mission planning that came to mind now were the many trip wires and pressure plates al-Qaeda would have spread throughout their complex, as traps set against anyone who thought to storm their stronghold.

"Sector watches, report in," Lima X-ray One stated as they neared their target less than two hundred metres beneath them now. With their oxygen tanks now removed because the outside air had enough pressure to breathe comfortably, they spoke in low voices through their radio comms. Lima X-ray One through to Six each reported that their sectors were clear.

When they touched the icy rock, Pierce stumbled, then slid ten metres on a forty-five-degree angle towards a sheer drop before his hand caught a rock, barely stopping himself from experiencing a sudden and undignified death.

"Watch it, X-ray Seven," came Killefer through the radio. "Get on your feet and get your chute hauled."

Pierce twisted from lying on his back to his front, then found purchases with his other three limbs, and scrambled back up the rock until he was on flat ground again. Once on his feet, he quickly curled up his chute and packed it. He silently cursed himself for pulling off the deception of being an old hand at a HAHO jump, only to stumble and trip on the final descent.

Zang came up to him and whispered out of mic, "Are you okay?"

"I'm fine!" he said a little too abruptly.

She nodded, but it was difficult to read her frame of mind with the NODs obscuring her face and making her resemble some kind of cyborg-like monster. "I just thought that perhaps you had your shakes again?"

Pierce grimaced. "Sorry!" He'd forgotten she knew about his infliction that sometimes bothered him in stressful situations, a medical condition he had still failed to report to anyone inside the CIA. His hands and legs weren't shaking, but that didn't mean they wouldn't in the coming minutes and hours if he didn't keep his focus on the mission and not on his fears. "I'm good."

She nodded. "Then let's move."

57

The team split into two, with Killefer, Sledge Man, Pierce and Zang in the first that moved around to a cave entrance on the western side of the mountain, and then Toxic, Bragger, Waxer and Random in the second team, taking another cave entrance on the southern face. From here on in, radio comms would be limited to short distances within the tunnels, as the many layers of rock above them would soon be too thick to allow bouncing of radio comms back to the Predator drone circling in the skies above.

As they moved with almost no noise, Pierce watched Killefer and Sledge Man, Lima X-ray One and Two respectively, sneak up behind two al-Qaeda guards, then cover their foes' mouths as their knives slit open their throats. Each Ground Branch paramilitary operator caught their corpses so they wouldn't fall hard upon the rock, not that the noise of them falling would carry far with the wind now picking up and blowing over the tops of the mountains.

Pierce couldn't believe how cold it was. It brought back

memories of training and fighting for years in landscapes as unforgiving and as desolate as the lands of the Hindu Kush. He preferred fighting in hot deserts and in the tropics, but it was not a soldier's lot in life to choose where they fought, so he followed the team leader as they descended, and compartmentalised his thoughts on the matter.

They entered the first cave, barely wide enough for a large man. Its roof was so low they all had to constantly crouch. Pierce was last in the line of four, constantly covering their rear should enemies sneak up behind them. They covered fifteen metres before Lima X-ray One slotted two enemy combatants with two well-placed shots from his suppressed HK416 rifle.

"Wait!" called out Two. He stepped forward and pointed to a trip wire, which One had almost activated. One stepped back slowly and carefully, and the tension in the wire remained. Everyone sucked in a breath of relief. Two sprayed the trip wire with a can of Silly String, making it easier to identify, and then they each carefully stepped over it and moved on.

As the team descended further, the tunnel twisted and turned, then opened into a marginally wider natural cavern. There were oil lamps here, so they raised their NODs. Pierce spotted woollen blankets, crates and hessian bags of food, most likely rice.

"Contact!" shouted One.

Soon the tunnel lit up with the muzzle flashes of weapon fire, and Pierce heard the distinct sounds of Kalashnikov assault rifles firing. Pressing himself against a rock face, Pierce readied his weapon and waited for One and Two to drop and advise they were reloading. Through the smoke and flashes and noise, Pierce spotted al-Qaeda insurgents, in their traditional mountain garb and turbans, ahead of them and shooting back. Then an explosion rattled further down the cave from where al-Qaeda had engaged them. The insurgents vanished in a fireball that raged like a dragon's breath towards them. The shock wave hit them and sent Lima X-ray One and Two hurling backwards, collecting Pierce and knocking him to the ground.

The impact winded him, and the soot now thick in the air hurt his eyes. Blinking away the dust and debris collecting in his tear ducts, Pierce had only just enough sense in him to notice Zang behind him, slipping and scrambling on loose rock, as the ground next to her gave way, and she slipped further.

Pierce realised almost too late what had happened. The blast had dislodged a rock face on the side of the mountain, and suddenly the tunnel they had been traversing had become a ledge. The rock beneath Zang's feet was still shifting under her, and then it and she dropped.

Pierce rolled and caught her by the wrist. A second later, and she would have fallen three hundred metres into the Solangi River. A fall no living being could survive.

"Stop struggling, Zang! I've got you!"

She was twisting and struggling in his grip until she realised that he had her. "Pierce?"

"I'm here!"

Then he felt the shakes building in his arms and legs.

"Mark? Are you okay?"

He gritted his teeth and held on to her tight. It took him a second to realise, with only starlight now to guide him, that the ledge he lay upon was barely the width of his shoulders, and one side disappeared into a long fall into nothingness.

But a more troubling problem was that he lay on a slope, and he was gradually sliding downwards. Up ahead, about a metre from him, the ledge ran out. If he kept sliding at this rate, he'd topple over the edge with Zang in less than a minute.

"Mark!"

"Don't struggle! I've got you."

He dug in his toes, which marginally slowed his slippage, but not enough.

He heard more shooting, then more grenade and rocket blasts. He had to get Zang back up with him soon, or he would face a series of impossible choices: let go of her, fall to their deaths together, or die under the volley of sprayed bullets that would inevitably come from behind them.

Now his arms shook violently, and it took all his will not to lose his grip on his friend.

"Mark! There's a ledge."

"A ledge, where?" He couldn't see anything now, with his NODs still above his head and the lanterns of the tunnels vanished with the blast and shearing of the rock face.

"Zang! There's just... one more foot... left!"

"When I say, let go of me."

"You sure?"

"Yes, I'm fucking sure. We're about to both go over."

Now Pierce heard footfalls behind him, and the distinctive sounds of soldiers swapping out magazines and priming their weapons. His back was exposed to the only path that returned inside the mountain, and he was still sliding.

"Ready!"

Pierce grunted. "Yeah, I'm ready." He slipped again, and the ledge ahead ran out. His head went over.

"Now!"

Pierce released her.

He didn't have time to check on her, as he heard men coming up behind him. With Zang no longer pulling him, he wasn't sliding so fast, so he turned and fired the Glock 19 semi-automatic pistol he had procured in the US Embassy. Two al-Qaeda soldiers turning their AK-47s now danced like ragged dolls as bullets churned out bloody meat holes inside their chests. They both toppled, then vanished into the night.

Pierce reached out with his left hand, finding a crack in the rock, and dug his fingers in. That was enough leverage to stop him, and he wasn't sliding anymore.

"Zang!" he called out.

"I'm down here, Pierce."

She sounded to be at least five metres away, but then Pierce figured he had probably just made this number up, for he had no idea how far away she was. "You okay?"

"Yeah! I'm on another ledge. I can't climb up to you though."

Pierce pulled himself up into a crouching position, then scrambled awkwardly until he faced the other way, and pulled himself up the ledge that only minutes earlier had been a tunnel. "I can't come down. Head back in, and I'll find you."

"What about Killefer and Sledge Man?"

Far away, Pierce heard further shooting and explosions, but the noise seemed to be moving away from them now. "Can't see. They might have gone down with the rock, or they might not." He tried his radio, but he only got static. Was Karson running a radio jammer nearby? It wasn't beyond possibility.

Then a large dragonfly creature, forged of metal and

slick edges, flew up close to him and hovered nearby. He immediately recognised it as a Black Hornet nano surveillance drone, which Ibrahim had described during the briefing. Its forward-facing camera lens now neatly captured an image of his dumbfounded stare looking back at it.

"Cover blown, Zang. Karson is onto us."

But she didn't answer.

Instead, the world beneath him erupted in further, closer, gunfire.

58

Now Zang shook like Pierce often did, but in her case, she knew why. She had almost fallen a thousand feet to her death, and only Pierce's quick dexterity had saved her. He had deposited her on a ledge barely a foot and a half wide, one of many that al-Qaeda had carved out here in the side of their mountain stronghold, so that the entire complex resembled a termite mound with tiny humans appearing and disappearing as their journeys alternated them from tunnel to ledge.

Getting carefully to her feet, Zang advanced. More gunfire and explosions rattled in the tunnel ahead. She heard Pierce call out from the darkness above, but his words were muffled to incomprehensibility with all the other battle noises erupting around her.

A soldier appeared on the ledge, illuminated by the light now shining out of the tunnel behind him. An al-Qaeda fighter with fear in his eyes, not because of her, but of the threat advancing behind him.

Zang was about to shoot when his body was peppered

with multiple bullets, and he fell bloody and silent into the night.

"Copy that, Black Dog!" echoed an American voice from the tunnel ahead.

Karson's Executive Believers were already here.

"Advancing."

Deciding that she had no intention of engaging US military-trained mercenaries on a precarious ledge, Zang moved backwards until she could take the next tunnel leading into the mountain. There she waited, with her NODs back over her face, readying herself in the green-lit world for engagement with the operators who would soon advance upon her. Her breathing sounded loud and heavy in her ears, and her heart seemed to explode in her chest with each beat. She realised she was hyperventilating, and her neck and shoulders were tensing. "Fuck!" she exclaimed through gritted teeth, knowing these were the first signs of a migraine. Pierce had his shakes, while she had her debilitating headaches, both of which could be death sentences in a battle like this one. But that didn't change the facts in front of them, that they just had to fight until they died or won. There was no other choice.

A soldier turned the corner and pointed her M4 down the tunnel towards Zang.

She fired and watched the female soldier under Karson's command grunt, twist and then stumble back before she dropped screaming into the night as the ledge ran out behind her.

Zang moved, knowing that the next Executive Believer to turn that corner would be more cautious in taking cover. This tunnel was narrow and low like the first one and too low to stand upright. She heard further controlled fire behind her, and while no bullets hit her, it did mean that her pursuers were close enough to spot her.

After a minute of frantic crouched running, Zang stepped into a large cave, half of which had been carved out to provide flat surfaces. Two men, badly beaten and dirty, and wearing the ragged tatters of western clothes, lay side by side, cowering from the sounds and lights of battle flashing around them. On each of their left ankles were manacles attached to chains, which were securely adhered to bolts pounded into the rock walls. She smelled shit and piss and spotted the buckets where the two men had to relieved themselves from time to time. Both men she recognised immediately from their CIA files, Fawad Jahandar and Nigel McMahon.

The DARPA engineer raised his hands in a surrender pose. Tears gushed from his eyes as he called out, "Are you American? I'm an American!"

Zang could hear the Executive Believers team advancing behind her. She turned and fired several blasts back down the tunnel she had come from. "Take cover!" she called behind her. Return fire echoed down the tunnel as bullets spat out of the darkness. Not bothering to check what either man had done to protect themselves, Zang pulled a fragmentation grenade and tossed it far down the tunnel.

The blast that roared seconds later shook the rock, and flames burned out of the gap near Zang, heating her face momentarily.

When the blast subsided, Zang turned back and fired off another three-round burst into the tunnel. When there was no return fire, she glanced down and saw there had been a cave-in. No one was coming for her from that direction now.

Jahandar sneered as he scrambled to his feet. "You're lucky you didn't bring the whole cave down."

Zang looked the former FIA intelligence officer up and down and ascertained he wasn't much of a man. He was soft of skin and rotund of belly, and his hands were too smooth for him to have ever performed any hard work in his life. "I'd say you're lucky to be alive for more reasons than just that."

McMahon's eyes grew wide with hope, for Zang and Jahandar were speaking English to each other, and her accent was clearly American. "Is this a rescue mission?"

Zang turned her nose up at him. "You're the traitor who got us into this whole mess in the first place, McMahon!"

As if a cold hand had just gripped her heart, Zang realised that if she killed McMahon now, then the voice-activation code to unlock the CIED device would be lost forever.

In response, she raised her HK416 and pointed it at him but found she couldn't pull the trigger, not when he was chained up and helpless like he was.

"Wait!" he exclaimed, raising his arms in another surrender pose. "Traitor? Me? Do you even know what really happened?"

Zang paused, sensing that McMahon was speaking the truth, or at least how he saw it from his perspective. Meanwhile, in the distant tunnels, she heard further fighting that was growing louder and closer by the second. She only had a minute at most to resolve this dilemma. "Explain?"

"They set me up! They framed me. Yeah, I gambled, but never any more than I could afford. Those assholes took money from the Mafia, then lied to those criminals and told them I stole it. What else was I supposed to do?"

"Who, McMahon? Who are we talking about?"

"I don't know who they are. He said he was a Russian."

An explosion rattled the caves perhaps a hundred metres behind them now. There were screams both of fury and pain. Curses were in both English and presumably Pashto, and they were getting closer. "Give me a name?"

McMahon rattled his chain. "Please get me out of here. I don't want to die. Not like this. Not when I have no idea what has happened to my family."

"The name, McMahon?"

"Just gag him!" offered Jahandar, as if he thought his words were of use to her. "I know where the CIED device is, not him. That *is* why you are here, correct?"

Zang turned her weapon on Jahandar, surprised at his rapid ability to ascertain what motivated her. She didn't sense he was book smart, but cunning like a fox, and that was exactly the vibe he oozed at her right now. "Where is it?"

Now Jahandar rattled his chains. "I'm not stupid. You get me out of here, and then I'll tell you."

Zang turned to McMahon. "The name?"

"I don't know! Something Russian."

"Try to fucking remember!"

He trembled now and cowered at the HK416 she pressed up close to his face. "It was... It was... Chernyy Pes, I think?"

Chernyy Pes. The name caused Zang to pause. She spoke Russian well enough to know the words literally translated into "Black Dog". Brad Karson had not just jumped at a chance to steal and sell American nuclear submarine propeller schematics when they became available on the market, but he had also orchestrated the entire operation from the get-go.

Both McMahon and Jahandar now looked past Zang. Their eyes grew even wider at the sight standing behind her.

"It's you!" McMahon cowered as spit dribbled from his quivering lips.

Jahandar said nothing, just turned paler with each passing second.

Zang felt the barrel of a weapon press into the back of her head, and knew without having to look that Major Brad Karson stood behind her, and he now had her life in his hands.

59

Noises. Flashes. Vibrations. Coppery scents. Tremors. The world that Pierce found himself in was a cacophony of sounds and visions and scents that assaulted and confused all his senses. Every time he operated with the NODs, sudden bright explosives lights would momentarily blind him. Every time he operated without them, darkness became absolute for long minutes where he could see nothing.

But fight on Pierce had. He'd shot, stabbed and strangled his way past a dozen al-Qaeda insurgents and Executive Believers mercenaries, in the three-way battle that made no sense and lacked any form of coordination beyond individual efforts. He'd stumbled across Waxer's and Random's bloody bodies, Lima X-ray Five and Six respectively, their corpses ruined by explosive compression waves that must have ruptured all their internal organs all at once while leaving their outsides intact. He'd tried to reach Zang, Toxic and Bragger on their radio comms, but got nothing. As for Killefer and Sledge Man, Pierce was convinced they'd fallen with the rock as it had sheared off the side of the mountain, and their bodies were now buried under hundreds of tonnes of rubble and near icy water three hundred metres below them. Their bodies would never be recoverable.

Pierce heard another gun battle up ahead. He was searching for Zang so they could team up and go after Kaajal Khan, who would have taken his half from Jahandar, or Brad Karson or Nigel McMahon, any three of the moving parts that could effectively lock the CIED device forever should he shut one down. But whichever path he took, nothing led him to the lower levels.

Figuring he needed to get past this next group of combatants, Pierce advanced. He was approaching from a shadowed tunnel just behind a group of Executive Believers mercs engaging in a heavy gun battle with al-Qaeda forces in the tunnel ahead.

Pierce pulled a thermite grenade and lobbed it into the battle line established by the American mercenaries. He didn't wish to collapse the tunnel in front of him, but needed a weapon that would do its job. A flash of intense pyrotechnic heat incinerated the combatants while leaving the rock intact. Some screamed and wailed, but most died too quickly to know what had hit them. Pierce quickly put the few screaming survivors out of their misery with single, carefully placed bullets to their heads. Then he ducked back into the tunnel and waited again.

The al-Qaeda forces the Executive Believers mercs had been engaging with were predictable when they advanced rapidly to assess what had taken out their foes. Pierce lobbed another grenade, which repeated the process.

He waited a minute for the smoke and heat to clear, then advanced into the carnage. Most of the bodies he couldn't recognise because they were too badly burned, but he did notice that one of the foes he had put a mercy bullet through the head was Captain Gang Keng. Around him lay many scattered and defunct micro drones, which Keng must have been deploying to find their targets and assess enemy movements and positions. Pierce didn't see anyone who resembled Karson or Sanders or Suwan, but in the carnage he had just caused, he might never know the answer to who had survived and who had not thus far in the conflict. He could have destroyed one or both halves of the CIED device already, but again didn't know this for a fact. Until he had exhausted all options, he decided to push forward and complete his mission as best he could.

A shadow lunged at him from the darkness. A kick collected him in the chest. Pierce felt his lungs scream for the air that had been knocked out of him as he rolled backwards and hit the ground hard on his arse.

He looked up only just fast enough to block a series of kicks aimed at his head with his arm.

It was Master Sergeant Kwang Suwan, employing every dirty Thai kickboxing trick she had ever learnt, inflicted upon him now with the single purpose of beating him to death. Half her face was singed from the thermite blast, and her clothes were in tatters. She carried no weapons, and Pierce figured she must have lost them in the carnage he'd caused earlier, but in Suwan's case, her body was her most lethal weapon.

He blocked and parried, but more kicks and punches got through compared to those he deflected or blocked, and soon his forearms and legs were a mass of bruises and points of searing pain. If he didn't get to his feet soon and fight back, she would soon beat him to death. He had no doubt as to her skill and tenacity, and it was all he could do from his supine position to block and parry, allowing through only a few painful blows between the half dozen he deflected.

Trying another tactic, Pierce tried to reach his firearm, for the HK416 was pinned under him, and his Glock wasn't in its holster.

Taking a break from the exertion required to beat a man to death, Suwan stepped back and wiped sweat from her forehead. She must have felt she had already beaten him and was now playing with him like a cat who had grievously wounded a mouse now cowering in its reach.

Pierce scrambled back, panting heavily himself and growing increasingly aware of the blood trickling across his eye from a cut he had sustained on his forehead.

Then he remembered as she did that he sat upon his HK416.

She rushed him. Instead of going for his rifle as she'd expected him to, Pierce pivoted and kicked out with his right leg.

Suwan's knee collided with his strike, sending her into a spin.

The few seconds it afforded allowed Pierce to clamber to his feet.

She regained her balance, then turned in an acrobatic spin and came for Pierce with fists and kicks flying. A foot hit him in the chest. The ceramic plates in his harness absorbed most of the kinetic force behind her powerful strike, but he still stumbled and tripped over the pile of smouldering bodies behind him.

Then he was rolling, tumbling down roughly hewed, descending steps. His NODs flew off his head, and then he was rolling in darkness.

Until he hit a rock face and stopped. He tried not to grunt, but the force burst all the air in his lungs straight out of his mouth.

"Fuck!" he exclaimed in a wheeze.

But there was no time to recover, for Suwan already pounded down the steps towards him.

Knowing she would be the better fighter in a tight space with almost no light, Pierce sucked in a lungful of air and rolled again. He crashed further down and along the deepening steps until he rolled out into another cave partially carved into a rectangular chamber.

The room was lit with discarded flares, likely left behind by Karson's mercs as they secured this area. At least he could see, but the sights that greeted him turned his stomach. This was an al-Qaeda torture chamber, with a slab of rock shaped like a pagan altar, adorned with chains, manacles and a deep rivet where the neck of a human body would line up.

There was a body on the altar, dressed in the same Afghani garb he had seen all the al-Qaeda fighters wearing during his assault on the stronghold. Only this body had no head, and blood spray patterns adorned every surface.

Remembering that he was still participating in a fistfight, he rolled as Suwan catapulted herself into Pierce and pummelled him with more kicks and punches.

This time Pierce didn't block. Instead, he threw his weight against her, knowing his relative bulk and strength was his only advantage. Up close and personal, her spit was soon splashing in his face as she groaned and struggled to hit him harder in his soft spots.

Pierce found a purchase under her left armpit, and then spinning and rolling her across his back, he flung her at a stone wall.

Suwan hit the wall hard, and most of the impact was taken by her head and shoulders. She crumpled on the rough floor, moaned and rolled.

Panting hard and feeling his exhaustion and pain, he staggered over to her, then lifted her from behind and wrapped his right arm around her throat while his other pressed down on the back of her head. She resisted, but the choke hold soon restricted the flow of blood and oxygen to her brain. Within seconds she was unconscious. Pierce released her.

He could have held the choke hold for a few seconds longer, starving her brain of oxygen and killing her, but Pierce didn't have the conviction to follow through as he normally would have done with an enemy combatant. Instead, he took several cable ties from a Velcro pouch and hogtied her. It was only after he had immobilised her that he realised she wasn't breathing or moving at all, and therefore he must have choked her too long anyway, and she was already dead.

He heard voices echoing off the rock, coming from deeper inside and below in the dark narrow tunnels that beckoned.

And one of those voices belonged to Rachel Zang.

He grabbed his fallen NODs and HK416 and raced towards the sounds.

60

Zang held Brad Karson's stare as he held hers. There was no life in his black eyes, and his face was like stone, expressionless. She could see there was nothing inside him that made him a feeling and caring individual. He lacked the emotions almost all other humans on the planet experienced on an almost continuous basis. Then she noticed the object held in his left hand by his side, wet and sticky and covered in damp knots of hair.

Zang almost vomited when she realised what it was that he gripped so tightly.

He threw the object at her. It hit her shoulder as she tried to deflect. The blow didn't hurt, as it was designed to shock. When the object fell and rolled into a corner, its resting position was side-on, and the eyes were still wide and seemingly focused on her. Karson had taken Kaajal Khan's head as a trophy, and al-Qaeda's regional commander was no more.

Drawing in a sharp breath and refocusing, Zang turned and focused again on Karson. In his right hand, his Glock was still aimed casually in her direction. Jay Sanders next to him, with his M4 raised, looked as disgusted as she was at Karson's actions, but said or did nothing in response. Behind Karson and Sanders were three more mercs, all combat ready, and their M4s were also aimed firmly at Zang. She was all out of options.

Karson snarled, "Khan had the other half of the CIED device. He paid for that, and now I have both." He studied the cavernous room, laying eyes first on Jahandar and then McMahon. He smiled when he saw they were both manacled to the stone walls. He was about to speak to McMahon, but instead turned to Zang. "Sanders was right. If I'd left you out of this, I wouldn't have taken as many hits as I have."

"You mean people, Karson? We're talking about thinking, caring, feeling human beings here. To how many of those people you talk so casually about have your actions caused death and suffering? Do you even care?"

"Of course I care. Someone has to stand up to the corruption and mismanagement of the government. I'm the only one who's doing anything about it."

Zang shook her head. She wanted to dive for and snatch up the HK416 she'd thrown at Karson's feet, but that was a suicidal move. Instead, she sneered and said, "You going to tell me all the money you make selling America's secrets will pay for your campaign of justice. That's just bullshit."

The muscles in Black Dog's face — or Chernyy Pes's face as he would have been known in Russia — quivered, as if Zang's words didn't fit with his internal narrative of how the world worked.

"Yeah, Karson. You know like I do, it's all bullshit. The money's just for you." She turned to Sanders. "You know he's just got to get McMahon here to give him the voice-activated password and then he has everything he needs. I don't know how many millions he thinks he's going to make out of this, but he's not sharing any of it with any of you." She glanced to the mercs behind Sanders and held their returned stares. "He talks the talk, but it's all hollow sentiments."

Karson suddenly raised his pistol and shot Jahandar through the torso, twice.

The Pakistani grabbed at his chest as he stumbled backwards and stared at Karson with shocked surprise. Then he slid down the rock surface, leaving a thick trail of his own blood smeared across its surface.

"You're right, Zang, my list of assets are all quickly turning into liabilities now, including you."

Zang tried not to glance Sanders's way when she spotted his moment of comprehension to the reality of the situation as it washed over his face.

Then she noticed the pistol in Karson's hand pointed at her, and wondered why the Black Dog hadn't shot her either. She had never been his asset. The only reason, she thought, she was still alive was because he wanted to enjoy her suffering by prolonging this moment for as long as he could.

No one had spoken, and the seconds now dragged. In her fear, all Zang could hear now was her own breathing and heartbeat pounding rapidly and violently in her chest.

Eventually Karson's expression seemed to calm as he turned his attention to McMahon. "Right, Nigel. If you want to leave this hellhole alive and in one piece, the only way that is going to happen is if you speak the words now to unlock these submarine schematics."

McMahon, his face speckled with Jahandar's sprayed blood, trembled as his face sank. "But once I tell you, you'll just kill me too."

"You're right." Karson raised his pistol and shot McMahon through the muscle in his upper arm.

McMahon cried out and crumpled to his knees. "Oh God! Oh God, that really hurts."

The mercs behind Karson now shifted uneasily. It wasn't just Sanders who was beginning to realise this scenario smelled bad.

Oblivious to everyone else, Karson took a step closer to McMahon. "Okay, I am going to kill you once I have what I want, but I can make it quick like Jahandar here, or slow and painful like Kaajal Khan over there. It took me about three minutes to cut his head off, and he screamed the whole time, even when I thought most of his sinew was no longer attached."

"Okay! Okay, the words are... 'Chernyy Pes is a special cockhead'."

Karson blinked and raised an eyebrow. Then with his free hand, reached into a Velcro pocket and withdrew the two halves of the CIED device, now locked together. A tiny green light flashed on the two adjoining parts. "Looks like you've delivered, McMahon." He pointed his pistol at the DARPA engineer's forehead and, with a single bullet, disintegrated the top of his head, which sprayed the rock wall just above Jahandar's corpse with brain matter, skull fragments and more blood.

Zang knew she should have reacted, but also knew it was too late when Karson turned the pistol on her and fired.

But no bullet hit her.

Sanders was suddenly in front of her as Karson's rounds impacted in his chest, once, twice, and then a third time. Simultaneously, Sanders depressed his trigger and sprayed the cave with more bullets. The three mercs were in the line of fire, and suddenly everyone except for Zang and Karson were dead or nearly so.

Sanders fell on her and grunted. She struggled to hold his weight.

Behind where the mercs were falling, lifeless or seriously injured from the bullets they had absorbed, appeared Pierce. He came crashing into the cave from a tiny tunnel, brandishing his HK416. He assessed the room in under a second, then fired off a volley of rounds into another tunnel that Karson was now disappearing into.

Zang dropped, with Sanders's unresponsive body now flopped on top of her and weighing her down.

Pierce meanwhile killed or ensured that the three fallen mercs were actually dead, then turned to Zang. "Are you okay?"

She nodded. "Get after Karson. He has the CIED device now, and it's activated."

"Roger that... Ronin!" Pierce turned, then vanished into the dark tunnel pursuing Karson.

Zang lay for a moment as tears welled in her eyes. She fought against the wash of horrid emotions she knew she was about to endure. She knew Sanders was dead, Zang couldn't hear breathing, and there was no heartbeat. She tested his pulse in his throat, but her fingers disappeared into a meaty, bloody hole that opened into his exposed throat.

Suddenly she was gushing tears. She had liked Jay Sanders, a lot, and if she'd let herself, she knew she could have made a life with a man like him. But now he was gone, forever, in a sacrifice to save her.

Her thoughts turned to Pierce. The Trigger Man was the same kind of man Sanders was, a man of action and conviction, but also gentle and caring where it mattered. Zang knew she was stupid to not want him in her life as a lover, friend and companion, but distancing herself from him, she knew, was exactly what she would do because it was her nature to do so.

Pulling herself together, she gently rolled Sanders off her and laid him down in a comfortable position, not that the dead cared about any of that.

Still, she closed his eyes so he would look to be at peace, kissed him gently on the forehead, and whispered words to him that only they would ever share.

Then she lurched to her feet, gathered up her HK416 and loaded it with a fresh magazine.

With a snarl and a growl, she took off after Pierce. She wasn't planning on two ex-lovers dying on her in the same night.

61

Pierce propelled his aching and beaten body through the claustrophobic tunnels of darkness in pursuit of his enemy. Karson was ahead, sometimes out of sight as he turned and ducked through the twisting passages. There was little ambient light for the night optical device to enhance, but it was enough to outline his enemy. Many times, Pierce thought to stop and take a shot, but the tunnel was never long enough for a clean kill. Then Karson turned a corner, and Pierce lost sight of him completely.

Pierce sprinted, figuring if there were any improvised explosive devices booby-trapping the path ahead, Karson would set them off.

Suddenly he found himself on a ledge, with icy winds howling around him.

The full moon was out, but clouds were passing over it constantly, altering its brightness.

Pierce paused to assess his surroundings. He was on another ledge on a sheer cliff face, with no railing and averaging only a metre in width. It turned right and snaked up the mountain. To his left, the ledge disappeared into darkness, and he felt it safe to assume any fall would be fatal.

Still wearing his NODs, Pierce turned right and spotted Karson's green illumination half walking, half jogging up the carved trail. Pierce tested the ledge, discovering both loose gravel, compacted snow and icy surfaces. To move rapidly in this environment was to invite a slippage and a long fall to a crushing death.

Judging that Karson was approximately one hundred metres from him, Pierce crouched down on one knee and fired a sustained burst of bullets at his enemy.

Karson flattened himself against the rock, then returned fire with his M4.

Pierce ducked back into the cave, but no bullets pinged around them. They were too far apart in the windy conditions to have any effective chance of hitting each other. So he loaded a free magazine and took pursuit.

The ledge soon proved harder to navigate than Pierce had expected, with more ice to slip on in too many spots. The ledge narrowed to less than his body width, forcing him to sling his military rifle and purchase the rock with his hands so he wouldn't fall, half walking and half mountaineering to maintain the chase.

After Pierce had covered fifty metres, the path ran out.

He looked up and across the two-metre chasm where a rockfall had taken out the original carved-out ledge. Then he spotted Karson raising his weapon and aiming at Pierce. He'd been lying in ambush, ready to shoot when Pierce reached this very spot.

Pierce pressed himself hard against the rock as bullets pinged around him.

One bullet clipped his left shoulder but left no serious

damage despite the short-lived red mist that was quickly consumed by the storm. Pierce let out a grunt, winced, then turned his HK416 and laid covering fire in Karson's direction. For several seconds they exchanged gunplay, but neither could get a clear bead on the other with the slippery ledges they stood upon, while the wind constantly threatened to throw them both off balance.

When a lull in the shooting came, Pierce realised it was because his magazine was empty. It seemed Karson faced a similar predicament.

With icy fingers that were partially unresponsive because of the cold, Pierce dropped out his empty magazine and fumbled for his last full replacement. He called out into the darkness as he worked. "You know, Black Dog, your ideas on how to look out for your men and women were never bad ones. You failed, though, because you were doing it all for the wrong reasons."

"I never failed, Trigger Man."

Pierce chuckled as he fitted the magazine and cycled a round into the firing chamber. "From where I'm looking, I'd say you will in about three minutes." He turned and fired another burst to where he estimated Karson's voice had originated from. He didn't hit his target, but it was enough for Karson to take off at a sprint, leading him further up the mountain, and then turn a corner until he was out of sight.

Pierce stepped out from the undulation that had kept him partially hidden during the shooting, ready to take a better-aimed shot, but Karson was nowhere to be seen. He looked again at the gap separating this side of the path with the other. How had Karson crossed it, because in these winds and with the slippery ice, there was no safe means to cross the distance?

Then Pierce noticed weird shapes flapping off the cliff edge on his side.

Removing his NODs for a clearer interpretation of what he saw, Pierce now recognised the remains of a rope bridge. Karson must have cut it when he had crossed over.

"Fuck!" Pierce swore. His words were immediately swallowed by the howling icy winds increasing in intensity around him. He had to cross, now, or Karson would make his escape.

Then Pierce notice a rope hanging from the hook in the rock on the opposite side, where the rope bridge had been attached. He didn't know why it was still there, perhaps Karson had missed it when he had cut away the bridge, but it hung about a metre from the lip of the opposite path to about three metres down.

Hyperventilating, and trying not to focus his attention on the minor wound in his shoulder, Pierce knew what he had to do.

He checked the ice underfoot. It was too slippery to move fast on, so he couldn't make a running jump to clear the distance.

Then he had an idea.

Pierce fired the remainder of his bullets into the path before him, exploding away the ice until only rock remained.

Abandoning his HK416, Pierce tested the path again, finding the grip he needed. But with the icy winds howling around him, he knew that grip would last minutes at most before more ice formed.

Before he talked himself out of it, Pierce took five steps backwards, then sprinted and propelled himself across the abyss.

Halfway across, he realised he was going to hit the other

side at chest height, and there was nothing he could do to prevent this.

The impact was jarring, and he slipped and slid down the rock face. His hands fumbled for the rope and caught it two metres below where he had wanted to land. Stopping suddenly, his downward momentum turned sideways, and Pierce crashed into the rock. The NODs on his head cracked, then fell off and disappeared into the pitch blackness of the world beneath him.

"Fuck!" he exhaled again.

The last time Pierce had found himself dangling on a rope about to fall to his certain death, his shakes had taken over and had almost defeated him. Determined for this not to happen again, Pierce grumbled, spat, complained and growled until out of sheer determination and pig-headedness, he clambered up the rock to the other side.

When he turned around, he found Zang on the opposite side of the abyss, staring wide-eyed at him. "Pierce! What the hell?"

He thumbed toward the path he had crossed over to. "I need to stop Karson. Throw me your rifle."

She nodded, unslung it and threw it hard.

It was a clean throw. Pierce would have caught it easily, but a sudden powerful gust snatched it, and it crashed against rock that was beyond his reach before dropping into the same unknown abyss that had taken his NODs.

"Oh well," he said with a grin. "Still have my trusty Glock 19." He felt his sidearm holster, but that weapon was missing too. Then he remembered he had lost it when he had fought Suwan.

"Pierce, I'll call in a drone strike. Karson has both halves of the CIED device now, and it's activated."

He nodded. "Okay, that's an option. But there could be more caves up there, where a drone can't reach him." He turned and took off up the icy track, with murderous intent on his mind.

Zang called after him, but whatever she said, it was lost to the winds.

62

The path ahead did not disappear into further caves, but snaked into a narrow ravine, perhaps three metres wide and at least a hundred metres deep on Pierce's left and fifty metres high above him. The winds here weren't as intense, sheltered as they were. He wondered where the path led to, because this direction took them further into the mountains and into more inhospitable terrain than they had already experienced. Eventually, as Pierce suspected it might, the path ran out at the point where the rock breakers who had carved this path had reached their most recent work front.

Karson waited patiently at this point, with a fighting blade ready and glinting in the moonlight in his right hand. Was he out of bullets too?

Pierce advanced cautiously as he touched his own KAMPO fighting blade in the sheath he'd kept strapped to his left arm, a deliberate show so Karson wouldn't miss it.

"It comes down to this, Pierce. Man versus man, at the most primordial level."

"Maybe."

"You know, it was I who slaughtered your Navy SEAL team. Every single one of them. It was a mistake to send my kind after me to kill me, because I trained them in everything they knew."

Pierce didn't mention that Karson was Army and not Navy, as Killefer and his team had been, but that fact was barely a point worth mentioning.

"And now, Trigger Man, I kill you."

"Like you did your wife and two sons?"

He shrugged. "Yeah, you were right there. I did kill them, but they were slowing me down."

Taking another step closer, Pierce allowed his hand to slip into a pouch on his plate carrier. "You are one sick fucker, aren't you?"

"I'm a better fighter, Pierce. You can't beat me."

"No, but a grenade can."

Popping the pin with his thumb, Pierce lobbed a grenade at Karson.

Karson didn't hesitate as he flung his knife through the air at the grenade, hitting it straight on.

Now Pierce stared wide-eyed, realising as Karson did that the grenade was equidistant between them. It detonated, and the chasm walls shuddered. The shock front knocked both Pierce and Karson from their feet, and they both struggled to maintain their grip on the rock as the paths around them crumbled further.

Pierce lost sight of what happened to Karson as he heard a cracking, thunderous noise above him. He looked up just in time to see sheets of snow crashing down upon him from where the grenade blast had dislodged it. Pierce dug his hands and boots into the rock. He held on for several seconds, but the weight of snow and ice building up on him was too much, and he dropped into the abyss.

He thought he was falling to his death until he hit another ledge some unknown distance from where he had been only seconds before. The snow that had gathered on the ledge cushioned his fall, and the distance couldn't have been too far; otherwise the force would have killed him. When the snow settled around him, Pierce shrugged it off. Most of it fell away and dropped into the dark abyss below him.

Then he heard Karson laughing.

Pierce glanced at his new ledge, merely thirty centimetres wide and about two metres long.

Karson stood on another ledge, slightly wider and slightly longer, about six metres below him but trapped on the other side of the narrow ravine.

Pierce looked around. There was no easy means for either of them to climb out from their trapped positions without using mountaineering gear, which he still carried with him. It would take time to set up and was why he hadn't used it at the fallen bridge earlier. But he had no time to use any of the equipment until he'd dealt with the Black Dog of the Hindu Kush.

"Seems that you've killed us both, Pierce."

He laughed and pressed himself against the rock. "Except my people will come for me. Other than Zang, all your people are dead, and I will deal with her personally long before she has any thoughts on coming after me."

Pierce felt the rock beneath him shift. He saw a crack suddenly appear. If that turned into a shear, he was a goner.

Karson laughed out loud. "At least you'll die first."

As the ledge beneath him groaned, Pierce undid his belt

and looped it through his chest rig. With his knife, he found a sturdy fissure in the rock, then impaled his KAMPO knife deep in it.

"You know, Pierce, I might die, but al-Qaeda will still find my body and, with it, the schematics of the submarines. You still lose."

Pierce gritted his teeth. The ledge shifted under him. He'd only just managed to loop the belt over the knife handle as the ledge gave way and crashed into the unseen valley beneath him. He was left hanging from a vertical rock face, dangling from a jury-rigged piton of his own making. He knew he looked undignified, but at least he was safe for the moment.

Pierce rotated as he spun slowly until he faced Karson.

"You look ridiculous."

Pierce grinned. "But I'm still here."

"I should throw rocks at you. I reckon I could hurt you a lot during the many hours we'll get to spend together before the end."

"Except," said Pierce as he rotated again so his back now faced Karson, "I still have one more grenade."

When he turned again and faced his enemy, he held his last fragmentation grenade primed in his hand.

Karson said, "You're too close. Throw that at me and the blast will kill us both."

"Yeah, I thought of that, but those rocks above you, they look precarious and should crush the CIED device when they come down on you."

Karson tensed as the veins in his face grew prominent and bulged. "It might not be me who ends your life, Trigger Man. But one day, someone deserving of that task will, and it will be unpleasant for you, I'm sure. I just regret that I won't get to watch."

Pierce lobbed the grenade high and up over Karson's head.

The concussion front, light and noise hit Pierce hard and threw him around like a rag doll.

But he had his wits enough about him to watch through the carnage as hundreds of tonnes of rock sheared down the side of the ravine, pulverising Major Brad Karson, burying him deep in a rubble pile of destruction somewhere far down in the abyss beneath where Pierce hung dangling like a fool in the chilly night.

And then, when it was all over, he fumbled for his pitons, rope and carabiners and prepared to mountaineer his way out of this hellish abyss.

63

Black Sea

Pulling her parka tight around her to fight off the chilly winds blowing off the rough waves rising and falling in the Black Sea, Karen Dwyer kept glancing back the way they had come. She should have felt comfort in the presence of the Navy SEAL team that had collected her and the four grateful members of the Pavlenko family and sped them out into the vast oceanic unknown. What bothered her was that they were still within the twelve-nautical-mile limit of the Russian state, and the lights of Sochi were still visible on the horizon despite the broiling clouds and light drizzle that provided a modicum of cover. There would be drones and satellites watching for them, and Russian naval vessels operated in these waters in their efforts to control the ongoing land, sea and air battles underway in neighbouring Ukraine and the Crimean Peninsula.

Daniil and Katerina Pavlenko huddled with their children under a blanket, and at times Dwyer thought they wept together as a family. Was it from relief to finally be away, or was it from the same fear that she experienced, that this was not over yet?

Their two thirty-six-foot-long rigid-hull inflatable boats sped through the water at forty knots, crashing through waves like a fist shattering glass pane after glass pane. The turbulence brought on seasickness, and Dwyer tried her best not to vomit. Not that she would bring anything up, for in her fear, she had not eaten in the last twenty-four hours.

She spotted the Navy SEAL lieutenant, who had introduced himself earlier as Nathan Silby, as he crawled up next to her and made a deliberate play at staring at his flashy diver's watch. "And there you have it. We are now officially in international waters."

Dwyer felt the tension wash off her like a snake shedding its skin. Her breaths became longer and deeper, and she felt herself relaxing. Despite it only being an arbitrary line on a map that the Russians were not so stringent at abiding by anymore, she did feel the worst of their ordeal was behind them now.

Silby crawled closer to her so he wouldn't have to yell as much to be heard over the wind and crashing waves. "Ma'am, I can tell you now, the data breach on US Naval submarine technical specifications is no longer in play. USS *Pasadena* will be rendezvousing with us in the next five minutes, and then the Russians will never be able to reach you or the Pavlenkos ever again."

Dwyer nodded, not certain how true that was, but at least for the Pavlenko family, they had escaped. Unfortunately, they had not all gotten away. With sadness croaking in her voice, Dwyer said, "What about Wilks? He was a former SEAL. Do you know his fate?"

The lieutenant grimaced. "Wilks was an excellent operator. I regret to inform you, ma'am, he didn't make it. His body turned up in no-person's land in the Ukrainian-Russian battlefronts just outside Bakhmut. He was—"

"Horrifically tortured?" She finished his difficult words for him.

The officer nodded. "Yes, ma'am."

"But he was a brave man to the end, held out long enough for the five of us to get away."

The lieutenant checked his wristwatch again, then made a signal with his hands, which prompted the pilots of the two inflatable boats to cut their engines. Several seconds passed before antennas, a periscope tower and diving rudders foamed up out of the water. Then the hull of the black metal beast emerged from the churning sea.

Submariners emerged from the submarine's escape hatch and threw ropes to the inflatable boats. As they were pulled up close, and the operators and submariners helped Katerina, Anatoliy and Emiliya up on the deck, Daniil moved up close to Dwyer so they could speak. "I don't know if we'll get the chance to talk again, but I wanted to thank you."

Dwyer blinked, unexpecting of his gratitude at this juncture.

"You put your life on the line for us, Dwyer. I have to admire that."

She nodded, smiled, then squeezed his arm affectionately.

Two submariners helped them up on deck as Daniil watched his family disappear below. He turned to Dwyer again and said in Russian, "Sixteen years ago, I was approached by two of your CIA officers stationed in Moscow.

Did you know they tried to turn me, make me a double agent?"

Dwyer nodded, then smiled again. She answered him in Russian too, for they were speaking his native tongue to lessen the chance of an operator or crew understanding them. "I did know that, but I didn't know you knew."

His expression turned serious. "They were a couple, probably husband and wife. I could tell, even though they tried to hide it. They worked too in sync with each other not to be."

Dwyer kept her face impassive with this revelation, because what Daniil had guessed was correct.

"I also know the SVR had them murdered a short time afterwards. I know you know this, but what you don't know is why."

Now Dwyer couldn't keep her impassive stare any longer, for this was indeed news she did wish to know, to fill in gaps from that very traumatic and turbulent time back when she was a permanent fixture of the CIA's Moscow station. "And you do?"

He nodded as his mouth curled into a sardonic grin. "I do, and when I tell you why, it will make your skin crawl."

A submariner approached and gestured that they both needed to head below so they could dive again to a safe operating depth.

Daniil Pavlenko nodded and thanked him in English, then turned to Dwyer and said, "But I would say that is a conversation for another time, when we are all safe and snug in the glorious United States of free America."

Dwyer nodded, knowing that she would get nothing from him now, but later, what would she learn?

She watched the Russian activist disappear below deck,

and she followed, grateful to finally get out of the wind and the cold and the fear and the terror. But how long would sanctity last, because nothing ever remained static and stable for long, and that was the nature of her work, and everyone else's work, within the CIA?

Even the Trigger Man knew this.

64

Singapore

Abdul Ibrahim called it "decompression time", Zang called it "me only time", and Pierce called it "post-dramatic rest disorder", but whatever name it was labelled with, Pierce knew he and Zang needed a week or more of just relaxing to come down from their latest mission.

Ibrahim had sent them to Singapore and told them to be contactable there, but to relax and otherwise enjoy themselves in the meantime. They did so on a no-frills government per diem allowance that got them cheap hotel rooms in a not-so-pleasant side of town. It smelled of stale cigarette smoke, and the sounds from a busy kitchen downstairs were incessantly of chefs barking orders at seemingly everyone else on the payroll.

Pierce lay on his lumpy bed and remembered Roshini Jahandar, and how she had kissed him, and later, how he had watched Brad Karson execute her. He felt her loss of life and the unborn child inside her to be the most poignant loss for him on this mission. He imagined Zang likely felt the same about Jay Sanders.

But these were morose thoughts he didn't wish to endure in this moment.

Jumping to his feet, he dialled Zang on her newest burner phone. "Want a drink?"

"Sure," she answered unenthusiastically. "But nowhere around here."

"What about the Marina Bay Sands hotel? I hear the bar at the infinity pool lookout is nice."

"Don't jest. I know you can't afford that. And neither can I!"

Pierce had never told Zang he had come into significant cash funds during a recent past operation, stolen from corrupt individuals who had attempted to frame him as an international terrorist wanted by every western power on the planet. That money safely ferreted away in multiple bank accounts across the globe would allow him to retire very comfortably if he needed to, or fund him if he needed to run and go into hiding again. But tonight, he'd dip into it for a bit of much-needed relaxation. "But I can, Zang. Drinks are on me tonight."

An hour later, they sat at a bar at a height of fifty-seven stories, with gin and tonics in their hands, looking out over the huge swimming pool that seemed to disappear into the sky, with the skyline of the modern neon city lit up at night.

"How did you get us in? I thought only guests could access the pool?"

Pierce grinned and chinked her glass. He didn't tell her that he'd paid for a room for the night, which he would retire to later. The room provided him with access to the bar.

"Let's just say I know a guy who knows a guy…"

She play-punched him on the arm. "Bullshit, Pierce. Tell me."

He sipped at his gin and tonic, then said, "What's the special access program code word?"

She made googly-eyes at him. "Fuck. You."

"Close," he said, shrugging.

"Tell me?"

"No."

"Fine, have it your way."

"Just enjoy yourself for a change."

She nodded and turned to take in the spectacular view again. The hotel was supposed to be one of the most luxurious and most expensive hotels ever built, and Pierce could see why.

When they hadn't spoken for several minutes, he turned to Zang and noticed she wore a sleeveless blouse, cotton pants and flat shoes. "You know, Zang, I've never seen you in a dress. Or a skirt."

Now she smirked and sipped at her gin and tonic. "And you never will."

Pierce raised an eyebrow.

Zang said, "Come to think of it, I've never seen you in a dress or skirt either."

"Not really my style."

"And there is your answer."

They returned to their silence, which at first Pierce had interpreted as comfortable, but now he wasn't so sure that it was.

When Zang realised he was staring at her, she made a face. "What, Pierce?"

He leaned over and kissed her.

She responded for a few seconds, then stiffened and tensed. He did too, and they both pulled away.

Pierce realised he had no desire to talk about what had just happened, so he returned his attention to the skyline as he failed to enjoy the view that only a minute earlier had given him great comfort.

Zang reached over and squeezed his hand. "Pierce, I don't... I can't..."

"Too much trauma?" he asked her.

She nodded. "I know what happened to Mackenzie Summerfield almost destroyed you, and Roshini's execution was a shock to us both, but to you particularly. I could see it in your eyes when it happened."

"And Jay Sanders," said Pierce. "I figured it out; he was a bedroom playmate like I was. Losing him cut you deep too."

Another nod. "Surely, you've had other bedmates too, since we first hooked up? That was our understanding?"

Pierce remembered the past encounters she referred to clearly, particularly the woman he had briefly enjoyed time with during a mission in Israel and Yemen.

"You and I, we don't work as lovers, but as friends, Pierce. I rely on that. As a friend, you were far superior to Sanders in all respects."

The conversation was becoming increasingly uncomfortable for Pierce despite him silently conceding her points. "I don't know about that, Zang. He gave his life for you. That's not something I can ever compete with."

"You don't need to compete, ever. And besides, you have given your life for me plenty of times. It's just that you survived each instance, and he didn't."

Pierce sipped again at his gin, watery now that the ice

had melted. He watched a young couple swim to the edge of the infinity pool, each in their tiny swimsuits and toned bodies, and as they stared out at the same magnificent view that Pierce and Zang enjoyed, they kissed with an embrace that lingered, then hugged and whispered promises to each other that he and his fellow CIA operator never would.

He threw the remainder of his drink down his throat and leaned forward. He couldn't look at Zang when he spoke to her next. "You're right. This isn't working. But I don't regret anything that happened between us. I wanted you to know that."

She touched him on the shoulder. "I don't either. And thank you."

He glanced over his shoulder at her. "For what?"

"For making this easy. My friend."

Pierce nodded, then handed her the key card for his room. "You enjoy that."

"What, you booked a room? Here?"

He shrugged as he stood. "That's how I got access to the view." He gave her a casual salute. "See you on the next mission... Ronin."

She smiled. "You know, I do like that code name."

He smiled too. "I know you do."

And then the Trigger Man disappeared, as if he had never been there in the first place.

65

Koh Samui, Thailand

For the next sixteen days, Pierce relaxed on a tropical beach lined with coconut palms, pristine white sands, and crystal-clear oceanfronts, where he drank beers outside his rented bungalow in the afternoons and swam in the mornings for exercise and relaxation. The island of Koh Samui was a tropical paradise that attracted tourists from all over the world, so no one noticed him as being unusual, and he relished this. With his bullet graze on his left shoulder now nicely healed, he'd gone diving, trekking, and basically allowed himself to fully embrace the tourist lifestyle. He ate good food at local restaurants, took in DJ sets playing on the beaches, and failed when he tried to pick up a twenty-something New Zealand backpacker the night before. The latter fail was a first for him in a long time, and he wondered if he was losing his seductive techniques. Then he did his best to not think about Rachel Zang, knowing that it would take time to get over her, and getting over her was perhaps why he couldn't get with anyone else, even for a night of fun.

But get over her, he would.

On the sixteenth day, as he sat outside his beachfront bungalow sipping on a soda water while reading a chapter of Yuval Noah Harari's *Sapiens*, he spotted Abdul Ibrahim approaching him from all the way down the far beach. He'd come alone, and like Pierce, he wore a T-shirt and cargo shorts. When the chief of the CIA's Special Operations Group was within speaking distance, he opened his daypack and withdrew a six-pack of Singha lager. "You thirsty, Trigger Man?"

Pierce nodded and took one as Ibrahim popped the lid. "Thanks, sir."

Ibrahim laughed as he fell into the deck chair next to Pierce. "You've found yourself a cosy little spot to disappear into."

Pierce took a long swig of the cool, soothing beverage. "I did."

"Not exactly Singapore, where I told you to stay?"

Pierce shrugged. "You found me easily enough, though. But why the personal visit? A phone call or a text message would have had me on the next flight, ready for the next mission."

Ibrahim drank from his own beer. "I wanted to make you an offer. I know you like working alone, but I think you are better working in a team."

Pierce made a snorting noise as he watched two attractive women in bikinis walk past, admiring their bodies. It was shallow of him, he knew, but he was a heterosexual man and saw no harm in it. They had probably checked him out too. "I'm not working with Mitch Hawley. I told you he was bad news, and too many people died unnecessarily because of his incompetence, including everyone in Lima X-ray and Roshini Jahandar."

"That's okay, Trigger Man. He's off the team."

Pierce paused as he considered this news. "You fired him?"

Ibrahim shook his head. "I can't. He's too well connected with the powers in Washington and old money. I had to promote him to get him out. He detests you now, and you've made an enemy out of him. This isn't the last time you'll have to deal with Hawley, but at least he's no longer with the Special Operations Group. I made sure of that."

Pierce shook his head. "Well, that's fucked up, then."

"It's politics, Pierce, and you'd be better off navigating it much more smartly than you do."

Pierce studied Ibrahim's attire. "With all your fancy tailored suits and ties, I always pegged you as part of the same Ivy League educated and old money circles, too?"

Ibrahim laughed riotously. "Trigger Man, you have no idea! I act like money is important to me so the heads of the CIA accept me. Most of Langley's seventh-floor executives can't stand the idea that a Muslim is in charge of the SAC/SOG. They only tolerate me if I act and behave like them. I'm on the outside too, just like you, Pierce. I just hide it better."

Pierce nodded, gaining a new appreciation for his boss. "I guess, then, I'm not the only one who's operated under cover and alone for too long?"

"Yes, we'll get to that. I've watched you and Zang on this last mission. You two work perfectly together as an integrated team. You're inventive, direct, and you get fast results."

Pierce tried to imagine what it would be like to work with Zang again when what he really needed was space to get over her. "I'm still not convinced."

"You worked well with Akash Parab, too."

Pierce shrugged. He had appreciated Parab's technical and information-gathering skills, and his coolness under stressful circumstances during their time together in India. "Maybe."

Ibrahim leaned forward. "What if I told you I need a team that reports directly to me, that I send on special missions outside of what Ground Branch normally does? Out-of-the-box instances like Karson are becoming more and more commonplace, and I need a team of out-of-the-box thinkers and operatives like you and Zang and Parab, who can resolve those instances fast, by any means necessary."

Pierce shook his head as he finished his beer. "We have a history, sir. You know me, and you know I don't play well with others. Just put me back to what I was doing before. A singleton operator, with a decent handler for a change, that I don't have to second-guess has my back all the time?"

Ibrahim grinned as he took another beer from his pack and handed it to Pierce. "You mean someone like Mackenzie Summerfield?"

Pierce raised an eyebrow but didn't take the beer.

"That's right. I need you in Spain straight away, Trigger Man, for the next out-of-the-box mission I need to resolve quickly. Summerfield's fully recovered from her injuries, and she wants to come back to the CIA. Specifically, she wants to work in my new team, with Zang and Parab already agreeing to join it too. But more importantly, Summerfield wants to work with you again. For some reason, she thinks you're the best operator the CIA has ever had. So, are you in or not?"

Pierce couldn't believe what he was hearing.

He took the beer and chinked necks with Ibrahim's bottle.

"Okay, you've convinced me. I'm in."

ACKNOWLEDGMENTS

Special thanks to Bodo Pfündl, Terrill Carpenter, Kenneth Karcher, Roxy Long and Kashif Hussain for early feedback, and Kronos Ananth, Deep Ranjan Sarmah and Diwaker for their first-hand advice on India, its people and culture, as their advice has been invaluable in this book. Mistakes, as always, lay solely with the author.

Once again, I'd like to thank everyone at Inkubator for their fantastic support and professionalism in getting this series out into the world, and those I have engaged with directly include Lizzie Bayliss, Shirley Khan, Brian Lynch, Claire Milto, Carol Mulligan-John, Garret Ryan, Stephen Ryan, and my editor Alice Latchford. I thank you all.

Other thanks go to Ian, Ann, Megan, Aron and again, as always, Bec Short, for her ongoing support and encouragement with every step I've taken with the Trigger Man series.

The Trigger Man will return.

ABOUT THE AUTHOR

Aiden Bailey is an international bestselling thriller author from Australia. Formerly an engineer, he built a career marketing multi-national technology, engineering, and construction companies. His various roles have included corporate communications with the Australian Submarine Corporation, technical writing for several defence contractors, engineering on an outback petroleum pipeline, a magazine editor and art director, and engineering proposal writer for the Royal Australian Air Force's surveillance and intelligence gathering aircraft and drone enabling works. Aiden has travelled widely in six continents and his experiences are the basis of many of his stories.

Did you enjoy *Shock Front*? Please consider leaving a review to help other readers discover the book.

www.aidenlbailey.com

ALSO BY AIDEN BAILEY